Worldwide Praise for of John Patrick and

"Always hot and sexy, always well-written, and always satisfying...."
- Out Front Colorado

"...Just about as hot as homoerotic writing can get! (Some stories are) utterly shocking!"
- In Touch magazine

"If you're an avid reader of all-male erotica and haven't yet discovered editor John Patrick's series of torrid anthologies, you're in for a treat. ...These books will provide hours of cost-effective entertainment."
- Lance Sterling, Beau magazine

"John Patrick is a modern master of the genre!...This writing is what being brave is all about. It brings up the kinds of things that are usually kept so private that you think you're the only one who experiences them."
- Gay Times, London

"'Barely Legal' is a great potpourri... and the coverboy is gorgeous!"
- Ian Young, Torso magazine

"A huge collection of highly erotic, short and steamy one-handed tales. Perfect bedtime reading, though you probably won't get much sleep! Prepare to be shocked! Highly recommended!"
- Vulcan magazine

"Tantalizing tales of porn stars, hustlers, and other lost boys...John Patrick set the pace with 'Angel'!"
- The Weekly News, Miami

...the scenes too explicit; others will enjoy the sudden, graphic sensations each page brings. ...A strange, often poetic vision of sexual obsession. I recommend it to you."
- Nouveau Midwest

"'Superstars' is a fast read...if you'd like a nice round of fireworks before the Fourth, read this aloud at your next church picnic..."
- Welcomat, Philadelphia

"Yes, it's another of those bumper collections of steamy tales from STARbooks. The rate at which John Patrick turns out these compilations you'd be forgiven for thinking it's not exactly quality prose. Wrong. These stories are well-crafted, but not over-written, and have a profound effect in the pants department."
- Vulcan magazine, London

"For those who share Mr. Patrick's appreciation for cute young men, 'Legends' is a delightfully readable book...I am a fan of John Patrick's...His writing is clear and straight-forward and should be better known in the gay community."
- Ian Young, Torso Magazine

"...Touching and gallant in its concern for the sexually addicted, 'Angel' becomes a wonderfully seductive investigation of the mysterious disparity between lust and passion, obsession and desire."
- Lambda Book Report

Ah, the lure of the forbidden!

Taboo!

A Collection
of Erotic Tales
Edited By
JOHN PATRICK

STARbooks Press

Books by John Patrick

Non-Fiction
A Charmed Life: Vince Cobretti
Lowe Down: Tim Lowe
The Best of the Superstars 1990
The Best of the Superstars 1991
The Best of the Superstars 1992
The Best of the Superstars 1993
The Best of the Superstars 1994
The Best of the Superstars 1995
The Best of the Superstars 1996
The Best of the Superstars 1997
The Best of the Superstars 1998
The Best of the Superstars 1999
The Best of the Superstars 2000
What Went Wrong?
When Boys Are Bad
& Sex Goes Wrong
Legends: The World's Sexiest
Men, Vols. 1 & 2
Legends (Third Edition)
Tarnished Angels (Ed.)

Fiction
Billy & David: A Deadly Minuet
The Bigger They Are...
The Younger They Are...
The Harder They Are...
Angel: The Complete Trilogy
Angel II: Stacy's Story
Angel: The Complete Quintet
A Natural Beauty (Editor)
The Kid (with Joe Leslie)
HUGE (Editor)
Strip: He Danced Alone

Fiction (Continued)
The Boys of Spring
Big Boys/Little Lies (Editor)
Boy Toy
Seduced (Editor)
Insatiable/Unforgettable (Editor)
Heartthrobs
Runaways/Kid Stuff (Editor)
Dangerous Boys/Rent Boys (Editor)
Barely Legal (Editor)
Country Boys/City Boys (Editor)
My Three Boys (Editor)
Mad About the Boys (Editor)
Lover Boys (Editor)
In the BOY ZONE (Editor)
Boys of the Night (Editor)
Secret Passions (Editor)
Beautiful Boys (Editor)
Juniors (Editor)
Come Again (Editor)
Smooth 'N' Sassy (Editor)
Intimate Strangers (Editor)
Naughty By Nature (Editor)
Dreamboys (Editor)
Raw Recruits (Editor)
Play Hard, Score Big (Editor)
Sweet Temptations (Editor)
Pleasures of the Flesh (Editor)
Juniors 2 (Editor)
Fresh 'N' Frisky (Editor)
Boys on the Prowl (Editor)
Heatwave (Editor)
Taboo! (Editor)

Entire Contents Copyrighted 8 1999-2006 by STARbooks Press, Herndon VA.

All rights reserved. Every effort has been made to credit copyrighted material. The author and the publisher regret any omissions and will correct them in future editions. Note: While the words "boy," "girl," "young man," "youngster," "gal," "kid," "student," "guy," "son," "youth," "fella," and other such terms are occasionally used in text, this work is generally about persons who are at least 18 years of age, unless otherwise noted.

First Edition Published in the U.S. in September, 2000
Second Edition Published in the U.S. in July, 2002
Third Edition Published in the U.S. in April, 2006
Library of Congress Card Catalogue No. 99-094937
ISBN No1-891855-73-5

Table of Contents

DEVIL-MAY-CARE by John Patrick 1
BILLY DOES HIS BOSS by John Patrick 13
VOICES FROM THE TEMPLE STEPS by Lewis Frederick 17
THE ONE by Lewis Frederick 35
RIPE FRUIT by Rick Jackson 43
STRAIGHT TO BED by Mario Solano 50
GREATER THAN BEING ALIVE by Jack Ricardo 52
A VERY SPECIAL DELIVERY by Rudy Roberts 57
IN THE GANG by Jack Ricardo 74
MY BROTHER, MY LOVE by Peter Eros 80
A STRANGE LIFE by Sonny Torvig 88
R. I. MIN by Peter Gilbert 96
A SINGAPORE SURPRISE by Rick Jackson 109
NOTHING SACRED by John Patrick 115
TWINS HAVE NO SECRETS by Peter Gilbert 118
THE LAST TABOO by Jesse Monteagudo 129
THE ADVENTURES OF FATHER MICHAEL by Frank Brooks 138
ADVENTURES WITH BILLY BOB by David MacMillan 154
THE PROMISE by Ronald James 161
CAUGHT IN CYBERSPACE by Barnabus Saul 166
A LITTLE EXPERIMENTATION by Peter Gilbert 175
SEX WITH X & Y by Tomcat 188
SHOWERS by Kevin Bantan 197
SURROGATE SEX by John Butler 202
MY COUSIN LIAM by Thomas C. Humphrey 212
THE PLEASURE BOYS by Peter Gilbert 221
THE STORY OF S: The New Boy In School by Barnabus Saul ... 232
THE BOY COOK'S COMPENDIUM by Peter Gilbert 238
WORSHIPING GODS by Leo Cardini 255
LEAVE WELL ENOUGH ALONE by Antler 270
STARK NEON MEMORIES by K.I. Bard 271
ODE TO BOY by Kevin Bantan 276
jesus + the turtles by Carl Miller Daniels 277
CELEBRATION by Carl Miller Daniels 280
BEYOND IMAGINING by JOHN PATRICK 281

Editor's Note

Most of the stories appearing in this book take place prior to the years of The Plague; the editor and each of the authors represented herein advocate the practice of safe sex at all times. And, because these stories trespass the boundaries of fiction and non-fiction, to respect the privacy of those involved, we've changed all of the names and other identifying details.

"The audience is on its feet calling 'Author! Author!' my mother is calling 'Arthur! Arthur!' my father's eyes are wet and a handsome young actor has flown in from the Coast to share the night with me. My father wouldn't want me to see the tears any more than I'd want him to see the actor."
Playwright Arthur Laurents,
in his autobiography *Original Story By*

- - -

"...I crawled to the other side of my room where Giovanni slept. I put my hand on his crotch. He had a hard-on. I took his cock out of his pajamas and held it in my hand. But I had no idea what to do with his penis, now that I had gotten a hold of it. Night after night I'd go over to Giovanni's bed and stroke his hard penis. I'd smell it, fascinated with the acrid smell that emanated from it, then I'd place it next to my cheeks and stroke it tenderly. This went on for most of my thirteenth year...."
Jaime Manrique in the book *Eminent Maricones*

- - -

"It all started at age seven when a neighbor boy taught me how to masturbate: The sensation of tugging the loose skin up and down around my small, hard penis was purely thrilling in and of itself. I needed no image, no story, to bring me to a dry, electric climax."
Boyer Rickel in the book *Taboo*

Gore Vidal (right) with one-time lover, ballet dancer Harold Lang, in Bermuda in 1947, courtesy of Wisconsin Center for Film and Theater Research. This relationship, considered taboo at the time, of course, is explored in the biography *Gore Vidal* by Fred Kaplan, available from STARbooks Press. One associate said that Harold did not have a beautiful body but a "handsome one." Kaplan notes that Lang was "notoriously randy and random; he had affairs, usually brief, with both sexes." Vidal confessed, "I had never known anything like this ... I was loving for the first time and everything was new." Likewise smitten was Arthur Laurents, who, in his book *Original Story By*, says Lang was "the best sex I'd ever had. He was the sailor with the ingratiating boyish grin and the white pants molded to Nobel-worthy buttocks. How could the answer to 'What is art?' compare to Harold Lang's ass?"

INTRODUCTION:

DEVIL-MAY-CARE by John Patrick

"I have tried everything except incest and folk dancing."
–Hermione Gingold, in her devil-may-care way,
to Gore Vidal

In his memoir *Teardrops On My Drum*, Jack Robinson recounts his defying taboos as a cute youngster in Liverpool. He had two lovers as a schoolboy. One was Eggy, his school chum, and the other was Eddie, a cop. Jack says of his love of Eggy: "...the love we shared was indescribable. Sitting at his side in school, sharing our sexy little secrets, sometimes puzzled at our own strange feelings. One part of my chemical content drew me to him, strong and masculine for the beauty and youth he had; the boy made me feel strong and manly, even lustful ... alive! The other half of me drew me to Eddie ... My man! I was feminine and wanted him to love me, take me, be inside my body! It was all too much for my childish mind to cope with.

"I'd been involved in so much dickie licking lately that I decided to go all the way with Eddie–do everything he wanted and just love him to death. I mentioned it to Eggy. 'Eddie's got a whole week off. I'm going to suck it for him, love him silly and not get out of bed all week.'"

"'You'll like it, Jackie. It's better than bumming. I love it!'

"'Strange ... strange you and I haven't sucked each other.'

"'Do you want to?'

"'No ... I just want Eddie. I love you like hell!'"

Later, Jack describes his first night out on the town with his cop/lover:

"Eddie was waiting patiently. 'Take a shower, Jackie. Put something nice on and wear a good overcoat. I'm taking you out tonight,' he said impatiently.

"'Will you link arms with me, Eddie?'

"'Yes, dear boy,' he replied in a fatherly voice.

"'Promise!'

"'Honestly! Hurry along-we're having a chicken dinner in town. Get dressed, monkey-we'll be late for the theater.'

"...Boys linked to men just fascinated me. Linking arms probably gave me more satisfaction than making love. It has always been accepted in Liverpool. The only place I've seen it." This "linking" defied the class barriers so common at the time, and all its taboos.

In the book *Eminent Maricones*, Jaime Manrique recalls the time his uncle Giovanni came to live with his family: "He was a handsome young man in his late twenties (which to me was old). I was attracted to him. We shared the same bedroom. Giovanni was in there to try to get a job as a secretary (he had gone to secretarial school), but he didn't seem to have luck landing any kind of work. At night, before going to bed, I'd watch him undress and put on his pajamas-he wore only the pants. I'd go to bed feeling thoroughly aroused. ...I crawled to the other side of my room where Giovanni slept. I put my hand on his crotch. He had a hard-on. I took his cock out of his pajamas and held it in my hand. But I had no idea what to do with his penis, now that I had gotten a hold of it. Night after night I'd go over to Giovanni's bed and stroke his hard penis. I'd smell it, fascinated with the acrid smell that emanated from it, then I'd place it next to my cheeks and stroke it tenderly. This went on for most of my thirteenth year. Whenever I saw Giovanni during the day, I'd close my eyes and imagine his cock in my hand, my lips touching the tip of its head. When we went for rides in his Jeep, I'd sit next to Giovanni and try to press my body against his. He seemed repelled by my advances even as he tolerated them."

And speaking of taboos, according to Manrique, one of playwright Federico Garcia Lorca's lovers, Philip Cummings was once seduced by Dionisio Carias, who says he went to bed with Cummings because it was the closest he could come to being with Lorca. During their relationship, Cummings revealed many intimate details about Federico. Dionisio Carias has written that in addition to saying that Lorca a very big dick), and was "very good" in bed, Cummings told Canas that Lorca was "a passionate Spaniard."

Manrique says that "Double Poem of Lake Eden" also contains some of the more beautiful and heartfelt verses Lorca wrote: "I am not a man, nor a poet, nor a leaf, / but a wounded pulse that circles the unknown," he says of his desire to explore a subject like sexuality, which was taboo in Spanish-American literature before he came along. Federico had been disappointed by Cummings and other lovers he had taken in New York, and it wasn't until he went to Cuba, where he was charmed by the black men of the island, that he began to truly enjoy himself. In his biography of Lorca, Ian Gibson writes, "As for the mulatto youths, with their chocolate-colored skin and breathtaking bodies, Lorca was by all accounts almost speechless with admiration and ... he soon began to pursue them."

In his book *Taboo*, Boyer Rickel recalls it all started at age seven when a neighbor boy taught him how to masturbate: "The sensation of tugging the loose skin up and down around my small, hard penis was purely thrilling in and of itself. I needed no image, no story, to bring me to a dry, electric climax."

Boyer would beat-off to images from girlie magazines the way his buddies did. "When beating off at night in bed, I'd lie back on the pillow and close my eyes, imagining impossible circumstances–in her bedroom or mine, or at night in the park–the story's climax a literal one. Meanwhile, it was particular boys whose bodies sent complex feelings of pleasure through me.

"Gradually, through high school, I began to move boys into my fantasies. In plot, these were no different from my stories about girls, equally impossible, equally thrilling sex after school under the athletic field bleachers, sex in his bedroom, where we'd gone to do algebra homework. But what such fantasies might signify was literally unthinkable. I experienced this as forgetting: daily, automatic, painless. For all I knew, I was just like my friends, forever horny, forever hoping for the chance to go all the way with a pretty girl...."

But then into his life along came Tony, a chunky Hispanic, the class giant, with skin dark as potting soil and the broad face of a Navajo: "He pushed me to the floor of a restroom stall. We'd shared the toilet, peeing from either side. He latched the metal door, guiding me to lie face down. Then he lay on top of me, pushing and wiggling to get his penis in. It felt almost good, the warmth of his weight and the pressure, though the linoleum was sticky and cold.

"'Now you try,' he said, peeling me back with an oversized hand. As I got started, we began to slide, as if the earth had tilted under us....

"By the time I was in college, all my sexual fantasies were homosexual, though their meaning was screened from my conscious mind. My eyes scanned classes, concert audiences, waiting lines in grocery stores, tables in the student union beer hall, for men, images of men to call up when I needed them, to live inside my narratives. The search was automatic, unconscious, as if performed by some other, some separate intelligence....

After graduating from college, he met Tone: "Tone sat, legs extended across the couch, like Elizabeth Taylor in 'Cleopatra.' This allowed the shawl to part, the sheer tights so form-fitting that I could see distinctly his circumcision line.

"I like the shape this little part makes here," he said, interrupting. He ran his finger down the middle of the lump made by his balls. ...He talked on about things I didn't have the concentration to comprehend, cradling his balls and stroking his lengthening cock, gazing into my eyes as though disconnected from the manipulations.

"He stopped talking when I pulled off my jeans. I lay down along his legs, kissing downward from his navel...."

In the interesting, highly readable book *Flipping*, Richard Ramos talks about different cultures and how what might be taboo to some is natural to others: "Incest was no problem to Manuel and Miguel. Growing up in Modesto, Manuel was serviced by his younger brother, Pablo, 'Pablita.' Same as I serviced my older brother. Pablita had an Afro permanent, and was queerer even than me. He wore women's underwear under colorful unisex clothes. And he was crazy for cock. Worse than me! Any cock. I discriminated, but he took black cock, white cock, baby brown cock. If cock came in blue or green, he'd take as many of them as he could get, too!

"One day Pablita interrupted Manuel and me. Manuel answered the door naked. His cock was semi-hard, wet with my saliva. Pablita leant over and licked it as he passed....

"I heard that some Moslems specialize in fucking sweet young things. Or anything that moves and doesn't move fast enough to run away from them. I've heard that the oil companies recruit Filipino sex slaves. Many are willing, I'm sure. Money talks, and not many Flips balk. Especially at a hard dick. 'Slide it in me and wiggle it around, Mr. Sheik!' is probably what they say. If they say anything at all. In my own experience, you don't need to say anything, just not run away."

In his memoir *Firebird*, Mark Doty recalls a story told to him by Warren, a participant in a writing workshop Doty taught. Sixty years before, as a second- or third-grader, Warren sat beside a boy whom he admired, a popular and handsome kid, and one day Warren noticed something he had never before observed: "When the handsome boy wore a polo shirt, his arm filled the sleeve, so that the fabric stretched a little. Warren's arms did not fill a sleeve in this way; it had never occurred to him that an arm could fill a sleeve, and in observing this characteristic of the boy's body Warren realized that he found it remarkable; the muscle, in its taut encasement of cloth, was a beautiful thing.

"Struck by what he had seen, Warren told another boy, a friend, and was startled by his friend's indifference to this matter: no response. After school, puzzled, he also told his mother about the beautiful arm, and she responded with a discussion of the variations in human body types, how some are naturally more muscled than others. Her intention was to reassure Warren that his body was acceptable, which was not what he was after. He knew what he felt, in the thrall of the swell of that boy's bicep. He understood, through some echo beneath her speech, unstated but perfectly clear, that he'd apprehended beauty in a location she did not approve. Message: there are private forms of loveliness, there are things about you no one should know. Should you be ashamed, to see what others cannot? Does the delight–your new, secret possession–outweigh your sense of singularity?

"Or does the shame simply commingle with the pleasure, infusing it with something airless, covetous, irremediably solitary: the boy alone in the hothouse of his loves?"

Most of us turn to porn, even porn videos, to explore the world of the forbidden in the privacy of our homes, and producers are happy to keep the

action flowing. Recently, Club Inferno (Hot House) brought us "Fist for Hire," starring Chris Ward, Jason Anderson, Tom Vacarro and Nick Nicaste, who is also known as Steven Foster (Mr. Boston Leather for 1997). The video tracks a day and night in the lives of four San Francisco fisting hustlers.

Hot House also brought us "Dr.'s Orders: Manipulation and Dilation," which Mannet.com's Butch Harris called a "masterwork," a hybrid of porn, comedy, drama and documentary that "pulsates with the multilayered rhythms of an epic, a two-part fisting fantasy is so realistic it's like having your hand up someone's butt (or vice versa) without the mess.

"The video opens with the demented duo of Dr. Mark Baxter and Nurse Jeff Baron as they take on the case of Mike Fuller's 'parched pooter.' After a long, slow prep session, Dr. Baxter dilates Mike's snappin' sphincter and then delivers the ultimate 'hands-in' treatment. Elsewhere in the clinic, Nurse Thom Barron straps Marcus Iron onto a porto-potty and forces him to give a urine sample. Just as Marcus is about to let loose, Nurse Baron is called next door to assist Dr. Glen Hunter perform an emergency rectal exam on patient Frank Parker's muscular posterior (beautiful, hairy and pink!). During the course of the procedure the unsuspecting Mr. Parker is subjected to some highly unusual experimentation involving his own semen and some suspicious purple liquid. Nurse Barron then returns to Marcus to finish what he started–brutally fucking the resistant Marcus into submission with his big, uncut anal probe.

"As Frank Parker continues to undergo unspeakable invasive acts at the hands (and dick) of Dr. Hunter, in another part of the clinic the extraordinary Johnny Rider and Mike Fuller take turns shoving large latex suppositories into each other's canal. Johnny then proceeds to sit on a world-class three-foot tall dildo–an unrivaled feat of anal dexterity. The final case study involves two newcomers, the aforementioned Nick Nicaste and the astonishing Dean Rodney. Nurse Nick administers a 'hole' series of huge buttplugs to the demanding Dean before finally diving in with both hands! Dean has a booty that knows no bounds.

"In *Dilation* the cutting-edge experimentation is continued with Intern Will Clark delivering an award-winning performance as he subjects muscleboy Josh Perez to a deep enema as well as a double-headed dildo. After filling Josh's hole with one end of the double-header, Intern Will takes to he opposite end...."

The now-forbidden practice of "barebacking" was included in Gino Colbert's hugely popular "Men in Blue" video. In fact, former model Todd Gibbs does escort from time to time if it's in a "fun way." He says when he does escort, he *only* barebacks and, as far as films are concerned, were he to return to the industry, he would do the same.

As Will Clark reported, it's all about dick. "JT Sloan," Will noted, "will be getting a Prince Albert soon after the tit ring that he had installed heals up. It seems to be a trend: Jim Buck, Kyle Brandon and Kevin Kramer all

have them. Geez, Kyle got his on video in *Fallen Angel 2*. Yikes!"

Yikes is right! That reminds us of the time at a bar in Provincetown when comic Bob Smith was relaxing before he went on stage. He was sitting at the bar listening to a guy named John, who said he was an expert on the subject of body piercing. In his book *Openly Bob,* Smith recalled that John's optional bodily orifices "now outnumbered the set he had been born with. John had six earrings, a stud through his nose, his nipples were pierced with small bolts, and, according to the bar owner, 'His dick has its own door knocker.'"

Smith's pals at the bar encouraged John to "whip it out," and Smith recounted that John's smile grew as he started to undo the buttons on the fly of his cutoffs. "He quickly yanked down his white underwear, proudly displaying his cock as if he was a little boy and he had just caught a frog. Hanging through the end of it was a large silver hoop. John had mounted the family jewels in an engagement ring. We frankly stared in astonishment–not so much at what we were seeing, as the fact that he was showing it with such poise. Having someone display their genitalia for public admiration is usually a cause for alarm. ...When asked to admire penis mutilation, do you admire the look, the ability to endure the process, or the sheer insanity of it?"

And speaking of insanity, in the introduction to her book *Satyricon USA,* author Eurydice says that in doing her research for the book, she met lawyers who paid to be electroshocked during their lunch hour, bankers who dressed as cheerleaders during their lunch hour, politicians who liked to be hung on a cross, bagpipers (armpit-sex), genuphallators (knee-sex), furtlers (sex with pictures of celebrities), and pygmalionists (sex with mannequins). "I attended workshops where burly truckers learned to perform 'sacred spot massage,' and sexuality camps where yuppie couples studied felching. But, unfortunately, none of these ever appears in the book. No felchers, no armpits, no electroshock."

"Like a stripper wearing pasties," the *Village Voice* commented, "Eurydice exposes more than most people would, and shakes it all around to give us a thrill; but certain particularly interesting bits never see the light of day. She is something of a tease, this Eurydice, and it's all the more frustrating because the body of the book is extraordinary and arousing. When she does deliver on her promises (sexual cutters, wanna-be vampires) she elicits sweet nuggets of truth from her interview subjects, exposing the most private, transgressive behaviors. Their delicious confessions not only illuminate the human psyche, they also offer prurient thrills."

One of the author's subjects, Matthew, slated to become president of a major American Catholic university, is a sexually compulsive homosexual. "AIDS," he claims, "would be the end of my addiction and the start of my martyrdom."

Taboos eroticize the forbidden, according to the *Voice* article, both in the Catholic Church and in the morgue. And necrophiliacs, like sexually active

priests, live ordinary lives in ordinary places. "At a lesbian sex club, women called 'Daddy and her Boy' have intercourse with a dildo: Daddy pumps the Boy hard holding her by the hair, panting, groaning, and yelling, then suddenly stops, just short of climaxing, and pulls out. Boy keeps writhing. The smack of Daddy's paddle reprimands her. Through it all, Eurydice is silent about her own desires. Her erotic needs remain largely unspoken, her appearance and background a mystery.

"...Any sex writer must decide whether to make him–or herself an object of desire for the reader, and Eurydice has chosen a slippery position of near invisibility while generating a lot of voyeuristic heat. It's part of the tease; her sexual identity is one of the many intriguing things that remain hidden as her voice delivers unexpected erotic jolts, waves of repulsion, and glimpses of the human sexual soul."

Susan Crain Bakos, writing in *Kink: The Hidden Sex Lives of Americans*, says she went to swingers-club parties and talked to lifestyle s/m players. She found that the most outrageous sexual behaviors vanish into the ordinariness of the person who practices them, and that the originality of transgression is only a diversion from an underlying need for uniformity and safety. ...More than that, however, its forays into the underworld beneath the underworld make an archival contribution to sexology."

And speaking of forays into the underworld, Virgil Vang, in *Queer PAPI Porn*, describes a visit to a sex club where the guys can ignore the rules: "...We spread our legs, exposing our shaved assholes to Alain, who walked slowly around each of us, nudging and adjusting our positions with his blunt toes. As his big toe probed my hole, digging downward, it created a sensation and strange craving in me I could have never imagined before. He wanted his whole foot in me, his toes walking up my ass. ...One by one we bent over, as the two assistants rubbed aromatic oil into our assholes. I groaned. With a covert glance, I saw the others stiffen with excitement.

"As we danced slowly around each other's rope-tied cock, we began stroking each other, fondling balls and fingering asscracks. The assistants motioned us to walk on our hands and knees, in a circle. I imagined that we possessed the sleekness of a panther, leopard, horse, or tiger. The assistants took turns placing our cocks into their mouths, teasing us until we got hard.

"As we walked, or more accurately, crawled, Alain seized us up one by one. The rope jerked and I looked toward my left, where Alain was bent over, rimming Jorge's ass. I could not draw my eyes away from Alain's flushed, bulbous cockhead. Then Niyo slid under his legs, taking Alain's tool into his delicate mouth. But what I really wanted were Alain's muscular thighs around my waist, his thick cock pumping my hole. For that I would have to wait. But my ass was ready for Alain this time. I waited until Alain did Niyo.

"Then it was my turn. I relaxed my buttocks and let him in. Suddenly, with a twist of the rope and of his body, Solar erupted in front of me, unable to hold himself. His dark cock expanded to twice its size as he shot,

spewing droplets over me and on the concrete floor. He flushed and placed his palms together in mock apology. The assistants ignored him and motioned for us to keep moving in a circle. As we moved, Alain moved in on us, rimming Vander and Solar by turns."

As many have discovered to their delight, what may be taboo one place is perfectly all right somewhere else. India, for instance, is the land of the beautifully sensual and the ridiculously repressed, of sumptuous splendor and sickening squalor, according to Ganapati S. Durgadas, reporting for *Black Sheets*: "It is a society where for ages people have searched for Divine Truth and a society where its bourgeoisie have been in massive denial for decades, especially about the society's sexual history.... When I landed at Bangalore Airport from Singapore, this was one of the things on my mind. How would I, an openly bisexual male, fare in this state of affairs? Enforcing the bourgeoisie's denial is India's adoption of the British Penal Code of 1834, complete with its restrictions against sodomy. It is being challenged in the Indian Supreme Court, and routinely broken daily, even by the police, who bust tea room trade, then solicit free sex from the arrested men (which should give you an idea how widespread sexual activity is throughout the society). I realized that I was entering a sexual war zone where the ancient past is being rediscovered by contemporary queers as ammo in their battle against their brainwashed 'modern' government.

"Everywhere I went in South India, I saw young men walking arm in arm, even kissing one another in the parks and alleys of Bangalore, outside temple promenades, on the commercial streets. Such displays of male affection appeared to be a working-class phenomenon, allowing such shows of affection plenty of room to slide over to the sexual when in private.

"...Though romantic love has always existed in Indian society, arranged marriages are the norm. Marriage is more a business merging of two families' interests than that of the particular couple, so this puts pressure on single people to marry. Men get the better part of the deal, because once they are married, a gay or bisexual man can still carry on with same-sex relationships so long as they don't impede or fracture the marriage. Women have less freedom in marriage but engage in similar affairs, if so inclined, given the opportunity of their own same-sex social environs....

"One Brahmin I know left his new wife and infant son home every night to spend time with his male friends to attend parties where, his wife protested, there were other women, including old girlfriends of his. My 'gaydar' suggested something different when I met one of those friends, a pharmacist. Narayan was a dark and handsome Tamil man, in his late twenties, but with an older air about him ... He was short, yet muscular of frame, with thick, curly black hair. He had a bright smile that lit up his dark, cocoa-brown face, and an inquisitive yet friendly manner about him. Quite educated, he did not hide his displeasure with his country's failings, social and economic, nor did he hesitate questioning U.S. norms or policies. I immediately took a liking to him, especially appreciative of his efforts to

make me feel comfortable and at ease in this immense, sprawling country. I felt an immediate sexual attraction to him but had to be careful. I was staying at a pundit Brahmin's house, surrounded by the Brahmin's relatives. The Brahmin's family in the States knew about my bisexuality, but I was not willing or ready to test the tolerance of the local segment of the family.

"When we left on a pilgrimage drive through Karnatika and Tamil Nadu, Narayan accompanied us. Another male beauty was our car's driver, the chauffeur of a Bangalore real estate businessman who was transacting a land deal with the Brahmin's family. The businessman lent us his Indian-made Volvo clone station wagon for the trip. The chauffeur was a tall, angular man, slimly moustached, with the same thick Dravidian hair, but clipped shorter than Narayan's. He had the same thick chocolate complexion, and was a delightful, playful and affectionate soul. Many a time I felt his body brush up against mine, his arms affectionately on my shoulder, or tapping playfully on my back as we waited in line in a temple for darshan, or the ritual unveiling and fire-lit sacraments of that temple's particular deity.

"How to venture further? A wave of curiosity and desire stirred through me. I was on a religious pilgrimage, but I wasn't dead to what my senses said to me. The exquisite mountain terrain and far-flung rice paddies of the South Indian countryside, the incredibly verdant greens of the flora, the rich turquoise-blue skies which seemed to go on forever. They only added to the puzzling excitement. I definitely was picking up an erotic vibe, but had to play it cool because the Chief Priest was leading us on this tour. Meanwhile, the pharmacist constantly caressed and hugged, squeezed and ran his hands through the hair of the younger Brahmin with a fervor I suspected was more than platonic. I watched them from the corner of my eye as we sat in the back seat of the car, while we rounded narrow snaky mountainside roads, upon the stone walls of which, gray short-haired monkeys frolicked and carried their young. The younger Brahmin did not reciprocate the affection with the same fervor, so the pharmacist eventually cooled his attentions, turning to inquiring conversation with me, much to my delight, still puzzled as I was.

"When we reached Shringeri my 'gaydar' was confirmed, but not in the way I might have liked. ...Being an adopted Brahmin, I shared a large bedroom with the Chief Brahmin and his son. Narayan and the chauffeur were roomed elsewhere-where, I dared not ask. In the morning, when we woke, we were to set off, but could not find either. We asked other pilgrims in the building we were staying where they had gone to. We were answered that they'd been seen heading towards the length of riverside outside Shringeri's nearby tall, walled gateway. The Chief Priest, being impatient to get started on the road, sent someone to fetch them. When they returned they had the lulled, sleepy look of men who had sex, and the smell of semen was on Narayan. It was so strong it stung through my nostrils and sharp into my mind. Yet no one said a word...."

If you're seeking to defy the rules and don't want to leave the U.S., New York City has always been a great place to go. It remains on the cutting edge, according to Guy Trebay, writing for the *Village Voice*. He visited the Lure, a large and intentionally grungy leather and s/m bar in the meatpacking district of Manhattan, equipped with a permanently installed slave training cage, and handcuffs suspended from the ceiling.

Trebay was at the Lure on "Pork Night," a once-weekly theme evening celebrating the interactions of sex, culture, and community and everyone's inner sex pig. In the mix there is a posse of go-go boys from the Latino Fan Club, and porn veteran Donnie Russo, a sweet-natured guy whose video specialty is trussing up eager bottoms and tanning their behinds. "I've been reigning for a long time," explains Russo, who made over 200 films in the past nine years, has his own Web site, and who started out posing for straight skin rags. Arranging the zipper on his leather jeans so it's opened to the trimmed pubic patch that, in the biz, is called a Hitler mustache, he says, "I've really grown up in porn."

On this particular night, Trebay found, the fund-raising was to set up scholarships to help ex-prostitutes. "You definitely find out someone's true colors when they're confronted with sex workers," a prostitute named Che told Trebay. "Fifteen minutes in the back seat of a car is the limit of most people's interest in the life circumstances of the average hooker,"Trebay commented, which is what made it so extraordinary that the Lure would help out. Russo charged only $5 for each spanking, and, as might be expected, the line was long for the service.

"Just because Times Square has gone the pure and innocent way of the young, critics have decried the death of sex in New York. It's not so," reported *Unzipped* magazine. "While many of the sex emporiums of yore have closed their doors, there is still a thrill to be had, if you know where to look." They recommended attendance at the infamous Black Party, where "performances run the gauntlet from vanilla leather sex, where the boys just fucked while wearing leather) to serious 'edge play' (two civilian leathermen demonstrated piercing on their 'boy')."

Yes, when porn stars, and their ilk, defy taboos these days they get lots of press. Witness Ronnie Larsen and his popular plays "Making Porn" and "10 Naked Men." A 29-year-old erstwhile San Franciscan, Larsen told the *Bay Area Reporte*r, "We all get lumped into the category of nudie plays, but I've spent a year working on this. You'll see it has structure and a story, and it's not just people shaking their penises.

"I'm fascinated about the relationship between sex and money, and I don't think prostitution is a bad thing. I think it's an interesting thing. ...(The play) is very sexual and very nasty. Someone pays to get peed on someone else to get led around on a leash, and my character pays to get raped."

About Sebastian, recruited from the stage show at the Campus Theatre to appear in the play, Larsen says, "I needed someone hot to be our poster boy. I think of myself as much as a businessman as a playwright. I don't ever

want to be a starving artist again." He admits his plays are based on his experiences. "I'm obsessed with sex, and that's what I write about. But I have no fantasies. My plays are about reality, about pulling back the curtain. It's all about disillusionment." And defying taboos.

Of course, since many consider the hiring of a boy for sex is taboo, it can be a thrilling experience to defy them. A fan named Eddie says, "I agree that there's a certain 'taboo' thrill for me in hiring escorts, as well as a desire for what I want, when I want it, as was always stated. I'm 33, and have been told that I'm attractive; no spectacular body, but no slouch, either. I'm rather serious and a little shy in my daily life. I have only hired escorts out of town when traveling-I guess, in a sense, doing something exciting that I wouldn't do at home. On my home turf, I'm looking for a stable relationship, and therefore don't pick up at the bars (although some chance encounters do happen from time to time!). When I'm away from home, I feel like I can let my hair down, be somewhat anonymous, and satisfy my sexual desires without emotional attachments. I enjoy talking to the escorts I hire, and becoming friendly if only for an hour-makes the experience pleasant, still with no strings attached. One escort once questioned why I hired him. Said I was handsome and 'didn't need' to hire someone. Maybe I don't, but it's fun!" And taboo!

But what once was taboo is quickly becoming mainstream. What to make of this? "Lately trend watchers have been making noise about the fact that pornography keeps on-excuse the pun-popping up," Ingrid Sischy says in *Interview*. "And no question, the trend watchers are correct-in endless ways the existence of pornography is no longer hidden under the counter, under the bed, or under wraps the way it once was. ... But it's inaccurate to confuse sex with pornography-they're each their own subject. The fact is that it was because sex and the body were treated as taboo subjects that the concept of pornography emerged in the first place, and then really exploded with the industrial revolution.

"Since then, sex and pornography have often been wadded together with both of them often treated as taboo subjects. It's important to unwind them, and it's also important to get rid of the taboos around these subjects so that we can understand them. ...We're living in a culture that's obsessed with sex-and what's funny is that often it's the people who seem the most obsessed with it who are the ones who decry it, and want to call the censors out. ... Because of AIDS, it became clearer than ever how lethal ignorance, lying, and hypocrisy about sex can be. ...It seems to me that as a culture we haven't gotten much further in terms of having a healthy environment when it comes to these same old issues. We've still got major hypocrisy and name-calling. We've still got people whose first impulse is to censor and we've still got a lot of repression whenever sex or sexuality comes up. In other words, we still live in a world where sex is like a landmine that can blow up at the slightest vibration. ...(I) am a firm believer in the role of the provocateur (and I know well) the relationship between provocation and

change. Change, after all, is a form of hope...."

Editor Boyd (*Scum*, etc.) McDonald once heard from a Long Island man who said he was 72 and married 43 years. "During the depression years," the man said, "I was sent to a Catholic Home for Boys. There were about forty boys there.

"When I was about eight, one of the big guys forced me in a corner, pulled my pants down, and fucked me. I was glad it didn't hurt. Just felt sticky and ashamed. He came to my bed at night. Fucked me sideways. Told me to squeeze my cheeks after he had it in. I became good at it after awhile. I then fucked other boys and they fucked me. A lot of fucking was going on.

"The man in charge of the boys came to each bed in the Dorm. He must have sucked many cocks a night. He sucked me so much once I pleaded with him to stop. But after I looked forward to see him come to my bed.

"Nothing happened till I got in the army. The clerk-he was gay-and I were on guard duty in Germany during the war. I held his carbine [weapon] when he blew me. I couldn't get his huge cock in my mouth but I licked & sucked him till he came. Once in a cellar we were staying in he let me fuck him. He had so much hair around his hole it was like a Brillo pad.

"After the war, at the Hotel St. George [Brooklyn], they had a pool, sauna etc. Plenty of rooms. I was fucked by a guy with a monster dick. No Vaseline. It was great after he had it in. I was also blown a few times.

""'I haven't had sex with anyone other than my wife since that time. When I'm all alone, I finger-fuck myself. I also make myself bare-ass and smack my ass hard till it stings.... I love asses, men's or women's. Cocks are great too, but I'm basically an ass man. I put my finger in my hole and then suck it. Nice!"

McDonald said that he thought this was a major religious story: the manager of a Catholic boys' home sucking his way from bed to bed in the dormitory. "I wrote asking for a letter with details," Boyd said, "but the guy didn't put out. Some men put out, some don't. I guess this one's too busy sticking his finger in his butt-which is admittedly more fun than writing letters." Boyd died in September 1993, two months after completing his final book, *Scum*, and a major seeker of stories about taboo sex practices was gone forever.

BILLY DOES HIS BOSS by John Patrick

Eric was justifiably proud of his long, thick, veiny cock. Easing back the foreskin, he pushed the moist end between young Billy's pouty lips, ready to thrust straight into him. Billy pulled back a little, his palms against Eric's hairy thighs. "Wait a second."
Eric was now irritated. "C'mon, blow me."
"No, it's that funny smell in here. I don't like it. They haven't cleaned this place in days."
"Okay, we'll go into my office. It'll be okay there."
In a moment Billy rose to his feet, and Eric gathered him in his arms, and kissed him deeply. Billy moaned as Eric's tongue probed deeply into Billy's mouth. Christ, Eric thought, he was about to explode. All he could think of was burying his cock inside Billy's warm, accommodating young mouth.
As the door to the john creaked open, Eric was buckling his belt. As he strode across the hall and wrenched open the door to his office, holding it for Billy, Eric's cock vibrated with a sweet ache. He thought he could never get enough of the potent rush of sensation as he filled Billy's mouth with his cum. The fact that he was a married man and that Billy was in his charge made what they did even more exciting to him. Eric locked the door behind him. "We'll be fine here. Everybody's gone for the day."
Billy was still dubious. He had always blown Eric in the john. It was always furtive, the danger of it making Eric come in mere seconds. Now, in Eric's office after closing time, with the outside world locked out, Billy knew he was in for something more. Not that he didn't *want* something more, it's just that Eric never asked for more. After he had blown Eric and gone back to his desk, Billy would still be hard, and after Eric had gone back to work he would sit there, stroking himself, wondering what it would be like to have Eric's big cock up his ass, and he would mess his pants.
Eric took Billy in his arms and kissed him again. Billy shivered with delight as Eric stripped him, caressed him. Billy was feeling hot over every inch of on his skin. Even where Eric did not touch, Billy could feel him. And the burning touch of Billy was in Eric's mind too. His long pale fingers reached between Billy's thighs, expertly stroking him. Billy grew ever more swollen under his touch, his cock pulsing and throbbing until wanting him was agony. Now Eric did something he had never done, not in all the months Billy had been working here, Eric took Billy's cock in his mouth. Billy fell back, across Eric's desk, and his legs parted to permit Eric full access to his body. He wanted Eric to take whatever he wanted.
The sucking, nice though not as expert as his own, lasted only moments. Billy lifted up so that Eric could lick and probe his asshole with his tongue. "Oh, yes," Billy groaned, and Eric knew what the boy liked. He wanted to please the boy.

"Spread your legs," he ordered. Something in his tone of voice made Billy obey him.

"Wider!" he barked.

Billy didn't need a second bidding. His hole was stretched wide to receive the three horny fingers which were thrust roughly into him. Billy's head sank back on the desk

"Jerk yourself," Eric commanded.

Eric's nostrils flared with concentration and his face beaded with sweat as he finger-fucked Billy and Billy jerked his own cock. Eric had never finger-fucked anyone with such vigor. Meantime Billy rubbed himself like crazy. Before long, Billy felt his mouth opening in a long "Oh" of excitement, and he bucked himself to orgasm.

"Oh, shit," Eric cried.

Billy couldn't help himself, but the fact of the orgasm did not dampen Eric's intense desire to enter Billy.

Billy looked down and saw Eric's prick was hard and throbbing and aimed directly at his asshole, which was open and vulnerable.

Eric dipped down, then, when he straightened up, his prick went straight in, up to the hilt. It took Billy's breath away. Billy's head went back and he gasped out loud. But before Billy had recovered from that first thrust, Eric had pulled his cock out and then rammed it home again. And again. Soon he had a rhythm going, a good steady fucking. Billy felt his warm, panting breath in his ear.

After a while, Eric swayed back from Billy so he could get a grasp on Billy's hips. It also meant his cock was angled for even sharper thrusting. Every now and then he would stop and grind his pelvis against Billy's. In turn, Billy gyrated his hips against Eric's. Billy could feel the thick prick twisting and squirming inside his body. He was amazed at Eric's self-control, because several times he thought Eric would come, but he stopped, held back, went back in again. But, all good things come to an end and Billy was overwhelmed by Eric's thunderous orgasm.

Eric helped Billy off the desk. Billy's clothes were all rumpled and there were papers everywhere, but Eric looked cool as a cucumber in his pinstripe suit. He sat in the armchair and sipped what was left of his coffee, looking at Billy through narrowed eyes as Billy dressed. "Just remember who's boss around here," he said quietly.

And that was the start of it. From then on, it became a regular occurrence, which suited Billy just fine. Before five o'clock, it was all business, getting the stock orders filled, boxing, tagging. Billy worked hard. But after five, when the building had cleared, they got down to the real business of the day.

Once, out of curiosity, Billy asked Eric where he had learned to satisfy a man so thoroughly. He narrowed his gaze and gave Billy a penetrating look through those clear blue eyes. "Many years of experience, my boy," was all he would ever say.

Several weeks later, Eric was becoming careless, and on a Saturday, when he had brought Billy in on overtime, he had forgotten to lock his office door. In fact, he had even left it ajar. They were hard at it when Billy looked over and saw the hunky driver Aaron Slater standing in the doorway watching them. Aaron's cute face was expressionless as he tried to comprehend what he had stumbled upon. Billy smiled at him in mid-fuck and Aaron winked back. The desk was at an angle to the door, so all Aaron could see of Eric was his back and his clenched white buttocks dipping in and out between Billy's stretched thighs. Eric quickened his thrusts and started panting his way towards orgasm, and Billy, even though he had already come, began jerking his cock again, mainly because being watched by Aaron turned him on. Billy started moaning even louder than usual in time with Eric's thrusts.

Aaron stepped inside the room, and his breath quickened. Suddenly Eric realized something was amiss. He turned and saw Aaron. In surprise Eric jerked his organ out of Billy's ass. But he had already gone past the point of no return. With a grunt, Eric grabbed his cock just as it exploded.

Aaron's eyes were wide with excitement as he watched the boss achieve the heights of ecstasy before his eyes. Aaron by now had his own cock out of his pants and was stroking it. Coming down from his high, Eric smiled at him. "Well, Aaron, I got it warmed up for you...." And he stepped aside, giving Aaron a clear shot at Billy's now sopping-wet ass.

"Oh, man," Aaron said, approaching them. "I've been wantin' to do this for weeks."

As Eric stepped back, Aaron took up a position between Billy's legs. With a cheeky grin, he took hold of Billy's ankles and stretched his legs wide apart, peering straight down into his bunghole. He gave Billy another wicked smile and a wink as he stroked his cock to full hardness. Aaron's longish fair hair flopped down attractively over his forehead as he aimed his thick prick at the target.

Before Billy had time to admire the cock too much, it was in him, all the way, and Aaron's hairy balls were slapping Billy's buttocks. Eric was impressed with the earnestness Aaron applied to the job. He had never shown much sign of eagerness about any of his other duties, but this he excelled at. Eric's cock began to twitch again, and Billy reached out and took hold of it, bringing it to his mouth. As Aaron screwed him, Billy went at sucking Eric's cock with renewed interest. Cum soon was jetting from it, and Billy backed up to allow the sperm to fall on the dark mahogany desk.

At just about the same moment, Aaron withdrew his cock and fisted it until a geyser of cum spurted into the air and landed on Billy's hard, hairless stomach. After that, Billy came again, and the two of them massaged the resulting cum into Billy's trembling body.

Thus began an after-hours routine that often turned into a threesome. Sometimes Eric would fuck Billy while Billy sucked on Aaron's cock. Or

else Billy would suck Eric while Aaron fucked him. As Aaron was so much younger, only nineteen, and single, he was able to meet Billy out of the office, and a short romance began. Seeing how the young beauties got along, Eric often would simply sit in his chair and watch them make love, jerking himself off.

As Aaron plunged into Billy, Billy arched his back, matching him thrust for thrust. Billy became shameless in Aaron's strong arms, rotating his hips and rubbing himself against the base of his shaft. Eric laughed aloud with delight at the wantonness of young Billy.

In the aftermath of their fierce lovemaking, Aaron would hold Billy tight, feeling a vicious delight that Eric, always hovering somewhere nearby, had to content himself with a pleasure solely of the senses. All too brief and empty.

Aaron and Billy had found love after taking their pleasures in any way they could in the past. As their love blossomed, as Eric thrust his cock strongly into Billy's mouth, the glimpse of the past relationship between Billy and Eric added fuel to the flames of Aaron's desire for Billy. As time wore on, Aaron came to see Eric as someone apart, cold, and often ruthless, a boss taking advantage of his position. It was inevitable that this would happen, and it was also inevitable that Billy and Aaron would eventually leave their jobs and start a new life-together.

VOICES FROM THE TEMPLE STEPS
by Lewis Frederick

The first time the oracle passed through our village, I knew I would see her again someday. I had one of those feelings that visit me often, ever since a childhood fever ravaged me. The sensations come suddenly, something between seeing and smelling a truth, though every known fact shouts it cannot be.

So I sensed that the priestess would return my way, not just once but many times in years to come. I could not know then how deeply our lives would intertwine. No one could have imagined that, not even the oracle.

A harsh idea reared its Gorgon head at me. Perhaps she did foresee her own fate, just as she understood everything else so clearly. Perhaps she knew and yet asked me to join her anyway, out of the inestimable love in her limitless heart.

I struggle to drive the notion away, but it haunts me daily, even in my dreams. And I have such colorful dreams these days, late in a long life, with little else to occupy me.

My grandmother, the village crone, saw the look in my eye that warm spring evening the temple party first found our village. Scampering with a host of naked boys along the beach at high tide, I left my friends in the rosy sunset of the Aegean without a second thought. Something special was happening overhead and I had to be there to see it.

Scrambling up the hillside, I landed in the midst of a rare community crisis. A herd of asses blocked the single road through our village. Townsfolk pulled on the animals' ears, kicking them from behind, shouting curses and waving rags at them. To the side, the grandest palanquin I had ever seen stood waiting for the impasse to clear.

Six blue-black men held its poles on their shoulders so effortlessly the litter might have been made of fleece. Talking amongst themselves in some unknown musical tongue, they chuckled at the villagers' antics with the beasts.

A glittering gauze swathed the palanquin walls but blew apart now and then in the soft evening breeze. Approaching the litter in small, steady steps, I smelled the heat of the black men's bodies and saw their sweat dripping from muscled arms and thighs. Close to the palanquin, all was quiet except for the whisper of jeweled curtains rippling in the wind. When the dancing fabric parted once more, an arresting face met mine in a penetrating gaze.

It was Elena, temple priestess, en route to her new summer home. Never has a more marvelous creature graced this earth. She defies description to this day. She is quite simply Elena, a demi-goddess, and she has been the source of my greatest torment these many years since. The woman, Elena;

the spirit, Elena. How I have hated her sometimes–and loved her so many others. I would give her my life. Maybe I already have.

These intense feelings pale against a far greater force, the love we both felt for another, the king. And that is how our journey really began.

It seems to me now so much hinged then on matters of beauty, her beauty and his, though generally men aren't spoken of in that way. But if ever there were a man who could be called beautiful, the king was that man. His beauty, in fact, may have outshone Elena's. At least it did for me, many times.

There were always two limits to Elena's charms. She was not a man and she was not of our people. In the world where we lived, there were no greater impediments to power than being female and a barbarian. Yet she did the best any woman could do in such an unkind age. Some say that she did very well in fact.

Grandmother whispered all of this to me that day on the road in our village. Even as I stood staring at Elena's amazing face between the parted curtains, the old woman hissed her story in my ear.

"She is the first temple whore, most holy woman in the land, though she comes from Asia Minor, captured by the king in a raid on her city."

Tiring of the crone's hot breath, I shrugged her off and ran to the other side of the road. Hobbling after me, my grandmother continued her story *sotto voce* loud enough for the entire village to hear.

"They say that she loves him nevertheless ... though he raped her and slew her family ... she is married to the oracle though and pledged to service the temple pilgrims. When the king comes to worship, she closets herself with him for days."

From this side of the litter, I could only see her profile as Elena watched the sun set swiftly over the sea. At that angle and in that moment, she had a soft, dreamy look, a little fragile perhaps, hardly the most powerful and holy woman in the land just then. A profound sadness settled over me as she put one hand to her brow and looked down wearily at the other in her lap. Was she weeping, or simply lost in thought, I wondered.

There was no time to find out. The villagers had finally cleared the roadway and the litter-bearers fell into their paces once more. Through the wind-tossed drapes, I saw Elena look over her shoulder as the litter took a bend in the road and disappeared. A shriek broke from my grandmother, and I turned to see her pick something from the ground.

"A gold coin!" she crowed. "The priestess has left my boy a gold coin!" She waved it triumphantly over her head several times to make sure everyone saw it, then placed it into my grubby palm.

Sure enough, it was a solid gold piece bearing the Semitic face of some Asian monarch on both sides, clearly none of our local currency. I ran down the road a bit to see if I could catch the runners, but they were already out of sight.

Why? I puzzled. What had the priestess seen in me to show me such

favor? Surely it was merely some gesture of largesse, nothing personal. Grandmother stumped after me, puffing loudly.

"Elena *noticed* you," she said. "And you had one of your feelings about her too, didn't you? I saw it in your eyes. It's a sign of some sort. Something great will come of this."

"So you wish, old woman," I shouted and ran with the coin to the beach, where I promptly threw it into the tide as an offering. I wanted no more of signs or portents tonight. For now, I wanted only to remember that face.

- - -

Years passed before anything more of significance occurred, but when it did, Grandmother was far from pleased. I had grown to near adulthood but remained small and hairless as a piglet with the soft, soprano voice of a boy. Passionate impulses stirred inside me, but I remained uncertain how to express them except in furtive explorations with other youths or alone on my pallet late at night, my grandmother's snores nearby posing a foil to anything but the strongest erotic urges.

I still thought of Elena daily, constantly in fact. But her palanquin never stopped in our village again, though it sometimes passed through, under heavier draperies than before. No more gold coins appeared in the roadbed and I resigned myself to the truth: she had never given me a second thought. Then one day I returned to my grandmother's hut to find a strange visitor waiting there. A gigantic, bald man sat astride a sagging horse in front of our door, fanning himself with an ostrich plume.

Grandmother saw me first and interceded. "Come here, child!" she said and pulled me to her ample bosom. I wrestled against her girth, examining the exotic visitor between her unwelcome hugs and kisses. He was the most impressive human being I had ever seen, not beautiful like Elena, but infinitely more provocative. In a first flash of adult insight, the word came to my lips ☐ *eunuch.*

I stood entranced. Our people did not tend to perform male castrations; we valued a whole, lusty male too much. But our soldiers took hostages of all sorts from other lands, bringing them home to work where they seemed best suited, in domestic service, or temple business. This particular one was tall but plump, masculine but soft. A certain cold cruelty danced about his eyes, though he wore a greasy smile and spoke in courtly language.

"So this is the one, then?" he said to Grandmother.

"No, *this is not!*" she threw back at him rudely.

"The one for *what?*" I asked between Grandmother's protestations. "What are you both talking about?"

The eunuch dismounted and hunkered down on his haunches. "Wouldn't you like to come live in a palace and eat meat whenever you want?"

Grandmother placed her imposing person between us. "Ask him what it will cost you," she screamed at me. "Your *manhood*, perhaps? Have him tell

19

you how *that* feels!"

The eunuch took on a wounded air. "Am *I* not a man then?" he asked softly. "Am *I* less than human?"

Grandmother didn't like the direction this dialogue was taking. "Don't listen to him," she spat into my ear, clutching me so tightly I choked.

He continued in a sorrowful voice. "I have always been treated well. The lady Elena has seen to it." He looked at me sharply as he threw these last words out.

I was lost to my grandmother at that moment. "You know the high priestess then?" I asked.

"We are ☐ how should I say it? *Familiar*," he said, and looked smugly at Grandmother.

"When can I go?" I asked the giant. In response, he simply smiled, while Grandmother commenced to keen.

Within the hour, I was ensconced on his broad lap, riding a wheezing horse to a new life. I would never see Grandmother or any of my people again. I shudder sometimes now to think how heartlessly I left her. But it was not my time to love yet. Those feelings would come later, with Elena and the king.

Soon enough I would know the pain of longing. Soon enough I would learn it was possible to want someone too much.

- - -

Soon enough I would also learn that a temple can be a very strange place. People say that gods live there, that the gods hold court within them. But some very surprising and human things occur in temples too.

Imagine a city filled to overflowing with people and beasts of burden. Smells of garbage, human sewage and animal dung fill its air. Now imagine a multi-colored palace, perched high on a hill above this world. Imagine yourself walking slowly among ordered columns, reaching out now and then to touch their cool perfection. Overhead, doves flutter and coo in dulcet tones. Imagine yourself sighing, knowing for a certainty you are among the gods.

Only don't look to the left, for there you will see a lamb's throat being slit, his blood draining into a cup for a priest's ceremonials. And don't look to the right, for there you will see a whore astride a soldier, her knees gripping his thighs while his loins grind hard against hers. And don't listen too closely, for everywhere you will hear the clink of coins changing hands, making deals, buying time, grace, blessings.

For weeks I wandered this alien land like a visitor from a different world, which in fact I was. Left largely to myself, I saw to my colorful education with enthusiasm. Both temple-goers and staff alike proved remarkably eclectic people, open to a host of possibilities, especially those involving a spry pubescent boy. Priests and eunuchs invited me to attend

animal sacrifices and ritual libations. Temple whores welcomed my watching as they serviced pilgrims. Sometimes I helped them and their partners reach fruition to the process, or merely brought them sponges and water to bathe afterward. I learned a lot in this way about human bodies and love-making, though at that point in my development, I found it all a curious business indeed, more comical or athletic than sensual, to be sure.

As always, Elena made the difference there. I saw little of her, yet lived for the moments when she sent for me. From the beginning, her manner toward me posed a puzzle. She was indescribably tender then suddenly aloof. Sometimes she held and stroked my head for hours, singing a nursery song in some strange, foreign tongue. The next day I would run to her as she stood at the altar, and feel her look right through me when I whispered her name.

I believe she communed with the gods, perhaps far more than she talked with other mortals. I was miserable without her, but unsettled in her company as well. One thing I always knew. She was clearly my protectress.

Not long after my arrival in this strange world, two things happened that convinced me of Elena's commitment to me.

A band of assorted eunuchs roamed the temple corridors at all times, serving in some intermediary spiritual-aide role which I never quite understood. They held great authority with worshipers, collecting moneys and directing ceremonials. Priests and priestesses too relied on their help heavily. But they also occupied some strange, dissonant social strata, neither man nor woman, neither child nor adult. I soon saw that they were the butt of many jokes. However, to their faces, the temple-goers treated them with deference. They were, after all, generally quite huge.

Which was just the problem the night I awoke with one nuzzling my neck as I lay on my palette behind the altar of some lesser god. Certainly I was no stranger by then to the vagaries of temple love. I had seen and sampled a variety of experiences. But a eunuch in my bedclothes with lust in his eyes was more than I could manage that night. I protested, he cajoled. I resisted, he insisted. I tried to wriggle free and he pinned me beneath his bulk. I wasn't sure what came next. Weren't eunuchs supposed to be disinterested in such pursuits?

"*Enough!*" An imperious voice rang out against marble walls.

That was all it took. My great bedfellow wilted and slunk away in the shadows along the corridor.

I looked up to see Elena clasping a clay oil lamp in one hand and a fur wrap around her shoulders with the other. A storm was building outside and a breeze lifted the dark, tangled hair from her face. Now that the eunuch had exited, she allowed herself a wry laugh. Then gesturing me to follow, she said over her shoulder, "Come-lie in safety."

We wound through painted columns to her bedchamber, a place she had never invited me before. Blowing out the lamp before we entered, she led me with a warm, tiny hand to her bed. Placing me between the covers, she

fussed over me till I was situated comfortably. At last she climbed in beside me and pressed my head against her breast.

I felt myself battling conflicting primal needs; a great commotion stirred in my loins, at the same time a surprising urge to sleep besieged me. Sleep won out, and I slipped over some invisible line into dreams. It was then I became aware someone else occupied our bed, when a resonant voice rumbled drowsily nearby. "Ah, beloved, are the children all asleep now?" It was the last thing I remembered before plummeting into darkness.

Later .I would learn it was the king whose bed I had shared that night, though it would be some time before we met each other formally.

- - -

The second time the priestess came to my rescue was an infinitely more important story for me. Hard feelings apparently went into storage the night Elena thwarted my amorous friend. The next morning, I felt a subtle shift in my dealings with temple staff. No one made eye contact quite the way they had before, though ostensibly they spoke and behaved just as they always had.

Not long after that incident, the same eunuch approached me with an invitation. It was time to go gather sage from the hillsides but he and his brothers were too fat to clamber among the crevasses. Would I help them collect the herbs they needed? Off we all went in an ox cart one morning, deep into the hills, drinking wine and singing songs along the way.

Something miraculous had happened to my voice as I moved from boy to manhood. It grew beautiful–even I could tell. After an awkward time when it shifted on me suddenly, hopping octaves when least expected, it settled down to a deep, melodious instrument. Though I was clearly a miserably adolescent specimen, reed-thin and pock-faced, my singing voice could command legions. I could see its strong impact in surprised listeners' eyes.

All the way through the countryside that hot summer day, the eunuchs asked for songs from me. I honored all requests, sending my bold voice forth into the woodlands. As my companions put cup after cup of wine into my hands, I sang more sweetly than man has ever sung, or at least so I thought. Suddenly the ox-cart stopped. It was dusk and we were miles from the temple compound, though I could see the blue-green ridge of its copper roof sparkling in the sunset, far away.

"I think he is ready," someone said from the darkness. I stepped down from the cart and promptly fell onto my back. Staring up at the band of eunuchs from my supine place on the ground, I thought I saw the glint of metal change hands.

My head spun crazily. These were my friends. We had laughed, drunk wine and sung together. What were they doing now tearing off my tunic? Why did they hold a knife above my thighs? A glowering face pressed close against mine.

"You are *nothing*, boy," a malicious voice whispered. "Do you hear me? *Nothing!*"

Sometimes when one has had a great deal to drink, there is something very sobering about a knife. Lying there on the ground, I repeated this foolish thought to myself as if it were some great revelation. Meanwhile the eunuchs tossed one back and forth that evening, arguing bitterly over who should cut my flesh. Thank the gods for contentious fat men who cannot make a decision!

I went in and out of consciousness several times that night, but eventually awoke to find Elena kneeling over me. Somewhere just behind her, a tall male figure stood in shadow. I could not see him clearly, but I could smell and feel his presence. He was leather, horse-hide, and clean man-sweat. They had apparently had a hard ride tracking me down.

"Your geldings are acting up, dear," the now-familiar male voice chuckled. "Perhaps you should ride only stallions, then?"

I passed out at that point.

Soon I would learn that, again, I had been with the king, once more ignorant of the honor, through Elena's intercession.

- - -

The word seemed to be out through the temple community that no one was to trifle with the priestess's young friend. An indefinable change occurred in my interactions with just about everyone. Nobody said a word about my elevated stature, but I could see its evidence in the way they stepped aside for me. At first the change disturbed me. Then, little tyrant that I was, I began to take pleasure in the rare intoxicant of intimidating adults.

So many of the temple rabble were nothing but sycophants who sniffed at my dirty hands and provincial manners when I first arrived there. It gave me great satisfaction to see them grovel over the same country boy, mere weeks into my tenure there, all due to nothing more than the priestess and king having saved me from a scrape or two. I became a true bully, arguing with the eunuchs, contradicting holy men in mid-sentence, refusing to make eye contact with toadies who wanted only a kind word from somebody important.

The only redeeming feature of this fatuous adolescent time for me was the occasional evening I spent with Elena in her chambers. Having slept there twice now after near disasters with eunuchs, I seemed to have some special admission privilege. It was clear, in fact, that I needed no invitation, though I always waited for it nevertheless. Without her having said so, I knew that I could access Elena whenever I wanted , at least any time she wasn't with the king.

Many nights we sat together by her brazier, watching the coals, spinning tales and singing childhood melodies till we both fell asleep in each other's

arms. As an only child, orphaned and raised by an elderly grandmother, I had no experience of vital young women. Elena became something between mother, older sister and first love to me, though we never touched each other with passion in those days.

I didn't realize then how very little more than a child she was herself. I saw her, as did everyone else, for the icon that she was in a constellation of gods, great spirits and nobility. Not once through all those years did Grandmother's whispered story of Elena's rape by the king cross my mind. Now I think back to all the times I found the priestess alone somewhere, pensive and melancholy, and wonder with some guilt if the story ever crossed anyone else's mind either.

The only hard times I experienced myself in those days were when Elena and the king went off together, shutting me out of her life. It was the closest thing to death I could imagine, as if the sun had been extinguished, and all the earth's green pastures and flowing streams had dried up. The king's visits with Elena were all the more difficult to bear because they came so unexpectedly.

He was an active campaigner then, out on his travels round the world, conquering new territories and subduing other peoples. As a result, I could never know exactly when my comfortable life with Elena would be interrupted. Out of the clouds, the king would appear one day, running up the temple steps to make a quick visit to the altar, then disappear with the oracle for days at a time.

The only way I coped with this enforced solitude was through expressing my sorrow in song. In the still, dark twilight I languished on the temple steps, indulging myself in melodrama, singing sad ballads in the sweet, strong voice I had developed so suddenly. Though they were clearly narcissistic spectacles, these shows soon became popular with the crowds. I often had a gathering of people, lounging on the marble stairs in various stages of melancholy till late at night.

At last came an unexpected response to my prayers. Finishing a particularly morbid lament one evening, I looked up to a sea of faces watching someone behind me. I turned and there stood Elena, clasping the favorite fur to her neck again, while the night breeze ruffled her hair and linen nightdress. She reached out a hand to me.

"*Someone* wants to see you."

Responding to her urgency, I followed without question through the maze of temple columns. Finally we reached her hidden room. She threw open the door, then stood out of the way.

Inside, an oil lamp burned faintly beside a bed draped in netting. Despite the prominent shadows, I recognized an increasingly familiar friend, his hard, bare torso propped against soft, tufted pillows.

Stepping slowly forward, I found myself uncertain how to address him. He was the greatest man in the land, yet I had slept with him twice, all without having been introduced to him personally. So how did we proceed

from there? He settled the matter easily.

"Do you know any *glad* songs?" he asked me dryly. "Or must we all slit our wrists together?"

I fell prostrate onto the floor. "Stand up or sit down, but do get off the ground," he said. "And come join us, Elena. After all, it is you who has brought us together."

So it was that the three of us somehow found ourselves sharing a bed, all awake at the same moment for a change and looking one another directly in the face at last. Both Elena and I knew better than to speak first.

"You have the voice of a man," the king said to me. "In the body of a boy."

"I am almost sixteen," I said quickly, trying hard to be respectful, though my pride stung.

I saw him exchange a quick glance with Elena. "It doesn't matter whether a man is fifteen or fifty--if the gods favor any part of him, his mind, his body, his *voice*--he is blessed indeed."

I had the sense of having just passed some test without knowing I was taking it. Either way, it felt good to be over it.

"So I ask again," the king said, reaching out to clasp Elena's hand. "Do you know any *glad* songs?"

I couldn't remember any for the life of me, so I made one up on the spot. Something lifted me out of myself, beyond my self-doubts, and gave me the words and melody to a song about the king. Spirits channeled through me and made me eloquent. I watched the impact of the words and music on this sage, older man.

First he lay back listening, a bit amused, a bit cynical. But somewhere along the way, something touched him more deeply. I don't know what part of the song may have done it. I only know that at some point his face changed and he turned to Elena, tears gathering in his eyes as he pulled her to him.

I continued my song, never knowing from one moment to the next where the words and music would come from -- they just materialized. And meanwhile I watched while the milky white softness of my beloved Elena melted into the thick, hairy mass of the king.

It was excruciating in one sense, exhilarating in another. Here was the woman I cherished more than anyone in the world. Here was the man I revered more than any other I had met. Here they were together, twisted into one tangled entity, sharing their heat, tongues and genitals, murmuring soft, guttural, nonsense words to each other, while I sang a love paean to the two of them from some dark, primal place in my soul, curled on the edge of their bed, trying hard to fill as little space as possible.

Even in my confusion, I could appreciate the beauty of their joined bodies, his muscled back beaded with sweat, sinewy arms encircling her tiny waist; her sighs, murmured between the mass of her riotous black hair, celebrating him, encouraging him. When he began his thrust in and out of

her, I could not fathom my own ambivalence--hating him for the bull that he was just then, treating her like some animal, being an animal to her--hating her for her vulnerability to him, wishing I could protect her from him, wishing I could be him, wishing I could be her.

In the midst of my deepest loathing for the three of us, a strange thing happened. The king raised his lips from those of Elena and looked directly at me. There was a warmth and sweetness in his face I have never seen, before or since, anywhere, but in that deep, black gaze. Encircling Elena in one arm, he reached out the other to me. Still thrusting in and out of her, he grasped my hand, looking tenderly at me. The moment my soft, childish fingers made contact with his hard palms, he cried out in a great, strong voice, which rang through the colored rafters. He looked me straight in the eyes the whole time he poured his seed into her. Then he collapsed into her body, still holding my hand, to sleep till dawn, as innocent as any babe.

I fell in love with him so hard I lost my soul to him that night.

Elena shifted her weight so that she could cradle his head on one breast, then reached out for me and pulled me to the other nipple. The three of us fell asleep, locked in a moist embrace, sharing each other's air and body smells. It was the happiest night of my life. So began the happiest time in my life as well.

- - -

Once I had welcomed the king's absences on military matters, resenting his returns to the city and envying his time with Elena. Now she and I both awaited him anxiously, wondering where he was and what he was doing. When word spread through the city that the army was back from its travels, she and I would make eye contact across some marble room and exchange secret smiles. Then the best of all would come, seeing him jump down from his prancing stallion in front of the temple and race up its countless steps to the altar; watching him walk, move, laugh at some courtier's comment, throwing back his head and showing perfect white teeth inside a crisp black beard.

If truth were told, he was not a very spiritual man. One could see him fidgeting as he went about his worship activities. He tapped his feet and drummed his fingers incessantly. His eyes never left Elena as she guided him through each ceremonial. Only she and I knew what was really on his mind in those moments anticipation of her body and of the time to come in her room.

Eventually it would arrive, the moment when we could all be together. We would eat and be humorous. He would ask for a song from me and set me a theme. Something in my music seemed to cut through his normal reserves, and he would soon reach out for Elena, letting himself be soft or vulnerable in ways he would not have been otherwise.

She was as soulful in her love-making as she was about everything else

that she did, throwing herself totally into some deep place inside her, which she seemed able to access only through her sexuality. The king tended to be more playful, clearly enjoying his strong masculine body and using it like the fine tool it was, made to shine brightly, whether on a battleground, a playing field or a bed of love.

As a result, it surprised me that of the two, he was by far the more tender. Elena had nurtured and blessed me in a thousand ways, but something in her held her back from loving me entirely. I could feel the hesitancy, even when she took my head to her breast and stroked my hair. I wonder sometimes now if it was her history of violent abduction. Yet she clung passionately to the very man who had victimized her.

It was hard for me to imagine him in that rapacious capacity, watching him handle her so reverently in lovemaking, or wrestle with her boyishly among tangled bedclothes, laughing and tumbling to the floor together. It was only a matter of time before I joined them, and it was through one of these wrestling matches that our first real togetherness occurred.

The king had just come back from a particularly troubling campaign. He had lost men heavily, including his favorite aide, in a dirty, futile struggle with a faraway city-state. The journey back had been complicated by an outbreak of some fearful, infectious illness among his men.

Elena and I knew it had been a difficult time for him the moment he arrived at the temple. He didn't bound down from his horse that day, but dismounted slowly and took each step deliberately. Rather than fidgeting through his prayers, he prostrated himself before the altar with hands clenched tight on each side of his head. Normally intent on her work, Elena sought me out with wide eyes as she officiated over his prone form.

Once back with the king in her rooms that night, we both found ourselves taking special care of him. She was unusually light and amusing. I sang nothing but cheerful melodies. We each poured him a good deal more wine than he normally took. Little good accrued from these efforts until an accident happened.

"Show our lord your new trick," Elena finally urged me in desperation.

I knew exactly what she was thinking. "Yes, let's see if I can do it!"

I had been training several tamed ferrets to perform while I sang. The lithe creatures stood on their hind legs and ducked their heads to the notes in what looked like some strange ferret dance. The effect was thoroughly ridiculous but had never failed to amuse observers. I ran off to bring their cage and soon had a half-dozen of the mettlesome animals situated on the floor at the king's feet.

Something went terribly awry when I started singing this time, however. Perhaps it was the ferrets' unfamiliarity with the king, or perhaps I struck a discordant note. Whatever the cause, as I broke into song, the ferrets broke into pandemonium. Two chased each other around the room. Two others raced up the king's legs and into his tunic. The last two went for the dinner platter and began pilfering our meal.

Horrified, Elena and I looked to each other then dove for the dumbstruck king, reaching into his clothes and trying to lay hands on the weasels. Between our groping fingers and the wriggling ferrets, the king collapsed to the floor, uncontrollably tickled. Soon all three of us were there together, laughing till we cried, while the ferrets raced round the room wreaking havoc.

Normally I only addressed the king when spoken to, but I suppose the unusual circumstances emboldened me.

"Sire, it is good to see you happy again," I blurted.

He stopped smiling, making me fear I had offended, and scrutinized my face as if seeing it for the first time. Finally, letting out a deep sigh, he took my head in his hands and placed a long kiss on each of my eyes, of all places. Then tucking me against one side, he drew Elena to the other. The three of us lay with arms and legs entwined on the cool ceramic tiles, forever it seemed, just holding, murmuring and chuckling to each other occasionally. The ferrets were long gone by now, the gods knew where. I was glad to be rid of them.

Eventually casual touch turned to sexual tension and laughter to lovemaking. Only this time I was no visiting minstrel. Tonight, to my surprise, the king and priestess welcomed me as an equal. My skin had cleared recently and Elena often told me how handsome she found me. Still, I could look at myself in a shield and see what an unappealing youth I remained, far too thin, and gangly to boot. Surely Elena was just being kind.

But tonight, two celestial creatures, one male, one female, made love to me, a common boy. None of us ever made it to sleep that evening, nor to the pillaged dinner tray. Yet something more nourishing than food or slumber fed our bodies and souls that incredible night. Certainly, none of us was ever the same afterward.

- - -

Poets say that human lives plays themselves out like seasons; this time in one's life is spring, that time, full summer. I will always think of my days with Elena and the king as autumn-- warm and abundant with celebrations of plenty, all juxtaposed against the knowledge that barren cold loomed ahead. A timeless quality settles over that whole period in my life, and though I have lived many years since, I know that our all-too- brief spell together was the true total of my life. The days leading up to it were just foundation, the days following it, mere aftermath. Important things have happened in the years intervening, but nothing like my minute with the king and his oracle.

Countless comfortable meals passed for us around the coals in Elena's brazier and countless loving nights among the pillows of her bed. Though the days were clearly numbered, I remember them as limitless. Maybe we thwarted the gods by being too happy. Maybe we had no right to be so smug

in our enjoyment of each other. We were far too open with our feelings and demonstrations, wandering the marketplace together at dusk; beaming at each other across the temple's great hall; rushing away from convocations to be together, each on a different pretext. After all, the king had a jealous wife and a host of rambunctious children. Elena had committed herself to a life of worship.

I alone was free to make choices, but no one else wanted me. So the decision was moot for me; I would stay where I was with people who cared for me. Whatever the consequences, at least there I knew love.

Then as suddenly as he had arrived, the king was gone again. He had never overcome the stalemate of his last campaign. In the weeks since his homecoming, he had been incredibly soft and fragile, yet incredibly eager to do battle again. He left Elena and me still asleep one morning, long before dawn and without good-byes.

News traveled poorly in those days and we listened eagerly but futilely for word of the king's progress. When notice finally came, we wished that it hadn't. No mere stalemate had occurred for the king this time, but a miserable defeat with terrible losses. Horrible tales filled the city streets; hundreds of men impaled on barbarian lances; horses slaughtered for buzzard feed; the king in retreat, nursing another bout of the plague among his dwindling honor guard.

- - -

For many long weeks, we waited for his return, planning together the ways we might comfort him. Still he did not come, and the constant watching began to wear on us. Finally we could stand no more, though Elena was the one who decided at last what to do.

I awoke one moonless night from a dreamless sleep to find her standing over me. Her familiar clay lamp and fur wrap were again in hand. They had come to be important symbols by now.

"Something is afoot," she whispered. "Come with me."

I followed her to the altar where she fanned the fire hastily. Throwing herbs and minerals into it while I yawned nearby, she watched the coals as if observing a play. I had just nodded off when a sharp breath from her startled me. Biting a knuckle, she clutched the comforting fur and watched the fire intently. Then whirling suddenly, she began to issue orders.

"Go and get two horses, the fastest you can find. Meet me as soon as possible at the bottom of the temple steps. We are going to the king, *tonight* ... right away."

I knew nothing of horses, nor of how to choose two game ones. But I did know enough to sniff my way to the palace stables and waken an aging groom to put him to the task. Soon I was standing beneath the temple, striving to keep a pair of dancing mares in hand. Fortunately I didn't have to work at it too long, for there was Elena running down the steps.

Without a word, she grabbed the nearest horse and leapt onto its back. Digging her heels into its side, she was off before I could mount. After cajoling my horse in circles for several moments, I finally managed to throw a leg over its back and kick it into pursuit of Elena. The rest of that ride is a blur.

I remember images of forests and marshlands whipping past too fast to see them. Villages and small farms, too, came and went. I had no idea where we were going but some intuitive map seemed to guide Elena. Sometime before dawn, the landscape became still and empty. It had been miles since the last signs of humans.

As far as the eye could see, all was desolate. This was a war zone. There ahead at last were the colors of the king, emblazoned on numerous tents. I felt a sob escape me the moment I saw them. Elena merely kicked her horse harder and rode with greater determination toward the distant campfires.

We dismounted at the king's tent and she entered without hesitation. I hung back and saw to the horses, which were lathered and heaving mightily. One died before dawn and the other was ruined for any future purpose but cart-pulling. After doing all that I could for them, I found myself at a loss. Pacing about the tent, I eavesdropped without shame but could hear nothing from within. All was silent inside.

The sunrise came and went. We moved from dawn into a blistering hot day. Still, no word came forth from inside the king's tent. Soldiers milled about the campsite, uncertain how to behave. I think all of us knew the king was dying at that moment. It was just too quiet, and he was not a man of silence.

It seemed like forever before Elena emerged. When she did, she had a vacant, distracted air about her. She shook her hair, then wordlessly stretched her hands toward the sky. Eventually, she seemed to remember where she was and looked about her. Laying eyes on me, she came to me and took my arm.

"Let's walk a bit," she said and led me away from camp. We strolled slowly for a time while I listened to her breathe. I think too I could hear her heartbeat in those moments− strong, steady and true. At last we stopped by an abandoned olive grove. After sitting a spell on the ground with me in silence, she finally spoke.

"He has been gravely ill, but he will live, I am sure."

Something broke in me then and I found myself weeping, clutching great clods of earth, shuddering uncontrollably. I think I half expected she would hold and comfort me. But I spent my tears on the soil without response from her. When at last I looked up, she was watching the king's tent. For the first time, I noticed the difference in our ages. There were dark circles under her great, luminous eyes and fine lines forming around her full, sensual mouth. I had never seen these parts of her. Had they been there before?

"I have a difficult task," she finally said. "One the king has put before me."

She turned and looked me in the face. "He has asked me to send him *you*."

I hung on her last words with a questioning look. "That is all," she added. "He wants you. Alone. Not me. Not the three of us. Just you-to be with him, to be close and give him solace. Something has transpired that he cannot stand my touch."

I sat for the longest time, tears still on my face, earth still beneath my fingernails, trying to absorb this thing.

"But what about you?" I finally managed.

She threw me a sage glance. "Yes, what about me?"

We sat in pensive quiet, watching soldiers mill about camp, and birds dart among olive leaves overhead, all the while really watching dreams die away.

"It's no matter," she said at last. "I know what is in his heart. It is easier this way. He can take you wherever he goes. That is not the case with me-though heaven knows I'd follow him into hell. Our world won't support my sharing his earthly battles. *You* can do what I can't. So do it, now, please, for the love of the gods-for the love of the king."

I mulled all of this over till I could do no more with it, then rose with an effort at looking resolute. Elena saw through me. "There is one more thing," she said softly. "He says that you must *commit* to this first."

I threw her a puzzled glance. "I don't understand it myself," she admitted. "But here's how it appears to me-our king is only human."

A thoughtful silence followed before she resumed. "In all the known world, men love mainly women. Something cosmic has happened in these small islands, though, such that strong men are drawn to one another. Oh, they may well *want* women, but we are not their true *focus*. Your men are notorious for their love of boys. The king is fragile just now, for it has never been true of him. He is troubled to have it happen to him at last." She smiled with an afterthought. "I believe it was your voice."

She drew a deep breath. "I thought that he was different. I thought we three were different. I see now, though, quite clearly, we are all mere clay. And so we must go on-being mortal, being limited. He cannot be with you unless he knows *you* have made the choice. Otherwise, you can come back to the temple with me. We will all just pretend that this talk never happened."

It was monstrous. He was asking me to make an impossible decision. Somehow I found myself angry at Elena.

"Stop!" I cried. "What is all of this rhetoric, 'men *must* do thus-and-so and women must bear it!' You are nobody's puppet. What is *your* choice?"

She watched me with a sad smile while I answered my own question in my head. She had never had any choices where the king was concerned. He had plucked her unwillingly from another world, then after she came to love him, abandoned her in the end. When these truths became apparent on my face, she resumed.

"There is only this last piece," she said. "He asks that you be sure. If you have any doubts, don't even try to see him."

We sat again in silence for what seemed like an eon. Finally, Elena stood and shook the grass from her gown. "I must find a fresh horse and go back to the temple." I let her wander off, lost in my own thoughts.

The royal cavalry was depleted and an ox cart was the only conveyance available to her. I avoided her, pouting, while she made the few preparations needed to return, mainly saying good-bye to the king and leaving medicinal herbs with one of his aides. I happened to be by the flap to his tent, so that when she made her final exit, we almost collided.

She had never been more beautiful to me. Her hair was still tousled from our wild night ride. She wore a flush on tear-stained cheeks, and her lips trembled like a child's. Wordlessly, she placed a hand to those lips and then to mine. Still holding the tent flap, she asked me with her eyes, was I entering or not?

I believe I saw curiosity on the faces of the guards around the tent, but they were too skilled at concealing their thoughts for me to be sure. Something crystallized in me at that moment and I felt a shift occur in my loyalties. I had thought I loved Elena as no one else in the world. But I was close enough just then to the king to sense his physical presence; I could even smell his scent, that mixture of leather and horse and man that was uniquely his own. Even though he had been sick, the essential goodness of his body overcame all, reaching out through the open tent flap, reminding me of his touch.

So the question was resolved, without my ever having to ponder it. Squaring my shoulders and lifting my jaw in an effort to show a confidence I didn't feel yet, I went into the tent to be with the king. I never looked back at Elena that day, and I never took my eyes from the king's as I approached his bed.

- - -

For the rest of the joint time we were to share on this earth, I would seldom be long or far from the king's side. Going into his tent that afternoon was the best decision I ever made. Maybe it was the only real choice I ever had as well. It was not always an easy one to live with, as it cost me and many others a great deal. Fortunately, the first to pay the price were the enemies of the king who had brought him so low.

As Elena had predicted, he survived the plague. I like to think I had something to do with that. Surely having someone adore him is good for a man's health? At any rate, he rallied a new army in record time and was back at his vanquishers' gates for revenge.

For me, it was a frightening start to our time together. Having just committed my life to this man, it was bone-chilling to see him so soon afterward, standing atop a mountain of bodies, swinging the severed head of

a foe high in the air. I was determined to follow him wherever he went, though. That was what he had asked of me through Elena, and that was what I delivered. Climbing up beside him on that grisly mound I raised his bloodstained free arm and led his men in a song of praise for him. I will never forget the look in his eyes for me then, something between amazement, amusement and admiration.

I came to know dark and empty places in his heart, times when he was distant or unfeeling, times when he could even be cruel. But somehow there was always something noble about him to me. Even in his worst times, he was, after all, my king. And now in addition, he was also my lover, or rather I was *one* of his. He was a magnetic man with strong appetites and a host of admirers eager to indulge them. But he always came back to me eventually, which was more than one could say of his other liaisons.

Even his lawful wife died an embittered shrew after raising a brace of spoiled royal brats alone. Sometimes years occurred between his visits to her. I felt little sympathy for her as she made their scant time together miserable, whining and complaining about his absences even when he was right there beside her. She didn't know what she had in him, and so didn't deserve to hold him.

Only one who loved our king deserved better than she got, and that was Elena. Never has any heart loved more truly than hers; never has anyone paid so dearly for love. That day by his tent, I thought I might never see her again, but I was wrong. There would be one more time, though we would not speak.

It was the king's homecoming from a stellar military coup. He had swept the farthest reaches of the known world and annexed vast new territories with hardly a battle waged. The streets of his city were filled to overflowing with well-wishers who spilled into the parade route. Some had to be rescued from near-trampling beneath the horses' feet. The procession wound around the city a number of times then stopped at the temple steps for the king to thank the gods.

Though still not much of a horseman, I grew better daily at riding. I considered it important to learn at least enough to keep up with the king, and it gave me great pleasure that he allowed me to ride beside him that day, declaring in this fashion my status in his life. Many eyes watched me speculatively from the cheering crowd that morning, and I worried what questions might linger behind them.

As we stopped at the bottom of the temple steps, the king dismounted. After starting to give his reins to a military aide, he reconsidered and threw them to me. A great shout went up from the crowd then, and I knew that they had embraced me. I had never been more proud.

The king was not long at the altar and I understood why. Meeting in that way must have been painful for him and Elena, playing roles in a formal rite with so much intimate history behind them. Soon he emerged once more from between the painted columns and bounded down the steps to the

renewed roar of the crowd.

    It had taken me some effort to control both his spirited horse and mine, and I was very glad to see him again. We moved away from the steps, guiding our horses gingerly through the mounting press of people. Suddenly I found it terrifying, seeing the fierceness of the crowd's fervor. Such tremendous devotion could easily go wrong, I sensed. They could overwhelm him. They could crush us both without intending to, all out of love, all out of merely wanting him.

    My horse caught my fear and started to dance. The crowd was unaware that I was losing control of my mount. He started snickering, lifting his front feet off the ground and jerking at the reins. Still, the people pressed against us, clutching from all sides. The noise was truly deafening. Even if I called for help, there was no way the king could hear me, though he was only an arm away. I began to give in to panic.

    Just then I heard my name spoken, only once-like a gong sounds. I heard it uttered clearly, in a calm, familiar voice, even over the roar of the people and clatter of hooves and swords. That was all, just my name, and my horse grew suddenly quiet. I turned in the saddle to look over my shoulder, and there I could see her at the top of the temple steps.

    Even from this distance, I could capture every detail of her. Once more, she was exquisite, clutching her collar of fur with one hand and reaching out to me, waving with the others. Then she put three fingers to her lips and gave them a kiss. My heart found peace at that moment and it has been quiet ever since.

- - -

    Sometimes I find myself in dreams, magically transported back to the temple, walking the marble halls between its towering pillars. There were noises echoing everywhere between those cold walls of stone, so many sounds reverberating they confounded one's senses.

    Yet out on the temple steps, everything could be heard and seen so clearly; a king's hearty laughter, hastening to his bed of pleasure; an oracle's whispered blessing, redeeming the very souls who hurt her; a youth's rising song, weaving a tale of loss and love.

    The players are all gone now, but I still hear their voices.

THE ONE by Lewis Frederick

Sometimes his name seems irrelevant now. When I remember, I just think of him as The One-that first, forbidden, straight man from the past who had eyes a mile deep and sweat that smelled good.

Maybe you knew him too, the college roommate or co-worker who gave off an erotic glow just saying hid in the hall. As you came to know him better, you found him ready for any adventure, sudden road trips, or late-night jaunts to dangerous bars. Most times, he navigated the usual topics: sports, work, and women. Then he broadsided you one evening with a startling disclosure you never expected from such a great slab of man, a taboo sexual fantasy or profound spiritual insight. Soon he wandered off to the john, or the woods, or whatever. He was always wandering off somewhere, leaving you alone with a knot in your gut, hating yourself for letting it happen, falling in love with a straight friend.

Maybe it wasn't much of a problem. He fled, or you did, at the first real glimpse of things bubbling to the surface. But years later, you would still get that half-sick hunger whenever you stumbled onto a photo of the two of you, arms around each other at some celebration, hoisting beer mugs, or the giant bass you had just landed, the first and only fish you ever caught, reeled in under his tutelage on a weekend trip with him, the same weekend you shared a sleeping bag because it got so cold, and you woke to find him nestled against you for warmth, knowing he was unaware of the turmoil he was causing you, believing he was unaware, probably.

Next morning he acted as usual, but he brought you coffee in the tent and sat very close, forever it seemed, talking about some dream he had of backpacking around the world then writing a book about his travels. You asked a hundred questions just to keep him talking, just to hear the husky timbre of his voice, see the dreams soften his weathered face, and watch thick, hard hands hold a speckled enamel cup.

Lots of us have one of those guys somewhere in our past. The only problem is, sometimes they don't stay there.

Lots of us have a Jake in our lives too; that longtime we fall in and out of love with but somehow can't shake-unless they die on us anyway.

Jake's funeral would have brought out all the ham in him if only he'd been able to perform. So many visitors came, the funeral home had to schedule additional hours. Imagine, all of those people coming to see a body they hadn't spoken to in years.

Most of them were probably just checking. They needed to make sure they'd heard the last from him. Jake's nocturnal phone tirades were legend. Drunk and hysterical over the latest rejection, he'd pursue what had become known as "Jake's reign of terror." Working through his Rolodex, he would

resort to mere acquaintances, looking anywhere for a sympathetic ear.

"Why do you stay with him?" friends asked.

"He's not so bad," I'd sigh. I had a little of the ham in me as well and wasn't above playing martyr.

Truth was, there were too many of those arm-in-arm photos of Jake and me plastering our walls. Though we hadn't been sexual in years, the pictures stood testament; frozen faces beaming from holiday parties; hands clasped beneath toothsome smiles; silhouettes joined at the hip against blood-red ocean sunsets—*always* the faint trace of smoke from Jake's constant cigar hanging about his head like a fallen angel's halo.

We had been a good thing for a long time, before the drugs and boys got to him. No matter how much younger I was and how hard I partied with him, I could never be young or drunk enough for Jake. None of our old crowd could believe he died from anything but AIDS. He'd checked out as he'd always hoped to, in pursuit of the perfect orgasm, panting in a rented room with a hustler he'd found in the park. Scared the shit out of the kid. I guess that boy's gone Southern Baptist since offing Jake.

Then too, there were tender times, right up to the end, rare moments between the shouting when Jake's big heart shone through in a silent look or gesture. We might be reading or listening to music, when he'd reach across the space between us and touch my arm. Despite all the hurt and anger, he could still hook me with a touch.

I was remembering that touch when I glanced up at the gravesite and saw him staring at me through the crowd—not Jake, but The One. He stood there alone, drilling a hole in me with those bottomless green eyes, gifts from some shadowy Celtic family ancestry. Funny how one look can make so many other things seem unimportant.

He had changed a lot, the leathery face more lined than ever, a distinct thickening in the torso. But the eyes were the same. No, that's not right. They were better somehow— warmer, sadder. I could still get lost there. We made it across the crowd to each other only to find ourselves inarticulate. He looked over both shoulders, doing a quick double take on some mourners in drag—simple black dresses, pumps, little veils—all very understated and tasteful.

"Can we get out of here?" he asked. I discharged the funeral parlor limo and joined him at the cemetery gates. We struck off in a purposeful stride, walking several blocks without words before he cleared his throat.

"I was in town and saw the news," he said. "'Famed novelist dies—longtime companion remembers.' "

"That would be me?" I asked. "Or was there another one?"

As always, he missed my humor. "Why didn't you tell me?"

"About what?"

"About you."

"I wasn't out then, much."

"*I* knew though," he said.

"How?"
"There was something."
"That bothered you?"
"No, *intrigued* me."
 With that, we went another several blocks in silence when I spotted a landmark. "There's a good place to eat next corner," I suggested.
 He smiled and put a hand on his little belly. "I'll try anything once."
 An old red flag went up; I had always hated it when he said that.

 DeVicenzo's may not have been such a wise choice after all. I'd forgotten the place was something of a shrine to Jake. The maitre d' seated us in a familiar booth lined with memorabilia, framed caricatures of Jake puffing on a cigar, the back of the menu where he'd first penned the opening lines of his Pulitzer novel, a few photos of him with me–more photos of him with others.
 "Is this okay?" I asked my companion.
 "Sure, no problem." He scanned the cluttered walls around us. "I don't get it though. You and Jake, I mean. So much older than you and, and so, so ..."
 "Unattractive?" I ventured.
 "Well, yeah," he said, flushing. "That big nose, those bushy eyebrows. I don't see it." He caught himself. "Sorry ... bad timing."
 I let him off easy, remembering all the times friends said similar things about *him* to me. "Don't trouble yourself. I've heard it for years. Jake wasn't about looks–he was about soul." I examined the photos behind us too. "Funny thing though, he was never alone long."
 "Yeah," he said. "I read how he died in a room with some kid." Now he *was* being insensitive. "What does that mean? Where did things stand between you?"
 Cocktails had come and I downed a big gulp. "Not well at the end. We were roommates, business associates. I typed and proofed his work ... got him to Betty Ford now and then. Mostly cleaned up vomit the rest of the time."
 I could see I'd put him off. He pushed the bread sticks away and looked around the room for something to change the subject.
 "Why did you come?" I asked.
 He scratched his nose, an old sign he didn't like the direction a conversation was taking. "I really don't know. You may find this hard to believe, but I've never forgotten you-- the way we were friends, the way you left. What was the deal there? You just vanished."
 A sudden sick headache took hold at my temples and spread across my brow. I'd forgotten this part, how he could sap my psychic energy. "I was in love with you, *okay*?"
 Aware of heads turning in the next booth, I lowered my voice. "I was damned near suicidal sometimes. Does that answer your question?"

Some personal power surged back with this confession, till I saw his reaction. Clearly pleased, he sat back against the leather, swirling his drink in his hands, a little smile playing about his chapped lips. I watched the way he held the glass, remembering those hands around a coffee cup, smelling fallen leaves, tent cloth, a smoldering fire.

Standing up, I threw down some bills and turned for the door: "This was probably a very bad idea."

Somehow I found myself at the curb, hailing a taxi, fighting some dragon lady in a business suit for it, then agreeing to share. We were just pulling away when he opened the door and jumped in beside me, shoving me hard against Ms. Laptop.

"Why did you do that?" he asked between clenched teeth.

"My last document better be intact," she hissed, "Or you'll be dealing with my attorney."

Our fragrant driver decided to play peacemaker: "You people ever eat camel belly? Sweetest meat in the world! My family have restaurant close-you try?"

I declined, gave him my address, and held my breath the rest of the ride.

- - -

Just get centered! Feel the elevator beneath your feet ... jiggle the key into the door ... finally inside, smell the books, beeswax, houseplants-cigars ... see the fading light pour through the rooms, how it falls on special pieces- the Mammoth tusk, the Cezanne, the Mycenaean boy in terra cotta ... something different though tonight- someone strange trailing behind me, curious, uncertain; no Jake greeting us inside to beguile the new traveler....

I could sense the revelations occurring inside him by the change in his footsteps. This was the way it always was, for anyone new who came to our apartment, Jake's apartment.

You met Jake at a lecture, or art gallery or bar-someplace. He drank too much and waved that awful death stick in your face. But he talked and talked and somewhere along the line you fell into his spell. He said "Let me show you something," and you followed him home, thinking home was going to be a Holiday Inn nearby.

Then the great door of his warehouse apartment swung open and he brought you into that incredible world, a world where anything could and did happen, where cultures met, clashed, and merged across ages, where wonderful sights, scents and sensations assailed you at every turn. Postmodern impressionists' work vied for wall space with relics from archaeological digs. Original manuscripts by Hemingway and Henry James lay like litter on side tables with back bills from phone-sex lines. It was almost too much, too many diverse stimuli. The only common denominator was Jake- and he led you by the hand to somewhere safe in the storm where he held you and touched you and made you believe in miracles. Only Jake

was gone now; the tour guide was gone.

My unwelcome guest was overwhelmed. I could hear his tentativeness behind me, the halting step, the sharp intake of breath as he rounded each corner. "What the *hell*...?" I heard whispered time and again.

He had followed me up to the flat, without invitation, after an uncomfortable trip with Laptop Lady, whom he'd battled non-stop. I had forgotten how pugnacious he could be, particularly with a strong-minded woman.

Eventually we found ourselves in the kitchen, probably the only place in the apartment Jake truly let me own. "Omelets wouldn't take long," I offered, half-hearted.

"That would be great," he smiled. "I'll pour drinks and make coffee."

Some unexpected blessing emerged in making a meal together. I cut and sauteed vegetables. He fumbled about the room, opening drawers, stumbling and dropping things, making a lot of noise, making me love him again, drifting just close enough for me to smell that peculiar personal scent of his: clean animal pelts and soil mixed together, with sandalwood soap and pipe smoke on the side.

In between, he talked about work, a fiancee, his racquetball game. I lost track of it all watching him move, seeing how the tough athlete's body had gone a little to seed, thick shoulders stretching his shirt, big thighs straining beneath the khakis. Strange that the combination could still seduce me so completely. It had to be pheromones.

Dinner finished, we dawdled over brandy. I thought of offering cigars but the act seemed a sacrilege. He went to the john so much I worried he had bladder problems. Several phone calls came in that I felt compelled to answer. We both spent a lot of time saying 'Excuse me' for something or other. Awkward silences lengthened as the night wore on.

"Sorry," he finally said. "I think I'm a little drunk." With that he was out cold.

I threw a handmade quilt over him, a patchwork thing, sewn up by a group of sexually abused women who had read Jake's work, decided he understood their pain, and elected him their mentor. I never quite got that one.

Looking down at my old friend's beautiful body, smelling his heat rise up amidst the woolen scent of the sofa cushions, seeing his face turn sweet in repose, it took tremendous willpower to walk away from him. I poured a last brandy, went out onto the balcony and dozed in an overstuffed chaise, watching the night cityscape. Lights flickered everywhere, jewels in a nameless queen's crown, till dawn dimmed their glow. That was when he came to me. The sky was just turning gray in the east when I felt his breath against my neck. Some cosmic convergence must have occurred that night between his soul and Jake's. Whatever the case, I have never felt so loved.

Having found him a poster boy for obtuse jock maleness, I expected a quick, recreational encounter. He surprised me with his tenderness. There

was a moment when he didn't seem to know what to do, then some primal instinct emerged. Slowly he began kissing me, softly at first, but with increasing urgency, probing my mouth deeply. He had a strong, patient tongue that insisted on admission wherever it chose to linger. It must have been more than a day since he'd shaved and I shuddered beneath beard stubble as his hungry mouth wandered over my face, ears and neck.

When he lifted my fingers to his lips and began sucking on them greedily, a quick gush of pre-cum soiled the pouch of my briefs. As he slowly slipped my clothes off, he teased me with each garment, letting the fabric linger like butterflies on the naked flesh he had just exposed. The tension mounted in me with this tactic until I could delay no more. I quickly slipped my body beneath his barrel chest, needing to feel the heat and the heaviness of him pressing me down, pinning me hard against the tufted cushions beneath us. Once I positioned myself there, the thrust of his erection grinding against my crotch struck me as strangely poignant, almost sad somehow.

. I continued working my body lower beneath him, fumbling with his belt and zipper, until my face was beneath his restless hips, arriving there just in time to catch the treasure that tumbled out when I yanked his boxers to his knees. His cock was just like the rest of him, not particularly long, but substantial, thick and comforting to touch, crowned with a dense black bush and graced with a fat, brown ball sack below. I drank in the rich smell of it, musky, moist, and heavily male. There was more than a little reverence in the way I held its mass with both hands, like a communion cup, guiding it between my lips, savoring the salty trail of silver that spilled from the slit. I reveled in the low moaning sounds he made as I worked the broad helmet head all the way to the back of my throat. Holding his full, hard cheeks in my hands I pulled him deeper into me. I wanted to taste every part of him, take every drop I could squeeze out of him. But just as he seemed ready to come, he let out a low growl, disengaged himself from my mouth and effortlessly pulled me up beside him.

We lay there for a long moment, staring at each other, breathing each other's air. Looking into those eyes once more, the cynic in me was surprised to realize that I would probably do anything in the world for him just then, anything he wanted. He must have read my thoughts as he gently laid me against the back of the chaise, threw my legs over his shoulders and shoved himself inside me, pushing all the way to the hilt in one single, fluid motion.

"Oh my God," he began murmuring like some sensual mantra. "Oh-my-God-oh-my-God-oh-my-God-oh-my-God."

I wove my hands through his hair and pulled his mouth down to mine. I could now feel him in every inch of my body, the wide plow of his penis digging deep inside of me, almost splitting me it seemed, the rough texture of his taste buds against my tongue, the startling silkiness of his hair between my fingers. I came long before I wanted to, hurling long, milky white ribbons across the place where our chests joined. As my sphincter

tightened around him he gave a loud sob and climaxed himself, filling me so full that the heavy load immediately spilled out and saturated my balls. He collapsed onto me in a sudden heap and we fell asleep in each other's arms, the sweet stickiness of spilled semen fusing our tangled bodies together.

Unsettling dreams filled my brief slumber. Jake cradled me in giant arms and sang me discordant lullabies, in Latin of all things. A tornado came and swept the apartment clean, Jake's manuscripts fluttering to the street below, while I wildly clutched the air, trying vainly to retrieve them. A tiger came prowling through our flat, confronting me in the bedroom, eventually jumping up onto the mattress and licking my face with clear sexual intent. I awoke at that point to the sound of the neighbor's miniature dog yapping next door, finding myself alone on the balcony, alone in the apartment.

He had left without a trace, not even an imprint of that big body on the soft chaise cushions. It was as if he had never existed. Now that he'd had his little walk on the wild side, just drunk enough at the time to blame it on alcohol, I would never see him again. Only the dregs of the coffee he'd made remained to convince me I hadn't hallucinated. After warming a cup in the microwave, I took it out to the balcony.

Sitting there, nursing a grudge, I watched the wide city stretch its contradictions before me, a complicated game board reaching to the horizon. Architectural marvels soared up amidst pockets of squalor. Gridlock paralyzed intersections beneath expressway overpasses that streaked with speeding vehicles. Homeless people huddled around oil-drum fires, while tinted-window limousines idled nearby.

Turning, I gazed through each of the great plate-glass walls surrounding the terrace, eyes lingering on the stellar rooms behind them. So many beautiful things, so much of Jake. A sense of dirtiness and dishonesty struck me, the stench and steam of the city on one side, the casual elegance of the apartment on the other. It was time to do something about it. Within seconds, I was pulling boxes from a shelf in the storage closet.

Knee deep in packing and labeling, I heard a racket rise up outside the front door. Somebody stumbled off the elevator and dropped an armful in the hall. Though I was in no mood to be helpful, the prolonged commotion eventually piqued my curiosity.

From a slit in the door, I watched him chasing assorted bagels down the corridor, stepping over stains from a spilled juice carton and kicking at the neighbor's dog between his feet. Wet rings stained the armpits of his wrinkled shirt and his spreading waist hung over the unbuttoned top of his pants. I went out into the corridor to see what I could do.

Kneeling down with him over the spills and scattered rolls, I caught that scent once more and looked long into his flustered face. He would never again beat me in racquetball, or best me in a rhetorical debate. He made terrible coffee and his clothes were a yawn. He was at least twenty pounds overweight and his hair needed styling.

But his eyes were still a mile deep and his sweat still smelled good.

Somehow I helped him get the mess up in the hall and got him back in the apartment.

We spent the remainder of the weekend putting Jake and other ghosts to rest.

RIPE FRUIT by Rick Jackson

"...The raven that stuck his head in when I answered was every chickenhawk's wet dream come true...."

We Marine helicopter pilots get enough tail that we don't have to fly out of our way to score. Sometimes though, a short side trip can turn up a good time where we least expect it.

Last deployment I was stationed aboard the carrier *Okinawa*. Four months into the cruise I was in the middle of special night-vision goggle operations off Comstock when a freak dust-storm whipped up and grounded my ass away from home. Normally being stuck in a strange rack for the night is a drag, but the Comstock Air Boss jumped through his asshole to make me feel at home. He not only set me up in a stateroom, but found one without roommates to cramp my style.

Scoring linen at that time of night was even trickier, but he managed somehow. Mid-rats was over by the time I got settled, but the guy was so thrilled at having a big-time Marine pilot aboard for the night, he even snagged me a load of seedless green grapes. Except for cock, grapes are my favorite food in the world-and one I hadn't seen since we pulled out of San Diego.

Looking back now, I half wonder if the sly bastard didn't engineer the rest of the night, too

I had gobbled about half the grapes before I decided to clean up a little and rack out. I shucked my boots and socks and was standing with my flight suit unzipped to the waist, bird-bathing my chest and arms, when suddenly there came a rapping at my chamber door. The raven that stuck his head in when I answered was every chickenhawk's wet dream come true. I hadn't blown a load in nearly twelve hours, so you can believe I paid him plenty of attention. Maxwell looked at my deshabille and did more than pay attention-the beautiful boy did everything but cream on the spot. When his eyes locked onto mine for a moment, I knew sleep that night was going to be hard to come by.

Max hung back, holding open the door, hardly daring to enter an officer's stateroom, hardly able to think. He finally managed to gurgle something about the Air Boss sending him up to be sure I had everything I needed. When I grinned and said, "I do now," the invitation was clear enough to penetrate even Max's lust-fogged enlisted brain. He gulped and eased all the way inside. By the time the door clicked shut, he was inches from me and the distance was rapidly closing as both our dicks went on the offensive.

Up close, he was so choice that my teeth hurt. I noticed his purple jersey and wondered for the first time whether the Air Boss might not have sent him up on purpose. "Grapes" are squids who wear purple jerseys to show

they pump JP-5, refueling aircraft that stop by for a drink. Max was so firm and prime that his juice just had to be ripe and sweet enough to spurt. He had sun-bleached blond hair that proclaimed his misspent surfer-stud youth, but hungry brown eyes shone out like beacons from beneath a healthy shock of blond. High cheekbones and a strong, single eyebrow, his perfect nose and gleaming grin, and the hand he pressed against my furry chest all promised my python a prime pumping like nothing it had felt in weeks. Even through the thick cotton of jersey, his nipples sat up and begged for my teeth.

His hands cupped my dog tags, worshipfully holding them hard against the rough red hair on my heaving chest. My eyes slid from his bone-bulge up across his narrow hips and hard belly to discover his hungry eyes, eager for everything I had.

My hand reached behind his head to silently stroke his soft, blond hair, matted now with the day's flight-deck grime and omnipresent oil fumes. Man-sweat came through strongest of all as his knuckles carelessly brushed across my own iron-tipped tits. Max gently lowered the tags and kept moving south, rippling across my belly, following the fur down to the zipper of my flight suit. He pulled outward, gently at first and then harder as my dick's struggle to be free put pressure on the cruel green fabric. When my lizard finally leaped up and smacked against my belly, Max's hand dropped the zipper, letting my flight suit fall abandoned and unmourned to my ankles.

Even through his cloud of sweat, I smelled the rich, musky scent of my own crotch as his face slipped down to lick me clean. His tongue and lips and teeth were dogged as any bloodhound and fierce as a congressman facing a pay cut. They raped my balls, sucking and tonguing and tearing as they worked, pulling my seed up into service. Max's desperate tongue slashed past my 'nads, slurping its way up my thigh until I ran out .of crotch, and he had to work his way back down one nut and start back up the other side. I stood still, my hands smearing his face against my balls, until I felt him go too far.

His lips began the nine-inch slurp up my snake. The guy's desperate need had made him ambitious enough to forget his place so I put a foot in the middle of his purple jersey and knocked him back onto his ass. "You're not getting my dick like that, you little shit. If you think you're man enough to make me happy, strip and assume the position."

In a way, it's too bad he was in such a frenzy; I didn't have time to enjoy the show of him peeling off his uniform to show all those hairless muscles and hard, enlisted curves. He had the perfect union of farmboy innocence, hard rippling muscles clad in soft skin, and a monster dick that is out of place in the real world. Only the darkest, most sensual wet dream fantasies deserve bodies like his–and it was all mine. The dark-blond bush that peeked out from behind his belly-up bone and a few strands of pit hair were the only fur keeping his beautiful body from being baby-butt bare. My teeth

craved the thick tits that towered from the dime-sized russet crowns of his powerful pecs. His full, wet lips were all but born to be wrapped around my shaft.

First, though, I needed to fuck him up the ass.

When I reached down to the emergency stash in a leg of my flight suit, I discovered I only had two rubbers with me and said a few apt but very naughty words. The guy grinned backwards over his shoulder and said he had more in his locker, but that we'd have to use mine first. He didn't want to risk some other tight hole happening along to take my load while he was gone. His tight, sculpted ass was already presenting like a bitch in heat, wriggling in my face as his hands clutched the porcelain wash basin for present support-and to help him bear the future he hoped was coming.

I bent over his quivering body and licked his neck, kissing my way to his tender earlobes. Faint trembles became quakes of lust as his body reveled in my touch. I slipped my way down his spine, licking the sweat from his knobby spine until I got to the class sweep of his firm, tight ass. Those mounds huddled against the world, flexing in instinctive uncertainty whether they were guarding his butt from insult or were desperate to clench my thick nine inches until I gave his hungry hole the protein it craved. I spread him wide and lost myself in the glorious spectacle of his pucker, pulsing and throbbing away like a Hollywood alien desperate for an unsuspecting snack.

Pre-cum was gushing out of my dick by now, dripping down my shaft to drizzle into my pubes. Only the urgency of the moment kept me from sucking his asshole as I wanted; but when I rubbed against him, slathering his tender cheeks with my lizard-lube and then slurping it up, the bumpy texture of my tongue and the silken feel of my lube on his cheeks made him beg and whimper to be fucked like a boot camp D.I.

Even with the mirror, though, I wasn't about to do him from behind. I wanted to look at that glorious young face while I did him hard up the ass. When I grabbed him by the balls and threw his butt onto my rack, a moment's disorientation evolved into the perfect picture of earthly bliss. His strong tanned legs lifted toward the overhead, deluded by need or hubris to believe he was ready for me. I was about to give him what he craved, but the bowl of grapes lying farther up my rack gave me an idea. I've always loved food. Fucking one grape with another would satisfy two needs: I could drive Max fucking frantic with desperation for my dick-and could enjoy myself with the old "Peel me a grape" ploy.

At first, the poor boy didn't know what to think as I forced his legs to the bed and popped some grapes into my mouth. When my lips met his, though, and that first grape slipped from my mouth to his, he started to catch on. I suppose he was used to furtive fan room fuck-and-run sessions aboard, but when my tongue snaked after it, crushing the ripe fruit against his teeth, splashing sweet juice down across his taste buds, young Max decided foreplay wasn't all bad. His hands wrapped hard around my butt, forcing my

dick against his hairless belly, flooding his bare, rippled muscles with a pre-cum catastrophe on the Johnstown model.

One grape followed another into his mouth to meet the same sweet fate until he was awash in grape juice and his dick was drilling against my belly, threatening to fuck loose at least two major organs.

When I knew we had to move on, I exploded grapes onto his tits and lapped up the luscious glory as his hands smeared my face into his hard pecs. Our supply of grapes and patience were both about gone; we both knew the time had come to fuck or get off the stud.

As I knelt between his legs, invention whispered to me again. The memory of cool juice exploding across Max's tits as my tongue teased them was nearly as seductive as the frantic flutter of the young squid asshole waiting so impatiently to possess my pleasure. In the middle of the Arabian Gulf, grapes were too precious not to use to maximum advantage.

I took five of the biggest, firmest, juiciest specimens we had left and rubbered them up with me. If that cool gush of sweet juice had felt good before, I knew it would be the best fucking lube in the world. After years of cursing the things, I'd finally come up with a fuck that felt better with a rubber. Not only would the luscious lube keep my lizard company on its prowl, but I'd have the added stimulation of that pounded pulp skidding across my peter every time I shoved my crank hard up Max's tight, tender hole. I dropped the first into the center of the rubber so it would fit right over my cum-slit. The rest fit nicely along my shaft, partly protected from abuse by the meaty overhang of my trigger-ridge.

Rolling the condom down the full length of my prick, pressing those cool, fleshy packs of soothing pleasure against my hot, throbbing peter was so deliciously kinky and wicked that I almost didn't need my bigger, juicier human grape to find satisfaction. But a single glance at the expression of desperate yearning on his face convinced me I shouldn't let him wither unused on the vine.

His legs were bent, feet bobbing in the air with the hurry-the-fuck-up impatience common to horny young men who have caught the scent of dick. I grabbed his monster root for a moment and lifted, partly to raise his ass higher and partly just to give his tender tool a twist to teach him patience. The soft skin gliding upwards in my fist made me promise to come back for a closer inspection of his uncut knob once I had pressed the fruit on my own stem. His massive joint was as flawless as it was long and thick, towering upward in a grand sweep like a unicorn's–and just as rare. Only the proud, strong, throbbing curve in his cock kept the comparison at bay. I've never been fucked by a unicorn's horn, but my asshole had long since been itching and twitching in anticipation of what I had in mind for Round 2. Just now, though, we were both ready to gush juice and, long past primed for Round One. Foreplay, delay, and faltering hesitation were all equally out of the question.

My hands locked tight around his ankles, swung his asshole into the air,

and I slammed my nine thick inches of hard cock through his hot monkey-lovehole. The one remote, silent corner of my consciousness that wasn't ravening savage recorded every sensation in such complete and exquisite detail that, in the months since, I've been able to relive the next several minutes in slow motion and stop-frame satisfaction whenever I felt the need to take myself in hand. Max's hole wanted everything I had, but no hole in history has taken my swollen knob without a strain. I hadn't gone through the usual lube-and-finger-fuck routine to prep his ass, so the first feel of my ramrod breaking down the gates of his virtue was a very considerable jolt. For me, it was an extra-special thrill. Not only did I get off slamming into Max's asshole, but the impact of my beaucoup boner against his quivering fuck-pucker smashed the living shit out of the grape I had stationed on point, sending an explosion of cool grape plasma ricocheting across my super-sensitive head.

I was through his ass so quickly, drilling deep down his spastic asshole, that some of the juice stowed behind my corona didn't gush out until I slammed back upwards against his sphincter. After grinding my short curlies against the ruins of his twitching squid-hole and pulverizing my grape pulp against the hard muscle at the blind end of his fuck-tunnel, I forced my hips backward, un-pistoning his chamber until my cruel cock-flange slammed solid against the desperate inside of his ass and juiced the last of my tender fruit.

You might think the cool juice on my hot rod would be distracting and shut down my pump-piston. Nothing could be further from the truth. The cool rush of juice cascading across my tender, throbbing tool felt as gloriously depraved and exciting as anything I had ever done. I'd read stories about guys who fucked food, doing a nice watermelon to pass the time or violating a slice of liver for amusement. I still didn't understand why anyone would want to screw food, but understand it or not, I fucking loved the wicked feel of that juice as the pulp left behind slid across my joint and I looked down into Max's boy-next-door face and felt his hot, hungry squid ass wrapped around the nine inches I know best in the world.

The dick inside my rubber was a rabid study in classic contrasts: the cool flesh and juice gushing along my bone with every throb and twitch and thrust; the hot, hungry grip of Max's guts as they scraped past; and, of course, the ancient throbbing from within as my nuts constricted and forced up sweeter cream to grace the grape.

Most guys clench up tight when I shove some of what I have up their asses, but Max's eyes slammed shut like the very Gates of Doom. His jaw sealed tight against the agony that rolled upwards through his soul, breeding the ecstasy only a man in lust can know. By the time my nuts were awash in hot, back-flushing grape juice, his eyes were open and sparkling with contentment. His lips were at my tits and neck and ears, greedily gobbling at anything he could reach to prove the sublimeness of his satisfaction. The feet I'd released early on ground hard into my Marine pilot ass, urging me to

mount him deeper and harder and faster in a stud-striding, hunk-humping gallop. His desperate hands were everywhere at once–stroking his nails along my spine, holding tight onto my ass as I ground into him, grasping at the Corps-cropped stubble at the back of my head, and pulling at the rough, red hair on my chest as he tore into my tits with fingers of steel.

The blowers couldn't keep our hard, naked bodies cool enough to keep sweat from splashing loose with every fuck-thrust until we were slipping and sliding skin against skin as much as we had flesh wrapped hard around bone. Our bodies slammed together, proving we were nothing more than jungle beasts breeding the conquests of the moment. Our lair was high-tech, but our instincts and the passions that fed them were older than time and twice as hard to control.

Only the constant purr of the ship's engines and the insistent whine of those feckless ventilators could have kept our rutting rampage secret. Every time my hips slammed into his cute little ass, driving my swollen joint home where it belonged, his body echoed a gentle grunt of satisfaction as his hard muscles shuddered under my impact. Within moments, though, those grunts had company–a long, almost feral howl of animal desperation. My fruity lube was keeping my dick from charring, but as I tore my latexed rake-rod across his asshole time after reckless time, it didn't take a boy scout to figure out that Max's poor little ass was about to ignite–and it didn't take a Marine to understand how fucking fine he felt.

I made the mistake of looking deep into the abyss of those cocker-spaniel brown eyes as I twisted around inside his ass to clip his prostate. The cute flicker of agony and ecstasy that rippled up from his soul was too much. My nuts seized up, my dick exploded in one frantic gusher of bone marrow after another, and I silently surrendered to the inevitable.

I climbed back down from the clouds and found my dick still reaming away. When I finally slowed down and regained enough control to open my eyes, I found Max's bare belly and chest awash in jeweled jets of his own jism. My body collapsed against his, content to rest for a moment wrapped in his arms and legs and let his seed smear against my sweat-soaked body. His asshole still rubbed my rod the right way, pulsing and puckering along its length, promising more good times on tap. I knew I would return to that gloriously uncut dick and teach it Marine tricks. His full lips begged for my tongue, and we both knew my cock had just begun to crow. First, though, I needed to tend to some unfinished business.

I eased out of Max's ass to take stock. Much of the juice had slopped back out of the tight, short confines of the condom and onto my balls, but every drop of my Corps-bred cream was still safely stowed away, awaiting disposal. I generally strip one load and get ready for another without a second thought, but the blend of nature's finest juices I found bouncing against my belly was too good to waste. I eased the rubber from my shank and dipped my tongue deep. My vintage was sweet and pure enough to make a French vintner weep in envy.

With a single slurp, I sucked the creamed grapes into my mouth and let the mixture ease across my tongue until every taste bud was aglow with the goodness of the grape smothered over in jarhead jism. I could try to describe the combination of tastes, but why bother? Better you should experiment for yourself. Let's just say that when young Max saw the expression on my face, he reached for my second rubber and the few grapes I had left. Unlike most Marines, I'm not much of a bottom, but I couldn't really blame the guy. After all, turnabout is fair play.

STRAIGHT TO BED by Mario Solano

He stumbles out of the bathroom, drunk and horny. His cock and balls hang out of his filthy Jockey-brand shorts in the same position they were while he took a piss. He falls onto the bed, reaches between his legs and plays with himself. His teenage son had been sleeping in a chair but is now at the end of the bed observing, as he's done many times before.

The man opens his eyes, sees the girl of his dreams standing before him. "C'mere, baby. Gimme a kiss," he says. The boy crawls in next to his dad and nuzzles his head in a pungent armpit. The man throws a leg over the boy, runs his hungry fingers through his hair, and kisses the soft neck. The boy feels both hard-ons on his belly.

The man reaches in the back of the boy's pajama bottoms and grabs his asscheeks and squeezes them, one at a time, allowing his finger to probe the tight, virgin hole. The boy is engulfed in sweat and the smell of beer. He doesn't mind. He's been waiting for this for a long time.

When the first finger enters, the boy winces, in pleasure and pain. He snuggles close to his dad. The man takes the boy's face in his hand and raises his mouth to meet his. His tongue slips inside the boy's mouth, which is wet with spittle. He pulls the boy on top of him and sticks his finger in his ass as far as it will go, then rolls over on top and spreads the boys legs with his knees. The top button of the boy's pajamas pops off and the thin fabric rips to below his crotch. The boy feels his dad's massive prick pressing between his thighs.

The man reaches down to finger his girlfriend's pussy and finds his son's six-inch hard-on. "Holy shit!" he says. He raises himself off the boy and looks in his face.

"Johnny! What the fuck?"

"It's okay, Dad," the boy says.

The man rolls off, laughing. "Good fucking God!" he says, still laughing. "What the fuck am I doing?"

"It's okay. Dad," the boy says again. He climbs on top of his dad's cock and gyrates his hips. The father lets out a short gasp, puts a pillow over his face and lies there. The boy's ass hole is moist from the finger friggin', and his own virgin juices. He guides his father's cockhead into his hole and slides up and down. The father's hands grab his son's waist and his pelvis begins to move. When his ten inches in as far as it can go, he pushes the pillow aside and fucks his son, wet, juicy and wild, for the first time, but not the last.

The father comes home drunk, with a sleazy broad. He wakes his kid,

shoves a few bills in his hand, and tells him, "Get lost, you pansy!" It's 3:00 a.m. "And take your fuckin' time," he orders.

The son sits in the hall, outside the shabby hotel room. He's groggy, sleep still in his eyes. From inside, he hears giggles, then heavy breathing.

He leans his head against the door. His moist tongue licks his open mouth as his hands move toward his crotch. The sounds from inside become rhythmic. His hands move up and down the inside of his thighs. He lifts his shirt and, with both hands, rubs his belly, his chest; he squeezes his nipples. He thrusts his hands into his pants and rubs the flesh on the inside of his thighs. His fingers massage his balls. His body convulses. He moves to the sounds of his father fucking. He fucks too, as best he can. One hand wraps around his throbbing cock. The other strangles his cum-filled balls. His closes his eyes and imagines his father on top of him, raising his legs in the air, entering his greedy asshole. He feels his father's lips on his, forcing his mouth open with his hot tongue. The woman shrieks. He feels his father plummet his big, fat dick inside him.

The boy pulls his pants below his balls and jerks his cock. His eyes now open and staring in awe at his own dick.

His father moans, "I'm comin', baby!"

The whore in his father's bed cries out, "Fuck me, you big stud! Fuck me with that big dick! Fuck me raw!!"

A guttural, "Fuck me, Pa," sticks in the boy's throat as they all come together–like a symphony of sexual pleasure. And now the boy's moans of relief intermingle with their voices. Finally, still jerking himself, the boy groans, "Pa ... Oh, Pa! Thank you, Pa! Thank you!"

GREATER THAN BEING ALIVE by Jack Ricardo

I had to be dreaming. I was feeling too damn good. I hadn't felt like that in ages. Not since I was alive anyway. My mind was spinning, my skin was broiling, my legs were shaking, I was tingling from my brain to my toenails, my balls were bubbling over. It was crazy. I was crazy. I opened my eyes but all I saw was the moon peeking through the leaves on the tree. But I was just feeling better and better and I didn't know why. Then I heard something. A sloppy slurping sound. And I looked down and there he was: this old geezer was kneeling down and leaning over me and his face was down in my crotch and his mouth was covering my cock and he was sucking me off! "Whoa!" I screamed, and he looked up and he saw me looking at him sucking my cock and that only made him crazier! He smashed his face down on my cock and before long I was moaning louder than I ever did in my life and my cock exploded, shooting all that cum in my balls right up the shaft of my hard cock and right into this old guy's mouth! He swallowed it, and I closed my eyes went to sleep.

When I woke up the next morning I thought maybe it was a dream, but, no, it couldn't have been, because there was dried cum all over my pants. I knew one thing: I more alive than I had been in weeks. I pushed myself off the grass and wiped away the morning dew from my shirt. I dug up my sign from the bushes and walked out of the park to the highway and stood there holding my sign that said, "Will Work for Food," even though it was a lie. I just wanted food and I couldn't work 'cause I didn't remember how to do anything any more that anybody would pay me for. All I wanted was money, really, so I could buy some eggs for breakfast. And I got it. Nobody ever stops and gives me a job to do for money though and they don't want me to work anyway. They just give me money. And not a lot of that either. But enough for me to eat again. And I chomped down on an egg sandwich at McDonald's..

All day long when I was doing nothing like usual 'cause there's never nothing to do, I thought about that blowjob I got from that dude last night. I never got a blowjob from a dude before. Sure, back when I was alive I got blowjobs from chicks, but that was so long ago I'm not sure if it really happened or if it didn't. But a dude, never! Hell, I wasn't queer back then. I don't even know what I am now! I guess I'm just kind of a helpless Joe, and a hopeless one at that! Even homeless, if you don't count the park. But I do.

And I'm skinny; well not *real* skinny, like to the bone, but when you don't eat three squares everyday and don't get much meat in your gullet, you don't get much meat outside your gullet either. But I think I'm a good looking kid anyway. Hell, I can see that when I look in the mirror in the john in the park where I go to wash and get my drinking water. I got dark hair that maybe needs a haircut but I don't have a beard. I try to shave at

least once every week, whether I need it or not (hahahaha) with a razor I found sixteen weeks ago in the bin outside the cake factory. So what I'm telling you is, I don't look so bad, that is if you don't count the clothes I wear, which I guess are shabby and grimy but they keep me warm in winter.

Okay, maybe I'm a little dirty cause I don't take a bath but that old man who sucked my cock last night sure didn't care. Yeah, that was some blowjob! You kno, I didn't even know my cock was alive until he did that and I was glad to know it was. Just thinking about that guy sucking me is waking up my cock again. So that wha's like to be alive? Well, I'll take it.

Okay, now, before I get too excited, like I've been saying, all day long I was thinking about that wildman's mouth sucking my stiff cock and I began wondering why a queer sucks cocks and drinks cum anyway. Well, maybe I'm dumb but I ain't stupid so I think I figured it out: He sucks cock and drinks cum cause he likes it! And if he likes it, then it must be something nice to do. So I decided I'd try it and see what happened. I mean, why the hell not? What have I got to lose?

Now to set the stage for this I should tell you I am not the only guy who sleeps in the park at night. I share it. It don't matter though, cause there's room for a lot of us here. Which is good, cause there's a lot of us here! I even got some friends. Well, not real friends, I guess, but guys down on their luck like me and we talk sometimes and share our food when we have more than we need that day.

One of my friends is this guy who calls himself Ricky Mertz. He's a bit older than me, but he's still a young guy. Anyway, he's skinny too. Anyway, I saw this Ricky's cock when he pissed at the lake and it looked something like mine, with a big head and all. And I decided I was gonna suck it that night, that is if Ricky didn't mind me sucking it and I don't think he would. He never minds anything. He's a little crazy. Not like me.

I knew Ricky slept over by the big rocks by the lake so I went there and sure enough he was there, resting. He saw me and didn't say a word when I sat next to him cause he knows I won't hurt him or try to steal his stuff either. So he was just laying there with his hands behind his head looking up at the moon that wasn't shining too much cause it was kind of cloudy that night. And I just sat there for a couple minutes thinking about his cock and what it would be like to suck it and my own cock started coming alive again.

Maybe even Ricky was glad I was there because when I reached over and started playing with his cock through his pants he still didn't say anything. Not a word. But he did look at me kinda funny. I think he was just like me: We both thought we had dead cocks that we only use to piss with and I guess he never had a guy play with his cock before either. But as soon as I started diddling with his dick, it started growing bigger and bigger. It was a real weird feeling but good. I could also feel my own cock growing, real fast and real big and real hard. This is what it means to be alive, I thought to myself.

I didn't have to unzip or unbutton Ricky's pants 'cause all I had to do was take the clothespin off that kept his fly together. And when I did, it was easy to just shove my hand in his pants and pull out his cock. So here I was holding a guyn's hard cock and really liking it. His cock felt hot and hard and soft all at the same time. Then it kind of leaped around in my fist. My own cock was leaping around in my pants too, so I pulled it out of my fly and let it leap around all it wanted.

Now Ricky was looking down at me playing with his cock and then he was looking at my cock leaping around. He moaned. He moaned again when I leaned over like I done it a thousand times and opened my mouth and stuck out my tongue and started licking his big cockhead. Now my blood started boiling again cause it tasted so...so... well, just so *hot*, I guess is the word. Ricky was liking it too, I think, cause he was groaning now, and when I covered his whole big cockhead with my mouth he groaned even louder and so did I even though I had a mouthful of him, which I never had before in my life. Now I liked this so much that I began to wonder why I had never tried this before. It was good that I wanted to eat all his cock. And I wanted to take all of it right down to his balls. So I lifted my head and united the rope holding his pants up and pulled his pants right off without even taking off his shoes. It's a good thing it was summer cause otherwise Ricky would have frozen his balls off, and he had a lot of balls to freeze, two big hairy and baggy globes that were settled on the grass between his legs like a glob of melted wax.

I took my pants off too so Ricky wouldn't feel all alone being almost naked, and he saw that my cock was hard and bobbing around like it was really alive. And it was. I was proud of it like a dad is proud of his son which my dad never was. But who cares.

I knelt between Ricky's legs and grabbed his balls. Man, if I thought hanging onto this guy's hard cock was a great thing, playing with his balls was greater still. They almost melted in my hand and my brain almost melted too. I leaned down and wanted to see if they would melt in my mouth. They didn't. But wow, they tasted better even than an egg sandwich on a cold morning. I licked his balls all over, then gobbled them in my mouth and Ricky was mooing like a cow while I did it. And he lifted his knees and started squeezing them around my neck which felt so great I had to stop to catch my breath.

So I sat up on my heels but kept holding onto Ricky's balls and my chest was heaving up and down and I knew I was smiling even though I couldn't see myself and I never smile. Ricky was smiling too, and grinning, and looking like he was having a ball. But it was me who was having the ball, two of them, Ricky's. And I wanted more of them. And I got hungrier that I ever been in my life when I had one and grabbed his ass and lifted him up until his balls were hanging low down between his legs. I smashed my face against them and started adoring them again–eating them, licking them. Then Ricky started screaming kinda loud, telling me he was gonna shoot.

And I wanted to taste his cum so I took my mouth off his balls and planted my mouth full down on his cock again until I felt his sweaty cock-hairs on my forehead. Soon cum was shooting down my gullet. It was twitching like a bitch and Ricky was grunting like a pig, and I was swallowing all his cum like a beggar. I was almost screaming too 'cause my own cock was shooting off with me not even jerking on it like I used to when I was alive and the guy not even sucking it and we both got off.

That night I slept next to Ricky and that's the first time that ever happened. We both woke up with our pants off and we both went to the highway and got our money for the day and had some eggs together.

We walked around all day but neither one of us talked much. But that night we went back to his big rock together and we both got naked and hid our clothes in the bushes with my sign and his bag. Then we laid down on the grass and I started playing with Ricky's cock again. And it got hard fast again. And Ricky started playing with my cock too!

And soon I was laying on top of him and sucking his cock while he was under me and sucking mine. And if you ever had your cock sucked while you were sucking a cock too you know that's it greater than even eating a piece of steak you found that was still warm.

We were both sucking along nice and easy and wonderful and just feeling my cock sliding between Ricky's lips and feeling my cock sliding inside his warm mouth. But no matter how good it was feeling having that cock in my mouth, I knew what I wanted to would be even better. I let Ricky's cock slip from my lips and I pushed my head down real low and over those great hairy balls of his and started licking his ass. Licking Ricky's ass was a lot better than eating his cock 'cause my balls started really boiling as soon as I stuck the tip of my tongue into that puckered little asshole.

Ricky was loving it too and I guess he was wondering why I was doing it and why I was liked doing it too 'cause my cock flopped from his mouth and I knew he was straining his neck and his head 'cause soon I could feel his warm, sloppy tongue sliding all around my asshole. I don't even know how we were doing it. But we was just rolling around in the grass holding onto each other's legs and stuffing our faces up each other's ass, just slurping and licking like it was a holiday and we were fireworks.

I slobbered all over Ricky's asshole, both inside and outside while hanging onto his legs with all my might, just stuffing both my nose and my tongue deep inside him sometimes, and he was doing the same cause I was pushing my ass down on his face and he was squeezing the cheeks of my ass apart so he could get more and more of his tongue and his mouth up there. He was tongue-fucking me so beautifully I could have died happy then and there.

And it got better 'cause, just like that, with our mouths eating each other's ass out, and our cocks pressed someplace against each other's bodies, my cock shot off like a loose cannon and I was creaming between us and shooting up his asshole and Ricky was holding me tighter than ever and I

knew he was coming too 'cause I could feel him and hear him. And when we were all fired out we collapsed on the ground like a lump of shit.

Well, I gotta tell you how this ends now, even though it doesn't ever really end. No, not really. It just goes on and on. Like life.

Well, me and Ricky we stay together all the time now. We both use my sign to get us some money and we eat our eggs together and we walk around together all day and we sleep together. But before we sleep, we jerk off together, or I suck his cock or he sucks mine, or I eat out his asshole or he eats mine out, or we do both together. I guess it's greater than even being alive!

A VERY SPECIAL DELIVERY by Rudy Roberts

I had lived in the neighborhood for only a month when I decided to take home delivery of the daily newspaper. I called the customer service office and was promised the commencement of the paper's delivery the very next day. Of course, as it turned out, no newspaper arrived as had been promised. When I called back to inquire, I was told that the delivery boy had just quit his route, but that a new boy would begin the following day. With profuse apologies, the service representative offered to suspend my first week's fee. Gladly, I agreed. And I awaited the following day's delivery.

The morning arrived clear and warm. I was anticipating the arrival of the newspaper so that I could take it out onto my deck with my morning coffee. I was just finishing up my work-out when the doorbell rang. Out of breath and sweating, I went to the door. Framed by the glow of the early-morning sunlight, a teenager stood with a crisply folded newspaper in his outstretched hand.

His speech sounded memorized, half-heartedly apologizing for the delay and introducing himself as my new carrier–Matthew. His voice was surprisingly well-adjusted and rich, despite his youth. His hair was golden, and cut fashionably short with just a touch of gel to hold it in place. His lips were bright and moist; a flicker of a smile played at the corners of his mouth. He was tall and thin–lithe but gangly–the typical teenager.

"So," he concluded, "if there's anything I can do to be of service to you, just call me at this number." And he passed me a card with his name and phone number printed out neatly below the newspaper's logo.

"Should I call you Matthew," I asked, "or Matt?" I wiped my perspiring brow with the back of my hand.

His long lashes fluttered a few times and he looked down momentarily at his feet, as though embarrassed for some reason. "You can call me Matt if you like."

"All right then, *Matt*," I said. "I'm Drew."

"Hi." He brought his bright blue eyes back up to meet my gaze. For some reason, I stretched out my hand to shake, as though we were finalizing a business transaction. To my surprise, Matt's grip was strong, his fingers long, cool and dry.

"I'll see you, then," he said, turning to leave. A handsome mountain bike was perched against my front gate, a satchel of papers flung over the seat.

"Hey," I remarked, "nice bike. You do a lot of riding?"

"Yeah, pretty much. I like to hit the trails after school and weekends. Now that it's summer, I've got all sorts of time."

"Aha," I commented, "so, you'll be out on the trails later this morning?"

He nodded. "I might head down to the beach for a while."

"Sounds good. Well, have fun! And I'll see you tomorrow." With a

friendly wave and grin; I turned and shut my door, returning to my workout. And Matthew straddled his bicycle and slowly resumed his paper route.

After a late night of sitting in front of the computer with a particularly cantankerous script, I slept later than anticipated. Still groggy, wearing only a T-shirt and loose cotton pajama bottoms, I half-staggered down the stairs to answer the front door.

There, in what seemed brighter sunlight than usual, stood Matt sporting a huge grin and a folded newspaper.

"Good morning, Drew," he said. "Here's your paper."

I accepted the proffered paper and stifled a yawn.

"Up late?" he asked, lingering, shifting his weight from one foot to the other. He was wearing black, baggy walking shorts and a striped T-shirt, and looked particularly radiant. His skin glowed as golden as his hair. His eyes sparkled more brilliantly than I'd remembered.

But all I could muster at that moment was little more than a simple nod and a few words. "Yeah, that's what you can expect from a writer, I suppose–odd hours."

"You're a writer?!" he remarked, his eyes widening, his interest piqued. "Wow! That's really neat!"

"Well, it keeps me busy, if nothing else," I replied. "And it's been known to pay the odd shekel here and there."

I wasn't sure, but I thought I could see Matt looking me over with a curious stare. But he was cautious about being discovered.

"Well, I'd better get back to my papers," he said suddenly, breaking away and turning to go. As he reached the gate, my door half-shut, he turned around and called out, "Did you maybe want to ... I dunno ... maybe go for a bike ride later on? I'll be done with my route in about an hour."

Rubbing my neck, suppressing another yawn, I thought briefly. The suggestion was innocent enough. And the kid seemed genuine. Deciding that I could use a solid workout to start my day, I accepted his offer.

"As long as you stay for breakfast afterwards," I added.

"Sure!" he bubbled, almost leaping onto his bicycle; I thought he'd injure himself.

"Then, I'll see you back here in an hour."

"Okay!" And he sped off.

Before Matt's return, I'd managed to change into more appropriate riding clothes–cycling shorts and a tank-top. I'd just tied my laces when the bell rang. He was indeed a pretty boy, eager to please and refreshingly alert and energetic. I ruffled his hair and locked the door behind me.

Our ride was vigorous. This kid was no slouch. He obviously cycled a fair bit from the way he kept up with me on the cycling paths. We barreled through some fairly steep and turbulent terrain and he kept abreast of me the whole way. After about an hour, we ended up back at my house, glistening

and famished.

"I don't know about you," I said, grabbing a towel from a rack in the kitchen, "but I need a shower before I can even begin to attempt breakfast. You're welcome to one, too, if you like."

Matt's T-shirt was wet down the spine and under the arms. A tiny damp spot had just begun to appear between two slimly-defined pectorals. His tongue flicked against those perpetually wet, ruby-red lips.

"Yeah, okay. Sounds good."

"I've got an extra T-shirt, if you want," I called out, climbing the stairs two steps at a time. "You can bring it back tomorrow."

Matt followed me up the stairs, maintaining his distance, looking around at the decor and the pictures lining the staircase. I chatted with him briefly about our ride, complimenting him on his prowess and stamina. All the while, I was grabbing clothes to wear after my shower. I set aside a spare T-shirt for Matt.

Standing in the doorway of the bathroom, I turned back and said, pointing, "There's plenty of towels in the linen closet there. I won't be long. Take a look around if you like." And I shut the door behind me.

The hot spray felt good against my muscles. But I didn't linger. I was also aware of my growing hunger. Within moments, I was finished. Wearing just my boxer shorts, toweling my hair vigorously, I emerged from the steaming bathroom. Matt was nowhere to be seen. I checked my bedroom and saw that he'd picked up the T-shirt I'd laid out for him. But he wasn't there. Casually, I walked down to the den and found him leafing through one of the books on my shelf-lined walls, seemingly engrossed in the pages of Charles Dickens.

"Ah, I see you've found my secret," I said, draping the towel over one shoulder, leaning against the door jamb.

Matt jumped slightly, startled at my presence. But his face broke into a wide smile. And he blushed.

"You sure have a lot of books," he commented, looking around at the several bookcases lining the walls of my busy, little office.

I sighed at his observation, recalling the move and the back-breaking cases of books that I had to bring with me. "Yeah, I know. Sometimes I'm not entirely sure it's all worth it. But that's the reality."

"I really like Charles Dickens," he added, putting the book back onto the shelf carefully, as though the volume were sacred or fragile. "We just read *Tale of Two Cities* in school this year."

"Would you like to borrow one?" I asked. "As long as you're careful, I mean. I don't generally lend my books out, but as long as you're careful, it should be all right."

"Yeah? Are you sure?"

"Sure, I'm sure. Go ahead. Take Mr. Dickens home with you and get him back to me when you're done. And now, get your ass into that shower, 'cause I'm famished." And, jokingly, I snapped my towel at him. He deftly

dodged the sharp corner and broke into a refreshingly boyish giggle.

I followed him into the bathroom, preparing myself to brush my hair and clean myself up to meet the day. Without hesitation, Matt stripped down and climbed into the shower. I didn't want to appear overtly lascivious, so I kept my stares to a minimum, using my peripheral vision as much as possible to catch a glimpse of his young, naked body. I noticed a tan line across his slender hips and pert buttocks. I didn't catch sight of his crotch, though.

His shower lasted only a few minutes. He emerged dripping wet. Casually, I looked over at him and smiled, being careful not to look directly between his legs. Without saying a word, I tossed him a towel and he immediately began drying off. He seemed sure of his body, calm and relaxed about his nakedness. And I smiled.

There was a lengthy pause as we both attended to our appearance. Combing and adjusting, side by side in front of the mirror, we were soon ready for breakfast. Every now and then, I'd catch him looking at my chest. I wasn't sure, but I thought I caught him at one point trying to see something beyond the opening in my boxer shorts.

"You look like a swimmer, too," I observed, nodding at his slimly defined chest.

He smiled and blushed once more, lashes fluttering like two delicate butterflies. "Yeah, every now and then."

"You've got a nice build." And I turned around, sitting on the edge of the vanity, crossing my arms across my own well-developed chest.

"So do you," he said, biting his lower lip nervously. He looked fresh and golden, scrubbed and pretty.

"Well, a person has to keep fit. Come on." And I led the way down the hall to the bedroom, where I grabbed my clothes. Matt popped his head out of the T-shirt just as I stuffed my hand down my pants to adjust my crotch. I paused slightly when I caught him looking. And then, sensing his nervousness, I smiled broadly and said, "Just adjusting the equipment. Don't mind me." And I openly fumbled with my crotch until it comfortably fit inside my pants. Then I zipped up.

"Now, let's have a go at some breakfast," I said, tucking my shirttails in, descending the stairs, Matt at my heels.

Within moments, I had two bowls of cereal and some sliced strawberries dished up, and a pot of coffee brewing. We sat at the round kitchen table, overlooking the back deck and my garden. We were both quite hungry and neither of us spoke for the longest while, content only to eat.

"So, Matt," I began, wiping my lips with the back of my hand, "tell me a little bit about yourself."

"What do you mean?" He almost seemed shocked at my question.

"I mean, tell me a little about who you are, what makes you tick, where you come from, what you want to do with your life, what your family's like, whatever. All the insidious details." I rose and crossed to the stove to prepare scrambled eggs.

"Well, my parents are divorced. I live with my mother a couple of blocks away in one of those high-rises near the bridge. My sister's just finished high school and is probably moving out this summer. My mother doesn't know this yet, so that should be interesting. And I have a dog named Ryan. He's a black Lab."

"Ah, nice dogs, those. I can remember my grandparents having a Lab when I was a boy. And, I suppose, you must have lots of friends, too?" I asked. "I mean, other than the four-legged type."

"I have a few," he replied, smiling. "But I guess I kinda keep to myself a lot. I don't generally take to people all that quickly. It's different with you, though, because ... well, I guess because you're older and I generally get along with older people better."

"Do you see your father much?"

"Not too much. He moved to Vancouver last year. I saw him at Christmas and that was it. But he calls every now and then to see how we're all doing."

"I guess you must miss him."

"Yeah," he replied, noncommittal. "But I'm glad he's gone, too, in a way. He used to ... well, he used to hit my mom. Sometimes, he'd even knock us around. He's apparently got some help since the divorce, but it's hard to forget what happened before."

"I guess so. That must make you and your mother pretty close, then."

"Oh yeah, we're good friends. Now, my *sister's* another thing altogether." And he giggled, rolling his eyes.

"Do you have a girlfriend?" I asked, spooning the eggs into a hot skillet.

"Naw, I'm not really ... well, I haven't found one that interests me too much, yet."

"How old are you?" I then asked. "Sixteen?"

"Seventeen," he replied.

"Hell, you've got lots of time to find somebody who interests you. I know it took me longer than all my friends before I got involved with someone."

"I would've thought that you had lots of girlfriends."

I shook my head and stirred the eggs as they cooked. "Well, I had lots of *offers* but girls weren't something I really cared for, to be honest. In a sexual sense anyway."

"Yeah?"

"Yeah. When I was growing up, I was pretty much focused on sports–and books. When I wasn't in the pool or on the bench-press, I was in the library."

"What about now?" he asked. "I mean, you don't spend all your time now in the library or on the bench press, do you? You must have at least a dozen girls hanging around."

"Well, Matt," I said, pausing, looking up at him for the first time since I'd started preparing the eggs, "I'll level with you. Okay? I'm not really all that interested in girls– if you know what I mean."

I gently scooped the eggs out onto two plates. The toaster popped out two dark, poppyseed bagels.

"I think I ... I think I know what you're getting at," Matt replied, cautious, it seemed, about jumping to the wrong conclusion.

"Well, you're a pretty smart kid; I thought you might," I said, setting the plates down on the table, straddling the chair, reaching for more coffee.

Matt munched on his bagel silently for a long while. I sipped my coffee and added another splash of milk. I thought then that I'd better make myself absolutely clear before he tortured himself to death.

"When I was about your age," I began, "my parents brought a boarder into our home to make some extra cash while my father was laid up from an accident he'd had at the foundry where he worked. They needed the money and my brother had just moved out, so that meant we had an extra bed-my brother and I shared a bedroom. And, so, a university student moved into my room. His name was Chris. I'll never forget Chris. He was tall, with black hair and the bluest eyes I'd ever seen. He was studying Philosophy or Poetry or something like that. And he loved playing chess and tennis. He was also the one who got me interested in working out, swimming, cycling and all that. Anyhow, one night, I heard Chris across the room jerking off. And I watched his silhouette in the moonlight. And I thought that was the best thing I'd ever seen. That was when I first started having any sexual thoughts. And every single one of them involved Chris.

"Well, after Chris moved out, the feelings didn't go away. If anything, they grew stronger. So, I decided to check things out for myself. And I joined the Drama Club at school-because I'd heard that lots of gay guys hung out there. And there was this one guy in particular-Mark-who I was kinda stuck on. So, as the year progressed, Mark and I became close friends. He'd stay over at my house sometimes. And I'd stay over at his.

"And this one time when I was staying the night at Mark's place, we were sucking back a few beers-his folks were working late and we had the house to ourselves. And suddenly I felt a hand on my leg. I looked over and saw Mark staring at me with this weird look in his eyes; I'd never seen him look at me like that before. And, before I really knew what I was doing, we were having sex. It was really the first time for both of us, but it was good. A bit clumsy, but we enjoyed ourselves.

Later that night, after his folks had gotten home and we'd gone to bed, we kissed and fondled each other for hours before going to sleep."

As my story progressed, Matt became more and more curious. He silently chewed, careful not to miss a word of my tale.

"So, that's my situation. I guess I've always been gay and it's what I prefer. I can't say that I understand it all, but that's the way I turned out. And I'm quite content with my life."

"Do you have a boyfriend?" Matt asked, his voice wavering and hesitant.

I shook my head. "Nope, not right now. I broke off with a guy about six months ago. But it wasn't anything really long-term. A couple of years."

"Oh."

"So, what do you think about all this?" I asked. "Does it bother you? Do you think it's wrong? Do you think it's sick? Do you think it's neat? What?"

He was visibly struggling for the right words, looking around the room as though they were waiting for him on the wall or the tea towels. Finally, when he'd gathered his thoughts, he spoke. "Well, it makes me feel kinda weird. Not that I think it's wrong or anything. I don't know. It's something I've thought about before ... I mean, about myself. But I kept pushing it away because I couldn't deal with what it meant. I mean, it's not the easiest thing to be gay in high school."

"You've got that right," I agreed, munching and smiling, remembering.

"How did you know you were gay? I mean, how did you know that's what you wanted? I don't see how a person can just tell that."

"Well, how does somebody know he's *straight*?" I countered. "I don't question those people. I assume that they know what they want, what feels good to them, what turns them on. All I know is that what feels good to me happens to be another man."

"I've never really ... well, done ... anything before. With anyone."

"I wouldn't have expected you to have done anything before. After all, you're only seventeen. You've got plenty of time to decide what's right for you. And, who knows, you might even wish to experiment with both boys *and* girls. Find out what feels good for you."

"Well, sometimes I like to ... play with myself in the shower," Matt confessed, looking down into his plate, pushing his food around now, blushing and smiling. "And I think about this senior at school. His name's Michael. He's the captain of the basketball team. He's black and he's got a great body. And I get kinda ... well, excited, I guess ... thinking about him."

"Do you jerk off about him?"

After a brief pause, he nodded.

"How does that feel?"

Matt shrugged. "Okay, I guess. I dunno."

"What do you think about when you're jerking off?"

Again the shrug. "His body. His chest and his legs. I imagine what it would be like to ... touch him." His voice had almost trailed off to a whisper. But I caught every word.

"It's confusing, I know," I added, "but it's not *wrong* to feel these things. On the contrary, it's extremely healthy to feel sexual urges–these ones just happen to be towards somebody of the same sex. Do you think about this guy often–what's his name, Michael?"

The corners of Matt's mouth curled, and a mischievous glint appeared in his eyes as he sat silently, staring into his plate, his hands in his lap.

"Almost every day." And he giggled nervously. "It's crazy, but I make believe we're together. I mean, I know he's straight and all that, but I still imagine being with him."

I smiled back, relieved. "Well, it sounds to me like you've already answered your question."

And he looked up at me, an eyebrow cocked, a smirk smeared across his face. "Yeah, I know."

Rising suddenly, I said, "Let me give you a few of my magazines to look through." And I raced upstairs, two steps at a time, to retrieve a handful of porno magazines from my bedroom. "You'll probably want to keep these hidden from your mother," I said, winking at him. "They're liable to give her ideas."

"As long as they give *me* ideas, that's all that matters." And Matt took the glossy magazines and leafed through them.

"This one's one of my favorites," I said, pulling out an Olympic-style edition that was full of hot jocks in provocative poses. There was one photo of a bald mulatto man on the parallel bars, naked and powerfully erect, his body arched and taut with years of muscle definition, his penis gigantic and curving gracefully upwards. He shimmered with sweat, his face intent and sharply handsome, dark and brooding.

"Holy shit, yeah!" Matt agreed, flipping back and forth to see the layout of that particular model. "This guy's *amazing!*"

"I've spent many a lonely evening with that one," I commented, making the appropriate hand gestures, feeling those all-too-familiar twinges in my groin as I recalled the many nights I'd spent with that particular magazine clenched in my one hand, and my aching cock in the other.

"I can't imagine you *ever* spending an evening alone," Matt said, voice lowered, turning the pages with fascination.

"Hey, it happens to the best of us," I replied, reaching across and ruffling his hair.

His eyes rose then to meet mine. He was damned hot. But I kept reminding myself that he was, after all, just a boy. And I'd been involved with too many boys in my days.

"Do you think those will keep you busy for a few days?" I asked, plopping the magazines into a double plastic bag.

"Oh, probably," he replied, still smirking. "If your paper's late tomorrow morning, you'll know where I am."

This time, we both laughed.

I was somewhat surprised when Matt didn't ring the bell the next few days. When I got up, I found my newspaper, neatly folded, sticking out of my mailbox. After the second day, I began to think that I'd perhaps confused him even more about his sexuality. But I didn't have to wait long for Matt to drift back into my life once again.

It was early evening, seven-thirty, when the doorbell rang. I hadn't been expecting anyone so I approached the door cautiously, wearing just a pair of shorts and a T-shirt. And there, through the peep-hole, I could see him standing on my front stoop, a knapsack flung over one shoulder. I quickly

opened the door and ushered him inside.

"Matt," I said, surprised and genuinely pleased to see him, "what brings you here at this hour? Making a special delivery?"

He chuckled at my weak joke. I shut the door behind him and bolted it. Silently, I led him out to the deck. Classical music was wafting serenely through outside speakers. En route, I grabbed a beer from the fridge and offered him one. To my surprise, he accepted.

He sat on the edge of his seat, chugging on the beer as if it was soda pop. I climbed into my chaise and settled back. After a brief pause, I spoke.

"So, where have you been keeping yourself lately?" I asked.

"My dad came into town kinda unexpectedly and we've been doing stuff together. And, at nights, well, I've been keeping *myself* busy." And with that, he pulled the plastic bag of porno magazines out of his knapsack and plopped them onto the table.

"I see," I replied. "You haven't gone and stuck all the pages together, now, have you?"

He chuckled again. "Not too many."

"Well, I know you're not in school, but would I be out of place in asking for a report on them?" I took a long draught from my beer then, settling back.

"I liked that Olympic one so much," he said, "that I had to go out and buy one of my own. So, I did. Yesterday."

"You *did*?!" I exclaimed. "How? Where?"

"I went downtown to that gay bookstore and just walked in and bought one. They didn't even ask for ID or anything. I was surprised."

"Oh, dear. I seem to have created a Frankenstein."

"Well, let's not go that far. But I think you've helped me clear some things up about myself."

"Yeah?"

"Yeah. I mean, after having looked through all those books –time and time again– I really got to thinking about my sexuality. And I guess I've come to the conclusion that I *am* gay–or at least I'd like to experiment with it. And I don't really feel all that freaked out about it any more."

"Why's that?" I asked.

"Well," he said, pausing to drink some beer, wiping his lips with the back of his hand, "probably because you've helped me realize that I'm not alone. I mean, there are lots of gay people around. At least I don't feel like some sort of deviant. I also found an ad at the bookstore yesterday about a gay youth group and I'm thinking about calling them up."

"That's not a bad idea," I added, impressed by his resourcefulness. "You might just find the young man of your dreams there."

"Maybe."

"You can never tell. Don't write them off just yet."

"No, I didn't mean that. I just meant that I ... well, I guess I'm just more into older guys."

"You know that already?!"

"I sort of always did."

"I see. Anyone we know?" And I smirked at him.

He blushed but didn't look away this time. He, in fact, met my gaze and held it with his dazzling blue eyes. His lips curled deliciously and his tongue flicked against the corner of his mouth.

"Well, I was thinking that ... well, if you don't have a boyfriend right now ... and I don't have one either ... that ... well, we could ... I dunno...." And he stopped, losing his nerve, sensing perhaps that I wasn't into what he was suggesting.

"Aren't there guys your own age who you'd like to get together with?"

"Yeah, a few. But I don't know how to go about asking them. At least with you, I already know."

"How convenient," I replied, half-serious, half-joking.

"I didn't mean it like that. Really. I'm sorry. It's not that you're a convenience," he clarified, "so much as you're ... well, you're really good-looking. And I thought you might find me ... well, good-looking, too." His voice faded towards the end, beginning to sound dejected.

"Well, that's more like it," I said. "Now, don't take this the wrong way either," I began, sitting up, "but I've been with lots of younger guys before and-for whatever reasons-I guess you could say that I felt taken advantage of."

Matt almost panicked. "That wouldn't happen with me," he insisted. "I don't want to take advantage of you, Drew. I really like you. And I really am attracted to you. I was just wondering if...." This time, his voice trailed off completely, cracking finally into silence. I thought he was going to cry.

After a brief pause, with Matt gathering his emotions and calming himself down, and me choosing my words carefully, I spoke. "You're right about one thing," I said softly, "I do find you quite ... attractive." His face lit up. "From the first day I laid eyes on you, I thought that you were an extremely cute guy. And now that you're sitting here with me like this, I have to admit that I can't think of one good reason to stop us from doing something about all this."

Matt was relieved to see a smile develop on my face. Even I wasn't entirely sure what my response would be. Part of me just wanted to turn and run, but then I looked at those slim legs of his and remembered that supple, defined chest from the other morning. And I gave in to my lustier instincts.

"You mean it?" Matt asked, incredulous.

I nodded.

Matt let out an enormous sigh and wiped his forehead. After taking another deep breath, he said, "Do you wanna go inside?"

"Sure," I said, rising. I led the way, sure that Matt was watching my butt swing back and forth in my shorts. Silently, I stepped aside, allowing Matt entrance into the house. I quickly followed, pulling the screen door shut behind me. And then, nonchalantly, as though we'd been doing it all along,

I slipped an arm around his neck and gently squeezed his shoulder. We headed for the stairs.

To my surprise, Matt wrapped a slender arm around my waist and cuddled next to my body. He felt hot to my touch, hot and dry. I instantly began to have stirrings in my crotch, anticipating the moment I got this boy naked.

"The other night," Matt began as we ascended the stairs, "after you gave me those magazines, I imagined that it was *you* on the parallel bars."

"Yeah? Well, I'm flattered. I only wish I were as well-built as that guy." I crooked my arm and cupped my palm over the top of his head, feeling the silky softness of his hair. As we walked down the hall together, I stopped by the bathroom and said, "Maybe we should get cleaned up first."

"Okay," he said, slipping past me into the dark bathroom.

I turned the lights on low. Matt looked golden. I pulled my T-shirt up and off, pleased to see that Matt followed suit. Deftly, he kicked off his shoes and peeled off his socks. I leaned against the vanity and braced myself with my hands, one at either side of me. This pose, I knew, made my biceps flex and my pectorals tighten. This time, though, Matt didn't try to hide the fact that he was fascinated by my body.

"You're fucking hot!" he whispered, bringing tentative fingers up to touch my chest.

I cupped his smooth shoulders and ran my fingers along his lithe arms. His touch was electric. When he grazed my nipples, he looked up into my face, smirking.

"Kinda like that, huh?!" he asked.

I chuckled and inhaled deeply, filling my chest.

"How about this?" And he bent over and brought his tongue into contact with my left nipple. I exhaled raggedly and pulled his face closer, feeding my fingers through his hair.

"That's it," I coaxed. "Oh, yeah!"

Then Matt stood up, licking his lips. I spread my thighs, one on either side of him, and pulled him closer, my hands firmly planted on his buttocks. And before I knew it, our mouths were locked together in a frenzied kiss. My strong tongue delved deep into his mouth, lapping and jabbing. We were hungry for each other, it seemed. I held his delicate head firmly in place with both hands, kissing his delicious lips and sucking on his writhing tongue. Matt floated his palms down my sides over the ribs. Momentarily, we broke for air.

"Where did you learn to kiss like that?" I implored, smoothing a stray lock of hair from his forehead.

He shrugged, flattered by the compliment. "I dunno. I just do it that way."

"Well, I wonder what else you just ... instinctively do," I added, pulling his butt closer, feeling our mounds of cock-flesh grind hotly together.

"Aren't we going to get cleaned up?" Matt then asked, pushing away and reaching for the waistband on his shorts. With one quick thrust, he stood in his white briefs, a large knob straining outwards.

I deftly unbuckled my shorts, stood free of the vanity, and shifted my weight in order to free them from my body. They fell away cleanly and I stepped out of them, fully naked, my cock beginning to grow.

Matt stared wide-eyed at my growing cock. I loved the look of absolute delight on his sweet, boyish face. He slipped his hand down the front of his own shorts and squeezed his cock. Taking careful breaths, he pushed his shorts down over his slender hips and tossed them aside with his big toe. And there we finally stood, both naked, in the warm glow of the halogen lights.

"God, but they make some teenagers look really good these days," I commented, taking in his beautiful, hairless body. His cock was fully and proudly erect; I was delighted to see how big it was. "You really *are* built well!" And I reached for that cock, wrapping my large hands around it, pulling slowly on the length of the shaft.

Matt's breathing became ragged. He closed his eyes and his face contorted. I thought he'd pass out. But he was just savoring the sensation of another man's hand on his aching erection for the first time. I used caution, though, wary of a young male's uncontrollable orgasms. I wanted this encounter to be more than a quick hand-job. With some reluctance, I released his hot cock and turned towards the tub.

I turned the water on and adjusted the temperature. When I turned back, I could see Matt squeezing his cock to make him come.

"Shall we?" I beckoned, stepping into the shower.

Matt didn't have to respond. He almost leapt into the shower with me, pulling the curtain shut behind him. I reached for the soap and soaped his back, feeling his satiny skin against my kneading fingers. Matt's exploring fingers reached behind him, rubbing up against my thighs. As he narrowed the gap between his eager fingers and my eager cock, I hardened. Leaning forward, I stuck my tongue into his ear, pressing my chest against his soapy back.

Quickly, he turned around and frantically embraced me, pulling our bodies tightly together under the hot spray of the water. Once more, we found ourselves kissing each other passionately and wetly. Suddenly his fingers found my cock and crept along its length until it reached the low-hanging balls. My tongue dragged across his cheek and once more filled his ear. He pulled on my cock with insistence, urgency.

"Yeah," I whispered, "oh, yeah! Pull on it!"

"I don't really know what to do," he confessed, not relinquishing his treasure for a moment.

"We'll take our time, then," I said, cupping his beautiful, pert ass in my hands, kneading each cheek like bread dough. And my lips latched onto his neck, nibbling and slurping on his soft, succulent, golden flesh.

"Holy shit!" he hissed.

But I didn't want us to shoot our respective loads down the drain. I did want us to get cleaned up so that we could romp on my bed for awhile, so

that we could explore the joys and mysteries of each other's body, so that I could perhaps teach Matt a few things about sex with another man while savoring the delicious flavors and aromas and sensations of his young body. Presently, our kissing still active, our hands blurred across our slippery bodies as we cleaned and scrubbed each other. I took special care in soaping my fingers and sliding them through the slick, hairless crack of his beautiful little ass. He was tight, of course. But I just wanted to get him clean enough to eat. For now.

After we had exhausted ourselves in the shower, we quickly exited and toweled each other dry. I particularly liked the way his spring-like cock bounced up and down when I rubbed the towel over his flat stomach. I also liked the way he wrapped a toweled hand around my cock and stroked me dry. During all this, however, we still managed to find each other's mouth, delving into the delights of our passion.

I hit the light switch and grabbed his hand, pulling him out of the bathroom into the hallway. Looking back, catching a glimpse of his excited face, I led us to the bedroom. And, silently, I sat on the edge of the mattress and spread my legs. Once more, though this time kneeling, Matt wedged himself between my outspread thighs, our eyes locked together. He pressed his face close to my chest then, inhaling the aromas of my body deeply into his lungs. Then I felt the steamy point of his tongue journeying across my pectorals once more. And I held him close, reaching along his arched back to that sweet ass.

"Where should our lessons begin?" I hoarsely asked.

"I want to know," Matt replied, breathing wetly against my ravaged nipple, "how to suck your cock."

"Perhaps you should allow me to demonstrate first," I offered, kissing his long, slender neck.

"Yeah?" he asked, breaking away momentarily, looking earnestly into my face. "Would you?"

"You don't have to ask twice," I said, smiling broadly. "Why don't you lie down and hang your legs over the end of the bed. That way, I can get onto my knees and get right at it. And you can watch from above."

"All right!" Matt exclaimed enthusiastically. He flopped onto his back and held his rigid dick out for me, licking his lips, his bright blue eyes wide with wonder and anticipation.

I lowered myself to my knees then and, bracing myself against his outspread thighs, got reasonably comfortable. Up close, his cock had a heady aroma that sent chills coursing through my body. In fact, the first thing I did was drag his cock across my face in order to inhale its sweetness before continuing.

"Now," I began, feeling peculiar in my role as instructor, trying to distance myself from my own growing desire in order to give Matt a sense of what to do, "there aren't any cut-and-dry rules about sucking dick. You don't always have to be on your knees. We could both be lying on the bed

together and suck each other off just as well. But, for demonstration purposes, I thought this way would be best."

"You should videotape this," Matt joked, finding the situation comical as well as erotic, "and sell it on late-night television!"

"Just shut up and watch!" And I grabbed his cock and held it perpendicular to his body. "I always like to get a taste of the dick I'm about to suck, just to get my juices flowing–so to speak." And I kissed the tender ridge along the underside of his fat cock. Then my tongue-tip traced a slow and steady route along the length of the shaft, stopping at the plump, sensitive head. Holding his cockhead against my lower lip, I continued in my explanation, "Then I like to play with the head a bit." And I slipped the dark head past my lips, encompassing it, bringing my tongue up against it to taste the free-flowing pre-cum that drooled from the end of it.

"Holy fuck!" Matt nearly screamed. He fell back onto his elbows, eyes shut, face ecstatic.

"Hey," I said, breaking away, "how can you expect to learn anything when you aren't even watching?!" I smiled hugely. "Now, after I play with the head of it for awhile-tasting it, mingling my saliva with that delicious pre-cum that's just drizzling out of this baby–then I take the cock into my mouth –always mindful of the teeth–and relax my throat to press it in as far as I can. Now, it took me a couple of years before I was able to take a cock this big all the way to the root. Watch."

And, relaxing every muscle in my throat, I slid his rigid cock slowly into my gullet until my nose was buried in his curly blond pubic hair. And, tenderly, I stroked his penis with my throat. With strong and urgent lips, I hugged the girth of his fat pecker and pulled back, relinquishing what promised to be a delicious assault.

"What do you think?" I asked, licking absently at the fleshy head, fingering his churning balls.

"Fuck!" was all he managed. "I could never do that with your cock!"

"Never say never," I smirked, opening my mouth wide for more. "After having played this trick a few times -- the deep-throat thing–I like to run my tongue along the ridge underneath: still just getting a taste for it."

And I brought my tongue flat against the base of his cock, licking at his balls, lapping at the length of his dick, matting the soft hair with my spit. Then I brought the tip of my hot, shimmering tongue into the deep slit of his cockhead and wiggled it around. Matt's legs were trembling as his breathing increased.

"You're amazing!" he rasped. "You're going to have me shooting my load before long if you don't watch out."

"I thought you might be a quick blow," I replied. "And, as much as I'd like to taste the fullness of your cock, I think we'd better just stick to the lessons for now."

"If you feel you have to," he said, joking. "I mean, far be it from me to hold you back." And he licked his lips with a great deal of lechery.

"You are such a slut," I whispered, speaking into the head of his cock as though it were a microphone. "And these things are a weakness of mine," I added, wagging his stiff cock around.

Reluctantly, I stood up and sat beside him. "So, after playing with it like that for a while, I suck on it and lick at it and kiss it and slurp all over it. That sort of thing. Get it real wet. Get it real hard. Sometimes I suck on the balls for a little while. Lick the inner thighs, too. That's always nice. Take it to the root again. And by that time, your partner should be ready to blast the back of your throat with a white-hot load of cum. How's that sound?"

"Sounds fuckin' amazing! You want me to try it on *you* for a while?" he asked, always the eager student.

"I'd be a fool to say no," I replied, leaning back, my cock semi-erect, stretching across my leg.

Matt leaped off the bed and crawled between my spread thighs, bracing himself with my knees as he knelt. He looked hopefully into my eyes and then back at my dark and powerful cock. Licking his lips to get himself ready, he reached for my cock and took the tube of flesh between his hot, dry fingers, bringing the head up to his mouth. With a quivering tongue, he tasted the tip of my dick, breathing hotly the whole time.

His movements were quick and excited, ravenous and frantic. Although he could not fit the entire length of my dick into his mouth, he valiantly managed to stuff over half of it inside. I could feel his teeth scraping along the sides of my dick, something that actually thrilled me more than alarmed me. His wriggling tongue was ecstatic. Saliva drooled out of his mouth and down his chin. His bright red lips were a sharp contrast against the dark column of flesh which they circled. His sucking was surprising adept. I could feel my arousal growing. Without thinking, I placed a large hand against the back of his head and pushed him farther down. He gagged slightly but relaxed enough to accept another inch or two of my hot dick flesh.

"Oh, yeah!" I hissed. "You're a natural! Mmm!"

His fingers played with my balls, weighing them, juggling them, tickling them. His attention made me all the more eager to shoot. But, just as I hadn't wanted Matt to shoot too soon, I certainly didn't want to be guilty of the same crime. Sensing that my orgasm was mounting faster than I'd at first anticipated, I gently pushed his hot mouth off my slippery cock.

Looking up with confusion on his face, Matt sat back on his haunches, his stiff cock in his hand.

"You were great," I said, ruffling his hair, setting his mind at ease. "I just didn't want to shoot too soon."

His face registered delight at having been so complimented. Then he wiped a stray string of saliva from his chin, licking his lips. I saw a curly pubic hair on his cheek and tenderly wiped it away with my thumb.

"What's next?" he asked, exuberant, bouncing to his feet, his dick stiff against his stomach.

"Well, unless you really want to," I said, lying back, my glistening prick rising above me, "I think it might be best to put off your anal lesson until later. I'm not sure it'd be the best thing to do for your first time."

"So, let's suck cock!" And he leapt onto the bed beside me, standing aloft, giggling, eyes sparkling with mischief.

"Are you sure you want to stand way up there?" I asked, lying flat on my back, licking my lips suggestively.

"Did you have any particular place in mind?" Matt replied, straddling my body, standing tall.

"Why don't you bring that pretty little butt of yours down here and rest awhile." I tapped my chin and smiled.

"Are you sure I'd be comfortable?" he said, squatting, his balls dangling closer, full and heavy.

"You tell me," I said, reaching for his thighs, pulling him down into position.

His winking and puckered asshole slipped up against my lips. I gently kissed it, smelling the clean yet pungent flesh of his tangy ass. With my tongue elongated, I traced the perimeter of my target, holding fast to Matt's legs as he squirmed and squealed with delight at the new sensation.

"Fuck!" he screamed. "Holy shit! That feels so good!"

I laughed deep and throaty. Then, taking careful yet sloppy aim, I shoved my long, pleasing tongue straight into his asshole. Matt squealed with glee. I slurped and sucked on the young flesh, wriggling my tongue inside his sweet young ass. His smooth legs were slippery with sweat. His butt cheeks were slick with my spit.

Suddenly, I felt Matt's mouth back on the end of my straining cock. I swung my legs up then, linking them around Matt's slender neck, pulling him closer, all the while digging my hot tongue into his fiery butthole. My maneuver was accepted with great excitement as Matt reciprocated, slipping my dick further into his hungry mouth, sucking ferociously. His fingers pried my own ass cheeks apart and pressed inside. I tried to accommodate his eager digits by relaxing my asshole enough to encourage his entry. As though he could read my mind, he shot a finger inside with ease, wiggling it around like a tiny cock.

All this was too much for me to take. Much to my surprise, my orgasm was rapidly charging to the point of no return. Not wishing to hold off much longer, I relinquished that tasty boy-hole and craned my neck to get Matt's throbbing cock into my mouth instead. I swallowed it whole and sucked frantically as my own juices boiled. I thought about warning Matt but thought that he'd have to learn sometime. My moans were indicative enough, and so were his, but neither of us pulled off.

With one tremendous lunge, I shot my load heavily and fiercely into Matt's sucking mouth. His first reaction was, not surprisingly, to gag, but he quickly adjusted to the amount of hot cream spurting from the tip of my slippery cock. Holding it like a handle, he pulled the head from his mouth in

order to capture the spewing nozzle for the remains of my load. This was too much for him to take and his own pent-up load of cum spurted from the tip of his dick into my willing and waiting throat. I'm always surprised at the amount that a boy's dick can produce. But the sweetness that accompanied this particular boy's cock made the experience delicious and enthralling.

After cleaning up our mutual mess, Matt climbed slowly off my body and laid himself down beside me, placing an arm across my rising and falling chest. His fingers toyed with my dark nipples as we relaxed together. I stroked his flat stomach, lingering in the soft hair between his legs.

"Sorry I didn't warn you," I said, running my thumb across the sticky head of his still-hard dick.

"That's okay," Matt replied, kissing my pectoral. "I liked it." And he giggled again.

"Well, you *did* seem to be able to take care of it," I added, holding his stiff pecker in my hand.

"That was amazing," was all he said.

"And *this* beauty doesn't seem to have had enough yet."

"I'm sure it wouldn't mind if you were to suck on it some more." His fingernails clawed lightly across my nipples, sending chills through my body.

"I guess staying the night is out," I commented, checking the clock on the nightstand. It was almost ten.

"We've still got an hour or so." And Matt reached down for my heavy cock, tugging on the sticky flesh with his hot fingers.

"If you really want the practice," I said, struggling to suppress a laugh, "I'm sure I could fit you in somewhere."

IN THE GANG by Jack Ricardo

The kid jived into the store just before closing. He was a wily little shit, stomping around like he owned the place, sneering, lighting up a cigarette and grinding the match on the floor. He wasn't wearing a shirt. His baggy pants were hanging from his ass and showing off a pair of dark print boxers. His black peaked cap was turned backwards. He thought he was so fucking "cool."

"Whatcha looking for?" I asked him, my attitude matching his, rude and indifferent.

"Whatdafuck you think? A goddam tattoo."

"What kind?"

"That's why I'm lookin', asshole."

Asshole, huh? I smiled to myself and watched the fucker strut around the room scanning the walls of tattoo designs. Exactly 18, unlined face, arms popped with muscles, a muscled chest centered with budding black fur. A raspy scalp surrounded the edge of his cap. Couldn't gauge his ass, the damn floppy pants cut off that view. Same with his front.

"Dis one," he said. I walked over. A small red heart with a banner awaiting a name. "And I want my girl's name in it," he demanded. "Ya hear dat, prick?" He smelled raw, a muddled aroma of sweat, dust, and confused anger. "On my ass," he added arrogantly and stood tall, lifting his chin in a dare.

"It'll hurt," I told him, anxious already.

"I can take any fuckin' thing you can dish out, man."

"Almost closing time, so...."

"Closing time?" he shouted, waving his arms, pacing the shop. "Shit, man, I wanna...."

"I didn't fucking finish," I yelled right back. His mouth snapped shut. "So I'll lock the door. Follow me."

I pushed the curtain aside. He sat in the folding chair next to my machine and my inks. A drop of sweat rolled down his neck. He was scared and hoped I wouldn't see it. "Get off my fucking chair," I said. He stood up, grumbling with attitude.

"Take off your cap," I said.

"Shit, man, ya ain't gonna fuckin' tattoo my head."

"Take off your goddam cap, dickhead."

His eyes grew wide, his brow folded, he bit his bottom lip. I thought he might slug me. He didn't. He snatched his cap off. A close-cut scalp as erotic as a hairy ass. I sat in the chair, enjoying the sensation that was seasoning my balls and priming my dick with gorging blood. "Turn around and drop your fuckin' pants."

He didn't hesitate. He spun around and unbuttoned his pants. They fell to

his ankles. I grabbed his boxers and pulled them down.
"Fuck, man," he muttered to myself.
"Where you want the tattoo?"
He brought a hand around and touched the side of his left cheek. A coarse coat of dusky fuzz roofed his ass. Thicker fuzz bunched at the base of his spine and scrambled into his crack. I kneaded both cheeks, firm, hard, pliable, until his ridged and hairy asshole winked at me.
"Hey, whatcha doing, man?" he said, craning his neck.
"Gonna have to shave ya?" I said.
"Shave!" He spun around. "No fuckin' way, man. I ain't counted on dat. All I wanna do is...."
I tuned him out. The hair on his chest narrowed over a flat stomach, burst into a full bush, and topped a dark, cut, soft dick with a big, round head. His balls were hefty, hairy, and hung low, long, and fat. I wondered if he spied the hard-on lifting the leg of my pants. I pawed it. He spied it.
"Can't work on ya with all that hair on yer ass," I said.
"My ass ain't hairy."
"Bullshit, ya got enough fuzz there to fill the downtown precinct," I told him. He laughed.
"Okay, man, but this is fuckin' weird." He muttered to himself, "A fuckin' dude shaving my ass, shooot."
"Lift your arms."
"What?"
"Lift your goddam arms, cocksucker. I don't want you flapping around like a goddam monkey." My voice was angry, a practiced anger.
"Okay, okay, okay." He lifted them. His underarms stunk. I stood up and inhaled him, reached to the rafters and brought down leather straps attached to thick chains. I snapped them around each wrist. His body quivered, both in fear and anticipation. I sat on my haunches in front of him and told him to lift his legs. He did, one foot at a time, while I pulled his pants and shorts off his feet. He didn't ask why. He was buck naked except for sneakers that might have been white at one time. They stank too. I trembled at the prospect.
"I don't fuckin' believe this!" he cried, angry yet defiant.
"You want the tattoo or not?" I said. If he said, No, I'd unchain him. If he said, Yes, he'd get the full treatment. Just like his buddies before him.
"Sure, man, gotta but...."
"Then shut the fuck up, piss-brain." I stood up and slapped his ass. He yelped. I slapped his ass again. He barked, "Shit, stop it, man." I slapped him again and again. The sound, the sting, fused the room like electricity through water. He rattled his chains. His cheeks were bright pink, shaded by black fuzz. "Warming ya up," I said, more to myself than him. "Heating you up."
"I know, I know," he mumbled.
I walked in front of him and took off my shirt. I took off my pants. My

hard cock popped up. "Hey, no, man, shit, no," he blubbered, he pled, tugging the chains. "No, way man, I changed my fucking mind. Nope, shit no."

"And let your buddies know you punked out?" I countered, as light as a breeze. "You fucking faggot," I spat.

"I ain't no fuckin' faggot."

"Wanna bet?" I spit in my hand and lubed my cock, slowly, sensually, stroking it till it shined. It was solid gleaming steel. I felt the head popping in and out of the foreskin and leaking like a sieve. His eyes were glued to the sight. I bent my legs and tugged my balls, pulled my cock.

"Oh, man," he moaned. Tears were brightening his eyes.

"Oh, yeah." He watched me like a hawk when I went to the sink and rinsed a clean towel under hot water, then grabbed my can of shaving cream and a sleek straight razor.

"Jeeezzz, what da fuck ya gonna do with that?" He was staring at my razor like he was a whore and I was Jack the Ripper. The chains jangled. Music to my ears.

"You know what I'm gonna do." I sat behind him and faced his ass. "I know what I'm gonna do. And I'm damn good at it. Ever hear any complaints?"

"No, man, but you sure better be fuckin' careful, man, cause that's the only ass I got."

"And a fine ass it is," I said. "Best I seen in ages. Ripe, like a tomato. Better than Jimbo's and sure better than Turf's. Beautiful hard fucking ass ya got there, Mingo."

"Thanks, man," he preened. "I got da best ass of all. And I'm gonna tell 'em dat, too."

"You do that." I pressed the hot towel against his ass, one cheek at a time, taking my time, time to enjoy, savoring, almost tasting that hot ass. I glopped the cream over the skin, kneading each cheek like it was dough and I was a master baker. "Nice, huh," I muttered. He hummed quietly. I swept more cream down the crack of his ass and lower. I palmed his balls and coated them with shaving cream.

"Hey, whatcha doing, man," he said. "Ya ain't gonna shave my fucking nuts." He was protesting but even he knew it was useless. I fondled and soaped his balls then mashed them in my fist tightly. He barked, "Yoooowie." I reached farther and wrapped my fist around a hard cock and yanked. The fucker got turned on faster than I figured. He yelled, "Heeyyy." His cock fought back, throbbed, pulsed. So did the cock standing up between my legs. I also coated it with cream and slid my hand down the full length, coughing up a slick stream of precum juice which wormed from the dangling foreskin like paste from a tube. I worked both cocks with care, diligence, and a helluva lot of love. He was trying to stifle a moan. I didn't stifle mine. I dropped both cocks and stropped the razor. The cheeks of his ass contracted. He tensed.

"Relax, punkboy," I cooed. I stroked the razor over one cheek at a time, cautiously, carefully, skillfully, scraping his skin clean of hair and fuzz. The sound of a finely honed razor scratching against bare ass was loud and enticing. My innards were heating up. My hand was steady. My cock was bobbing. My mind was reeling.

I moved the chair around and faced one thick, dark, very hard cock with a giant mushroom head. Beautifuckingful! Not only the best ass of all his buddies, but the biggest dickhead. He stretched his chin down and watched while I slurped his dickhead between my lips and slopped a handful of shaving cream over his cockhairs, his belly, his chest. His dickhead was a hot magic globe that filled my mouth. I gnawed it while I lifted my eyes and watched him watching me gnawing and massaging his chest with shaving cream. His lips were parted, his mouth was open, the fucker was drooling. I slurped up the juice seeping from the pisshole of that huge dickhead. He pressed his hips forward and tried to plant his cock clear down my throat. I pulled back and lapped my lips. His cock wobbled in front of me, as excited as my own. I grabbed the razor and stood up.

The hair on his chest fell to the floor while my razor slid over his dark skin. He didn't move one muscle when I scratched the thin blade under his arms. The stink hit the floor. He let out a deep relieved sigh when I sat again. I latched my fist around the hard brawny flesh of his cock and shaved close, very close to the root. His cockhairs splattered on the floor. He was again holding his breath, his cock was throbbing. It was alive and willing. I held his balls tight, taut, the most difficult part and the most fun. I held my breath as well while I scraped his nuts clean of hair, the flesh fondled in my fingers, the musky aroma potent, the blade slowly, carefully scraping over his nuts.

I stood up, overheated by the sight. A gang punk, all my own, scraped raw, splotches of leftover shaving cream spotting his body like clouds in a night sky. I became lost in the image while stroking my cock and yanking my balls. My mouth was watering like a sieve. I gulped down my spit, went to the sink and rinsed a large towel in hot water, then came back and bathed him clean until his body was quivering. So was his bigheaded dick.

I stepped behind him, sat down again, washed his nuts, the crack of his ass, and before he knew what hit him, slipped a finger inside his asshole.

"Ohhhh ... shit...!" he screamed and strained his chains, trying to swirl his body around. I reached under and pulled his balls down, pulled them longer and lower than they already were. He kept screaming. The more he strained, the more he squirmed, the harder I fucked my finger up his ass and stretched his balls, until the fucker was groaning and pushing his ass back, damn near begging me to feed more finger up that unsullied asshole. He spread his legs wide, slammed his ass back. He was crazy swinging back and forth in the air, his feet scuffing the floor.

"Ohhhh....shiiitttt...wwwoooowwww...." he kept muttering, with unexpected heat and fierce passion.

I plucked my finger from his hole, stood up, slid my hands around his chest and my palpitating cock between his legs. My dickhead hit his balls and set the fire; my cockhairs ground into the smooth cheeks of his shaved ass. He snapped his head back, mumbling, "Ohhh, fuck, fuck, fuck, fuck...." I sucked his neck and mumbled back, "Ya got that right, faggot." I fingered his nipples and pinched. His yell was mixed with a groan. He swiveled his neck; I kept sucking it. No more yells, pure groan. I let go and pulled back, keeping one hand on his smooth, flat gut. I hawked into my hand and lubed my cock, pulling the skin back fully to expose a dickhead larger than his. His head sank onto his chest when my dickhead barely touched the rim of his asshole.

I stood there, holding his waist now with both hands, looking at and loving that cockhead pressed on the brink of pronging that bastard's asshole. I edged forward just that little bit and felt the tension in the muscles of his asshole fight back and clamp up.

"Shit face," I shouted.

His concentration broke. His asshole lost its tension.

My cockhead plopped inside.

He screamed, loud, too loud.

I told him, "Shut the fuck up, you dirty prick! Take it like a fuckin' man not like the goddam punk you are." And I rammed my entire hard cock home free. He screamed again. I clamped one hand over his mouth and the other round his cock. The chains were clanging over head erratically while he wrestled about and tried to break the hold. Too late. We were asshole buddies and were gonna stay that way until I let loose. His struggles only increased the sensation raging through my cock, my nuts, as that giant dickhead of mine tapped every tender wall inside that fucking punk's asshole. The more excited I became, the more I stroked his cock. The more I stroked his cock, the more he relaxed. The more relaxed he became, the more his screams of pain turned to moans of goddam joy. Pure pleasure, pure asshole pleasure. For both of us.

His body was still moving, swaying unevenly, but he wasn't struggling anymore. He swung his torso back and forth to fuck his cock into my fist, to screw his ass onto my cock, until I began banging the fucker, shifting my hips back and pulling my cock out before slamming it back inside the kid. The smell was acrid, was erotic, sweat, sex, anger, lust. He grunted like a snared animal and his cock expanded in my fist and grew harder than granite before the head started spitting out great globs of cum that flooded the floor and smeared my fist. My own cock felt the surge and leaped inside that cocksucker's asshole, spitting out a load that fucking filled that punk, that laid that fucker out like a ragdoll.

Fifteen minutes later, I tattooed the heart on his ass. The name "Buck" centered the banner. Me!

I covered the tattoo with gauze and told him how to care for it. He pulled on his pants. I unlocked the door. He had his hand on the knob. I said,

"You're in."

He hesitated before opening the door and mumbled quietly, "Yeah, thanks." And then he was gone.

Odd ritual this gang has. They have to be fucked by me and have my name tattooed on their asses before they're in. I head the gang.

MY BROTHER, MY LOVE by Peter Eros

My brother Rich is lying beside me now, breathing gently through his mouth, not quite a snore, more a periodic snuffle as he exhales. He's brown-skinned and tightly muscled, his chestnut hair with sun-bleached streaks is tousled in waves against the pillow, one arm flung up against the headboard. Even asleep he gives off a tangible erotic charge. I'm still aching with pleasure from our sweaty lust, at peace with myself, as my eyes urge attention downward, seduced by the shapeliness of his hips and massive, even when flaccid, purple-veined cock. I reach out and stroke the slumber-warm flesh and he murmurs and smiles.

Six years ago Mom died. I was twelve and Rich was fourteen. Dad was devastated and Rich took over running the house and us. He cooked and washed and cleaned the house, and still managed to get good grades at school. He helped me with my homework and found time to shoot hoops and to surfboard with me as well as spotting for me when I was weight training, a discipline we both enjoyed in imitation of Dad. Rich and I were not just brothers, we were best friends. I enjoyed his beauty and his promise and loved to praise and pamper him, and to tackle as many chores as I could to relieve his burden. There weren't too many other kids around us. Mom had inherited her mother's house in what has become a retirement community twenty miles north of San Diego, only a couple of blocks from the beach.

While Mom was alive, Dad drove trucks for a local construction company, but once she was gone he followed his dream and bought a rig, driving cross country, often away for a couple of weeks or more. I guess if the authorities had known, he'd be accused of abandonment, but Rich looked after us better than Dad could.

Before long Dad grew a mustache, weight-trained even harder, acquired some tattoos and began wearing raunchy tank tops and butt-hugging 501s. He hired younger guys to accompany him as relief drivers on the long hauls. They often stayed with us when Dad was home, sleeping with him in his king-size bed. I guess I was pretty innocent in those days and thought nothing of it, even when they horsed around in the bathroom and slept in each other's arms. But looking back I realize Dad's companions were all of them pretty hunky with their muscle tanks, tight jeans or leather pants and tattoos. They still are.

I was a late developer. My balls didn't drop till I was nearly fifteen and it took another year before a wanking session produced my first alarming spurt of cum.

I had wondered why Rich didn't have a girlfriend, but I assumed he was too busy looking after us in addition to his studies. I wasn't interested in girls yet and concluded that the inclination to date would come along

naturally sooner or later.

I'd heard about *gays* but thought that just meant effeminate sissies. That a regular guy could have sex with another guy hadn't occurred to me, though I did enjoy seeing other good- looking guys, especially at the gym. Half-fledged desires lurked in the dark corners of my mind, and even while denying them to myself, I yielded to their influence, careless of the consequence. I often got an embarrassing hard-on in the locker room as I regarded naked guys from the camouflage of downcast lids. At the gym I stole sidelong glances with a circumspect, yet wistful scrutiny, which, had I known, demonstrated the impulse of my hormones. I couldn't stop myself, and really enjoyed the pleasurable feelings in my crotch and the hackles that my reconnaissance provoked. No doubt my own arresting looks, with my well-proportioned, muscular body, handsome face, and Mom's auburn thatch and startling emerald eyes, aroused interest in others, but I was too green to recognize the signs.

The revelation came when I was home alone with a mild bout of flu. I'd finished my SATs, so school wasn't critical. Dad was on a trip and Rich was at college during the day. I was bored. The TV was all talk-show crap and I didn't have anything to read. I wandered into Dad's room, randomly looking in drawers and closets. The drawer of the nightstand on one side of the bed contained a stash of condoms, lubricant and poppers. As I opened the door of the cupboard, an avalanche of gay sex mags and videos slid onto the floor. The picture spreads puzzled me as well as turning me on, but the text was sufficiently explicit to make me hot for some action of the kind described, as cock in hand, I read myself to overstimulated climax.

Dad had a VCR in his bedroom so I put on a video. It educated me better than any still photos ever could. Jeff Stryker in "Powertool" made my mouth water.

Over the next three days, I ran 'em all; my favorites got several viewings as, with manic energy, I jacked my rigid prong and lubed and probed my virgin butt with thumb then fingers. The rubber dildo I found in the drawer of the night stand the other side of Dad's bed initiated a deeper penetration of my virgin butt, and an overwhelming sense of loss when I shot my load and removed the flexible probe from my rectum.

The third day I got a real shock. I had a prowl through Rich's bureau and found a video under his briefs. The star was my brother, renamed Randy Slicker. Seconds after the credits rolled, Rich, with his brazen, white-toothed smile and vaguely guilty, gleaming blue eyes was stripped butt naked. He was playing a security guard. Rich and his equally studly sidekick ripped off each other's uniform. They had interrupted their patrol on a tree-shaded, grassy knoll before an angled corner of the gleaming metal and mirrored-glass facility they were supposedly guarding. They fell into a clinch on the verdant lawn, their energetic coupling reflected at various angles in the glistening glass behind them.

Rich's round, tight buttocks and rosy butthole invited more than a finger.

It was a sweaty outdoor fuck with the sun kissing the rock-hard muscles of the turned-on buddies as they body-slammed each other, Rich's heels reaching for the sky. His buddy poked Rich hard in the center of his adorable steamy ass. He split Rich's legs wide and slammed into his hunching hole. You could hear the guy's spunky balls slapping Rich's ass. They switched to doggie style, Rich's seeping dick banged against his belly, bobbing and dribbling in time to his partner's teeth-jarring shoves. I longed to reach between his legs and help him out as his soundtrack voice screamed, "Yes! Yeagh! Yeeees! Fuck me, fuck me, fuuuck!"

I tried a firm banana, sheathed in a condom, up my own ass, taking an experimental hit of poppers to relax me, a tip I'd picked up from my reading. As my body flushed with unexpected heat and my heart palpitated, with hip-thrusting panache I shot my load all over the TV screen. Even after I'd cleaned up I thought I could smell spent sperm.

By the fourth day, I had managed to wangle at home, pleading illness, Dad was still away and I'd screwed up my courage to come out, to Rich. I'd memorized the most seductive come-ons from the videos and the sexual techniques that seemed to produce the most satisfaction. I was getting anxious and agitated by the time Rich got back from college. His normally sparkling sapphire eyes were dull and violet shadows encircled them. He'd been studying hard, and I knew he had suffered a lot of sleepless nights lately.

As I'd learn later, Rich wasn't tired from studying so much as he was from renting out his versatile butthole and hugely satisfying dong, initially to earn more funds for college, but more recently from sheer enjoyment. He'd been recruited as a call-boy by his gym coach, who ran a male escort agency on the side. Following a private audition, a strenuously gratifying sampling of Rich's anal and oral aerobics, and having encouraged him with optimistic estimates of the potential financial rewards, the coach marketed him to a well-heeled and discriminating clientele and to the video producers.

I was desperate to let Rich know how much I appreciated him and all he'd done for me, and I wanted to reward him with my new-found knowledge. I was sure that I could bring him real joy, and more than a little pleasure and relief for myself too. Simmering as I was with testosterone and ego, I hoped to graduate from groping my own endowment. I dreamed of breaking into movies, like Rich, fucking with all those spunky bucks who seemed to me like so many trophies to be won.

As Rich dumped his backpack, I told him I was feeling much better and had thawed out a pizza for us to eat. He gave me a grateful smile and headed for the shower, shedding clothes as he went. When I heard the water jetting I peeked in the bathroom to make sure he was showering, then stripped naked and headed for the steamed-up glass door, my cock already bouncing in front of me with anticipation.

As I slid the door open Rich turned to me with a gasp, his soap-lubed prick clutched in his slippery grip.

"Todd, what're ya doin?"

I didn't reply. I just slid the door behind me and pulled him to me, thrusting my tongue in his mouth as my hands clutched his shapely butt and our cocks bounced against each other. He gripped my shoulders and pushed back for a moment but I didn't give an inch and he suddenly surrendered. He reached up and stroked my hair, putting his two hands on the sides of my face. They felt warm and caressing. A sense of absolute tranquility came over me as he kissed me voraciously, responding to my attack with equal passion. My mouth suctioned his, my tongue savoring, probing and exploring his perfect dentition, exalted by the rapturous, insatiable feelings enveloping me, far more exciting than I'd ever imagined from the videos.

Rich's mahogany hair was free and clean, shining clean. His sad and faintly troubled eyes looked at me from his beguilingly tilted head. The smooth boyish cheeks, the wide and full-lipped succulent mouth invited a tongue bath. He gazed at me, filled with love and apprehension and a confident calm, despite what he must have feared for me and for him. His eyes were haunted, but I could feel his uncompromising desire, like a dog who has caught the scent of a bitch in heat–and that's what I surely was. Hunger overcame judgment as he crushed me in his robust and suddenly predatory embrace.

Rich slid down my body and sucked on my bloated throbber, which looked like it could blow at any minute. The crown of my plump, dimpled, extended cockshaft balmed his clasping lips with pre-cum. His cheeks hollowed out as he hungrily siphoned my cock to the balls. Wet, mouthy sounds sludged out of his throat until, with his hand wringing cum out of my raw dick like a sponge, and the other hand pulling on my aching nuts, my cum-sherbet spouted and gurgled and Rich's tongue spooned the jizz into his throat.

Spent, but far from satisfied, I moved to return the compliment. But Rich pulled me first into a tender embrace, then dragged me from the shower and roughly toweled us both before pulling me into the bedroom and throwing me on his bed. He fell on top of me and held my hands above my head as he scrutinized me.

"How long have you known?"

"About Dad, three days. About you? Since yesterday."

"You're a fast learner."

"I want to learn! Shit. I want to do *everything*. I want to fuck and I want to be fucked. Teach me, Rich. I've tried a banana and Dad's dildo, but I haven't been properly fucked yet and I haven't fucked anybody."

"We'll see what we can do. First slurp on this."

Rich straddled my torso, his sumptuous, gym-wrought body towering over me, his gorgeous dick bouncing in my face. It was deliciously long and thick, with an arching swoop to it convenient for any cock-sucker's mouth, and I was one hungry dick-sucking initiate. I licked and chewed his balls before going down on his bobbing throat-opener. I tongued the cock slit and

circled the ridge of the crown. Following Rich's instruction I took a deep breath and managed to suck him right in without much gagging, thanks to his careful tuition. I opened my throat to receive the full length, pausing at the base till I needed to take air. I bobbed my head, sucking the pulsing rod until I reached the crown, deep breath, then back to the base. Rich instructed me how to caress his cock with my tongue and to play with his tits.

Abruptly Rich slid around and began to 69 with me before lifting my legs and probing my pucker with his agile tongue. I groaned and thrashed about, unable to control the tremors of pleasure pulsing through me. He uncapped some lube and thrust two fingers into my spasming hole. He lay back with his prick bouncing tall and positioned me astraddle him. He gently pushed me down until he could insert the head. I gasped. He was much bigger than the dildo.

With great patience, Rich talked me through it as his man-root slowly, deliberately eased into my core, spreading, penetrating and expanding. He taught me to use my butt cheeks to squeeze the prick, to massage it, to give it pleasure. He played with my tits and caressed my arms. He pulled my face down to his and kissed me voraciously, chewing on my lips and dueling my tongue with his own. Then, all discomfort dispelled, he urged me to ride him to ball-busting climax. As Rich's cock exploded up my ass, buried up to his trim, tanned balls, my aching dong jetted a creamy pattern across his chiseled torso. He scooped it with his fingers and tasted it before feeding me my first pungent glob of tangy cum. My taste-buds relished the salty savor and the delicious aftertaste.

We lay awhile in each others arms, gently exploring with hands and lips, before showering. Then we headed to the kitchen and devoured the pizza. I confessed to my clandestine discoveries and Rich owned up to fucking with some of Dad's buddies before acquiring his professional prowess. Honed by a number of sexual gourmand clients and three or four skilled video directors, Rich was the veteran of more than thirty videos. The one I had found in the drawer just happened to be his current favorite.

I was going to wash the dishes when Rich's hand nestled on my thigh and eased into my crotch, massaging and tweaking my instantly revived prick.

"The dishes can wait. We've got some unfinished business."

He took my hand and dragged me into Dad's bedroom, pushed me down on the bed, then switched on the TV and loaded a video.

"It's your turn to stuff some ass, but first you can swab me with that oral probe of yours."

He lay back on the bed, his head at the foot. On the TV a muscular duo were demonstrating what he intended to teach me. As I moved in to sniff, bite and tongue his asshole he raised his feet and rested them over my shoulders, placing a bolster under his butt. His pucker was prominently ridged, like a tightly furled rosebud, almost callused in appearance, and very inviting to a first-time rimmer, despite a slight but understandable concern about being messy. But I had experienced the pleasure of rimming from the

receiving end, a pleasure I wished to return in full measure.

My face pressed down between the splayed thighs, inhaling the spunky aroma. My tongue laved the ridges of flesh with solvent spit before pressing against the sphincter, kissing it, sucking it. Rich moaned his pleasure, writhing on my tongue-tip. The tight asshole relaxed, allowing my tongue to enter all the way in, drilling deep.

As I licked and stabbed his ass with my tongue, I grabbed his bobbing cock, swollen and red, straining again with the sting of impending release.

"Enough, Todd. You'd better fuck me now or I'll shoot before you get started."

Rich's lubed fingers took hold of my hugely expanded rod and guided the head down between his thighs to his spit-slicked hole. I felt the tight pressure bite down gently on the head of my cock. Then it slipped in easily as the tightness of Rich's sphincter relaxed its grip on my glans. I felt myself expand and stretch in the slippery, moist conduit as it slowly engulfed my entire shaft. It felt like my cock was all the way up into his stomach. Then his ass clamped hard around my swollen probe.

"God, you feel great in there, kid."

Rich reached up his hard, thick arms, clasped them around my lithe trunk and squeezed me hard. He pulled my head down and kissed me, his mouth hungrily sucking on my wet and probing tongue. I felt light-headed with euphoria as primal instincts took over. My hips bucked furiously, pounding Rich's firm, tight asshole with accelerating momentum. My greed and need were fueled by the rhythmic slap-slapping sounds of my hips pounding his spread buttocks and the contraction of my nuts as they smacked against his hot flesh.

Rich's cock rubbed vigorously against my stomach, pumping his shaft between our sweat-slicked bellies. My whole body spasmed and I yelled with joy as I slammed myself into him to climax and he simultaneously erupted with thick spurts of creamy, steamy jizz, splattering my stomach and his own chest. I collapsed onto him as his hands clutched my butt, anchoring me, holding my spent prick inside him.

"Oh God! I can't believe you're so good at this, Todd. Stay there Kid. Oooooh! I just love the feel of you up there."

- - -

Of course, Dad knows all about us now. He can hardly object, but he does worry, and cautions us all the time to be safe and careful. But now everything's out in the open it's relieved a lot of tension, for Dad as well as for us. He doesn't have to pretend about the guys he brings back and neither do we. The only tension now is the undeniable fact of a mutual sexual attraction that Dad seems scared to acknowledge. Rich and I would both get it on with him in a shot, but I guess Dad's conscience is more conventional than his lifestyle. You could call our environment a morality-free zone.

With seventeen inches of well-matched cock between us, Rich and I, I reckon, have got more cock and appetite than four average men.

With our video and escort earnings Rich and I have bought matching Harleys and our own king-size bed and VCR. We often share a mutually acceptable partner. We've found we both like being the meat in the sandwich. Tomorrow Rich graduates *Magna cum laude*, so I planned a pre-celebration. After a delicious roast dinner, I gave Rich a thorough massage, followed by 30 minutes or so in the spa.

By then, we were both well and truly primed and fell to devotional cocksucking. Each of our straining cock-poles disappeared deep into the other's overstuffed throat, enjoying the velvety wetness, mouth-fucking each other, gently at first and then a little deeper with each stroke.

But Rich was anxious for my stiff monument to brotherly love up his twitchy butthole. He gently pushed me off and smiled up at me as he spread his legs and undulated his hips in invitation. I dove tongue first into his inviting asscrack, licking and kissing his rosebud until it blossomed open. I sunned myself in the passion emitted by his eager, lustrous baby blues, so clear and candid, reflecting unconditional lust.

Anticipation and desire electrified the air as Rich slowly lubed my meaty cock, and caressed my cum-filled balls. He positioned me to probe his welcoming orifice. I slid easily in until my pubes nestled against his crack. I felt the muscles of his ass ripple around my cock.

When Rich began to grind his ass around my mightily aroused cock, I knew it was time for some heavy-duty ass-slamming. So I rammed him hard, the unique curve of my shaft massaging his prostate pleasure-point with every hard-driving thrust. As he cried out and shot a load that spattered him from head to crotch, I came in small spasms leading to big ones, filling Rich with copious sperm.

I sponged the delicious cum from his torso with my tongue, swallowing his plentiful offering. As I slipped from anchor, Rich, unwilling to give it up, stroked my cum-coated prick and engulfed it with his mouth. As the cock began to harden again he sighed and closed his eyes, sucking on me like a contented baby with a milk-filled teat.

I swiveled my body and took his long cock in both my hands, hand over hand, and brought my lips to its head. I kissed it. I opened for it, very slowly exciting the shaft until my lips were anchored around the root. Then I was astride him and he was inside me before he could protest. As I rode him, clenching and unclenching my sphincter, Rich sighed and groaned and swung his hips from side to side, grinding into me, his personal boytoy for the night. I urged him on, twisting and manipulating his tits. He groaned and cried out as he rammed it deep into me. As I came in thick gooey globs, he shuddered, filling my colon, writhing and bucking with each spurt of cum, crying, "Oh ... yeah! Yeah!"

We fell asleep in each other's arms, and when I woke I found I had my mouth on the evocative nape of his neck. I was lying there in that sweet

reverie, halfway between slumber and waking, between desire and satiety. It had to have been one of the grandest feelings imaginable, the rewarding aftermath of our unbridled instincts and gift for debauchery. How many brothers, I wondered, could find such peace and release in happy dissipation with each other?

A STRANGE LIFE by Sonny Torvig

Mine is a strange life, but one that suits me. It just seems a great shame that, like a basketball star or football pro, I have a limited shelf life to cash in on my greater assets. The good side is that it simply means a life packed from dawn till dusk. And then some.

Now every job has its downside, and mine is the working time between breaks, the weeks spent earning my mobility. Those are the times I spend on one of our offshore rigs as a diver. It is an eerie life of strange silences and pressures, a life no shore-bound man can imagine. The only reason I continue is the compensation; that pays for my mobility.

Today, though, I am ashore, three days into a break and already into the swing of it. I take great care of myself for this side of my life; image is everything on the road. With a sharp suit and a well-groomed appearance I can catch any fish, from the biggest to the smallest. I get them all.

But back to today. Thankfully it's dry, the wintry sun trying its best to tear through the thin, gray full-time clouds. I stand waiting, my expensive suitcase close by my feet, folder of papers in my free hand. A car rushes past, the driver giving me a shake of the head. No matter, this isn't meant to be foolproof. I see a Jaguar sweeping out of the gas station and try that little bit harder. I smile as it closes in on me, and extend a thumb carefully, as if this whole thing is abhorrent to me. The Jag never falters. I open my hand and shrug, an 'I understand, I wouldn't want to either' kind of gesture. The Jag falters. I raise an eyebrow. The Jag dips its nose, and swishes just past me before stopping halfway onto the slip road.

In the rush to clamber aboard before we are under the axle of a truck, I carefully hold my case and paper's on my knee, pointedly struggling with the seat belt.

"Just put the case in the back, but don't forget it when you leave." He smiles at his featherweight joke.

I take a better look at him as I carefully swing it past his ear, onto the floor behind our seats. He is a little older than forty, well groomed, well maintained. He has grey at the temples, but a shock of tawny blond hair with no more hint of seniority than that. I say my thanks, explain why I am in such unusual circumstances.

"Bloody hell, that takes courage!" The driver glances across at me. "You've just abandoned a company Merc and walked away from a job, just because you disagreed with a superior?" He was sizing me up, curious if I was a dangerous maverick or a man of high standards.

"Oh this isn't the first time they have tried to screw me before an important meeting. This time, however, I made a stand, and turned their advantage to mine." I chuckle. "I'll send the keys back in with my resignation papers next week. Let them sweat a little."

The Jaguar is cruising. I had noted the headings on papers on the back seat, and await his next question. He coughs. "What is it you specialize in?" I look across at his inquiry, and smile.

"I act as interface between manufacture and consumer. The official title is that of operating systems consultant. Basically I listen hard, ask questions, and solve problems. I'd like to act independently, ideally, but circumstances aren't ideal just at present."

There is a silence. It is warm, so I ease my jacket off my shoulders and reach back to hang it in the rear. "Why not at present?" This is like playing a washboard. "A feud with my partner. I'm living out of a suitcase for a few weeks, until I find a small flat nearer London. Once I'm set up I can concentrate on starting freelance."

"Where is it you are heading for now?" He looks concerned, one of his own kind in trouble pulling all the right strings.

I recall the address on the papers, and take the chance. "Manchester. I'll find a hotel in the center somewhere I'm sure. Anywhere will do while I work some 'damage limitation'. We both smile, fellow conspirators now. He suddenly looks over.

"You don't need to bother with a hotel. I've two spare rooms you could choose from." He awaits an answer.

I take my time making a decision, then say, "Honestly, I do appreciate the offer, but...." He shakes his head. I offer more lame excuses and he batters them all down, this having become something more for him. I bow to his good-heartedness and eye his goods. "Thank you. My name is Brad, by the way." I reach across to offer my hand, and a little awkwardly he returns the brief shake.

"It's not a problem Brad, and I'm saddled with the name Edgar." He looks a little apologetic, as if he is waiting for my laugh. All I see is a chink of light in the bedroom door for later. The Jaguar cruises north with ease. As we pass over the Cheshire plains, canals cutting through its rich farming land, we go into more depth about each other. He is single, a workaholic, has a big house south of Manchester, admits to feelings of aloneness sometimes. Especially as he gets older. He asks what I like in the way of food. We share similar tastes. I always have similar tastes to my ride.

South Lancashire rushes past the dusk-shadowed windows, and we grow quieter together, comrades in arms. Men set on self-made pathways. The first course has been consumed and enjoyed, the company pleasant and a little intimate by way of confidences. The ground is prepared for later.

I am shown around his detached property, a tastefully simple home with little evidence of being lived in. My bedroom is next to his. I change my clothes for a casual outfit he has offered me for the evening and descend to help with the meal. I call it tea, he calls it dinner, we trip over the gap that temporarily creates. But a glass of cognac quickly rubs off the rough edge.

We eat opposite each other at his beautifully handmade table, a meal that may be simple, but fills a need.

Afterwards, I sit back and sigh, content, eyeing my host with renewed intensity. He wears no rings, and there is no visible evidence of any women in the things I have seen so far. He places his knife and fork symmetrically on the plate, and pushes it slightly forward. "Have you had enough?"

I momentarily consider a come-on, but I leave it for later. "Yes, thank you, I appreciate this very much." I sip my wine. "This sure beats the cold sterility of a hotel as an evening's resting place." I rise to clear the plates, and my hand brushes his as I reach past him. He leaves his hand where it lies on the maple surface. The cleaning-up I begin without a prompt, a means to an end, I have found. Manners and being good company can slip me into most homes, like a credit card under a door. I raise my cognac in a toast, and follow him as he turns back to the large room. We stand close at the window, comparing notes on the view and its merits. It is certainly a beautiful house, and idyllic surroundings. I yawn pointedly.

"Sorry, I think the stresses of the day have taken a greater toll than I had anticipated." I lay a hand on his shoulder, lightly, a thermometer to judge the temperature. Still a little too cool. "Do you mind if I have a quick shower? It would wake me up for the evening. I think seven a little extravagant a time to end the day. A shower'd do me good."

"Of course." Ed leads me up to the main bathroom, and I accept the silk robe offered, warm on my bare arm as I close the door behind his departure. I strip again, wondering why I was not left to use my own room's bathroom, then shower for a long time. dry myself for even longer. I now need to create a question in his mind: Why the long absence from downstairs. I sit on the side of the bath and wait, the catch on the bathroom door left off. I hear the footsteps on the landing. They falter by the door for a moment, then move on. I stand in readiness, a towel covering my head in preparation, my nakedness tanned and perfect. I hear the footfalls return, and begin to rub my damp hair.

"Oh, I'm sorry, Brad. Very sorry!" I hear him bluster. I let the towel slip from my head and grin. He stands still, one hand on the door one on the door-frame, his eyes fixed on my body. I half turn and fold the towel onto the side of the bath, my ass being one of my best assets.

"Not a problem, Ed. It's nothing you won't have seen before, I'm sure." I pick up the robe, but just toss it over my arm as I pad towards the door. "I certainly don't need this for modesty's sake now." I make a point of grinning as I step up to him. "I have to say I feel a new man after that." He hurriedly steps back out onto the landing and tries to look away. Without success. "You seem tongue-tied, Ed." I stand still. My cock's already twitching from the electricity coursing through me.

"Sorry, very sorry. It's just that you took me aback. I wasn't expecting to see you....I didn't think....what a fool I feel. I'll go back downstairs, now I know you are all right."

I raise an eyebrow. "Did you think you'd find me dead in the shower from slit wrists?" I tease him now. He is backing against the banister, shaking his

head. "I'm pulling your leg, Ed! But thanks for the thought." I step nearer to him and offer my hand. He shakes it in relief, and relaxes a little.

"You'll have to excuse me; this is a little unusual as situations go, you have to admit." Ed looks me in the eye, and I see the moment blossom like a meadow in the summer sun.

"You look lost, Ed. You have all this wealth and success, and you still look lost. You hate the name given to you at birth, and you lose all the surface confidence when faced with something unexpected." I put a hand on his shoulder, keep on looking him in the eyes. "I think our meeting was destined, because what I see is the solution to one problem straight away." He visibly jumps. "You must decide on a new name, and tomorrow, without fail, you ring for a form and change it by deed poll. Job done. No more Edgar." I step to one side and towards my own room. "What do you fancy as a new name?" I pad over the soft carpet and turn to sit on the bed, pointedly throwing my robe onto the duvet. "Any ideas."

Ed leans on the door frame and looks distant, one hand in a pocket, the other unconsciously rubbing his chin. "I like the sound of Ray, it sounds a lot more of a success name than Edgar." He continues to think for a few moments, and I notice in his distraction the pocketed hand is being quietly reassuring. "No, I'll stick to Ray." He steps away from the door frame and smiles back at me, present again. "You do realize that even if I go through with this stunt, it will cost the business a packet. Just think of all the printed material that will have to be scrapped and redone, not to mention the legal department kicking up a fuss."

"You have to stick to your word, Ray. See it as a positive business move. Just you feeling better about yourself will pay dividends."

I rise from the bed, and turn away, pointedly bending to reach for some moisturizer. I turn back, filling one palm with the cream, smoothing it over my upper chest and shoulders. I see that Ray is a little uncomfortable, and stop. "Am I embarrassing you?" He smiles, a little sheepishly.

"It's not that, Brad. It's just that it's been a long time since I had company, let alone company as open and uninhibited as you." He shrugs, unaware of his understatement. "I'll go and mix us a drink while you get dressed."

Then he hesitates, and I jump at the sudden opening.

"Look, Ray, will you do me a favor? I have a pulled muscle in my back, can you oblige and rub some of this into the area. It's just where I can't reach." I turn away and wait. I feel his warmth on my back as he stands behind me, and pass him the tube of muscle relaxant. An old trick. He asks where to start. I feel the firmness of his fingers as he begins to massage the ointment between my shoulders, and I sense his ease with this intimacy. "A bit lower." He is soon into the lower concave of my back, and I feel warm breath on my skin. The rhythm of his hand is slow and easy, and I rock on my feet to his steady pressure. I murmur thanks, but Ray doesn't stop. He reaches the base of my spine before he seems to snap out of a trance.

"Sorry, I was getting lost there." He pats my back and holds out the ointment. I turn to say my thanks, and am taken by surprise by his instant closure. He steps into my space and touches my cheek. Another step, I remain frozen. This is too good to be true. He brings his lips to mine and a hot tongue slips across the frontier. From a close friend's kiss to a lover's. I stifle my shock, matters taken out of my hands a very rare occurrence. He stands back a little and puts his head to one side. "You didn't mind that at all, did you." He isn't asking a question. His hand reaches forward and touches my chest, a finger stroking downward over my abdomen. His eyes run down my body and come to rest on my suddenly alert cock. Without a word more he sinks to his knees, his fingers unbuttoning his shirt as he kneels before me. He slips the pristine white from his bronzed shoulders and reaches forward. Warm fingers encircle my growing length, and wet lips push back my foreskin, the head of my cock slipping into a dark, damp heat.

I groan in delirium, no longer having to orchestrate matters. What I have here is a more-than-willing partner. I feel my knees quivering as my entire length is sucked down a hungry throat, a hot vacuum that instantly has me teetering on the brink. It has never been as instant as this, and my whole body is on fire. My balls boil to let loose their full load, my cock being sucked and licked with a real passion. Fingers enclose my hot and tight balls, tickle behind them at the damp trigger spot. A digit pressure against my puckering ass makes me jump forward, Ray moans in delight as my curls grind into his face. The inquisitive finger slips wet and rigid into me, and with a shout of release I slam forward, what feels like a torrent of cum siphoning into Ray's mouth. He just gobbles it down with an ardent lapping and sucking that would go platinum if put onto disc. My entire being is in flames.

With equal certainty, Ray pulls me down to his level, his wet and oozing lips shining in the light from the window. Cum slowly runs down over his chin; his tongue laps out to capture what he has lost. I reach forward to his waistband, unclip and unzip. While he slides his arms around my shoulders and pulls me into his salty kisses. I work his clothes down *en masse*, a lush and bushy-based cock leaping from its confinement and into the evening air. It presses against my groin as our embrace becomes more fervid. My face is slicked with my own cum, the smell of mansex heavy between us. I reach down and grip his thrusting, urge him to his feet before me. The clothes flop behind him as he kicks free, and with an enthusiasm fuelled by a willing partner and quickly charging balls, I lap at his rigid cock.

Ray's hands close in my hair tugging me closer, my nose pressed flat against his belly as a twitching length of manhood slithers about my mouth, digs rigid into my throat. I seize his hanging balls and urge him on. Not that he needs much help with letting go. With a hot rush my mouth fills with his gushing cum, his grunting and lunging pumping me full to overflowing. I urge him on, more and more frenzied as he pounds against me. He tastes so good. He tastes so good that I want to eat him all night long, suck his

copious balls dry of every drop they have to offer me.

With a last quivering jerk, a softening length of sex slips between my lips and into the cooling air, the scent of orgasm deep and musty in my nostrils, themselves coated with his cum. Our eyes meet and an understanding passes between us. Ray steps back from my kneeling appetizer and unfolds himself onto the bed, his ass perched where he knows I will want it. Need it. I ease to my feet and apply a little by way of brakes. I want this to last. Some I just want to fuck, or be fucked by and then gone. But Ray, he has something about him. A vulnerability? A softness? He cares, and just for a change, I want to be cared for.

I slip into his warmth, his hands cupping my ass cheeks as I nuzzle against his neck. He squeezes. I nibble. He slaps lightly. I feel myself hard against his thigh. He slaps again, and a hot mouth clamps over mine. His tongue is eager; it batters me, slavers the flavor of sex out of me, licks me clean and rampant. A strong grip urges me above him, my weight pinning him into the soft bedding. He bares his teeth, and brings his legs up, heels drumming my ass. "Fuck me! I want you to fuck me!" He writhes beneath me, his arms slip to my waist; nails rake my lower back. I suck in a breath at his urgency, and my cock screams to be buried deep inside him. I arch back, and up his legs come, ankles meeting behind my neck, backs of his thighs pressed hot against my chest.

He pulls me nearer, and my need meets his with a powerful force. He is reaching down to coat my cock with my gel, no hesitation, no doubts. I reach down and nudge against his waiting rosebud, tight, hard muscle. Which relaxes, to drag me in, his grip pulling me deep inside in one long suction. He groans and shuts his eyes, head arching back as I touch base. I feel a little delirious, my cock suddenly getting all it's been dreaming of for the last four weeks. I buck against him; he clamps my face in his hands and grimaces. "I said fuck me, not just play at it. I need to be hammered into submission, I need my insides to be flooded with you!"

I need no more encouragement, pounding home again and again. I feel soaked in high octane fuel, the growing heat about to ignite an inferno. Ray is arching back at me with every beat of my hips against his slicked asscheeks, his violent submission to explosive sex increasing the fury of my thrusting rhythm. I feel the burst of heat in my balls as, far too soon, I lose my last control, hot cum bursting deep into Ray. I roar in unchecked glory, wet slapping and slithering joining the symphony of delirium we sing together. A burst of thick running cum erupts onto my chest as Ray joins the roaring heat I'm ablaze with. We collapse into each other's sweating embrace, teeth biting deep, nails raking raw. This is a case of victimless rape. This raw sex-primal, urgent, delirious and addictive.

We bite, we suck, we nip and nibble; we scratch, we rake, we pump and pound; we writhe, we cling, we grind and struggle. "We are the best, we are the hardest," Ray mutters in my ear as he finishes licking; he is erect against my slippery stomach. I am trapped between his thighs as he grips my hot

length. I nuzzle his neck again, add another mark for good measure. "Now it's my turn to play the boss." His grip on my ass digs nails in, and our weights shift. I roll under him, slick with cum and licking. He keeps me turning, onto my face, nose pressed into the warm bedding. His weight descends on me, hands pressing my shoulders down. He shifts again, onto one hand, I feel a drop of cool goo splash onto my ass. Some more oozes from the tube into my crack. Fingers slither between my cheeks, and I wriggle in anticipation. Ray presses closer, and his cockhead between my parted cheeks. I raise up my butt, prepare for a fucking like I've never had. My head still swimming with adrenaline, I want desperately to be overpowered, obliterated, owned!

With a nudge, then an unstoppable penetration, his cock spreads my defense wide and slips into my hungry hole. I welcome him, and his length is soon pushing farther and farther up inside me. His belly touches my ass, but still his cock pushes onward. Firm hands grip my hips and pull me back, and more throbbing flesh slithers into me.

At last I feel complete; Ray buried to the balls inside me. Hot and thick I bathe in the sensations of being overpowered. For once, it is not me in the position of power and decision, and it is a feeling I find I like. And want more of. My insides gradually empty of their heated invasion, only to have the hard flesh slip back again from the beginning. Ray has a knack of withdrawing and then overcoming the restored resistance to fill me again.

Again and again, and more and more heated.

He is panting now, and I am moaning into the muffling duvet. We bounce to a primal rhythm that increases to a heartbeat. Nearer and nearer to orgasm, my balls jiggle and roll between my widely spread thighs. My cock is rubbing back and forth against the damp fabric, oozing appreciation for Ray's tricks. He wiggles his hips, stretches me deep. His panting is becoming more a rasping breath, his weight increasing against me. I lose the ability to raise my ass to meet his beat as his grip on my hips increases. Teeth suddenly bite into my shoulder, and his weight pins me down fully. It is now just his jerking hips and his gripping hands that fuel our fucking, and the thrusting is becoming frenzied.

On and on, we rise together. We swear blindly, and we lash and writhe in a joint orgasmic crescendo. Like an incoming wave littered with surfers, the abundance in our balls heats to detonation, and with simultaneous pent-up enthusiasm we thrash to that moment we all crave. Like a detonation in my belly, hot juices flush into me, and my own cum pumps furiously between my impaled flesh and the fabric. We buck and writhe against any cease to our ecstasy, longing for forever. Flooding and flooded with essence of sexual celebration. The weight of another pinning me down under his ravishing lust is an experience new to me, and one I want to return to time and time again. Again cum bursts from Ray up inside me, my ass running with our juices. His belly against my cheeks slaps wetly, as with painful finality his cock loses its urgency within me.

We rest in a breathless and sodden mass, sated, satisfied–but just for a moment.

The rest of the evening stretches out before us, full of promise and exploration. I hope in my heart to feel this much again, this hot and damp haven of excess. I feel Ray slip from me, and a warm hand slide over my smooth cheeks, his lips are near my ear, and I catch a whispered wish: that I should return.

Well, to be honest, that won't be a problem. No, at this moment, what will be a problem is leaving....

R. I. MIN by Peter Gilbert

"The cock that had felt so hard and alive on the previous day lay limp on his thigh. Even in that state it looked beautiful."

They are in the garden just underneath this window as I write. David, my son and Andy his new partner. They're holding hands and seem to be laughing at something. Perhaps David is telling Andy about Phong. I'll be in for some leg-pulling later today if he is.

David was born in 2547. That's right. Slap bang in the middle of the Gay Revolution. We couldn't have chosen a worse time to get married and have a baby. When she was pregnant, my wife and I stopped going out altogether. People that knew, or guessed that we'd done 'it' the natural way shouted foul abuse. It was a horrible time for both of us and, when David was getting towards his teenage years, our worries increased. We said nothing to him. Perhaps we should have done. I think we hoped that he would settle down properly if we let him think he had been conceived in a lab like most other kids. More probably, I was scared of broaching the subject.

He started dating girls. There. I've put it in black and white. Maybe that will make it easier to tell the story. One of his tutors told us about it at first. He was worried. All the other boys in his tutor group did all the things one expected boys of that age to do. They sat in the class holding hands and, if the tutor couldn't hold their attention, their roaming fingers soon found an alternative source of interest. My son, on the other hand, spent his free time standing by the fence that separated the boys from the girls and tried to attract their attention.

Things got worse. When he was fifteen he was spotted walking with a girl among the old ruins on the outskirts of town. We put a stop to that of course but not without a hell of a lot of difficulty. David shouted, screamed, slammed doors and called us every bad name he could think of. At that point there was nothing else I could do but consult a psychiatrist. He was a nice enough guy. Having to tell him that David had been conceived in the old fashioned way wasn't easy. He wasn't shocked–or didn't appear to be–but he admitted that it was almost certainly the cause of David's perversion.

"Tell me," he said, "Have you never been attracted to people of your own sex?" Just the way he said "never" was enough to convince me that I'd be the subject of conversation at his home that evening. "What a weirdo!" his laughing partner would say after hearing about me.

I had to tell the truth, and the truth was "No. Never." I had never even done the things that all boys did in high school. You were a complete outcast at my school if you hadn't had a cock in your mouth by the time you were fifteen so I lied and told my schoolmates about a non-existent

forty-year-old uncle. By the time I'd gotten to the ripe age of seventeen I made sure all the guys at school knew that I was being regularly screwed by 'Uncle Steve'. That seemed to deter them from making any advances in my direction and I put up with their taunts: "He lets his uncle fuck his ass. He lets his uncle fuck his ass!" I just got on with my studies. I never hung around in the changing room. I never stood on the side of the sports field with high- powered binoculars clamped to my head and I never collected pin-ups of boys and young men.

Both my wife and I, you see, come from old-fashioned families. Writing the date in four figures has given me away I guess. I can't get used to this New World Order system of writing the date. As for Eurodollars, what was wrong with the old New Dollar? But I digress.

"So, what do I do?" I asked.

"Buy a boy," he said. "Go out and buy a really good-looking boy. Put him in the same room as your son. David will soon find out what's good for him."

I was appalled. I think, if I am to be truthful, that we had shut our eyes to the traffic in humans that was going on at the time. It was all to do with the Great Land Clearances of course. History was never one of my strong subjects.

I know that we were told in school that the slave trade of the 18th and 19th centuries wasn't a bad thing. How could it be when the World President and Vice President were both black.

When I was young, the whole business had been a bit shady if you know what I mean. You'd see adverts on the screen for

teenagers (suitable for all types of house duties–day and night.) We sniggered knowingly and turned to something more interesting, like the gladiator contests or man-hunts.

I didn't need to be told that Phong was dazzlingly beautiful. I knew, from the moment he climbed up onto the inspection plinth, that there was something about him that was quite different from the boys and young men that had preceded him. The whole business was one huge embarrassment. It had started within minutes of my stepping into the vast reception hall of Male Order, Inc. I stammered out the reason for my prospective purchase. I hadn't expected to be asked that. I thought it would be a question of "That one there. I'll take him with me." but it wasn't like that at all.

"It's for my son," I explained, "Not for me." The clerk behind the desk laughed. "A bit like a model space station, eh?" he said.

"Sorry?"

"They say that every father who buys one for his son spends more time playing with it himself," he said.

I overreacted. That was stupid. I see that now. I was furious –so angry that I hardly glanced at the first lad that mounted the dais. It shut the salesman up to an extent, but he pronounced the words 'your son' in such a way that I could see he wasn't convinced. I became more horrified as each

one succeeded the other on the dais. First at the salesman's patter and then- if you know what I mean-at my own mounting interest. The tall African really did have a beautiful cock. A stocky little Scandinavian was put up. "Just look at his lovely soft little buns," said the man. "Imagine feeling them pressing against your hips. Your son's hips I mean." I am ashamed to say that I wasn't thinking about David.

Then Phong was led in. "From the far east," said the salesman. "A very popular line for what you have in mind- for your son."

Everything about Phong appealed. He was tall and slim and he had the most beautiful eyes I had ever seen. They were deep brown and fringed with long lashes. He was the first boy who actually smiled. It was a sad little smile, but compared to the glowering looks the others had given me, I felt as if the sun had suddenly come out. I loved his color. He was as brown and as shiny as the pies my wife makes for World Liberation Day. I loved the way he put his manacled hands down to try to hide his pendulous cock and when they turned him round I didn't need the salesman's spiel. Even I could see that his buns were beautiful. His long legs were not by any means thin but they and his remarkably slim waist set his butt off to perfection. I didn't need to see any more.

The formalities took a little time. Finally Phong, dressed in a tiny pair of shorts and wearing the compulsory identification and tracking anklet was officially David's property.

The first problem surfaced as I flew home. He spoke no English. I hadn't thought to ask about that. The second problem met us at home. David threw one of his tantrums and said there was no way; no way at all, that he was going to share a room with Phong. My wife said she had spent most of the day trying to persuade David to act like a normal young man but with no success. Thus Phong went into the spare bedroom and we both came to the conclusion that we had wasted a lot of money. Phong would have to be re-sold.

"What you could do," my wife said one night, "is have a doorway made between their rooms."

"What good would that do?" I asked. She said it was worth a try. So I did. Yet another expense.

David was furious but we were getting used to his reactions. "What the hell is that for? If you think I'm going to even touch him, you've got another think coming! I'm not like that. I never will be. It's revolting!" he shouted.

I said that if perhaps he couldn't sleep, he might like someone to talk to.

"How the hell can I talk to someone who doesn't know a word of English?" he snapped.

"Then you can teach him," I replied. David stormed out of the house.

Things went from bad to worse. David seemed to calm down a lot over the next year. It was Phong that caused all the trouble. There was no problem when they were both at home together but David took to spending

nights away with his friends, and in his absence, Phong became unmanageable. It was particularly infuriating because we'd done everything we could to make him happy. I took him out whenever I had time, and we let him sit with us in the lounge in the evenings. Perhaps things might have worked out better if we'd continued, but the walks had to stop. Invariably we'd meet people I knew. "Come to your senses at last?" they'd say, sniggering. The lounge evenings were an embarrassment too. Phong had a habit of stretching out on whichever chair or recliner he chose and the sight of his long, brown legs, or the soft-looking bulge in the front of his shorts disturbed me. It didn't really worry me. All that was needed was a hint to my wife that an early night might be a good idea and I'd forgotten all about Phong when I woke in the morning–until he misbehaved in some way.

David's absences from home became longer and longer. It had to be a girl or even girls, we decided but neither my wife nor I had the courage to ask him. In some ways it was reassuring to think that the old ways of life were being continued but neither of us wanted David to suffer as we had suffered. The prospect of having natural grandchildren instead of laboratory-mated ones was attractive, but we'd also been saving up for David's prom season and it didn't look as if there would be one.

Then came the weekend in the summer. My wife had gone to visit her sister, and David decided to take off for the weekend too. I was looking forward to a quiet time. I went out to buy a few things, came back, and Phong was nowhere to be seen. I was disappointed. I'd bought him some new shorts and a new collar. I'd gotten quite excited on the journey home thinking how nice he'd look in his new white shorts and with a white collar round his neck. As it was, after searching the house and the yard, I threw them both into a drawer and settled down to watch the sports on the holovisor. The boy racing was quite good. I'd put a bet on 'Lovely Legs'–the twenty-year-old favorite–and he came in an easy first. The gladiator contests bored me. Everyone said they were rigged anyway and I was quite glad when the loser, having had both arms and one leg broken by his giant opponent, was put down.

I made myself a meal, ate that, and then realized with a shock that it was evening and there was still no sign of Phong. The curfew was due to sound at any time. I had visions of Security Policemen at the door. "Excuse me sir. Is this yours? We found him wandering. You are aware of course that it's a criminal offense? We'll have to ask you to come with us."

Twenty hundred came round. Still no Phong. Twenty one hundred. I'd have to do something. I accessed 'Crime Reports' on the computer and sat wondering whether to or not. I had just made up my mind to call my wife first to ask for her views on what I should do when I heard the outside door slide open. Convinced that my wife or David must have returned unexpectedly, I sprang to my feet.

"Have you seen...?" I started but it was neither David nor my wife. It was Phong–dressed in David's clothes. I couldn't believe my eyes. In the first

place he shouldn't have known the PIN to open the door. That was bad enough but to see him in David's gear made me feel quite shaken and very, very angry.

"Where the hell have you been?" I asked. He was about to go into his room but stopped, stared at me and then shrugged his shoulders

I can't remember the exact words I used. I felt as if I had lost control of my own household. Things were happening round me that I couldn't even understand, let alone stop. I remember telling him to take the clothes off and I remember the enormous effort I made to stop myself hitting him.

"You stay in your room! Okay? Understand? I'll deal with you later," I shouted. His big brown eyes opened wide. I shoved him through the open doorway and closed the door behind him. Then, with my pulse racing, I went back into the lounge to let my temper cool. If David had been at home I could have taken it out on him, I thought. It was all at least half his fault. And why the hell hadn't he secured the door between his room and Phong's? That would have kept Phong from stealing his clothes. Perhaps I should have beaten David when he started to rebel. Phong too. When the salesman tried to sell me a whip, I'd given him a lecture on humanity and kindness.

In the strange way in which the human brain works, my temper became more and more directed towards David. The more I thought the thing over, the more David seemed to be to blame. David must have given Phong the PIN. It was even conceivable that David had given the lad permission to wear his clothes. Maybe David had told him he could go out alone. Something would have to be done of course. The situation couldn't be allowed to continue. I decided to do nothing until David came back. I could find out the truth then and deal with both separately and fairly.

But then I thought again. The weekend wasn't even half-way through. If I didn't act, it was possible that Phong would go out again the following day. I could almost hear the voice of the Security Police Prosecutor. "Are you seriously asking us to believe that after the boy came back, dressed in your son's clothes, you did nothing?" Then he'd ask me where Phong had been. That was a point. I ought at least to find that out. Something had to be done. I stood up and strode down the corridor to his room.

I stood, rooted to the spot as the door slid open. He was obviously expecting the beating of his life. He was lying face-down on his bed and he didn't have a stitch on. Not even his shorts.

"It's all right. I'm not going to harm you, Phong," I said. "I just thought we ought to have a little chat."

He didn't turn over or even look at me. He just grunted. I pulled the chair towards the bed and sat down. In the simplest English possible, I tried to get the reason for my disquiet across to him. There were rules, I explained, for everybody. They applied to me and my wife; to David and to him, and one of the most important–if not the most important as far as he was concerned–was that he must never go out unescorted. The matter of wearing David's

clothes was serious and I'd deal with that when David returned. All I wanted at that moment was his promise never to go out alone again. I stopped talking. He said nothing. He just lay there with his face buried in the pillow. That annoyed me. In fact it infuriated me. Any answer would have been better than that silence.

"Do you understand?" I asked. He said nothing.

It was a perfectly ordinary gesture. I really mean that. All I wanted him to do was to turn over and face me. I put out a hand and grasped his left leg. Myriad tiny hairs brushed against my fingers. I wouldn't say that I was especially tactile but even remembering the feel of his leg makes me shiver with pleasure. Nothing like it had ever happened to me before. I doubt if my hand had rested on his leg for more than a minute before I began to realize that strange things were happening to me. I could actually hear my heartbeat, and my cock started to react.

Phong got the message and, with a reluctant grunt, he turned over. If I was embarrassed, he must have been doubly so, for his cock was completely rigid. Something like eight inches of rock-hard flesh stood out from dense, black hair so extensive that it seemed to grow right across his body from one hip to the other. I felt horribly guilty. I couldn't bring myself to look at his face. The poor devil had obviously been masturbating when I walked into the room. I remembered being caught in the same state by my father when I was a boy. Perhaps it was from him that I acquired my attitude. Every lad, irrespective of status, is entitled to play with his own property in private.

Still gazing at his middle, I stammered out something about being sorry. His penis nodded up and down as if to acknowledge the apology. His balls, I couldn't help noticing, were a much lighter shade than the rest of him. I hadn't spotted that when I bought him.

"I'll come and talk to you later," I said. As I lifted myself from the chair, I put out a hand to steady myself and, this time, it landed just below his knee. Like tiny little springs, the hairs compressed under my touch, each one seeming to do it's weak best to keep my palm from the shiny brown skin from which it sprang. I pressed slightly harder.

"Are all the boys where you come from as hairy as you are?" I asked. Considering his lack of English, that must count as a really dumb thing to have said. I really don't know why I said anything. Phong smiled.

"Funny. There's hardly any hair here," I said. Almost without my knowing it, I had moved my hand up a few inches and my fingers were brushing over smooth, cool skin. There was a long muscle running up the inside of his thigh. It felt hard, but the incredible, satin-like smoothness of his skin sent mine into goose-bumps. Still Phong said nothing, but he was smiling at me in a way I can only describe as inscrutable. It wasn't an arrogant smile. It was the sort of smile David adopted if I told him something he knew already; a patronizing expression that said, "I know this and more besides, but carry on if it pleases you." I did-moving my hand a

bit farther upwards with every stroke.

"You're really ... strong," I said. I had to stop myself from saying 'beautiful.' I was beginning to feel light-headed. It was as if some spirit had taken possession of me. I knew I wasn't gay. I couldn't be, but my cock was pressing insistently against my pants, straining to be let out.

"All hard muscle," I said, sliding my hand up and down the inside of his thigh and moving it up a bit farther with every stroke.

And then he spoke. "Phong like R.I. Min," he said.

"Is that who you went to see today?" I asked.

He grinned. "R.I. Min," he said.

"Friend?" I asked but he didn't answer and, at that moment, I couldn't have cared less if he'd visited a thousand people. My fingers made contact with his balls. They were cooler than the rest of him and felt slightly damp. I looked at his face. He grinned again and then shut his eyes.

I shuffled the chair nearer the bed. His cock was only inches from my face. I took in the soft brown skin; the dark lines of his veins and the deeply puckered skin at the top. It was absolutely straight and pointed upwards and backwards. I touched it gingerly. He didn't open his eyes, but he smiled. David, I thought, was such a fool. It was obvious that Phong didn't mind what I was doing. Indeed, he gave every indication of enjoying it. How many times had my son seen that cock in all its glory and ignored it? I put all my fingers round it and slowly moved the skin downwards. Slowly, almost shyly, his glowing cock head appeared. It was the color of a ripe plum. I touched it. It was as smooth as a plum too.

It suddenly occurred to me that I was faced (literally) by the perfect opportunity to test this gay sex business. There was nobody else in the house and it didn't look as if Phong would object. Even if he did he'd only be able to complain by obscene gestures that my wife would probably interpret as being aimed at her. I moved the chair even farther forward.

I was right. He didn't object at all. In fact he let out a low moan of enjoyment as I licked the top of his thigh. I steadied it with the fingers of my left hand. That was entirely unnecessary. It felt like steel. I lifted my head and took the tip of it between my lips. I felt his hands on the top of my head and, for a moment, I thought I'd made the greatest mistake of my life. He pushed me away but he pushed gently. It slipped out of my mouth but not before I'd realized that my school friends had told the truth. The flavor on the tip of my tongue was unique.

He took his hands away, brought up his knees and parted his legs. I realized what he wanted me to concentrate on. They hung low; so low that they were almost touching the sheet. He put his hands under his buns and lifted his butt off the bed. I put out my tongue and made contact with the cool, crinkled skin of his scrotum. One or two wispy hairs touched my lips. I moved my head farther in. I sucked against one of his balls and he groaned. I did the same to the other one and he groaned again. All the time his cock seemed be exuding a delightful odor that filled my nostrils. It was a

bit like munching a bread roll in a restaurant while you're waiting for the main dish. You can smell it cooking. My main dish for that evening was only a fraction of an inch away and I was determined to stuff it into my mouth and suck every ounce of flavor out of it.

I lifted my head and looked along his belly and chest to his face. His eyes were still closed. I buried my mouth in his bush and then licked upwards along the shaft. He groaned. I did it again and he groaned for a second time. Then, taking it in my fingers, I popped it into my mouth and pushed my head down as far as I could go. That was a mistake. I gagged and had to come up for air. The second time was more successful. It slid over my tongue. I closed my lips round it and sucked as hard as I could. I think he said something. I'm not sure. I was in such a state that I wouldn't have known if a bomb went off. I pulled my head back again and licked the head. I tried without success to poke the tip of my tongue into the pursed foreskin. That having failed, I retracted it with my lips and the full flavor flooded my mouth. I could feel it on my tongue and on the insides of my teeth. It was warm and sticky and the taste of it just about blew my mind. I remember thinking that this was only the starter. If the starter tasted so good, the main course would be even better. It was about to be served too. He lifted himself upwards again. This time I moved with him and kept licking and sucking for all I was worth.

He grunted again–and then again. I could feel it pulsating in my mouth. I knew that the flood was coming and I was

determined to drink every drop. Another grunt–and then the whole of him went rigid. The first jet filled my mouth

completely. There was no way I could hold it all. I had to open my lips. It was just as well I did. The second, third and fourth jets would have choked me. I swallowed hard but not hard enough. Some of it ran down my chin. I just had to come off it. I didn't want to. Long streams of spunk dangled down from my lips to his belly and bush. The drops glittered like pearls on his brown skin. For a few moment, I sat there relishing the taste and realizing what I'd done. I, of all people, had enjoyed a gay experience with a boy young enough to be my son.

"You okay?" I asked. I expected a tirade of oriental abuse. Instead, he smiled. "R.I. Min good," he said. "Phong like R.I. Min."

That just about did it as far as I was concerned. I knew he couldn't understand a word I said and I knew that young people can be thoughtless. I felt guilty for what I had done and completely deflated. To be compared unfavorably to somebody else – an oriental of some sort by the sound of his name – was the last straw. I carried on shouting at him for some minutes. All he did was to calmly take a wipe out of the box next to the bed and dry his groin. I might as well not have existed. Totally deflated (except in one part of my anatomy) I left his room, sealed the door and went back to my own room.

I got undressed and lay down. For some reason, the pleasant sensations

and thoughts of my wife I usually enjoyed when I was alone wouldn't come. Phong kept intruding. His taste was still in my mouth. His scent filled my nose. The image of his long, brown legs kept recurring. At the moment I shot my load, I was imagining something that I had never done in my life and thought I never would. That worried me but, after I had cleaned up, I found I could think more rationally.

In the first place, I decided, Phong would have to go. Apart from leading me away from my wedding vows, I wasn't going to have some far eastern call boy in my house. That's what he was obviously. R.I. Min was an Asian name. I wondered how many times Phong had obliged him and how they had met. Slowly, the full picture pieced itself together in my mind.

Right on the edge of our township there is a little group of Asian-owned business. Everybody knew that if you wanted to do something taboo – if not actually illegal – those guys could fix it. The area had become known as 'Fixit Corner'. Obviously, David had got one of his girlfriends pregnant and had sent Phong down there, dressed in his clothes, to arrange things. He was the ideal person. He probably spoke their language.

I couldn't sleep that night. Not because of what I had done to Phong. Thinking about that was actually pleasant. It was what R.I. Min had done that obsessed me. I had to find the man–but how? And what did one say to a man that helped himself to other people's property? It was as if three separate voices were arguing in my brain.

"You enjoyed that, didn't you?" said Memory. "Let's go through it again. Remember how hard it felt? Remember how he lifted off the bed when he shot his load? Remember that salty tang in your mouth?"

"All very well," said Conscience, "but Phong isn't your property. The title deed states quite clearly that Phong belongs to David. You're in no position to get worked up about R.I. Min. You're just as guilty."

"No, no." said my vengeful side. "R.I. Min has to be found and punished. Min isn't even a Euro-American name. He's a foreigner. He must be found and extradited."

"So that you can have Phong all to yourself," Memory replied. "There's something rather wonderful about youth isn't there? Especially brown youth with hairy legs. Let's run that through again..."

On the following morning I staggered out of bed feeling completely drained. I took my breakfast pills and went down to wake Phong. There was actually no necessity for that. Phong had been with us long enough to know how to look after himself but I wanted to see what the new shorts and collar looked like on him. The door slid open. He was still in bed but awake. The sheet that covered him came up to just below the dark circles round his nipples. I'd been right, I thought, to select white shorts. White set him off to perfection.

He grinned and threw the sheet to one side. His cock which had felt so hard and alive on the previous day, lay limp on his thigh. Even in that state it looked beautiful.

"R.I. Min," he said, and the joy I got from just looking at him evaporated. I pointed to his little sanitary annex. He got off the bed, gave me a strange, questioning look and went in there. I sat on the bed and played with the collar, all the time thinking of the man that had helped himself to my property. "David's property actually," said Conscience. That was true, but it had been my money that had bought him. My money that fed him. The water I could hear spraying onto his body had been heated at my expense and he lived in my house. He was as much mine as he was David's. Anyway, I'd had his cock in my mouth. His semen was still in my gut. He'd shot it willingly too. Perhaps I wasn't as good as Mr. Min. Mr. Min was probably much older than I was. Mr. Min was the sort of person who preyed on other people's property. Small wonder that he was good at it. I heard the dryer click in as the water was turned off.

"You could be just as good as Mr. Min. You just need practice. You did reasonably well yesterday," said Memory and, as if to confirm the judgment, my cock began to swell in my pants. I envisaged the little beads of water running across Phong's skin and evaporating in the hot air blast. The hairs on his legs would be waving like corn in a high wind. As for that dense mat round his cock. My cock quickly swelled alarmingly. I looked down; I could actually see the outline of it moving towards my knee under the cloth.

"You are here to fit a collar. Just remember that," said Conscience and, at that moment, Phong stepped back into the room. He might have smiled. I don't know. All I was aware of was an eight-inch shaft of rigid flesh pointing upwards and forwards as he walked. I wanted to stand up. I had to stand up in order to fit the new collar. The problem was that I couldn't; not in the condition I was in. Phong would have to come down to my level. I gestured towards the bed. He grinned and lay down, again on his front. The old collar came off easily enough. He lifted his head to let me get it right off and then, when he was free of it, he kissed my wrist. He must have thought he was being freed for life. He struggled when I went to put the new one on. It was obviously going to be a two-man job and I'd have to wait for David to return. I gave up and put the collar on the side of the bed.

I'd never noticed his ears before. They were quite large; certainly bigger than mine and very flat against his head. I started to play with them, just running my fingertips round the edges. He made a little moaning sound. Then I tickled the back of his neck. He liked that too. I could tell by the way he

moved his head from side to side. I ran my fingers down his spine, trying to count the individual bones. Inevitably, my fingers found the soft flesh of his buns. He flung his legs apart. The collar fell on the floor.

"R.I. Min," he said. I slapped his rump. "No more R.I. Min," I said. "Understand? No more R.I. Min."

"No more R.I. Min," he repeated. Whether he understood or not was a different matter. I put my hands under his hips and

twisted. He got the message and turned over. If anything it looked stiffer and even more appetizing than it had a few minutes earlier. I took it gently between my thumb and finger.

"Go ahead," said one of my inner voices. He wants it. You want it. There's just the two of you in the house. The others won't be back till much later. Take your time. Show him what a true Euro-American can do to a boy."

"It wouldn't be a bad idea to take your own clothes off," the practical side of my brain added. "If you make a mess on those pants, you'll have a job explaining it to your wife." I didn't stand up. I couldn't but I managed to get everything undone and removed. Struggling out of your pants in a sitting position is not easy. They ended up, inside out, on the floor. Phong turned his head to see what was going on, grinned again and then took my cock in his hand.

"R.I. Min," he muttered. Angrily, I knocked his hand away. It took over an hour. They say, don't they, that the flavor of a good meal should be enjoyed in little bites? I didn't bite any of him with my teeth but I took everything I could between my lips.

Just when I realized that the meal was enjoying it as much as the diner I don't know. He lay still as I sucked on his ear lobes. I don't think he enjoyed having his eyelids licked but when I made contact with his fleshy lips he put both arms round me and pulled me towards him. I could feel his cock hammering against my belly. His tongue pushed into my mouth and I sucked on that. The taste was unmistakably that of David's toothpaste but at that moment I couldn't have cared less if he'd taken everything David possessed. Except himself of course. He was mine. All mine, and I could do what I liked with him for as long as I liked. He hugged me even tighter. My tongue explored his mouth. His went deep into mine and at that moment, he gave a sort of shudder. I felt it running down his body. I followed it. I nibbled at his nipples. He groaned. I moved down even further and sank the tip of my tongue into his navel. I hadn't realized what a source of delicious flavors a navel could be–but it was nothing to the bristly, still slightly damp hair I encountered next. His distinctive odor and taste got stronger and stronger. By the time I'd got down to his balls, there was no holding him–literally. He flung himself around on the bed, groaning and panting. He brought up his knees and I went in further. The feel of his smooth thighs against my cheeks and the musty, spicy odor down there were so delightful that I didn't want to stop, but a tiny spot of moisture landed on the back of my neck and I was all too aware that I was leaving a sticky trail somewhere. My balls and the insides of my thighs were aching.

I lifted my head and looked over the top of his tool at his face. His mouth was wide open and his eyes were closed. I lowered my head again. It touched my lips. I opened my mouth and, as slowly as I possibly could, I took it all. First the silky head, letting my tongue play on the slit until the salty taste became apparent. Then the ridge of still-retracting foreskin and

then the huge, solid shaft with its venous ridges. It touched the back of my throat. He shifted violently but I didn't gag that time. Maybe I'd gotten used to it already. I sucked. I sucked hard. He groaned and lifted himself up as if trying to cram it into my gullet but I moved with him.

At that moment, unfortunately, I came. I couldn't stop myself. For a split second, full consciousness personified by the voice of Conscience returned but it didn't seem as earnest as it had earlier. "That's David's property in your mouth and you are a married man," it said but then went on to say "but you might as well carry on now you've got so far."

I did. I somehow got my hands between his thighs and stroked upwards till my fingers reached his balls. He liked that. So did I.

By this time he was thrashing around so wildly and groaning that it was difficult to know which part of him my fingers were touching. I remember that during one convulsive heave my hand slipped forward, past his balls and I touched his anus. He groaned even more loudly and then, in successive spurts so rapid that nobody could have counted them, my mouth filled with his warm juice. I managed to swallow most of it. The rest cascaded down onto his belly and the top of his thighs.

We cleaned up as best we could, then bundled up the sodden bed linen and changed it for new.

He didn't say anything, he just grinned at me and strode into his sanitary annex.

I dumped the old bed linen, had a shower and settled down in my den and recommenced the search for Mr. Min.

I'd been at it for some considerable time when David returned. I'd found a Ming and several foreign names with the initials R.I., but I was nowhere near success.

"Good weekend?" I asked.

"Oh, not bad. Where's Phong?"

"In his room. I want to talk to you about him. He went out yesterday wearing your clothes."

David smiled. "That was a bit silly of him," he said. "He ought not to do that really."

My frustration at not being able to find Mr. Min surfaced. "A bit silly? A bit silly? It was criminal. He could have got us both in deep trouble. It's not to happen again, David. Do you hear me? You've got to deal with him very firmly indeed. I think that both of us have been far too soft with him."

("I wouldn't have said you were soft from what I could see. He certainly wasn't," said Memory.)

"Yeah. I guess you're right. I'll go down there now. I'll unpack later," said David and he left the room.

Chang, R I. Foo, R I. Xiaou, R.I. The names scrolled up the screen. It was no use. Pretty obviously, Mr. Min had given a false name to cover himself. I got up and wandered down the hallway towards David's room. If he had got some girl into trouble and had sent Phong to find an abortionist as I

suspected, then it was my job to help him put his life back together again. I didn't know how he was going to deal with Phong's unauthorized absence. I hoped he wouldn't be too severe although a good thrashing would have been in order.

I was just about to open his door when I heard his voice. I stopped. I couldn't hear what he was saying but it didn't sound much like an angry reprimand. For the first (and only) time in my life I put my ear to the door.

"God, I've missed this," said David. "Open them a bit wider. Bit more. Oh, that's it. Gee, you've got a glorious little butt! Ready?"

Phong gave a low grunt; then there was a long pause. Phong grunted again, and then again. I heard the bed creak. Phong gave a long, drawn-out groan. It was much like the sound a man makes when he's lifting something heavy – the sound of physical strain.

Then I heard David's voice. "Ah! I'm in," he said. "I'm *really* in!"

A SINGAPORE SURPRISE by Rick Jackson

"Once I felt his ass seize up and that second orgasm of his splash against the concrete, I knew it was time for me to take care of my own priorities...."

Before I stopped by on a sales trip, about all I knew of Singapore was that some American kid had been caned there a couple years back after a doubtful confession for vandalism. Signs everywhere promised stiff fines for gum-chewing and jaywalking. I didn't see any specific "No Butt-Fucking" signs, but in a place like Singapore, a guy doesn't need to read the writing on the wall to know he's not about to get any. My last night there, though, I got a surprise that taught me a man should never pre-judge and always keep his options open.

I'd just spent ten days in Sydney so I certainly didn't need sex badly enough to risk cruising crappers in Asia's most frenetic police-state democracy. I was just doing the shopping scene, stopping by the Plaza Singapura in Orchard Road to check out the exotic CDs. What I did need was to piss like a big dog with a bad attitude. I had no sooner wandered into the fourth floor john, though, than I had to start rethinking the program.

The john was divided down the middle with floor-to-ceiling stalls, leaving pissers along the wall on both sides. Force of habit took me to the far, isolated set and, as I rounded the corner, I saw three guys spaced along the wall. Each of them had his hands full of hard Singapore dick, pumping away while he leered at his competition. Ever cool, I pretended to ignore the electrified charge of mansex that had those dicks standing tall and proud as I headed for a pisser about midway between a couple of average-looking Chinese twenty-somethings.

Much as I craved the leak of a lifetime, I needed to tease those tight Singapore sluts even more. I stopped about eighteen inches back and slowly popped open the top four buttons on my jeans. I pulled my thick nine inches of uncut American pride out on display and took a moment to aim it for fullest show and advantage. When I arced a blessed yellow torrent of the most rapturous relief up through space and over into the pisser, there was zero doubt in my young mind where everybody's eyes were looking. I played to the crowd, easing my own eyes to mere slits of satisfaction as I painted one lurid design of golden ecstasy after another across the face of the porcelain. Once the first flush of relief had passed, I clamped down hard on my bladder, forcing every drop I had to leap up and across the space between my big Anglo dick and the cool white of the porcelain pisser.

At first, I didn't know whether my audience comprised piss-freaks or dick-freaks or just plain freaks. All I knew was that they were desperate for me to make their acquaintance-- among other things. The Chinese jack-offs

on either side had been so close that I lost track of the third guy for a time. When I finally ran dry and got down to playing slide-the-foreskin myself, though, that changed on the double and the Chinese weren't especially happy.

He didn't exactly push them aside, but eased just in front of me, his long brown dick shiny with lust and all but begging for love. He was about ten years older than I, but tall and built and exotic looking. He lacked a turban but wore the long hair and beard of a Sikh that spoke as much about his background as his delicious chocolate-brown skin. Unfortunately, he also wore the same horrible polyester that Indians always seem inexplicably to like so much. That polyester was stretched tight across a fine full butt, flaring out to tease my dick into being naughty. I never did learn his name, but somehow names didn't matter. I decided to myself to think of him as Singh-a good Sikh name and what he made my cock do.

Singh played slowly with his big dick, instinctively knowing how much I liked to see the crystal-clear pre-cum leaking out of his piss-slit and slipping in silvery threads of silken man-sugar down towards the floor. Sometimes the thread would grow too thin and snap; sometimes my tormenter would slip a finger against the thread and slurp it up into his mouth. Every fibre of my being needed to swallow that Sikh shank so far down my throat that we would be locked together always-but for once in my life, I was out in public without a rubber to my name. Who would have thunk a guy would need rubbers in Singapore?

Needing desperately to make some contact to prove to myself the vision was real and not some passing djinn, I reached out and cupped his huge, hairy brown balls for a moment, sliding gently forwards until his hot throbbing dick was lying ready in my hand like a gift of the gods. I eased my fingers up to trap it in position and began slowly jacking him along, fucking that leaking nozzle into my wrist at one extreme and prodding his balls with my fuckfinger at the other. I forgot all about jacking myself. The Chinese twenty-somethings might as well have been a highland mist in a tornado. All I could feel was the hot musky power of that big, brown dick in my hand and how good and right and messy it felt there.

After having my man in hand for a mindless eternity, I heard, as though from a great distance, "Will you fuck me?" I was so far gone from the heavy feel of his dick and the masculine smell of his musk that his plea didn't register at first. Then he moaned and I saw his hand holding a rubber. When he gave a little gurgle and begged again, "Will you please fuck me?" I decided to do my bit for international relations.

In a couple of gibbered monosyllables and a whole frantic lexicon of facial twitches, my meat du jour made clear we needed to go somewhere else-away from the audience and dangers implicit in a public toilet. I was all for that. If he wanted to take me home so I could ream his ass at leisure and make him scream like a dervish in a rusty threshing machine, I thought

that was a very good thing. Little did I know, though, that we weren't going home.

We quickly walked right through the mall's garage and down four flights of an echoing cement stairwell to find a small vestibule next to the ground-floor door. Anyone opening the door could see us, but Singh said not to worry. Could I believe him? This was his home turf, but it was also Singapore. What would happen to us if some little Malay grandmother or other decided to use the stairs and caught me slamming Singh's ass against the rough concrete walls and making him cry? Something told me that the Singapore police could think of an infinite variety of unpleasant things to do to us.

Something else told me, though, that the gorgeous brown butt on display not three inches from my throbbing knob needed some abuse, too. As I was trying to ease my overgrown American shank into his off-brand rubber, I noticed more than a dozen others scattered about the floor. That same something told me that Singh had been there before. Since he was still running around loose in public, he had to know what he was doing.

All the time I was dropping his pants and rubbering up, Singh was busy as a Midwestern circus tryout. One hand was whipping his shank like a runaway pile driver; the other was pulling at his left butt-cheek, forcing his hairy ass-crack to gape wide and so invitingly that not even a stoic could pass it up. All the while he was chanting his desperate mantra: "Fuck me! Fuck me! Fuck me! Fuck me-eeee!"

I wanted the moment to last hours past forever so I took my fucking time giving him what we needed. I started off up that ass-crack, sliding my fuck-finger deep to score the stiff glossy black hairs that live there into shape. I no sooner found Singh's desperate asshole than the monster tried to eat my defenseless arm for dinner. His gorgeous brown butt arched instinctively backwards onto my finger even as his body shivered in promised bliss and his lips gaped wide in a groan of almost Vedic wonder.

Soon, though, even having an ass filled with fingers wasn't good enough and he switched from groans and grunts of pressing contentment to a new "Hurry! Hurry! Please hurry!" mantra that begged desperately for a good fucking.

I should have held off and toyed with his ass, but that hot, clenching asshole locked tight around my hand and shook it with a welcome that was downright embarrassing. Singh's butt arched back, presenting it to me like the bitch in heat he was. Sometimes a man just has to let foreplay slide, forget about romantic finger work, hop aboard his mount, and gallop on down the trail.

Normally, I use a lot of lube. With my big dick, I have to slather it on to excess unless I want to leave a string of mutilated corpses and shell-shocked walking wounded in my wake. Since Singh had lured me off unprepared for his pleasure, though, there wasn't much I could do to grease the skids of our love but drop some spit along my shank and hope for the best. I only needed

a moment to take out my fingers, lock my hands onto his hips, and kick his legs wider apart so I could get some room to ream, but the racket Singh made with his whining proved even that moment was an eternity too long for him.

An instant later, he had another eternity too long--and too thick and too hard to bear. As I slammed forward against him, ripping his eager asshole wide with my knob and rubbing him worse with every inch of my blue-veined shank, our concrete stairwell reverberated like the living center of downtown Doom with Singh's harsh animal howls of agony. Once I was buried butt-deep, I reamed upwards until my dick lifted much of his weight off his feet and he temporarily had the noise just plain fucked out of him. My hands eased upwards along his flanks, coasting beneath the slick polyester to find thick handfuls of fur that begged to be ripped away from his stone-tipped tits. I snagged twin fistfuls from his pecs and held on tight, holding them like reins while I put the rest of his bone-happy body through its paces.

I had expected that ass without any grease to be a tight fit, but I'd never felt anything like the way the soft tissues of his guts scraped against my latex-clad lizard. I started off slowly enough. I'm not a total dick, after all. I can be sensitive. I know all about the '90s. Inside a dozen heartbeats, though, I knew the poor bastard was lost--and so was I. There was no way to be a kinder, gentler assfucker. The harder and faster and deeper I slammed his ass, the more that latex rubbed us raw and the louder the bastard screamed--but he did more than that.

His hands were all over my ass, trying like some greedy stockbroker beast from beyond to pull my body all the way into his so he could possess me absolutely. His hips lurched backwards to meet my every thrust and parry my few stabs at easing his pain. I fucked him harder, and Singh just screamed louder, at once telling me I was killing him and begging me to bone him even faster. I humped that hapless hole as his body writhed in torment on the end of my shank and shuddered with man's most basic of terrors in my arms.

Beneath the polyester, I could feel his pain-knotted body bathed in sweat as he struggled against the limitations of Nature to take everything I had. Now and again, his hand would slide low to jack for a moment -- perhaps to try taking his mind off the problem I was pounding his way. Once I really got going, though, he didn't have any hands free. I fucked him up against the grey concrete and into the position familiar to punks and viewers of police shows the world over. In Singh's case, though, we didn't need a neighbor's videocam to show how much damage my nightstick was doing. Every snarling breath and feral whimper and mindless grunt and drop of gushing sweat screamed volumes about what a good time the slut was having. The question was how much longer he could last without passing out-or drawing every cop south of Malaysia.

The dry, fiery insides of his guts were a rolling horror of sensation, but he absolutely would not let up. Every twisting fuck-thrust met nine inches of cock-craving tissue just begging to be abused. Even when the tightness of his butt was so severe that I thought my dick was going numb, Singh kept babbling and screaming on about how I was ruining him forever and how I should do it even harder. Since both his hands were braced against the wall by then, I reached down to take him in hand, but his pounding Punjabi unit was already a sodden mess of splashed sperm and good times quickly forgotten. I held tight, though, and felt him nut yet again within a minute or two as I pounded his dick into my fist with all the selfish brutality I could muster.

Once I felt his ass seize up and that second cum splash against the concrete, I knew it was time to take care of my own priorities. I hadn't come to Singapore to cruise, but now that it had been thrust upon me, I was determined to blow the nut of my young American life or rupture an aneurysm in the process. I was, after all, an unofficial American ambassador of good will. The rabid thrust of bone into muscle, the sweaty smack of two hard bodies at play, and the savory stench of man-musk choking the fetid tropical air all conspired to mesmerize me and make me quite forget myself. I felt my hands back on Singh's tits and my gritted teeth snarling trash-talk into his ear as my body crashed through his faster and harder with every passing moment.

Time lost its focus and spun awry, and I gave myself up completely to the best Singapore surprise any tourist could crave. I don't think the stairwell door opened–but I was past caring. Whether Singh blew more loads of spooge against the wall I have no clue. I only know that I rode that Punjabi pony harder than a mad Mogul with a new mallet and more chukkers than sense.

When the fog finally parted and I bred my way back to life, the stairwell was ricocheting with animal noises again–only this time they were mine. I tried to shut up and just hold Singh tight while I juiced his ass, but the harder I spewed that sperm, the louder I had to credit every god I could remember. My dick had fucked itself so raw and sore inside that rubber that my cum gushing back across my tortured flesh was a blessing in more ways than one. Having my bone balmed gave me the help I needed to finish the job in style. I lifted Singh's right knee towards his chest and eased about to finish him off fucking his ass sideways against the concrete. By the time I had finished what he had started, we were both worn mute, panting like asthmatic cheetahs, and sweat-soaked social disasters.

I pulled my tortured tool out of the ruins of Singh's butt and gave him a pat of affectionate thanks–and then leaned back to catch my breath as I added our rubber to the collection. Singh smiled back and quickly pulled up his pants to make his escape. As he headed back up the stairs, he turned around and looked back down at me and added, "Not a place to rest. Sometimes the customers use stairs on the way to the shops."

The bastard had lied to me. We had been at risk of discovery the whole time, yet, somehow, that made fucking him up that gorgeous butt of his all the more exciting-fun and exotic and something I wanted to do again soon.

I had to leave Singapore the next day, but you can believe the next time I pass through the country, I will have a lifetime supply of rubbers and lube when I head for the Plaza to piss. I have learned to be ready for anything in Singapore.

NOTHING SACRED by John Patrick

A Wicked Dream

My new neighbor, Jimmy, said he joined the youth group at his church, and invited me to a Halloween party they were having.

"Which church is that?" I asked.

"Ours."

"The Catholic?"

He grimaced. "Catholic? Hell, no, Catholics don't have parties. They wear black and worship rosaries and things like that. This is at our church, the big one, the Methodist."

"Oh, I don't think I can," I said. "I'm not supposed to go into other churches."

"You're not supposed to go in other churches?" he asked. "That sounds like some Catholic thing. You ain't Catholic, are you?"

"Yes," I had to admit.

"You should join our church."

"I don't think I can."

"Sure you can, if you want to."

"I don't think my folks would let me."

He was astonished. "You mean they're Catholic, too?"

"Of course."

"You mean you're going have to stay Catholic?"

"I guess."

At that point in my life, I wouldn't have considered changing my religion. I loved going into the confessional. My confessions were always heard by Father Anthony.

When I studied to become an altar boy and started to serve at mass, I became enthralled by Father Anthony, the youngest, handsomest, and most lenient of the priests. Eventually I feared that my feelings for him would overwhelm me.

In the sacristy before and after mass, as we dressed in our cassocks and surplices, the older boys would tell dirty jokes. Details from them kept me amused during the services, and later, at night, I'd become aroused thinking about boys and girls doing all those filthy things to each other.

Then one day Father Anthony wasn't doing confessions. He'd been "on a Saturday night howler," as another altar boy put it. That night, I had my first wet dream about Father Anthony. It was a wicked dream. It was night and I was waiting in the shadows of the fist pew. The shadowy place was brightened by a half-dozen perpetual candles arranged near the altar in tall

columns of thick blue glass. They released a weird scent unlike anything I'd ever smelled before, and a changeable light that gave everything a dreamy sheen.

Just then, I heard a rustling sound. The small door at the side of the altar opened and a figure slid in, shutting the door behind it. From the mass of curly hair, I knew that it must be Father. I watched as he leaned over the first pew to wrap his arms around the seated figure. He kissed the figure's shoulders for quite some time before he stood.

It was then that I saw it was Jimmy! In stunned silence, I watched the lovers climb the two steps to the dais that held the altar. Jimmy was lifted and placed upon the sacred table's highly polished surface. Next, Father Anthony slowly undressed Jimmy. When the boy was nude, Father's hands gripped the boy's little cock.

I watched in fascination as Father took the entire cock in his mouth and began sucking it while roughly tweaking Jimmy's pert nipples. All this was performed as if it were being done on stage. Then Father whispered something and backed away from the altar.

A moment later, the studly priest was standing behind the bench; he was nude and he possessed a sizable prick. Its rigid length was being slowly soothed by Jimmy's eager hands in preparation for what was to come next. When Jimmy finally took the hardening organ into his mouth, Father began to sway about as if drunk with lust. Father held Jimmy's head so he alone could direct the action. To begin with, the cockhead was slipped between Jimmy's waiting lips. The lad's mouth bulged in an attempt to contain its indecent burden. For a good while longer, I watched as Jimmy tried to swallow the heavily veined, dark cock with only limited success.

Soon, at least two fingers, coated with holy saliva, were disappearing into the tight ass of Jimmy. Jimmy continued to suck the priest's prick while he was being finger-fucked.

Before long, Jimmy went down on his hands and knees to place his chin near the edge of the dais the swollen prick directly before him. Jimmy sucked the weighty ballsac while he massaged the shaft.

After a few minutes of this, Father gave another soft order and, at once, Jimmy released the cock, which thrust upward immediately. Jimmy turned over on his back. In the dimly lit chapel, Father knelt between Jimmy's outstretched thighs. He clutched the solid shaft and pointed its head to the moistened slit. There was an anxious moment when I was sure Jimmy could see me in the shadows.

I stepped back a bit just as Father lurched forward. Jimmy screeched. Father's cock was in him to its very root. With arms fully extended and palms flat against the altar top, Father delivered a series of unrelenting thrusts. Now the candle flames were shaking to such a degree that they seemed likely to extinguish themselves, but their bluish glow continued to reveal every moment of the incredible fuck of Jimmy by my favorite priest.

After another round of savage thrusts, Father was heaving Jimmy's legs so much higher still that the boy's creamy, smooth butt had risen off the altar. Jimmy's eyes flashed open and then clamped shut as his head turned wildly from side to side. Just then, there was a sharp slapping sound as Father's bursting prick was wrenched from Jimmy's ass. As Father squeezed the last of the cum from his own prick, he was bringing Jimmy to orgasm. As Jimmy came, he screamed in anguish.

Jerking my own hard-on, I came right along with him. A groan escaped my lips and Father twisted his head toward me. At the same moment, Jimmy started to lick the cum from each of Father's fingertips.

"Did you learn much from your lesson, my sweet boy?" Father asked me from the altar.

But I did not reply. Instead, I stared for a few moments more then ran as fast as I could toward the exit....

I awoke with a start. My bedding was wet with cum. Normally I can't remember my dreams, but this one I would never forget. And the next time I saw Father, I got a hard-on, and I was sure he saw it tenting my pants, but he only turned away.

TWINS HAVE NO SECRETS by Peter Gilbert

"Mr. Barker's compliments, sir, and he asked me to give you this."

I looked up to see a fair-haired lad, tall, barely legal, with an engaging smile. I took the little manila envelope from him, settled my class down to writing some notes and tore it open.

"Return my compliments to Mr. Barker and tell him I wholeheartedly agree," I said. I crumpled up the note and envelope and put them in my pocket.

Even at this distance in time, the memory of our correspondence sends a little frisson running down my spine. We could have so easily been found out. Schoolboys, even older schoolboys, are an inquisitive breed. Any one of those unsuspecting messengers could have stopped in the washroom, steamed open the envelope and read the message.

"*I think you'll agree this one has very nice legs. Wouldn't mind getting between them. What about you? GB....*" Gordon had written.

Deeper down in my pocket, waiting till I got home and could destroy them safely, were the two earlier notes he had sent that day.

"*Knowing your partiality for tight bottoms, I am sending a particularly fine example. Try to get him to bend over for you. GB.*"

"I think something fell out of your pocket," I said.

The boy patted his hips. "Don't think so, sir," he replied.

"I'm sure I'm right. Maybe it rolled under the desk."

"He didn't drop anything, sir," said Michael O'Grady from his place in the front row.

"Better have a look to make sure. If it was money, this lot will have it in no time." My class laughed sycophantically.

The lad protested that he never carried loose coins in his pockets but he looked under the table and I sent him back to thank Mr. Barker for his thoughtfulness.

"*This one has an attractive bulge in his pants. Have a look at his fingers. If they're anything to go by, it's solid meat. GB.*"

That boy went back with the message that I thought Mr. Barker had guessed the dimensions correctly.

Gordon and I had both been on the staff for about three years. As I recall, I started in September of one year and he joined the school in the following January. He soon made his mark. He was the only math teacher I have ever known who could have a class roaring with laughter one moment and as quiet as mice in the next. The boys liked him enormously. He was always being stopped in the corridor and asked to explain something or to look at a half-finished exercise to make sure the lad was on the right lines. None of my English Literature students stopped me. I suppose I was slightly jealous.

And then there was Gordon's gymnastic class, which he held on Tuesday evenings in the school gym. It was open to outsiders too. He'd been a gymnastics champion himself when he was young-almost, so I heard, selected for the Olympics. You only had to peer through the circular windows in the gym doors at the boys on the trapeze, leaping over the vaulting- horse or swinging between the parallel bars to see that he was good.

Needless to say, the school authorities were delighted with him. Gordon was the only member of the staff sometimes to be invited to the Principal's office for coffee during the morning break.

Our relationship started with a ghastly error on my part. Looking back, I'm glad it happened as it did. At the time I was frightened to death.

Reports had to be written in a hurry. There had been some sort of hold up at the printing works-something like that. I thought it would make sense if, instead of going home straight from school, Gordon could come to my place and add his remarks about their math to my students' reports. He lived some way from the school. He thought it a good idea too.

We did the reports. I went out into the kitchen to get coffee and came back to find him sitting on the sofa looking at one of my collection. I remember the book well. It was called *Butt Patrol*. Page one showed a group of six sweating teenage boys, each dressed in some strange sort of camouflage uniform, marching along a mountain track towards a strangely Alpine- looking building. A few pages later, they had reached their objective and were lounging on expensive furniture in a large room. Small wonder that the hunting trophies looked down from the walls with expressions of surprise. Buttons and zip flies had been opened and eager hands were groping under the camouflage. By the end of the book, they were naked and their patrol leaders, dressed, incongruously, in strange leather harnesses and military caps, forced adult penises into their behinds.

"Oh that," I said, almost dropping the tray from shock. "I confiscated it the other day."

"Oh yes. Who from?"

"Oh, I can't remember. Anyway, I promised him I wouldn't tell anyone." The truth was that I'd been looking at it one evening when the door bell rang and had slid it hurriedly under a cushion and then forgotten all about it. For that slip of memory my career was about to come to an early close. Gordon would be with the principal on the following morning.

"There's something I think you ought to know, Dr. Roberts...."

"Some good ones in here," said Gordon. "I like the little fair haired one."

I couldn't believe my ears. I put down the tray and sat next to him.

"Or this dark one. He's taking it well. Probably been had a good many times before the picture was taken I guess."

"Are you....?" I stammered.

"I thought you'd guessed."

"No. I never dreamed."

"I always thought you were. All that stuff you teach them about Shakespeare's boy actors. The kids don't realize of course. They think you're a brilliant teacher."

I stammered out something about not being half as good as he was and we spent the next hour pleasurably discussing the photographs in the book, wondering where the building was, postulating that the rich owner had probably taken the photographs and wondering where and how he had recruited the patrol.

Then the notes started. Gordon to me. Me to Gordon....

"You're the math expert. How long do you think this one is? PG."

"Smaller than you might think. He's in the gym club. I've seen him in the showers. GB."

"Well, how big? Mathematicians are supposed to be precise! PG."

"5.654 inches by 0.89 of an inch, or thereabouts. GB"

"Are you sure? PG."

"Mathematicians don't make mistakes. Now can I get on with my lesson? GB"

...And then came the Sunday evening phone calls. Every Sunday evening, one of the channels–I don't remember which –did a program of hymn singing by famous church choirs. We'd sit in our respective apartments–two miles apart–with telephones clamped to our ears.

"How about that one fourth from the left? The one with the curls. I'll bet there's a nice ass under that cassock."

"Not keen. A bit too young. How about that tenor in the middle row on the left?"

Every call lasted a full half hour. I'd call him one week and he'd call me the next. Life had suddenly become fun. I found myself singing in the car on the way to school, looking forward to the first of the Barker missives and wondering which trusting youth would deliver it.

We went on like that for a little over a year. The new entrants to our classes must have wondered when we would actually start teaching them instead of using them as messengers. I stayed in school late one Tuesday evening for no other reason save that I wanted to bring my records up to date and put some new posters on the classroom walls. Gordon, seeing the light on, came in.

"Well," he said, "I don't know. I really don't know."

"About romantic poets ... or something else?" I asked, tacking up the portrait of Shelley.

"Romantic boys more like it," he said. He went on to explain that twin brothers, named Henry and Paul Munro, had joined his gym club. Neither was a student at the school.

"Well, either Henry's got the hots for me or there's something wrong with him," he said. "He's been grinning at me all evening, rubbing his crotch, winking. The lot. He even asked if I was going to take a shower!"

"Sounds a bit dodgy to me," I said. "I'd be careful if I were you."

"Oh, I will be. Don't you worry!"

But I *did* worry. Soon Gordon was talking of nothing else other than Henry Munro. What a fine build he had! What a nice kid he was...!

"And you should see his *cock*!" he said one evening. "*Absolutely* beautiful! I went into the showers with him."

"Is that wise?" I asked.

"Oh it was alright. There was no hot water in the staff showers."

"And how old is this paragon?"

"Sixteen. He'll be seventeen in July. They both will. Honestly, Peter, he's absolutely gorgeous!"

Weeks passed. I had the janitor look at the staff showers. The thermostat was working perfectly. I began to get worried.

Then, late one Tuesday evening, Gordon called from a bar in midtown. Could I come at once? There was something he wished to tell me.

Fearing the worst, I drove out there and found Gordon, not as expected, staring at the floor contemplating a prison sentence, but smiling broadly. He bought me a drink.

"Success," he said, raising his glass.

"To success," I repeated.

"Not 'to'. 'After'. I've done it."

"Done what?"

"Had it."

"You are not wont to be so vague," I said. "Had what for God's sake? Too much by the look of you."

"You can never have too much of what I've had," he said. He lowered his voice. "Henry Munro," he whispered.

"You haven't!"

"I have. I've had that lovely cock in my mouth. I've drunk his spunk. God! What a boy! And he loved it. He really loved it and very soon I'm going to fuck his ass."

I honestly didn't want to hear any more. Talk about thin ice. This guy was in real danger. Sixteen-year-olds are legal in our state–but not to their teachers and gym instructors!

He carried on despite my protests. I heard about every move from the time he blew the final whistle to the time he blew Henry. Nothing was left out. I even had a graphic description of the boy's shorts coming down.

"And next week it'll be the same," he said. "That's what I wanted to talk to you about."

"Me? What's it got to do with me?"

"It's the brother, Paul," he explained. "Up to now, you see, I've driven them home together after a meeting. As it happened, Paul wasn't there tonight but he will be next week. I thought, if you were to come into the school, I could send Paul down to you to wait. Don't want him near the gym for obvious reasons."

"To hell with that," I retorted. "I only come to school in the evening when I absolutely have to. You know that."

"How about if Paul comes to your apartment? It's within walking distance. That would be better. I can pick him up when we've finished."

Only a few days earlier, Dr. Roberts had warned the entire staff about inviting students to their homes. Apparently the editor of the school newspaper, a nice enough guy who taught sociology, was in the habit of inviting his "journalists" round on Sundays to discuss the news aspect of the forthcoming week.

"No way!" I said. He bought me another drink. Then another. I was far from being in a rational state of mind when I agreed to his proposal for that coming Tuesday only. Definitely not more. After Tuesday, he'd have to think of something else.

- - -

The doorbell rang at eight-thirty-five precisely. I'd gone through the apartment with a fine-tooth comb. Every cushion had been turned over, certain drawers locked. I'd even taken down the photo of my twelve-year-old nephew and replaced it with a shot of his sister.

"You must be Paul Munro," I said, opening the door.

"Yes."

He was not a beautiful boy by any means. I couldn't imagine sending him on his way to Gordon with a note. He had an open, friendly sort of face, curly hair, brown eyes. The sort of kid anyone would look at twice but not three times. He wore an old coat, jeans and trainers. I invited him in. He hung up his coat in the hall. I offered him a Coke which he refused and we settled down together to watch television.

Nine o'clock came. Then nine thirty. He looked at his watch.

"Henry and Mr. Barker are taking their time over it," he said.

"Probably some new exercise or they're talking," I said.

"No. Mr. Barker's giving him a blowjob."

"Rubbish! That's a terrible thing to say."

"True though. Henry tells me everything. He did it last week when I wasn't there. Henry says he's good at it, the lucky sod."

"Who? Henry or Mr. Barker?"

"Henry of course. He's never had sex with a man before but he said it's great."

I said something about his brother letting his imagination run away with him.

"Not Henry," he said. "Trust him to score first. We had a bet."

"What sort of bet?"

"As to who would find a man to do it first. We both wanted to try it. Girls are boring."

He grinned and spread his long legs out in front of him. "You don't know anybody, I suppose?" he asked. "I'm not keen on the idea of hanging around outside the bus station."

"Certainly not," I said. I tried to look at his face but found my gaze diverted lower down. He had quite a considerable packet between his legs.

And then the doorbell rang. "That's them," I said. "Let me get your coat." I helped him put it on and gave him a playful tap on the backside. Not a thing I'm accustomed to doing, and I felt guilty. He grinned. I opened the door and saw at once why Gordon had become so besotted. Henry was startlingly beautiful. You could see that they were twins. They had the same laughing eyes and snub noses but Henry was taller and somehow more graceful looking. Gordon, standing behind him, winked and made a thumbs up gesture. Paul said something about waiting too long. I stood, thinking, in the open doorway and watched the car speed away.

I didn't remind Gordon that we'd agreed on one Tuesday only. In fact I said something on Monday about seeing him the following day when he came to collect Paul, who arrived again at exactly eight-thirty-five. This time he accepted a Coke. I was watching a film on television.

"He's gay," said Paul as the actor concerned threw a table across the saloon.

"So what?" I replied.

"Oh, you're not homophobic then?"

"Certainly not. It doesn't stop him from being a bloody good actor."

"Or Mr. Barker from being a bloody good gym instructor," he said.

"Let's leave Mr. Barker and your brother's fantasies out of it, shall we?" I replied. For a moment or two he said nothing and appeared to be watching the film.

"Mr. Barker's taking Henry to some hotel for the weekend soon," he said at length. My heart sank. I hadn't thought that Gordon could be such an idiot.

"What for?"

"To fuck him up the ass. He reckons Henry's got a beautiful ass. He told him so and he said Henry's cock is the thickest he's ever seen. That's crap. Mine is thicker. We measured."

"Mr. Barker is a mathematician," I said, laughing. "Maybe you didn't read the rule properly."

"We did too. Mine's an inch and an eighth. His is an inch and a sixteenth."

"An inch and an eighth?" I said. I was beginning to lose interest in the California gold rush.

"Sure. You got a rule in the place? I can prove it."

Have you ever done something and known, as you did it, that you were being incredibly stupid? That's how I felt as I went into the study and rummaged through the drawers of my desk to find a pair of external calipers and a rule. I knew I had them. Just couldn't remember where they were.

123

English Literature teachers don't have much call for such things. Finally, I located them under a pile of old exam papers in the bottom drawer. I went back into the lounge.

"A dollar you're wrong." I said.

"I'm not wrong. Better get it up first." Without batting an eyelid-in fact he kept both eyes on the screen-he unzipped his fly, groped inside and brought out a remarkably long but totally flaccid cock. Still watching the television, he began to slide the foreskin up and down. I couldn't help watching as the purple head came into view and vanished again. It began to twitch upwards. So, under my pants, did mine.

"Better if someone else does it," he said. "Henry does it for me usually."

"Would you like me to?"

"Sure. It'd be quicker and better. Hold on. Let's get these right down."

He stood up. His jeans and shorts slid down to his ankles.

I don't think I shall ever forget that moment. Just the sight of his long legs, honey-colored lower down and startlingly white at the top, was enough to get my heart racing. My cock strained against my pants. He sat down again and held his shirt up. His balls were huge. I remember wondering if Henry's bush was the same as Paul's. If it was, perhaps it was that which my mathematical friend found so attractive. Paul's was a perfect inverted triangle, so straight at the top that it could have been shaved.

"Go ahead," he said. I reached over and touched his cock. It felt warm and slightly rubbery. I could feel his pulse. I exposed the head again, covered it, and brought it back into view.

"Gee, that feels good!" he said. "Go a bit faster." I did.

"Oh yeah! That's so good." Slowly, inexorably, it rose, hardening in my hand until it felt first like a vulcanized rubber truncheon and then like a piece of teak. The head was fully exposed and gleamed slightly in the reflected light from the television screen.

"Time for measuring," I said. It was pointing to the ceiling.

"You'll find I was right," he said. He was. Exactly an inch and an eighth in diameter in the middle of the shaft and six and a quarter inches long measured from his balls.

"That's a dollar I owe you," I said.

"Forget it. I don't do things for money. You goin' to carry on where you left off?"

"Do you really want me to?"

"Sure."

So I did. The California gold rush continued without us. He was panting. I suspect that I was too.

"Oh! That's so good. Oh yeah! Yeah! Not long now...."

I reached into my pocket for a handkerchief. "Oh yeah! Yeah! Yeah! Coming...! Coming! Now!"

There wasn't time to bring out the handkerchief. I just plunged my head downwards and took it into my mouth. He thrust upwards and I choked.

Semen splattered over the sofa but not before I got most of it. My mouth filled. I felt it running behind my teeth and under my tongue; warm and very slightly sour. I swallowed.

"So you are," he said with a smile. "I knew I was right."

"Just keep quiet about it," I said. "I've got a career and a reputation to consider."

He didn't. We had a very enjoyable repeat performance on the following Tuesday evening and, on the next day I received one of those familiar brown envelopes.

"I hear from Henry that you drank from the fountain of youth last week and last night. Good for you! Have a beer on me tonight to celebrate. Was it nice? -GB. P.S.: This one is rather pretty don't you think?"

"My compliments to Mr. Barker. I accept gladly and tell him it was very nice indeed," I said. "Oh! And tell him that I agree with his sentiments," I added. There was no time to sit and write a note. I had a particularly unruly class at that moment.

"So," said Gordon that evening as we sat in the bar. "Looks like we've both struck lucky."

I said I was worried about them talking to each other.

"Inevitable with twins. Nothing to worry about," he said.

We spent a very enjoyable hour or so, talking about the boys in low voices.

"What's a sixteenth of an inch between friends and between brothers?" he said at one point. "I'll tell you what. I've never known a boy enjoy an orgasm like Henry. He wriggles around on those judo mats like an eel out of water. Bloody marvelous. I can't wait to get him into bed and screw him."

"Paul said something about that," I replied. "A hotel or something?"

"Sure. As soon as he gets permission from home I'm going to make the reservations. Nice little place on the coast. My folks used to take me on holiday there when I was a kid. There won't be any tourists there at this time of year."

"What we could do," I said, "is go together. You with Henry and me with Paul. I could do with a break."

"And a nice little virgin ass," said Gordon. "Why not? Could be fun."

Again, that strange feeling of exhilarated fright swept over me. I felt like a kid stepping into a roller coaster car for the first time.

Paul was thrilled. Predictably, Henry had told him at the gym club that he and I were going too. He talked about it from the moment he stepped through the door.

"We can do much more in the hotel," he said later.

"We've not done too badly tonight," I said. I was kneeling on the floor between his thighs, wiping the odd splashes off the soft white skin.

"You goin' to have my ass?" he said. He might have been reading my thoughts. I could actually see his asshole from that position; a tiny little pink orifice hiding shyly behind his scrotum.

"We'll see," I said.

"Mr. Barker's going to fuck Henry. He gets a finger in his ass every week. Says it'll be real good once Henry gets used to it."

Not wanting to be left behind, I got some lube the next day and on the following Tuesday evening, Paul, completely naked for the first time ("Don't want to make a mess on your clothes.") lay with his legs over the arm of the sofa whilst I wormed a well-greased finger into him. He yelled at first but then, as he got used to it, he quieted down. His cock was stiffer than it had ever been.

"Oh! Ah! Oh! Ah!" he groaned. A drop of pre cum appeared.

"That's probably enough for now," I said, withdrawing about three inches of finger." Looks like you're about ready."

He was too. He'd never shot so violently as he did that night. Spurt after spurt filled my mouth. I couldn't swallow it fast enough, which accounts for the long stain on the side of the sofa, which my nephew remarks upon whenever he visits me.

It was whilst I was attempting to wipe it away that Paul dropped his bombshell. "We shall all be in the same room, won't we?" he said.

"I shouldn't think so. Gordon and Henry will be in one room and you and I in another."

"Oh no. We must be together. We're twins, see?"

I pointed out that, at that moment, Henry was having his ass exercised about a mile away.

"That's different," he said firmly. "In the hotel we must be together."

Apparently Henry had made the same stipulation. Gordon sent me a note to that effect on the following morning.

"It's a damned nuisance," I said.

"Oh, I don't know," said Gordon. "Could be rather fun. Look better too."

"How so?"

"I can book a double room for them and a twin-bedded room for us. They're going to need some sleep after all."

We've laughed a lot about that remark since then. Perhaps they slept during the morning. I don't know. The action started on the afternoon of our arrival. I was pretty tired after the journey. Gordon's car is comfortable enough but there isn't a great deal of room on the back seat. For almost the entire journey, Paul had been caressing my cock through my pants and whispering encouraging promises. The same thing was happening in front. I wonder we didn't have an accident.

That afternoon, I lay naked on my bed, hugging Paul and nibbling his ears. The towel beneath us was horribly damp and uncomfortable but we were both too exhausted to do anything about it. Gordon's voice came from the next bed.

"Ready for another one?"

"Sure. Go in a bit more slowly this time."

Both boys had cried out pretty loudly the first time. I was about to pull out but Gordon, obviously more experienced than I was, had no such intention.

"Just relax," I heard him say. "That's right. Oh, that feels good. A bit more."

He might have been talking to them both. Paul's ass loosened up against my thrusting cock. They yelled simultaneously as we drove in. That, somehow, made it more exciting. Henry's gasps merged with Paul's. I'd watched Gordon undress Henry out of the corner of my eye as I did the same to Paul. Henry was beautiful. His legs were longer than Paul's and more suntanned. I was wrong about his pubic hair. It was denser and darker than Paul's and extended upwards towards his navel. Paul, I thought, had the nicer butt. It was slightly narrower, a bit more jutting and, although there was no way of telling from that distance, I guessed it to be softer. It certainly felt so.

He pretty soon learned to use it too. The first time was a bit difficult. For both of them I suspect. I heard Gordon whispering to Henry. "Put your legs on my shoulders. That's right. Oh, yes. That's lookin' good. No, no; take your hands away. I'll do that."

The second time was better than the first. Paul actually grinned as another load of my spunk was discharged deep inside him. Almost immediately afterwards successive jets from his cock splattered onto my face and chest.

That was the afternoon. God knows how many times we did it that night. I know I was too tired to go down for breakfast. Gordon brought me up a cup of coffee.

"Change of partners tonight if it's okay with you," he said when I was sufficiently awake to follow what he was saying.

"Sure. If the boys don't mind."

"We discussed it over breakfast. They think it's a good idea."

It was, I thought that night, a very good idea. Paul's soft groans and Gordon's grunts came to us through the darkness, apparently turning Henry on much more effectively than I was doing. Gordon had been right about Henry. From the moment my cock was in him, he wriggled and squirmed like a worm on a hook. Muscles deep inside him gripped my cock, sucking it deeper and deeper into him.

He came with a triumphant cry as if he had won a race. I suppose he had. The next bed was creaking loudly and his brother was panting as if he was still running to catch up.

And so the weekend continued. Paul. Henry. Paul again. Henry. Paul. How Gordon managed to keep awake on the journey home I shall never know. The boys and I slept for most of the time.

We delivered them at their house, helped them to the steps with their bags and drove away.

"That was quite a weekend!" exclaimed Gordon.

Sleepily, I agreed.

He said it again in the bar a few days later. "Quite a weekend! Who do you think was better?"

I wasn't really concentrating. Sitting at the bar was the most beautiful young man I had seen for years. He was with an older man. Gordon, who had his back to them, was oblivious to their presence and I couldn't really tell him to look round for fear they might notice.

"I still favor Henry," Gordon was saying. "His ass is tighter."

The man at the bar put a hand on the boy's thigh. The boy didn't react. I was dying to let Gordon know. Then the man stood up and walked over to our table. I guessed he'd seen me staring. I wondered what excuse to make. The odd-shaped bottle on the shelf behind the bar maybe?

"Pardon me," he said. "Aren't you the two guys who are screwing the Munro twins?"

I think we both went white. I certainly did. Neither of us said a thing.

"I recognized the car outside," he said. "How did they perform?"

"Perform? How do you mean?" said Gordon. I was still dumbstruck.

"In bed of course. There's not a lot between them as far as cock size is concerned, but, really, Henry's got the nicer ass. In my opinion anyway."

It didn't seem possible but I had to ask. "You know them pretty intimately, obviously."

"I guess you could say that. You both had them, I understand. I'd like to have been there to see it. Nothing like the sight of a boy having his ass filled for the first time, eh?"

Neither Gordon nor I said a word. We just sat staring at our glasses. I wanted the floor to open up so I could drop right out of the world.

"Oh, there's no need to clam up," he said. "They told me all about it."

I was furious. So much for Gordon's assurances and knowledge of the psychology of twins. The Munro boys were obviously just a couple of big-mouthed whores.

"So, how long have you known 'em?" I asked.

"Since they were five."

"Five!" Appalled, Gordon and I both spoke together.

"Sure. I'm their *stepfather*!"

THE LAST TABOO by Jesse Monteagudo

I was born in Havana and came over to the States during the Mariel Boatlift of 1980, when I was only three. My first memory was being on a crowded boat ride from Mariel Harbor to Miami, with my Uncle Rey and other men who were just like him. All those men had spent time in Cuban prisons for "improper conduct" (homosexual behavior). Forced to open Mariel for the Boatlift, Fidel Castro used it to rid Cuba of "undesirables"- criminals and gay men. (In later years, Uncle Rey and the other men from the boat were to die of AIDS, but that is another story.)

Mom and Dad took me to Mariel Harbor to say goodbye to Uncle Rey and then, at the last minute, handed me over to him to take to Miami. Like many Cuban parents, they probably expected me to lead a better life in the U.S. than in Cuba, and for that I am grateful. Still, it was hard for a three-year- old boy to be sent away by his parents on a boat full of strange men; and that experience made me a loner for the rest of my life.

When I got to Miami I was placed in a foster home since Uncle Rey, besides being a *maricon*, was also a hopeless drug addict. My foster parents, Ernesto and Maria Ochoa, were a strict evangelical couple, who disciplined me, sent me to school and to church, and made sure that I stayed within the law. But there was never any love between us, so when I turned eighteen and graduated from Miami High School, the first thing I did was walk away from home, never to return.

Since then I've lived a lifetime in four short years: buried my Uncle Rey, served in the U.S. Army, and traveled the country with many jobs and many women. When I came back to Miami last month with my girlfriend, Olga, I was 22 years old and had tried almost every experience at least once. My year in the Army built me up; and I kept my build with workouts at the gym, running and playing soccer. But one thing I could not do was keep a steady job. The first thing I did after Olga and I settled down in an efficiency apartment off *Calle Ocho* was to get a job as a bagboy in Mora's Market. The second thing I did was get fired. Olga was pissed.

"I can't believe it! How could you be so stupid to lose your job after only a week?"

"Don't get on my case! Things like that happen all the time!"

"My ass! You lost your temper and hit the boss with a forty-pound bag of rice!"

"Well, Jimmy Mora had it coming to him! All he did was follow me around all day long, like a lost puppy, trying to get into my pants! I could tell the dude was queer for me from the moment he hired me!"

"Well, you could have humored him."

"It's so easy for *you* to say! You weren't the one he was panting after all day. Finally I just got fed up and said, 'Listen, faggot! You might get to

fuck with all the other bagboys but you're not going to fuck with me!' And that's when I hit him with the rice bag!"

"You're so macho!"

"I've had no complaints," I smiled. "Or would you rather I'd let Jimmy Mora suck my dick?"

"To be honest, I couldn't care less," she turned. "As far as I am concerned, you can let Jimmy Mora suck your dick every day. 'Cause I am not going to be here to do it for you!" To my surprise, Olga grabbed a suitcase and began to pack her clothes in it.

I was floored. "*Olguita*, what do you think you're doing?"

"I am going back to California! If I'm going to be with a jerk, I might as well get one closer to home." The next thing I knew Olga was out the door with her suitcase, leaving me without a girlfriend as well as without a job. Not wanting be without a home, I decided to swallow my pride and ask for my job back. Hell, I'd let Jimmy swing on my dick any time, if he'd only hire me.

I ran from my apartment to Mora's Market, only to find that my old job was already filled by a winsome nineteen-year old Colombian named Charly. Jimmy took one look at Charly's tight jeans, then at me, and decided that Charly was a better prospect. Still, I must have looked hungry or desperate, since Jimmy didn't let me go without some advice: "You look like you might be able to find work as a model. I know a guy who runs a model agency that I am sure could get you a job," he grinned. "That is, if you don't mind posing without clothes."

Posing without clothes. Leave it to a fag to come up with an idea like that. But, hell, I'd do anything for cash, even pose buck naked! No sooner did I get out of Mora's Market that I jogged a few blocks up *Calle Ocho*, to the model agency that Jimmy Mora recommended. There in a sleazy office sat a sleazy agent, Xavier Diaz-Ximenez, a disgustingly fat man who wasted no time trying to put his greasy paws all over me. After I pushed him away, I asked him point blank if he could get me a job.

"I think I can. Have you ever heard of Christian Borges?"

"No."

"He's the hottest director of gay adult videos. He specializes in hot Latin boys like you." I was flabbergasted. *Me* in a gay fuck video? Well, I've done worse things before. And I needed the money. "Tell me more."

Xavier Diaz-Ximenez spent the next half-hour telling me about the gay porn industry in general, and Christian Borges in particular. To make a long story short, the dude was just thirty years old and, like me, was born in Havana. He made a name for himself a couple of years ago with *Cruisin' Calle Ocho*, a video about randy boys in Miami. He's since made such classics as *Los Hermanos Pinzones*, about two brothers who sailed with Columbus, and the Mexican western *Max and Juarez* (Chi Chi LaRue had a cameo as the Empress Carlota). Borges's "performers" were young Latin muscleboys, mostly straight, who moaned and groaned a lot and sometimes

came without touching themselves. I was a young Latin muscleboy, certainly straight, and I could moan and groan with the best of them. I decided to do it. "When can I start?"

"Right away. It so happens that Christian is in Miami right now, taping his latest video." After I gave Xavier my vital statistics–and I was doing my best to keep his hands off of them–he picked up the phone and dialed a number out of his card file. A brief talk over the phone and I was ready to go.

"Christian wants you to come over right now. He's taping at the Club Miami, over on Coral Way. Here's the address." Not having bus or cab fare, I decided to jog the couple of miles to the Club Miami, down 27th Avenue and up Coral Way. It being a hot summer day, I was drenched in sweat by the time I got there.

"I am Victor Navarro," I told the bathhouse attendant, a swishy Cuban boy who wore too much eye makeup. "Mr. Borges is waiting for me." I must have looked sincere or desperate, for the queen didn't bother to ask me for a Club membership. Instead, he just let me in, pointing down the hall at the gym.

I followed the hall to the end, past the Club's sauna and shower area, and into the gym. There I found Christian Borges in the flesh, surrounded by his equipment, assistant, technicians, cameraman, and two swarthy young 'performers' who were quite naked and apparently disgusted with the whole thing. I held out my hand and introduced myself.

"Mr. Borges, I am Victor Navarro. Mr. Diaz-Ximenez sent me over to see you." I expected Christian Borges to be fat. Or ugly. Or fat *and* ugly. Instead, the director was handsome and muscular, with bleached blond hair that looked good on him. He sat on a director's chair behind the camera, and looked very comfortable. As for me, I was hot and sweaty, and very nervous. Borges noticed my discomfort and laughed. "Relax! We're among friends here!"

I managed to work up a smile. "Thanks. It's just that this is my first time doing videos."

"There's nothing to it. In fact, I used to be a "performer" myself, before I became a photographer and then a director. The money is better and I don't have to take my clothes off anymore."

Everyone laughed, which put me at ease. But Christian meant business. As he looked me up and down, he motioned for me to get closer to him, which I did. "You're a good lookin' dude," he said. "You certainly have potential. But tell me a little about yourself," he added. "How old are you?"

"Twenty-two."

"And have you ever had sex with another man?"

"I fooled around with a couple of guys in the Army. And I let a couple of dudes blow me, back when I needed the money. But I'm straight."

"So are most of the boys who work for me. Do you think you can perform?"

"You mean get a hard on?"

"Yes."

"I guess so."

"Good. Now take your clothes off. I want to look at you."

Though I hadn't expected to get naked so soon, I figured I would have to do it sooner or later, so I did. Fortunately, my jog up and down *Calle Ocho* and to the Club Miami had worked me up a bit so I was in pretty good shape. As my clothes dropped to the floor, Christian got up to take a closer look at me.

"Not bad! Not bad at all! Xavier was right, you have quite a body." As Christian talked, he reached over to feel my pecs. "You have a nice, smooth chest and tight abs, just what our viewers like. And you have a good tan," he added, as he moved his hands down my torso towards my crotch. "Your cock is nice and thick, too, and uncut," he added, as he grabbed my plump *pinga*. "The men who buy or rent our videos expect our boys to have foreskins," he added, while pulling mine back to expose my cockhead.

"I guess," I muttered. I was getting nervous. Not only was I stark naked in a room full of other men, but my *pinga* was taking on a life of its own, rising to its full eight inches under Christian's expert touch. As the director stroked my cock with one hand, he began to pull my low-hanging balls with the other. It was all I could do to keep from losing control.

"How did you get your body in such good shape?," asked Christian, as he continued to work my cock and balls. "You must have done something with it."

"Well, my years in the Army built me up. And I've been working out as much as I can. And I play soccer...." Meanwhile Christian was driving me nuts as he continued to play with my genitals, like meat in a supermarket. I began to feel dizzy, and I would have fallen if not for Christian's assistant, who brought a chair for me to sit down on before I hit the ground. Christian released me and tried to put me at ease.

"Don't worry, Victor. Performing in a video can be a trying experience the first time around. But you'll do just fine. In fact, I think we can use your experience as a soccer player in the video." Again he waved at his assistant, who brought me a cold glass of lemonade. "But first we need to give you a name."

"I like my name just fine."

Christian smiled. "But performers never use their own names! We have to give you one." He thought for a while before he looked up. "I know! Latin stars with first names only are very popular right now. We'll just call you ... Victor!" The assistant clapped, which I guess assistants do when their bosses come up with a smart idea. And it wasn't a bad idea. At least I could keep my name.

"Victor, you're made for porn! You're handsome, you have a nice, muscular body, round buns, a thick, uncut cock and low-hanging balls. And

I bet you're a bottom, too!" he giggled. "In fact, I predict that you will be a star in no time!"

"Thanks, but I'm no bottom! And I am not much of an actor."

"Nobody in porn is an actor. All you have to do is learn a few lines and do what feels good to you." I wondered what Olga would say, if she knew that her old boyfriend was working in a fag video. But a boy's gotta eat, and this seemed to be the best chance I had to do it.

"When do I start?"

"Right away. I just finished the scene with Arnoldo and Ronaldo," he said, glancing at the two boys who were now giving me lethal looks. "In fact, Arnoldo and Ronaldo were just leaving." Taking the hint, Arnoldo and Ronaldo walked out. I was alone and naked, with Christian, his assistant, technicians and cameraman. As I stood up, I thought of following Arnoldo and Ronaldo into oblivion, only to be stopped by Borges's assistant, who had a contract in hand.

"This is the standard performer's contract," said Christian, handing me a pen. "You get a set fee for each performance, and you give us the right to use your face and body to advertise the video. In turn you can use your experiences to sell your services. In fact, I could help you if you want to do so."

I turned down his pimping services. "When do I get paid?"

"My, are we impatient. Well, you get paid as soon as we finish taping. Is that soon enough?" I reckoned it was, so I took a deep breath and signed my body away. Victor Navarro, straight Cuban boy, was now Victor, gay for pay. Though I wasn't pleased with it, there was no turning back.

"Carlos, take Victor over to the showers," said Christian, as he put the contract away. "Wash the sweat and the dirt off him and make him up for the next scene. I'll see if Manuel is ready." The next thing I knew Carlos was pushing me down the hall and holding me under a steaming shower, washing the dirt and the sweat off of me. He then sat me in front of a makeup mirror as the makeup queen-the same one who worked the door at the club-did his magic on me, going so far as to cover up a birthmark on my face. (I though it was a nice birthmark, too. It made me look like Enrique Iglesias.) Before long I was back in the gym, where Christian was waiting for me, this time accompanied by a muscular *mulato* who was dressed in a soccer outfit.

"Victor, this is Manuel. He's the star of *Cruisin' Calle Ocho* and of our new video, *The Cup of Lust*." We shook hands. "And this is our newest discovery, Victor."

"Christian told me that I was gonna perform with a hot Cuban," said Manuel, as he shook my hand. "He wasn't joking." Manuel, as in turned out, was Christian's top performer. Just my age, he was born in San Juan, Puerto Rico, where he learned at an early age to use his body to get what he wanted. Though Manuel was just my height, five and a half feet, he was strikingly handsome and incredibly muscular, with a body that put mine to

shame. But what made Manuel stand out in the crowd was his monster cock: ten dark, thick, uncut inches of mouth-waterin' *pinga*. It was a cock that made itself noticed even when it was covered by a jock strap and shorts, and I could not help staring at it. Manuel noticed me noticing: "I hear that this is your first time."

"It is," I said. "I am straight." Christian and Carlos rolled their eyes, but Manuel laughed.

"That's okay. I am straight, too. In fact, my wife often comes to see me work." The thought of Manuel's wife watching me and her husband fuck didn't sit well with me, and it showed. "But don't worry. She's back in San Juan with her mother," he smiled, as he placed a muscular arm over my shoulder. "I am sure we'll do just fine."

"I am glad you boys are getting along so well," said Christian, "but we gotta work!" Carlos handed me a soccer player's outfit to put on, just like Manuel's but smaller, to fit my size. Now properly dressed, I joined Manuel on the set– actually, the back of the gym–which was made to look like the locker room of a soccer stadium. As Manuel and I stood in front of the lockers, Christian began to direct.

"*The Cup of Lust* takes place during the World Cup soccer tournament. Manuel is Latin America's soccer champ and you are a team rookie who secretly lusts after Manuel but doesn't want him to find out. Manuel didn't care for you at first but he's come to like you," he added. "Just take it from there. And don't worry about the dialogue. We'll take care of it later."

"Is there a script?"

Christian sighed. "Of course there is no script! We make one up as we go along. Now go ahead and do what you would do in such situations."

"I never had such situations."

"You'll think of something," he paused. "But I'll give you a hint. Your team just won a crucial game, thanks to your last-minute goal. All the other players have gone out to celebrate, leaving you alone in the locker room with the man you wanted to fuck for months. Do I have to spell it for you?"

"Don't worry, Christian," said Manuel. "I know what to do. Just roll the cameras." I could tell Manuel had done this before. Satisfied, Christian Borges moved himself back behind the camera, sat in his director's chair, and waved at the cameraman.

"Roll 'em!" I was about to say something stupid and ruin the take when Manuel turned me around to face him.

"You were great, Victor," he said, as he smothered me in a warm *abrazo*. "I didn't think you had it in you but I was wrong! You kicked the winning goal!"

I said the first thing that came to mind. "Oh, it was nothing, Manuel. I only did what I knew *you* would do. You are my hero!" Not exactly Academy Award material but I think it did the job.

"Well, your 'hero' has something for you." Taking my right hand, Manuel put it over his already-stiff dick. Though I instinctively pulled my hand

away from his crotch, Manuel put it back where it belonged. As he held my hand in place, Manuel pinched my right nipple with his left hand, sending an electric-erotic charge throughout my body.

"I've seen you look at my basket in the locker room, Victor. I know you've been queer for my cock and balls from the moment we met. Well, now you're gonna get them." Without saying another word, Manuel reached over and kissed my lips. Our moustaches brushed against each other as our lips locked and our tongues explored each other's hungry mouth. I had never kissed a man before and the effect was riveting.

"Now strip!," directed Christian, from behind the camera.

We took off our outfits. Manuel's cock was more than I had expected. I gasped as I stared at my Puerto Rican partner's perfect manhood, ten inches long and half as thick. Manuel's sausage was dark and strong and covered with a thick brown foreskin, while his massive balls hung low like two juicy brown plums. Though I've seen many pricks in my time, in the Army and elsewhere, Manuel's sausage put them all to shame.

"You like my *pinga*, don't you, boy," growled Manuel, as he tweaked my tits. "Now work on it!"

"Suck his cock!," ordered Christian.

I hesitated. "What if someone walks in?," I ad-libbed.

"Don't worry," replied Manuel. "The other guys are gone. It's just you and me." Firmly in control, Manuel's muscular hands pushed me to my knees. Though this was not the first time I had a dick in my mouth, Manuel's maleness seemed to be more than I could handle. I tried to pull back, but Manuel would have none of it. "Suck my dick, boy," he ordered. "*Mamame la pinga!*"

Manuel's word was my command. As I reached for my video lover's cock I took in his strong, masculine odor, the smell of a natural man. Encouraged by the odor, I took hold of Manuel's prick, pulling back the thick foreskin to lick the massive brown head beneath. Manuel groaned with pleasure as my tongue licked his cockhead, moved down the sides of his thick shaft and played with the sensitive spot where his cock meets his balls. I then took Manuel's balls into my mouth, working each sensitive egg the way I knew he would enjoy.

Having worked around the surface of his cock and balls, I took Manuel's ramrod deep inside my mouth and down my burning throat. Manuel groaned with pleasure, holding my head firmly in place as I continued to deep-throat him. My own eight-inch *pinga* remained hard, though I never touched it. Christian and his assistants remained silent as they watched a video hound's hottest fantasy: two young Latin muscle dudes taking pleasure from each other's hard bodies and thick, uncut cocks.

"Now suck *his* cock," Christian told Manuel.

"Get up, boy," Manuel ordered. As I stood upright, Manuel dropped to his knees, taking my cock in his hand and pushing the loose foreskin back to reveal my cockhead. I almost lost my balance as Manuel took my dick in his

mouth and began to suck. I leaned back against a locker and surrendered myself to Manuel's expert blowjob.

"*Mamame la pinga, Papi*," I begged. "Suck my dick." Manuel didn't have to be told. An experienced cocksucker, Manuel ran his tongue up and down my shaft, drenching it in saliva before taking it in his mouth. I groaned as my peter was enveloped in the warmth of my lover's mouth, who pleasured me the way no woman could ever do. Only a man knows what a man wants, and only a man can give a man the pleasure that he needs.

"Now eat his ass."

"Turn around, boy," Manuel ordered. I wasn't ready for this turn of events, and was about to bolt when I was pushed against the locker by my impatient lover. Manuel wasted no time taking control of my tight, virgin ass, spreading my legs and cheeks apart to eat my tender hole. Never before had I experienced a man's tongue in my rectum, and I enjoyed every minute of it. As I surrendered to Manuel's oral love, I spread my legs farther apart, exposing my asshole to whatever I had coming to me.

After he got my asshole wet with his tongue, Manuel then inserted a couple of fingers deep inside my virgin hole, massaging my prostate and readying my ass for what I now realized would soon follow. Again I tried to say something, to resist, only to be shut up by Manuel's command.

"*Yo quiero ese culo, Papi*," purred Manuel, as he stood up behind me. "I want that ass, boy! I heard Cuban boys like to get fucked in the ass. Well, I want to fuck that hot Cuban ass!"

Since getting my ass fucked was not in my contract, I wanted out, but Manuel would have none of it. While keeping my hole wide open with his fingers, Manuel put on a lubricated condom that Carlos tossed him. I yelled with pain as Manuel inserted his ten-inch *pinga* into my virgin *culo*. There's no way I could get that monster up my ass!

"Relax, Victor, and bend over" Manuel whispered in my ear. "It'll make it easier for you." To my surprise, it did. As I relaxed and bent over my rectum loosened up, letting Manuel's ten-incher go in deeper inside me. Before I knew it, Manuel's prick was buried inside my manhole, and the pain was gone. Pain turned to pleasure as Manuel's cock moved in and out of my ass, rubbing against my tender gland and fulfilling a need I hadn't known I had.

"Fuck me, Manuel!," I cried, as I surrendered myself to his dominating fuck. *Chingame el culo!* I didn't care what anybody thought. I was out of control, possessed by a Puerto Rican muscle god who was giving me the pleasure that only a dude can give another dude. As my lover continued to plow into my tender man-pussy, he pulled me closer to him, kissing me passionately with each violent fuck. I held on to the locker with one hand and furiously beat my meat with the other, keeping pace with Manuel's savage thrusts. Even Christian and his assistants got excited by our wild, uninhibited sex.

"You like that fuck, don't you, boy? You like the way my big Puerto Rican *pinga* plows your hot Cuban *culo*?" I sure did. To be fucked in the ass was a Latin dude's last taboo, his asshole the last thing he would surrender to the power of another man. But I didn't care. For a while we forgot we were on camera. We were just two savage animals indulging in that most uninhibited of acts, man fucking man. Soon the force of Manuel's cock, rubbing against my tender prostate, joined with my frenzied handjob to drive me beyond sanity and past the point of no return.

"I'm coming, Manuel! I'm coming!", I yelled, as I shot a load of cum all over the locker. Instinctively, my asshole pressed hard against my lover's cock, which led to his own violent orgasm. With a grunt, Manuel's pulled his cock out of my rectum, releasing the condom as it shot a full load of semen on my back.

"Cut!" yelled Christian. "Victor, Manuel, you guys were great! Manuel, you were at your peak and you"-meaning me-"really surprised me. Are you sure you were never fucked in the ass before?"

"I am sure," I said, as I looked sheepishly at a beaming Manuel. "But I wouldn't mind being fucked again." I was still straight, and I still liked pussy. But now I also liked to get fucked in the ass, again and again. "Does that make me queer?"

"I don't think so," said Christian. "It only makes you a good performer." We laughed. "I do believe this is the beginning of a great career."

As they say in Hollywood, a star was born.

THE ADVENTURES OF FATHER MICHAEL
by Frank Brooks

...At St. John's Academy

From the Journals of Father Michael X:

8 April 1976: St. John's Academy for Boys seemed to be in the throes of spring fever when I arrived late this afternoon. The gatekeeper, a smiling, shirtless young man, whom I presumed to be one of the students, turned out in actuality to be one of the staff–and a priest, no less. I'll admit that the day was unseasonably warm for early spring–muggy and close to 90 degrees–but still, you expect to see a priest appropriately garbed in black, his Roman collar in place, not naked from the waist up.

"Father Michael," he said, "we were expecting you hours ago. You must have got lost. Everybody gets lost in these hills. We're not easy to find." He introduced himself as Father Thomas–"Just call me Tom"–and gave me directions to Monsignor Roland's office in the main building.

Before driving through the gate, I noticed the sign still posted beside it, apparently a quaint remnant from the days not too many years ago when St. John's Academy was St. John's Monastery for Discalced Friars:

BY PAPAL REGULATION:
FEMALES NOT ALLOWED ON MONASTERY PROPERTY

I was surprised at how seemingly vast the property was, at how far I had to drive, after passing through the gates, along a twisting road through the woods before arriving at a large clearing with its lawns and buildings. As I came out of the trees, the silence burst into a cacophony of shouts and shrieks and laughter. The entire school of 200-some boys appeared engaged in a wild recess or after-school sport. And a bestial lot they appeared when I first saw them. Almost all were barefoot. Few wore shirts. All wore their wind-blown hair girlishly long. To cover their loins, most wore tight, very short gym trunks or threadbare jeans. Sunburned and sweaty as they ran around kicking or throwing balls, tackling each other, swatting each other, and so on, they impressed me as a chaotic herd of wild animals, and I offered a silent, questioning prayer: *Dear God, what have I gotten myself into!*

Could it be that in fleeing the trials and temptations of an inner-city parish I had taken on burdens just as trying, if not worse? My consolation is that my stay at St. John's will be a temporary one. As soon as a staff position

opens at St. Mary's Girl's Academy-less than five miles from St. John's-I am first in line to fill it. It was my understanding, when I requested a transfer, that I would be sent directly to St. Mary's, but complications arose and now I'm here, so I must make the best of it as I await re-assignment to St. Mary's.

As I climbed out of the car, I was hit by a soccer ball, which caused a great deal of tasteless mirth among the boys nearby. The sun-bronzed little beast who retrieved the ball muttered a "Sorry, Father" and ran off before I could say anything to him, leaving behind his sweaty, bestial, adolescent aroma. In fact, the humid breeze seemed ponderous with the earthy scents of sweaty boys and pine pitch, and I tried not to inhale too deeply of this potent miasma.

I paused before entering the main building, distracted by what I thought must be a hallucination. Not far away, sitting on the grass under a tree, two figures were embracing. I was shocked to see a girl on the Academy grounds, and shocked even more to realize that "she" was topless. But "she" had no breasts. In fact, neither of the two embracing figures-not only embracing, but passionately kissing!-had breasts. In fact, neither of these two good-looking, long-haired figures was female. They were both boys! Two boys, "making out" (as youth calls it) like a male-female couple in the throes of a demonic passion, like a pair of animals in heat. The two of them fell over and started rolling on the ground as if they were wrestling, their mouths glued together. My first impulse was to run at them and kick them apart. Instead, getting hold of myself, but shaken by the sight, I fled into the building, intending to report them immediately to Monsignor Roland.

In spite of Father Thomas's directions, I wandered up and down stairways and hallways for what seemed an endless interval as I searched for the monsignor's office. The old stone monastery was a sprawling monstrosity, even larger inside than it appeared from outside. At one point I wandered into a large open room that apparently was one of the dormitories, as there were at least 50 beds lined up in rows. The room was a shambles, with clothing, shoes, books, and whatnot scattered all over the floors and on the unmade beds themselves, and the air reeked of sweaty T-shirts and socks. On one of the beds a boy lay sleeping-a stark-naked youth!-his mouth slack, his legs spread, his large, grass-and-soil-stained soles staring me in the face. I stared in fascination and horror at the over-sized, snakelike erection that lay stirring and pulsing against his lower abdomen, the moist tip of it pecking at his navel. He had to be experiencing a filthy, wicked dream, and I expected to see him ejaculate (i.e. experience a nocturnal emission) at any moment. Turning abruptly, I fled in a shock. St. John's was turning out to be one surprise after another.

I wandered in a stunned daze for a while, hardly knowing where I was or what I was here for, and running into nobody. The hallways were eerily empty. Except for the naked youth dreaming filth in one of the dormitories, the building seemed deserted. Then, in one of the first floor hallways, a door

banged open and through it charged two boys in gym trunks and nothing else, shrieking and laughing. Behind them appeared a third boy, this one without a stitch on, in pursuit of them. I was shocked to see a large, semi-erect phallus swinging and flopping from the naked boy's groin as he ran, shouting: "Give it back, you fuckers! Give it back!"

The two boys in the lead nearly ran smack into me and stopped in their tracks. They looked at me, frowning, as if I were from outer space. Then one of them smirked as he held up a filthy athletic supporter (a jockstrap, as boys call them).

"It's mine!" shouted the naked boy. "Give it back!"

"Give it back," I managed to say in what I hoped was a commanding tone. "Now, if you please!"

"Yes, Father." The young thief threw the supporter at me, hitting me in the face with it. Then, before I could react, he and his thieving companion darted away and were gone.

The supporter was moist, and smelled as if it hadn't been washed in decades. Disgusted, I flung it away and the naked urchin caught it.

"Thank you, Father," he said, blushing, but grinning devilishly in spite of his embarrassment. There was almost a girlishly seductive tone in his voice, and I suspected that he took delight in his obscene nakedness as he stood before me.

"You'd better put that on," I said. "Now, if you please!"

"Yes, Father." Still standing no more than five feet from me, the impish young beast wriggled into his jockstrap and tucked his satyr-sized (and now fully erect) phallus into its meshed pouch, which then resembled a large tent over his groin.

I swallowed, feeling a hot flush spread over my face and torso. My embarrassment was boundless as the boy grinned at me as if pleased to fluster me. "Hadn't you better *finish* dressing," I said as coolly as I was able.

The boy shrugged and went trotting back toward the door through which he'd bolted, his round little bottom rotating in a most unseemly, very feminine manner, his grapefruit-sized buttocks–velvety smooth and white–dimpling with each step. Before he stepped through the door, he threw a glance back at me over his shoulder and hesitated–as if expecting me to say something. I turned on my heels and strode off in the other direction.

To say I was upset and disturbed by what I was encountering at St. John's would be an understatement. It was apparent that despite St. John's reputation as a top-notch private school–a school that scored high academically, a school that produced an inordinately large number of seminarians–it was apparent that St. John's was severely lacking in discipline, to put it mildly. It seemed to be totally lacking in decency as well. I wondered if Monsignor Roland really knew his school, whether he knew what was going on in the rest of the school as he remained (I

imagined) cloistered in his ivory-towered office attending to business matters while the boys he was in charge of ran wild below.

I found the Monsignor's office at last, tucked away in a secluded wing on the third floor, at the end of a long hallway. The building was so quiet-still full with the spirit of the discalced friars who had tiptoed these halls not so many years ago-that I moved silently myself, tiptoeing through an open door into what appeared to be an outer office or reception area. It was deserted. I heard voices and laughter coming from an inner office, and paused to listen.

"I'll make it worth your while, Monsignor," said a young male voice.

"I know you will," said a man's voice, "I have no doubt about that. But I'm afraid that letting you go over there would be like letting a fox into the hen house. You'll end up impregnating all 200 of those future nuns."

"I just wanna see Denise. I'll take her out in the woods."

"I'll bet you will! How's your supply of rubbers?"

"I've got two of 'em in my pocket."

"I wouldn't let you out of here unless you had a dozen of them. Make that six dozen."

"So give me some extras, Monsignor. Come on, Monsignor, I'll make it worth your while! Please, Father Superior, *sir!*" The boy's voice had a cajoling and yet a mocking tone.

"Maybe if I could watch?"

The youth guffawed. "No way!"

"If I could watch, I might be more easily persuaded."

"You're a pervert, Monsignor."

The man laughed. "I just want to make sure you're wearing a rubber when you mount her. The last thing I want is one of *my* boys getting one of *their* girls pregnant."

As I listened to this exchange, I moved in a trance to the inner door and I found myself peering into the Monsignor's office. A husky, bearded priest of about 40 semi-reclined in a plush, leather-upholstered chair behind a large desk. Seated on the desk and facing him was a long-haired blond youth dressed in nothing but tight, threadbare jeans. The youth's large bare feet rested on the man's lap and the man played with them as they talked. From time to time the priest lifted the feet to his mouth and kissed the boy's filthy toes.

"I won't get her pregnant!" the boy said. "C'mon, I'll make it worth your while!" He slid off the desk and onto the priest's lap. His bare arms encircling the man's neck, he rotated his buttocks against the man's lap and squirmed in the man's hairy-armed embrace. "C'm on, Father, give me a pass to get out tonight."

The priest fumbled with his Roman collar as if it were a strangling necktie he needed to loosen. His face had reddened and sweat beaded on his forehead. His hairy hands slid all over the youth's velvet-smooth, tanned torso.

"Please, Monsignor? I'll make it worth your while."

"It's hot in here," the priest said. "I'm afraid I must get more comfortable." He yanked off his Roman collar and tossed it onto his desk.

The boy, grinning, started unbuttoning the priest's shirt. The collarless priest unzipped the boy's pants.

Mechanically, I eased backwards and tiptoed out of the office and down the hallway. Once on the stairs I ran, and as if guided by built-in radar, found my way out of the building and to my car. At the gate a half mile from the main building, a startled Father Thomas let me out when I blew the horn.

"Emergency!" I shouted out the window as I passed him, breathless in my panic. "Have to go back! Have to go back!" Then I drove, blindly.

Hours later, after endless dead ends, I found myself at the gates of St. Mary's Academy for Girls, where I was welcomed with the respect due an ordained priest and was given sanctuary for the night.

9 April 1976: Hellish night! Endless nightmares! Yesterday's traumas at St. John's have polluted the purity and inner peacefulness I had gained during my drive away from the corrupt city into the undefiled countryside. Such dreams! I hardly dare write them down–not that I remember them in enough detail to do so coherently. I won't let myself remember! Let me just say that they were demon-infested dreams–demons in the form of wild, naked youths–youths from St. John's Academy. Horrible! It was from such demons that I fled the Purgatory of my inner-city parish. But now it seems that I've gone from Purgatory to Hell. My nightmares culminated in one of my dreaded nocturnal emissions, one so powerful that I cried out as I awoke. Dear God, I hope nobody heard me!

Later: I have just breakfasted with Father Hillsborough, head of St. Mary's Academy, a dignified, thin-smiling clergyman of impeccable good manners. He shares my misgivings concerning St. John's, which he has visited only once (years ago) and has not returned to in spite of frequent invitations. He finds the lack of discipline there abhorrent. In fact, he finds the laxity in the Church in general these days a travesty. Only disintegration and spiritual decline can come of it, is his opinion, and I'm inclined to agree with him.

I had intended to ask Father Hillsborough to hear my confession, to tell him all, but I lost my nerve. It's no excuse, I know, but I felt that he might be less than understanding were I to lay bare my soul before him. He does, after all, have the final say as to whether I am accepted here at St. Mary's when that position does indeed, once and for all, become available. All I told Father Hillsborough about the reason for my request for a transfer from the inner-city parish was that I had felt that I could better serve the Church in a more monastic setting.

"We are very monastic here," said the priest, sipping his tea. "In fact, I minister to St. Mary's as any abbot would to his monastery. You have certainly noticed the strict discipline. Our young ladies are as well-behaved and saintly as the good nuns who teach them and set for them an example of chastity and obedience, those cardinal virtues. There are only two priests besides myself on the staff. I am sure you would fit in nicely when the position does finally open up. (I am sorry for the complications and I apologize for any inconvenience.) Indeed, I will keep you at the top of my list. It is indeed regrettable that for the time being you will have to serve time at St. John's, but we must obey our superiors, mustn't we? Perhaps you will be able to instill some discipline among Monsignor Roland's unruly tribe during your, let us hope brief, stay there."

"Yes," I said, feeling sick to my stomach at the thought of having to return to St. John's. I had hoped that Father Hillsborough might somehow intuit the desperateness of my plight and intercede for me, possibly informing the Bishop that he was in dire need of another priest on the staff immediately. But then, how could he know my true plight? I had not confessed to him. I had not truly opened up to him. But how could I? How could I?

Father Hillsborough, I would have had to say to him, I am fleeing my inner city parish because of the terrible lust I experience upon hearing the confessions of all those horrible boys, all of whom seem addicted to the sin of self-abuse, and worse. Their hot-breathed confessions always excite me horribly. I cannot resist asking the details of their sins, and then to hear them describe–with my incessant promptings to "go on, my son, go on"–how they do it and why they do it and how they feel as they do it. Oh dear God, I have found myself sinning in the very confessional as I listen to them. I had hoped that by gaining a transfer to an all-girls academy I could put myself out of temptation's grasp. My transfer was granted, but due to unforseen complications I have ended up not at St. Mary's, but at–oh dear God, only temporarily, I pray!–at an all-male academy that appears even worse than the school I am fleeing. I can't imagine what the boys' confessions must be like at St. John's–or rather, I *can* imagine. Dear God, help me!

Late morning: I'm back at St. John's. Father Thomas, as shirtless as he was yesterday in the muggy heat, was again manning the gate when I arrived, listening to some abhorrent rock music on the gatehouse radio. He said he was relieved to see me, as would be Monsignor Roland, who had been making phone calls in an effort to track me down.

The Monsignor, standing at the edge of the soccer field and caressing the bare backs of the two nearly naked boys who flanked him, smiled at me as I drove up to the main building. Leaving his pets, he came trotting over to greet me in a manner most undignified for a member of the Church aristocracy.

"So there you are!" he said, nearly dragging me out of the car as he shook my hand with his hairy, sweaty paws. "Where did you run off to? We'd feared you'd got lost in the woods and had been eaten by a bear."

I gave him an excuse about having forgotten one of my bags at a motel, which he accepted without question, then ushered me into the building and up to his office, where he briefed me over coffee.

"We're probably a little looser here than you're used to, Mike-you don't mind if I call you Mike?-but I think you'll get used to that fast and come to appreciate it. We're not big on discipline and punishment at St. John's, but I think you'll find that we have fewer real problems than is usual in a place like this. Treat the students like adults, and they'll act like adults. Treat them like children, watching their every move like doting parents, trying to enforce a thousand and one petty rules, and they'll act like children, trying to get away with as much as they can. No, we have very few discipline problems here. Our main rule here is that there would be no leaving the property without permission. Our main concern is in keeping track of the boys, in not letting them sneak out to get lost in the woods or to invade the hallowed grounds of St. Mary's down the road. Father Hillsborough over there is, you might say, overly protective of his young ladies. For the most part, the boys have been cooperative in this regard. They like it here and rarely get the yen to sneak off and get into mischief elsewhere."

As he briefed on my teaching and other duties-for today I was just to settle in, to wander around and get acquainted with my new surroundings-I asked him about confessions. How often were they held, I asked, and how many priests were available to hear the confessions of so many boys? I was hoping I wouldn't have to hear the confessions of too many of these demonic young creatures.

"We have *general* confessions here," the monsignor said. "The boys gather together in chapel, confess silently to themselves, and we absolve them in one fell swoop." He made the sign of giving absolution. "Zap, you're all forgiven! No more of the tedium of hearing them one at a time-unless a boy wants to confess privately, of course."

This news came as both a surprise and a relief. Maybe life at St. John's will be less stressful than I had imagined.

Evening: I should not have allowed my hopes to rise too soon. No, I will not have to hear confessions here, but what I *will* have to deal with is a thousand times worse. The boys of St. John's are completely shameless and out of control, more so than I had ever imagined. Although they must wear shirts to class, chapel, and the dining hall, they are not required to wear shoes, so most of them go barefoot all the time. I must say, it is disconcerting to attend Mass where not only are most of the *worshipers* barefoot, but the altar boys as well! Although I haven't, of course, checked to verify my suspicions-how could I?-I suspect that both altar boys at this

evening's mass in the chapel were stark-naked under their cassocks. Sacrilege!

I have avoided touring the dormitories, afraid of what I might encounter there. I don't even dare imagine what I might find there.

There are six priests here at St. John's, in addition to our superior, Monsignor Roland. From the way they dress and act–all smiles and laughs, even sharing off-color jokes with the boys–it's hard to tell the priests from the students. I'm afraid I don't fit in here at all. I have nicknamed this place The Devil's Academy.

10 April 1976: I must say that in spite of their slovenly appearance and demeanor, the students here are scholastically above average. Perhaps this is in part due to the lack of a distracting female presence. Whatever it is, I was pleasantly surprised to find the students in my various mathematics classes both more attentive and knowledgeable than I am used to. However, there is a certain silliness or smirkiness in the boys that I find irritating. I might even call it "flirtiness." They don't seem to respect my priestly status, but rather, they treat me more like one of themselves than as a venerable clergyman.

In algebra class this afternoon, I was embarrassed to recognize that boy from yesterday–the boy who had *lost* his athletic supporter to the two young thieves. Today in class he was only slightly less naked than yesterday in the hallway, today wearing a tight, shoulderless T-shirt and extremely short, tight, ragged cut-off shorts. He kept staring at me during class, as if trying to attract my attention, but I avoided direct eye-contact with him and said nothing to him despite his constant squirming and grinning. His name is Fritz and he has a mop of shoulder-length dirty-blond hair that he is continually tossing out of his eyes. His legs are less tanned than those of the average boy around here, as if he spends more time indoors than out.

So, all in all today, when I wasn't teaching, dining, at chapel, or conversing with one of my fellow priests, I spent my free time in my room, reading. I'm under no obligation to patrol the hallways, dormitories, or grounds. I must say, the priests around here are a loose bunch and seem to delight as much in relating their own off-color jokes and pranks as they do in talking about the unsavory shenanigans of the students.

Despite my complaints, I must admit that St. John's is less of a hellhole than I'd feared. Perhaps my–short, I pray!–stay here will be less of a hell than I was so sure it would be.

11 April 1976: Again, I got my hopes up too soon. This place really is The Devil's Academy. One must be on guard every moment. Temptation lurks everywhere. Lurks is the wrong word. Temptation stares one in the face whichever way one turns.

In algebra class this afternoon–last class period of the day before the prolonged after-classes and pre-dinner outdoor games and frolics–I dared at last to glance directly at Fritz, who had been squirming most distractingly

all class long. The boy's face was flushed, and he was smirking at me in a most arrogant, yet coy, manner. When he saw me finally looking at him, he wiggled his toes and spread his legs, and my gaze was drawn under his desk to the junction of his thighs. I nearly gasped out loud. Protruding from one leg of his ragged cutoffs was the shiny, maroonish glans of his wicked young prick. As I gaped, the penis lengthened, sliding like a snake from its hole and twitching most emphatically. I coughed and turned my attention to the blackboard, praying that none of the other students had caught me looking at what I had seen. I dared not look Fritz's way again.

After class, though, he lingered behind as the rest of the class stormed out. Then, being the last to leave, he cast three glances back at me as he sidled out the door. I sat at the classroom desk and tried to immerse myself in tomorrow's lesson plan, but my mind would not let go of the image of that obscene snaky thing between the boy's thighs. Finally, after a quarter of an hour, as if I were possessed, I found myself walking in a zombie-like trance down the hallway, down the stairs, and down more hallways until eventually I stood outside the door of the lockerroom–the door through which Fritz had first appeared a few days ago. My legs had brought me here, but my mind–at least my conscious mind–had not. Some force, some demonic entity, had taken over control of my actions. The locker room door opened and several boys barged out, nearly bowling me over as they charged for the exit to the athletic fields. Hardly thinking, my mind a whirling chaos, I entered the locker room.

A few boys sat on benches, tying their shoes. They glanced up at me, but seemed unconcerned to have a priest in their midst. Moments later, they were up and gone, and now the locker room was deserted, and silent except for the sound of water dripping in the showers. A door opened and a boy came out of the restroom near the showers, adjusting his athletic trunks as he walked. His face was flushed and he started with surprise when he saw me, then let out a nervous laugh and ran past me and out into the hallway. Ten seconds later, the restroom door opened again, and another boy stepped out. It was Fritz.

He hadn't a stitch on. His long, thick young phallus was pointed straight at me. When he spotted me, his mouth dropped open for just the briefest moment, then settled into the most wicked, demonic leer I had ever seen. Licking his lips, he stepped backwards into the restroom and let the door swing shut.

I rallied all my willpower, determined to leave then and there, determined to flee not only that lockerroom, but St. John's Academy as well. However, my legs ignored my will and moved me with a will of their own in the opposite direction and, my heart sledge-hammering, I entered the restroom. It was a small restroom, with three toilet stalls and three urinals. It seemed silent and deserted, but I could see a pair of bare feet under the door of one of the stalls. Pushed by a force beyond my conscious control, I went into the middle stall and lowered my black pants. Although I settled onto the toilet

seat in the pose of Rodin's *Thinker*, it would be an understatement to say that I was barely capable of thought. I was possessed, in a state of temporary insanity, totally disoriented and trembling violently.

"Stick it through, Father."

I nearly jumped out of my shoes at the sound of the half-whispered words. To my left I spied Fritz's satanically grinning face perched in a large round hole in the stall partition. He opened his mouth and wiggled his wet tongue at me.

"Stick it through, Father–I'll suck it for ya."

Despite my clerical life, I'm not a total ignoramus in such matters. I'd heard the confessions of wicked boys, had listened to them describe ungodly acts committed in restrooms such as this.

"Ooh, it's a big, hairy, juicy one!" Fritz growled, licking and smacking his lips. "Stick it through and I'll suck it off!"

Suddenly his arm came through the hole, his hand reaching for my rigid cock. (I use that obscene slang word now because it suits the obscene filth I am about to write. In fact, when writing about such wickedness one is almost forced to use the language of wickedness.) His hot little paw fingered the swollen head of my cock, smearing the hot, sticky-slick fluid oozing from the partially open slit. His fingers gripped my thick, throbbing phallus and tugged. I stood up, allowing him to draw my raging manhood through the hole in the partition.

"Oh yeahhh!" the boy muttered, breathing hotly on my throbbing phallus as he toyed with my hairy, hugely swollen balls. His hot tongue began to lap at my ball-flesh and I gasped, pressing against the partition, trying to force my entire body through the hole.

As he tongued my balls, he gripped the shaft of my cock. It was so thick that I was sure that he could not close his hand completely around it. His nose and lips slid up and down along the shaft as he kissed, sniffed, and licked. What a filthy, wicked little demon he was! Suddenly, his mouth engulfed the head, then several inches of shaft, and pleasure such as I had never in my life either experienced or imagined surged through my throbbing prick and I gasped out loud, stifling the impulse to groan like a beast. The ring of the boy's hot, wet lips slid up and down my veiny cock-shaft as his nimble tongue twirled and churned and probed, titillating the most deliciously sensitive parts of my cock. Clinging helplessly to the top of the partition, I rocked my loins. The boy sucked loudly, juicily, growling like a hungry animal, exciting me even more. I began to thrust wildly and all at once I saw stars and such ecstasy gripped my loins and surged throughout my body that I nearly blacked out. Gasping, grunting, I exploded down the boy's throat, trying to thrust my entire body through the hole and down the boy's ravenous gullet.

"Oh yes!" I gasped. "Oh God!"

The boy sucked and sucked and sucked, until I nearly jumped out of my skin and had to withdraw my cock from his insatiable mouth before I

screamed. Exhausted, I slumped back onto the toilet, gripping my ultra-sensitive phallus as if to protect it from the very air.

"What a load!" the boy said, licking his swollen lips. Then, without even asking, he thrust his own rampant phallus through the hole, where it throbbed only inches from my face.

The shiny, flushed knob had swelled completely out of its foreskin, which was pulled back almost tightly. Veins bulged on the silky-skinned, ivory shaft. Clear sap oozed from the slit. The excited young phallus had a musky, boyish aroma that inebriated me as much as it repulsed me.

"Suck it!" the boy whispered, flexing that obscene appendage. "Suck me off!"

Though I had just experienced the orgasm of my life and felt nearly drained of strength, the sight and scent of that rigid young prick quivering so close to my nose and lips injected new energy into me. Excited beyond reason, I found myself pumping my still-swollen erection as I hadn't dared since my sinful teens. Hardly knowing what was happening, I found my mouth closing around that hot, hard, cylinder of boyflesh and I began to suck the juicy, pulsing young devil-cock.

"Oh wow!" Fritz panted, pistoning his rampant boyhood between my smacking lips. "Suck it, Father!"

My eyes crossed and re-crossed as my head bobbed and I blew the gasping, squirming, naked teenager. My hand jerked up and down my enormously engorged manhood. Never in my life had I felt such an all-encompassing concentration upon the task at hand, such all-pervading bliss. The boy's prick bucked and squirmed in my mouth, its underside grinding against my wet, churning tongue. I wanted that demonic youth–wanted all of him–his flesh, his juice, his soul.

"Ohhhh!" he sighed, humping with intense, screwing motions, his prick flexing with each thrust. "Awww yeahhh!" His prick pressed hard against the roof of my mouth and his hot love-juice began to squirt down my throat. As he fed me his holy communion, his cries of ecstasy became almost girlishly high-pitched.

The boy-sperm came in hot, forceful torrents, gagging me at first, but I regained control and managed to swallow, then to gulp, then to suck ravenously for all I could get. What a terrible and yet delicious juice, what a musky-sweet flavor! It had a peppery tang, as if spiced with powdered brimstone–surely the brimstone of Hell itself–and yet how wretchedly wonderful! I wanted more, more, more!

As I sucked, as I growled–without warning, my own viscous spunk spurted forth yet again from my pulsing manhood, and, as I pumped it out, writhing with the unholy sensation of it, I looked down and saw the boy's bare toes wiggling in it and smearing it as it splashed down hot on the stone floor. This obscene sight stimulated a few last powerful orgasmic surges in my tortured loins.

After that I suffered a sort of blackout. I only vaguely remember pulling up my pants and fleeing the restroom. Hours later I awoke in my room after a feverish sleep. It was time for dinner and then evening chapel, but I was too exhausted and distraught to leave my cell.

12 April 1976: I strictly avoided looking at Fritz in algebra class this afternoon. However, against my will I found myself paying closer attention to the other students than I had previously allowed myself. How wicked they are! How wicked are the boys in all my classes! I discovered-oh Lord, I could not tear my eyes away!- that many if not most of them sport erections during class, erections they don't attempt to hide-as if hiding such large, large slabs of young manhood would be possible in the obscenely tight shorts or jeans they all wear. From time to time, the shiny, engorged glans of one of these terrible erections would ease out the leg of a boy wearing shorts, its slit, staring at me like an evil eye. And, my Lord forgive me, I could not stop myself from staring back at it!

They knew I was looking; I knew they saw. These wretched students could tell I was eyeing them between the thighs as they slumped in their desks, and they would spread their legs wider, as if to taunt me. In spite of their wicked games, however, they managed to pay attention to the math lesson at hand-more attention than I was able to muster!-and this astonished me.

I spent the day sitting behind my desk in every class, unable to get up because of the maddening erection that throbbed in my own pants and that I dared not display. I called various boys to the blackboard to work out problems for the class as I sat safely concealed behind my desk and made comments. Boys called to the board could not hide the tented condition of their shorts or jeans, and this caused titters, but without being disruptive. I am starting to believe that a state of more or less permanent tumescence is the natural condition of male youth, also that that tumescence is somehow catching, like a fast-acting psychical virus. If a boy in a group gets an erection, soon most of the others in that group will be hard as well!

At lunch and dinner, I paid more attention to the other priests at my table than I had during previous meals, and I realized that every one of them was paying more attention to the boys in the dining hall than was proper or discreet for a teacher, not to mention for a priest. In fact, they stared shamelessly at certain passing boys, nearly drooling their perverted interest and apparently unconcerned that anyone might notice. Has every last one of the priests here at St. John's gone to the Devil's camp?

I was indeed shocked when, during dinner, Father Thomas winked at one of the barefooted, bare-legged, long-haired young demons wiggling past our table and who returned to the priest a most wicked, coquettish expression. Did Father Thomas then clear his throat, or was that a growl I heard?

After dinner I tried to enjoy a peaceful, calming walk alone along one of the many paths in the woods, but thrice I came upon boy couples seated on a

log or on the ground, arms around each other, mouths locked in an obscene kiss, faces red and sweating as their tongues dueled. Due to their long hair, I am always at first sure that I have encountered two girls, or a long-haired boy with a girl, but there are only boys here on the walled-in grounds of St. John's Academy. Instead of pulling apart and running away in shame when I chanced upon them, these kissing youths paid me hardly more than a glance, as if a passing priest was of little concern to them. Flustered, I walked on, not daring to look back at them as I passed again out of sight.

And then, oh Lord, I stumbled upon something I hardly dare write about. Passing a clump of bushes, I heard grunts and gasps, what sounded like two boys engaged in an earnest wrestling match. Pushing aside branches and peering through the foliage, I spotted two completely naked boys, one lying face-down on a blanket on the ground, the other mounted on his backside and rutting at him like a beast in heat. From the sounds they made as they performed their sodomitic rite, I could not tell whether both were suffering pain or an agonized ecstasy. I watched in frozen silence until the youth on top bellowed and grunted like a bull, his body jerking and shuddering as he poured forth his wicked seed into the youth pinned and moaning under him. As the top boy's motions slowed, and as he collapsed on top of his vanquished bottom, I fled the scene, my mind flashing as if with a thousand short circuits.

This Devil's Academy really is becoming too much, more than I can possibly bear any longer! I have spent the evening tossing and turning on my bed, refusing to let myself ease the painful, maddening tension in my loins. I must leave this den of iniquity or be lost forever! Tomorrow I must leave.

13 April 1976: Too late, I am lost. Forever lost.

It was after midnight when Fritz knocked on my door. Had I known it was he, I'd have pushed my bed and chest of drawers against the bolted door and cowered in the corner until he'd gone away. Thinking a fellow priest had come to deliver an important message so late at night, I opened the door.

The devil-boy stepped in, grinning, naked except for the tightest little threadbare rag around his middle. In his grubby hands he carried a small paper bag, which he opened immediately revealing a tin of Vaseline.

"I thought you'd come down to the lockerroom today after classes," he drawled, eyeing me suggestively. "I was waiting for you."

I shut the door, staring at him in amazement as he peeled down his cutoffs and tossed them aside. His fat, heavy erection pointed acutely up at me, throbbing with the rapid beat of his heart.

"You missed some fun, Father. I sucked off at least ten boys. I wanted to suck you off too."

The boy moved toward me as I stood there transfixed by an unholy spell and he pulled down my pajama bottoms. I gasped as he wrapped his hand around the vein-bulging shaft of my splitting-hard erection.

"You got a big, hairy one, Father!" He grinned up at me most wickedly, sliding his hand up and down my cock. Then, as I stood there helplessly, he unbuttoned my pajama tops and pulled them off. "Nice hairy chest and stomach too." He licked my abdomen.

In my panting excitement, I almost hyperventilated as the boy led me to the bed. Dizzy, I collapsed on the mattress. As I lay stretched before him like a sacrificial lamb, the demonic youth began sucking greedily at my manhood and my swollen balls nearly burst. Truly helpless, I lay there trembling so that I feared I was having a seizure. The boy's hot drool dribbled down my ballooning, hairy balls as his long-haired head bobbed, his hot, ringed lips rippling over the rim of my glans and the veins of my shaft. I gasped almost convulsively with each sucking descent of his ravenous mouth. I was on the verge of blowing his head off with a violent ejaculatory explosion when he released me, letting my heavy phallus smack hard against my abdomen like a hot, wet fish.

Smiling more demonically than I'd seen him yet, the boy dipped his fingers into the Vaseline container and lubricated my tusklike phallus with the slippery jelly. As he smeared and rubbed and worked the lubricant all over my hot venereal flesh, I writhed in pained sensation against the bed, as if lying there shackled and unable to resist his unholy ministrations. Climbing over me, straddling me at the hips, the boy held my greased phallus vertical and lowered his compact rump toward it. As my fist-like glans forced apart his buttocks, I tossed my head from side to side, moaning, "No! No! No!"

"Yeah!" the boy sighed. "Yeahhh!" Rotating his hot little behind, he worked the head of my cock into his bum. His eyes rolled back in glassy delirium as he impaled himself to the hilt on my rigid manhood and pressed his smooth buttocks to my fat, hairy balls. His own young phallus, throbbing wildly and oozing sap, pointed ceilingward and, as he began to ride up and down, sodomizing himself on my priestly scepter, it began to whack up and own, flipping hot sap across my hairy stomach.

I grasped handfuls of my bed sheet, writhing helplessly as the boy had his way with me, chewing my lips to keep from screaming out loud from the intensity of the raw sensation I felt. The youth was a seething cauldron inside, and so tight and slick as to make my phallus feel skinned alive, its every nerve on fire and quivering. Against my will, my loins rocked and I thrust upward to meet the rapid, downward, screwing descent of the boy's delicious bum.

My Lord, I must confess, I had never in my life experienced such ecstasy! Lord forgive me, but I could not help myself!

I sat up suddenly, crushing the boy in a loving embrace and kissing him as if wanting to suck the very breath out of him. His tongue was nimble and sweet, his saliva like honey. I could not get enough of him. Clinging to him, I rolled him over without disengaging my phallus from his love canal, and I pressed down on top of him. He hooked his legs over my shoulders so I

could penetrate him as deeply as possible, and, kissing nonstop, gazing into each other's eyes, we moved against each other, copulating in an unholy frenzy. As I fucked the youth, his hand moved between our bellies, pleasuring his boyhood.

"I'm gonna come!" he groaned, and his rectum began to convulse around my plunging manhood. His eyes rolled back and his body convulsed as he spurted his hot juice between us. "Ohhh!" he moaned. "Oh God!"

A whirlwind of seething ecstasy surged through my loins, through my phallus, through every cell of my body. My mouth gaping in a silent scream, I began to explode into the writhing youth, filling him with my priestly seed. A loud, drawn-out groan of pleasure at last escaped my mouth, then a bellow of release. All of St. John's might have heard me, but I didn't care. I no longer had any control. I continued to jerk and grunt and bellow until I'd emptied every drop of my molten love-juice into my gasping partner. Then I collapsed on top of him.

He started to giggle, then to laugh. He squirmed until I rolled off him, my phallus disengaging from his body. As he lay there giggling as if gone mad, I lapsed into unconsciousness.

He still lay next to me when the dim light of dawn coming in through the window woke me. For a few moments, I watched him sleep, then shook him awake as panic came upon me.

"You must leave," I said. "We must not be caught together like this."

Instead of jumping off the bed to flee the room, he smiled at me, then gripped his hard cock and began to masturbate.

"Come, you must leave!" I repeated.

"Why?" he asked, stroking himself.

"Because we must not be caught together like this. It's not right for a priest to be caught sleeping with a boy. It's sinful, criminal!"

"But all the other priests do it," the boy said. "I've done it with all of them, and they've done it with lots of other boys. They do it all the time." His hand moved more rapidly up and down his cock. "I've even done it with two priests at once. I suck one while the other one fucks me. It's great!"

I couldn't believe what I was hearing. As I stared in horror at the grinning, masturbating youth, his eyes rolled back.

"I'm coming, Father!" He pulled my head down over him and shot hot juice against my face. "Drink it, Father!" Pushing down on my head, he thrust his spurting phallus into my mouth. "Suck it!"

I swallowed greedily, watching the boy's grubby toes wiggle and clutch with his obscene pleasure.

17 July 1976: I today received word from Father Hillsborough at St. Mary's Academy that a position on his staff is about to become available. He asks that I make an appointment to see him to discuss arrangements for my transfer there. I have replied that I thank him for his offer, but, alas, I no

longer feel that St. Mary's is the right place for me, as I seem to have found my true calling here at St. John's.

ADVENTURES WITH BILLY BOB by David MacMillan

(OR, THE END OF CELIBACY)

I'd driven down to college from my home in New Jersey and got in a day ahead of any of the other students. Beginning somewhere in South Carolina, I started seeing this stupid billboard. Five or six football jocks of various races standing around with the same shit-eating grin on their faces and the King James version in their hands. And the caption: "REAL MEN DON'T READ PORN." Sure, they were all hunky-looking men; but their reading material told me they were all a little short on gray matter.

That damned billboard definitely brought home the fact that I was entering the twilight zone that was (is) the Bible Belt. But UGA had been the only grad program to give me both a lecturer's position and an apprenticeship.

I was lying on my bed the next morning and everything had been put away. I do mean everything–especially my collection of gay skin mags. I hadn't been about to take any chances on what the fates in the Dean of Men's office might deal me for a roommate.

The guy who walked in was a hunk. Blond, blue eyed, taller than my six feet, and perfectly developed–there were abs and lats and pecs on top of each other.

He smiled bashfully and stuck out his hand. "Billy Bob's my name," he drawled with so much magnolia juice and honeysuckle in his mouth I could barely understand him. "What's your'n?"

"Baruch." He stared at me like I was speaking in unknown tongues, and I probably was for him. I grinned. "It's a Jewish name–it means 'Bruce' in English."

"Can I call y'all that, then?" I nodded. "Where y'all from?" "Near the City." He looked at me with big, blue uncomprehending eyes. "New York, that is. How about you?"

"A little hole in the wall near on to Macon called Dry Branch." He plopped down on his bed, keeping his eyes on me like some kid seeing a tiger in the zoo for the first time. "What year y'all in?" he asked finally, seeming to take too many seconds to figure out what to say next.

"I'm starting a doctorate in Philosophy–I've got a teaching assistanceship, which carries room and board with it."

Now, he did look like a kid seeing a tiger for the first time–only, it was like I might nosh on him for a snack. "A teacher?" He turned bashful again, twisting on the hem of his T-shirt. "Maybe, y'all could ... uh ... *tutor* me?"

"Why?"

"I ain't got too much time for studyin' 'n' stuff with football and all." I almost groaned aloud. "Hey, Bruce, tell y'all what I'm gonna do...."

I arched an eyebrow in his direction. Yes, he did look good enough to eat; but he was going to have to change into a tutu in one hell of a hurry if he expected me to get into anything with him. I mean, the guy could bash my brains in with any of just those fucking muscles I could see through his shirt. "What's that?"

"Well ... see ... I belong to this group that meets every Wednesday night...."

"What's it called?"

"The Campus Crusade."

"What the fuck's that?" I asked sharply, breaking in on his slower thinking process.

"Why, Bruce ... you've never heard of us? We're the real Christian student group here on campus."

I did groan aloud. I would have to draw a Jesus freak for a roomie! That frigging billboard from the drive down stood suddenly in front of my mind's eye and I found myself wondering if I'd hid my stash of mags well enough to survive a quarter with this overgrown mental midget. "I don't think so, Billy Bob." I tried to smile. "You see, I'm Jewish and that isn't my kind of group."

He continued to stare at me-only now, his eyes reminded me of a lost puppy. "What's Jewish?" he asked. "Sorta like being Catholic or Jehovah's Witness?"

"Sort of," I answered, trying to staunch his questions.

Several weeks went by after our introduction. Classes had begun and so had football practice; and our lives took totally divergent paths. I slipped into the basically sexless lifestyle of a doctoral candidate, studying and teaching while Billy Bob grunted his way through wide receiver's training and P.E. classes. He didn't invite me to any more Jocks For Jesus meetings and I didn't allow myself to think about my hunky roommate-even if he did insist on getting out of everything but his underwear the moment he hit the room. I'd even forgotten my stash of porn mags-Wittgenstein had me by the balls. It was turning into a boring quarter.

I let myself into the room, my mind somewhere between dialectic materialism and Socratic natural aristocracy. My eyes told me Billy Bob was on his bed in just his BVDs like he usually was, but I didn't think anything about it. It was Friday and I was tired and, maybe, my mind wasn't working as fast as it usually did. What I wanted was a number of cold ones and, afterwards, a warm body snuggling next to mine.

He turned as the door shut behind me, and his face turned a bright crimson. "What're you doing?" I asked, chuckling. "Playing with yourself?" His face went white then and I became curious suddenly. "What've you got there, Billy Bob?" I demanded good-naturedly as I crossed the room.

Stopping at the foot of his bed, I realized two things with total, complete clarity all at once. This boy had a boner in his briefs that would leave a prized Angus embarrassed and he had one of my magazines open on the bed in front of him.

I groaned inwardly. I calculated the distance to the door and the length of time I'd have to open it before this jock for Christ could come after me. The problem with that was that he was a wide receiver on the football team and, although I wasn't a football nut, I figured that meant the boy ran and he did it well. I started calculating my chances of coming out of this alive.

Then, suddenly, from nowhere, anger welled up inside me. Why should I be torn limb from limb? Why should I have to calculate an escape? So what if I was gay? I hadn't done anything to him. And the son of a bitch had gone through my personal property to find my magazine!

"Didn't your mother ever tell you it was impolite to go through other people's personal shit?" I demanded, allowing my anger to grow. Billy Bob turned whiter, which was hard to do for a lily-white Southern boy.

"I was looking for some aspirin, Bruce," he offered slowly. "And, then, I found this–and the other ones just like it."

"Yeah?" I growled. "So...?" My anger kept me going now; I was on pure adrenaline.

"They sure don't have this kind of stuff back in Dry Branch."

"That still doesn't mean you've got the right to go through my things–or anybody else's." I stuck out my hand, demanding the return of my magazine. He glanced down at a particularly cute model's picture and, sighing, took a swipe at the two-by-four in his briefs and closed the magazine. He slowly handed it to me.

"I'm sorry, Bruce. I didn't know what to think when I seen them." He glanced down at his hands. "Then, I just plain got curious."

"Well, your mama and the boys at your Wednesday night prayer group wouldn't like your looking at them."

"You're right there." He chuckled then. "But, then, it sure ain't none of their business neither!"

I'd run out of adrenaline and I started realizing how close I'd let myself come to being, at the very least, maimed by this overdeveloped hunk with Jell-o for brains. Only, I was beginning to wonder just how accurate that assessment was.

"Did you see anything you liked?" I asked cautiously, allowing my curiosity to take me over.

He smiled slightly. "Well...." he drawled even more slowly than usual. "Some of the stories got me to thinkin'." He glanced down at his crotch and my eyes followed the direction his had taken. Billy Bob still had his boner and I was pretty sure it'd grown some since my last glance at it–it was closer to resembling the Empire State Building now.

I pulled my eyes away and they went to his face, my curiosity definitely getting in the way of sound judgment. "Yeah, well, Billy Bob, I don't go in

for being anybody's patsy ... and your boys sure aren't going to be happy with your trying out queer sex!"

"What they don't know ain't gonna hurt them," he answered back, watching my face now and consciously playing with himself.

"Like I said, I'm not willing to be just a warm piece of meat for straight boys, Billy Bob. So, I suspect we'd better forget it, okay?"

I turned and went over to my desk. I didn't look back at him. I put the magazine away and plopped down in the chair and picked up a dissertation on the meaning of Kantian symbolism. Of course, my mind wasn't willing to change gears; but Billy Bob didn't know that. I was praying he'd say something, do something, so I could get off my self-imposed celibacy. I might prefer reciprocity–but what the hell, I was hungry!

After the longest seconds I'd ever experienced, I heard him clear his throat. I still didn't look up from my book. "Y'all ... uh ... don't mean y'all ... uh ... want me to...?" I looked up then and saw the biggest, roundest eyes I'd ever seen.

"Billy Bob, that's exactly what I expect ... usually."

He fell silent then and I almost had my mind set to get into Immanuel Kant by the time he spoke again.

"I don't rightly think I'm ready to go that far." I glanced over at him in time to see him break into a real shit-eating grin. "But I sure am interested in findin' out more about that shit in that magazine of your'n, Bruce!" His grin became even more shit-eatin' than usual. "And I sure can keep my mouth shut when it comes to my friends."

I found myself grinning in spite of myself. "I guess that's good enough–for starters anyway. Only, I thought you people didn't think real men read porn."

"Shitfire! They just don't know what porn is all about then!" He laughed and stood up. I rose too and began to move toward him in a daze. It'd been so many weeks I'd forgotten how a man actually felt.

Billy Bob grinned as I approached him. "C'mon, Bruce. Come to Big Daddy!" He held his arms out for me and I slipped inside them like I'd always belonged there.

His paws circled my waist and pulled me against him. I was being pressed against his hairy pecs and was surprised to find the nipples were hard as my face pressed against them. Tentatively, I stuck my tongue out and pulled one in between my teeth. I grinned as Billy Bob grunted in surprise. I was also willing to swear that two-by-four caught between his belly and my chest had grown to the size of Pike's Peak.

I was ready to swoon, it'd been so long since I'd been this close to a man. Shit! Forget reciprocity! I was forgetting everything but that monster cock in his briefs and what it could do for me!

"Sweet Jesus!" my own personal jock grunted and pulled away from my teeth and what they were doing to his equilibrium. He stared down into my eyes. "That sure does feel good, Bruce, honey."

"Not as good as the rest of it is going to feel!" I growled in near frustration at not having him out of briefs already and me hanging ten on his pole.

"Show me, Bruce," he demanded, giving in to his lust and taking me by the arms and stepping backward toward his bed. "Show me everything. Please?"

Somehow, I caught my second wind then. I was suddenly no longer just another queen desperate for a sex-fix. I was this big panting wide receiver's trainer. I grinned as I helped him direct us onto his bed.

He pulled me down on top of him as he crashed against the mattress. Then he was holding on to me, wrapping his legs around me and gripping me in the warmest, gentlest bear hug I could imagine this side of Moscow. When I'd managed to raise my head enough to look down at him, he was grinning more broadly than ever.

"If we go any further," I forced myself to forewarn him, "there won't be any turning back for you, Billy Bob."

"Y'all trying to tell me I'm gonna be queer, sugar?" He stared up at me with the biggest, roundest eyes I'd ever seen. My fingers slipped inside the waist band of his briefs and I nodded slowly to his question.

He guffawed then and lifted his ass off the bed. "You ain't no queer till folks know it, boy! Y'all sure ain't telling. And I ain't neither!" He pulled me back against him and it had the effect of forcing my hands inside his briefs, exposing his ass.

He giggled and grabbed for my asscheeks. "Get outta them clothes, Yankee boy!" he grunted and wiggled his bared ass against his blanket.

I stood up and slipped out of my pullover and jeans. I looked back down at him and saw his two-by-four was still hiding inside his briefs even though the rest of him was bared. He stared at my cock and I started to get nervous. "Y'all be a whole lot bigger than I'd thought. And y'all be skinned as well!" I looked at his face and followed his eyes back to my cut, kosher hard meat.

"Let's see what you've got, Billy Bob," I suggested hoarsely then. I might be this wide receiver's trainer in the ways of gay sex, but I was also one horny New Yorker!

I inched that cotton along his legs as they rested against my chest until the fabric was under my chin. His cock hitting his abs sounded like an I-beam hitting a city street after falling more than ten floors. I gulped. Shit! I hadn't even seen his two-by-four yet, and I already knew it was fucking bigger than Mount Everest!

I was a frightened queen–but I always got hungry as shit when I got scared.

His briefs bunched at his ankles and I shoved them over his size-15 feet. He was now all mine. He was naked and he was mine! I glanced down at his dong then.

I gasped. All of a sudden I wasn't sure I was all that hungry.

He had what Southerners called the dick of death. The fucker was thick-almost as big around as my fucking wrist! And long? Jesus! The fucker was long enough to see daylight at the other end when inserted into an ass as deep as it would go. My first reaction was to back off. I started to pull back. But his legs circled around my hips stopped my retreat. I was fucking caught with the biggest cock this side of the Red Army only inches from either one of the two orifices it might choose to check out. Billy Bob was a perfect sample of a corn-fed product of American Phys Ed. He might be slightly short of gray matter, but he had definitely not been slighted in the equipment category. He grinned up at me and stroked all of it-more than ten inches!

"Y'all like it?" he asked, pouring on all the magnolia juice and honeysuckle he could put in it.

I reached around his thighs and took it tentatively at its base and stroked upwards, watching its skin come up and cover that helmet of red meat.

I nodded numbly, wondering if I could survive it when it came at me.

"I like the looks of your'n too, Bruce." He glanced down along his pecs and abs and other muscles until he could make out my cock between his legs. He frowned slightly and reached for it. "I guess it'd be all right if I tried receivin' first." He stared into my eyes. "That is, before I make quarterback in this game of our'n. You promise to make it feel good?"

I wasn't believing my ears. It sounded like he wanted me to fuck him. I stared down at him, not yet daring to speak, and waited for a sign from that two-by-four that I would give me permission to plunder his backside.

A grin spread across his face. "I want to try it, Bruce. I want to know what your dick up my butt feels like. Y'all mind havin' dessert before you get the meat?"

I nodded numbly as he slid his ass closer to its day of reckoning. I glanced around wildly then, realizing that this was a virgin ass. Only, there wasn't any greasy shit I could see anywhere in the damned room-just like there never is when you're in that hottest of moments. I gulped and spit in my hand and lathered up my cock, hoping it'd be enough. "This might hurt a little at first," I mumbled as I encircled my cock with my hand and took aim between his legs.

I was sliding in easier than I had any reason to expect with a virgin ass under me. My eyes were glued to his and I didn't dare look down at my progress. And he was staring right back at me, his face registering nothing as inch after inch of kosher cock made its way into his ass.

I was afraid he'd ball up one of those ham hocks and put me out of my misery if I kept going. And I was afraid he'd do it if I stopped. I kept giving him inch after inch of New Jersey prime and he just stared up at me. When my bush was scratching beneath his balls, I couldn't hold my curiosity any longer. "How's that feel, Billy Bob?" I asked fearfully.

His brows knitted and he wiggled his ass around on my spear imbedded in it. Slowly his face began to break into a grin. "That ain't bad at all, boy," he

chortled. "So far, I mean...." He eyed me suspiciously. "Of course, y'all gotta do a bang up job on my butt for me. Otherwise, I'm gonna be one evermore pissed homeboy! Now, fuck my ass good for me."

I grinned down at him feebly, still imagining a nightmare was going to come up and wallop me when I wasn't looking. But I started to plow that Georgia ass with everything I had. Billy Bob grunted and moaned under me. He grabbed his putz and pulled it with abandon. His assmuscle grabbed at my cock and made me wonder if I'd ever see myself whole again.

He shot all over the headboard of his bed and he was laughing as he was doing it. "Plow that ass, boy!" he hissed as his second rope hit him in the eye. And I kept on, afraid to stop. And not wanting to either.

When I'd finally come inside him and fell spent against his chest, he wrapped his arms around me. A few moments later, he started laughing and didn't stop. Finally, I lifted my head and looked down into his face. His big finger came up and traced its way down my nose onto my lip. "I know why real men don't read porn," he chuckled.

"Oh yeah, why?"

"Hey, it's simple: Why read it when you can do it, boy?"

He chuckled again. "At least I know how I'm gonna be spendin' my nights after practice from now on out." He lifted me off him and laid me back on the bed as he moved inside my legs and took his two-by-four in both hands and aimed it in the general direction of my butt.

–*This tale has been adapted from material that originally appeared in Stallion magazine.*

THE PROMISE by Ronald James

(The Last of Three Parts)

"...He's really hung big, I mean major dick-and he starts sayin' how much I'm gonna love his big dick."

On Thursday, my brother Frank blew me twice. On Friday, he did me three times, once before we left for school, once when we got home, and once just before we went to bed.

We had chores to do on Saturday: cut the grass, rake the leaves, wash Dad's car, wash Mom's car. We started first thing that morning, finishing just before noon.

Mom had us shower, then fixed our lunch; the rest of the day we watched television.

At 5:30, the folks left to join friends for dinner and cards.

As soon as they were gone Frank asked what I wanted to do.

"You know!"

"You horny?"

"Yeah!"

"Then let's go upstairs."

Once in our room Frank stripped naked, dropped to his knees, and started licking at my crotch even before I was undressed, licking the crotch of my jeans.

"Gimme a chance to get it out, will ya!"

"Know what I was thinking?"

"What?"

"I was thinking I'd suck you off then you could fuck me ... that way it lasts longer and feels better for you."

"I don't know Frank," I still wasn't sure about fucking.

"Frankie," he corrected me.

"Yeah ... I mean, Frankie. I don't know ... but you can suck me off right now."

I stripped off all my clothes and stood in front of him, hands on my hips, hard dick sticking straight out, my balls pulled up tight.

"No, Jamie," he whined, "it's what we planned. Really, you'll like it, it feels really great."

"Yeah, okay, okay, but do me now."

My brother went down on me, my dick, my balls, steadying himself with his hands on my ass.

"Jamie, talk to me."

"What should I say?"

"Tell me what to do."

"Do what you're doin'."

"You have to tell me ... come on Jamie, you know ... tell me."

"Suck me, Frank ... Frankie ... suck me, suck my cock. Ty said you really dig young dick so suck this young dick. Now my balls ... do my balls you faggot, you fucking queer faggot ... I mean...."

"No, it's okay ... just say it, call me anything."

"Okay ... I forgot. Faggot, you're a fucking faggot, eat me fag, you queer ... cocksucker, queer fairy ... dicksucker. I'm close, Frank, I'm gonna cum ... now ... now, right now!"

I came in his mouth and he swallowed my jiz.

"Was it good, Jamie?"

"Yeah."

"Really was it good? Am I a good cocksucker?"

"I said yeah ... you gonna jack off now?"

"In a little while."

"'Cause I'll watch if you want."

"I said, in a little while. While you fuck me I'll jack off ... that's when I like to do it best. Ty taught me that ... to jack-off while he fucks me."

"Does Patrick fuck you?"

"No, I just went down on him."

"How'd you meet him?"

We were sitting now on Frank's bed facing one another, both with hard-ons he said we shouldn't touch.

Instead he leaned forward and played with my balls, ran his hand over my lower belly, said how beautiful my hairless dick was.

"Tell me about Patrick," I said.

"He's Ty's friend...."

"He's captain of our football team."

"Yeah."

"So, what happened?"

"I did him, I told you already, okay? Look, Ty and him they had this bet ... I don't know, just some bet ... and the loser had to give the winner a hand job, see? And Ty lost but he wouldn't do it. So Patrick was gonna beat his ass. So Ty said a hand-job was for kids, that he knew a guy'd give him a real blow job 'cause the guy was givin' him blowjobs–that was me."

"How come you know all this? You weren't there."

"'Cause Ty told me later."

"So then what?"

"So Ty told me to meet him in the third floor boy's room during Study Hall. And when I get there he's with Patrick. So I pretended I just came in to pee, but Ty say's I'm the one.

"Then he blocks the door shut with one of those rubber wedges Mr. Bloomburg uses in shop to keep the doors open, and he says I should give them blowjobs."

"What did you do?"

"Nothing. I was kinda scared so I just stood there. Then Ty grabs me and starts shakin' me until I'm on my knees and he pulls it out and sticks it in my mouth and I blow him ... but not all the way."

"Why not?"

"'Cause Patrick pushes him away is why not, and pulls it out −he's really hung big, I mean major dick−and he starts sayin' how much I'm gonna love his big dick.

"Then he sticks it in my mouth and starts cussin' me doin' him, calling all the names like cocksucker and queer, and then he just starts sayin' fuck over and over and comes off in my mouth.

"Then Ty made me suck him again and I sucked him off all the way.

"Then Patrick makes me do it again only this time he just gives me the head and he jacks it off in my mouth. I don't like that. I like to suck off a cock but that's what he did.

"Then they let me get up, and Ty says I should go in the stalls and take care of myself 'cause they don't want to see a fruit come off. So that's what I did, and when I came out they were gone."

"You jacked off?"

"Yeah."

"You do it to Patrick after that time?"

"No. I kinda asked him once when he was alone at his locker if he wanted to fuck me, but he told me to beat it or he'd fuck me up bad ... but not you."

"Huh? They think I'm queer too?"

"No, I mean, what I mean is he said he was gonna fuck me up bad, and I know you're gonna fuck me good ... that's what I meant ... it's a joke."

"Should we do it now?"

"Yeah, but you gotta put something on."

"I just got undressed!"

"No ... I mean on your dick; you gotta put Vaseline on it."

Frank pulled a tube of Vaseline out from under his pillow and greased my cock. I squirmed as he did it.

"Hold still! You don't want to come yet."

"It feels good."

"I know but this is gonna feel better."

Frank lay back. "Get between my legs," he said.

I scooted up.

"Closer."

He raised his legs exposing his hole, and reached for me, for my dick, pulling me closer still.

"Put it in, come on, put it in now."

"Frank ...."

"I'm clean ... don't worry ... we took showers. Just put it in slow."

I hesitated.

"C'mon, Jamie, you promised."

I hadn't promised, but I was excited and suddenly I wanted to do it, so I did as he said, guiding my dick with my fingers. I rubbed the head against his hole making little stabbing motions. He draped his legs over my shoulders and pushed back as I pushed forward, and I was in.

He gasped, moved his hips slightly, "Oh, oh Jamie, fuck me now! Please, Jamie ... please ... fuck me now."

"What should I do, Frank?"

"Move your hips back and forth."

As I did my dick slipped out. Frank's hand shot forward guiding it back in. I got the rhythm, now I was fucking.

"That's it, that's it, fuck me Jamie. I knew it, knew you'd be the best. Look Jamie, look how hard my cock is ... that's you, that's you doin' it to me. Get the Vaseline ... quick ... squeeze it on your hand. Now rub it on my dick so I can come when you do."

I touched his dick lightly, then smeared it with the stuff, rubbing it in, moving up and down the shaft, jacking him off, "You do it now."

He took over. I closed my eyes and fucked.

"Jamie, Jamie watch me ... open your eyes and watch me. Yeah that's it, watch me jack off. Oh man, I'm jackin' off my dick while you dick my ass. Fuck me, man, fuck my faggot ass."

"Oh ... I'm gonna shoot, Frank, I'm gonna come off now."

"Me too! Watch me, watch me pop my nut with your dick in me."

I shot off. He was right, it was better than a suck job. I came off just as he shot his load, a big squirt across his belly, then another, then more jiz running down his hand.

"Fuck Jamie, oh fuck! Jamie it was good, wasn't it good, didn't I tell you? Huh? Wasn't it good?"

"Let's do it again," I said.

"Okay man, in a little while-you just shot off!"

"But I can do it again, look." My cock was still up.

"I gotta wait a little, man, 'cause fucking makes my ass kinda sore."

"But what about this?" My fingers were moving my balls, my thumb hooked over my slick hard-on. "You know you love young stuff without fur-look at it Frankie, look at it. Want it, Frankie boy, want some more dick, young dick, young peter up your ass? C'mon, Frankie boy ... take care of this."

And he did. And he took care of me for the next several years.

Even after I began to date girls, I could always use Frank for a blowjob or a fuck if they didn't put out, and even when they did.

Sometimes I gave him head. It seemed fair enough. Sometimes I even popped him that way. A few times, when I was totally drunk, I let him put it in me-my poor fucking fag of a brother, always running after my dick.

(The first installment appeared in *Fresh 'N' Frisky*; the second in *Boys on the Prowl.*)

CAUGHT IN CYBERSPACE by Barnabus Saul

You remember how your grandfather used to spend hours hunched over his stamp collection? The simple pleasure he got out of those little rectangles of colored paper, mounting and remounting them, rearranging them in various ways. The world of paper seems a million miles away now. I spend hours hunched over a gadget now that shows me an endless array of little colored rectangles, each one a youth proudly displaying his all. And just as grandfather had his magnifying glass, I can enlarge these thumbnails and explore them similarly in fine detail. But as for mounting and remounting them, that's all done in your head these days.

You collectors of fine youths, you'll know what I'm talking about. What staggers the mind is the sheer volume of boys out there ready to drop their pants for the nearest guy with a digital camera. It must have become one of the defining rites of passage for adolescents to get their dicks documented and registered in cyberspace for other guys to download. You look at their faces as they pose: mostly they're looking straight back at you, straight into the camera, and you can't help but wonder if they know how much pleasure they give just by getting out of their clothing and showing themselves. Perhaps they're not thinking of that at all; perhaps they're just enjoying the thrill of naked display, air currents round the buttocks. Either way I guess technology beats stamp collecting hands down.

Another thing about the net is how it brings folk together. This guy wrote to me; his name was Scott. He read some of my stories and did a search to see if I was on-line. It's not rocket science: there I was, Barnabus-underscore-Saul in the hotmail directory, where anyone could find it. He was very polite, and I was flattered. It's nice to have someone appreciate your work. He said he read one of my stories and got the best bone he'd ever had out of a piece of fiction. Ain't that the way to flatter a guy! He asked if he could send me his picture. He was a skinny kid with huge, smiling eyes and a cheeky grin.

That's the best pose, by the way, for you boys on your way to get your pictures taken smiling into the camera; sulky is okay, but smiling, enjoying your nakedness and enjoying sharing it, is tops. He sure didn't work out though; most of his physical effort seemed to have gone into growing his hair down to his shoulders. His chest was as smooth, flat and featureless as if it had just been ironed. You had to strain to see his nipples; they were just faint discolorations, and his bellybutton wasn't much more than an accidental tuck in a tablecloth. And he had no hips, the guy was just straight up and down except for where his hard little buns stood out against his otherwise plane geometry like a couple of hemispheres that had been stuck on as an afterthought.

Oh, and his dick of course, it was soft and small but still poking out at a good angle so you could tell it was real bouncy and elastic. He apologized for this in the e-mail, said he didn't know if it was polite to send a stiffer without being invited first, there's probably a FAQ about it somewhere detailing all the etiquette of how to expose yourself to strangers. He sent it later, at my keen invitation, and it lived up to its promise. He had quality balls too, low-slung and of a good size, in a sac that wasn't too hairy. He asked could he be in one of my stories and I said I'd give it some thought.

We carried on corresponding; he has a digi-cam, so I could watch him too, and sometimes I would log on just to see what he was up to. Not many people realize that a speaker is just the same as a microphone. Try plugging a microphone into your speaker sockets and if it doesn't blow you should hear a tinny little sound out of it. All you have to do is control the circuits right and you can use it both ways. It works with monitors too, the same circuits that shoot the electrons at the screen can be switched to suck them back in. That's another reason why I love the internet: you can get out there and control the technology. The hard bit isn't getting into a remote computer, it's switching the batteries so there's enough power to activate the monitor when it's switched off. The picture is always dark, but not necessarily low-quality.

Scott is a late riser. Often I tune in and see nothing more than a crumpled heap of bedclothes, as if some large hamster had done several energetic circles to create a comfortable pit.

Towards midday he wakes. He stretches, yawns, brushes lank, shoulder-length hair from his face, kicks the bedclothes aside and raises himself to of the edge of the bed. He has slept in his underpants, which are off-white from several days service. Moments later this lean, featureless, streak of skinny youth, sagging underpants clinging low on curveless hips, makes his way uncertainly towards the kitchen. He returns moments later with food on a plate and a small vacuum cleaner trailing its hose and lead behind him. Carelessly he abandons the vacuum cleaner in the middle of the room, sets the plate on the bed while thoughtfully scratching the contents of his briefs and then switches on his computer, settling himself into the chair before the monitor. He uncovers a long floppy tool and plays with it while the machine boots up. For me this makes the picture much brighter; the quality is almost real.

He goes on-line to see who is about, fiddling with the mouse while reaching for food with the other hand and scattering crumbs on the floor. He jumps up, plugs the vacuum cleaner into a socket and removes the crumbs, keeping an eye on the screen as the program sets itself up. Nathan is on-line and greets him. He settles into his chair, one hand on the mouse, the other caressing his semi swollen shaft.

"Calling Cyberwanker ... whatchadoin'?"

"Nothin'. Playing with myself," Scott answers, "you?"

"I been up all morning doing chores."

"There's a good little boy...."

"You ain't done your morning wank yet? It's nearly time for your midday wank. Then it'll be time for your mid-afternoon wank and your early evening wank...."

"I'm working on it, don't worry yourself. I must have come in my pants while I was asleep."

"Tell me when you next come, I'll put my fingers in my ears."

"I have to be careful. It took me half an hour yesterday to clean up my keyboard. I still don't know if it's working properly. There oughta be a faucet on the end of your dick so you could control it better."

"Hey, switch on your digi-cam! Let's see your meat!"

"You mean you wanna watch me jack-off?"

"Sure, Andy's on-line too. He wants to watch you JO, don't you, Andy?"

Andy's voice joined in "Sure, Scott, let's see you tug your little willy." Scott reached up to his digi-cam and now that he was aware of being observed, squared up to it, presenting his almost-erect rod and wriggling his hips to make it dance. "See that you guys? Nothing little about this baby. Watch and learn." He began to stroke the whole length of his rod extravagantly with his fingertips for the benefit of the digi-cam.

"Okay, big boy," said Andy. "Nice meat. Let's see you jerk it. Hey, Nate, five dollars says it takes more than 60 seconds."

"He came in his pants before he woke up. It'll take more than 60."

"Hey, Scott, when did ya come in your pants? Was it last night or this morning?"

"I dunno. I was asleep."

"Well, feel your pants, how damp are they? This is important; I could have money riding on this. You had your breakfast yet? Go get some protein," said Nathan.

"Hey, never mind that," said Scott, suddenly springing out of his chair. "I had an idea. Watch this you guys. I bet you never seen this before." He tugged the hose attachment out of the vacuum cleaner and thumped the 'On' button, kneeling up close to it so that his rod end was caught in the powerful suction current. "Can you see it? Wow, man you should try it." The observers, all three of us, watched fascinated as Scott's wooden shaft bobbed and danced, tugged this way and that by the currents of air and by his own muscular exertions.

"Jesus, man, are you abusing your vacuum cleaner?" gasped Nathan.

"You're sick, man. You are *so* sick. Shove it right in man. What does it feel like?" Scott stood up. "Hold on, man, I'm gonna get some grease on my prong." He crossed the room and rummaged for a jar of ointment, which was secreted under other junk in a drawer by the bed. His dick was one hundred percent rigid, clamped to his skinny, flat belly so that it pulled his nuts forward, outlining them separately in their sac. When he returned into view of the digi-cam he had discarded the underpants and was rolling a

generous helping of lubricant up and down his shaft, allowing it to slap with impressive force back onto his belly.

He knelt down as before and smirked up at the camera. "Hey, can you guys see this?"

"Go on!"

"Got your dick out, Andy?" Scott stretched out his long, unmuscled legs behind him, as if he were preparing to do press-ups, and inched himself forward so that his rod end bounced and swayed in the forceful currents of air.

"Sure thing, I'm about as ready to come as you are."

"Nate?"

"Yep, I'm ready, Scott! I'm warm and dribbling pre-cum."

Scott slid a little further forward, and a little farther. "Woooh, you should try this, guys. This thing has a mouth on it." When suddenly with a big swallowing sound the noise of rushing air disappeared and the vacuum cleaner's tone changed to a higher pitched hum which sounded very pleased with itself.

Scott yelled "Waaaaaaa" and started to tug frantically at the little box. Nate and Andy's jaws opened wide in disbelief and their paws worked overtime to see their mate wrestling on the floor to get free of the vacuum cleaner. His shaft had disappeared fully inside it by now so that his balls were clamped tight to the metalwork. His legs flailed about and his hard little buns tugged back as he used all his strength to try to extricate himself from the machine's pull, and then collapsed forward again as he lost the battle and his tool was sucked ever deeper into its metallic insides. Andy's voice was heard yelling, then "Wow, I shot. Wow, that was good. Great show, Scott! How you doing Nate?"

"Oh yeah! Here we blow. Ah ... ah ... ah ... ah!" There was a pause, then, "Shit, I got it all up my screen again. My whole computer's getting to be just a spunk dump. Scott, how you doing? Have you cum yet? Scott? Scott?"

Scott had ceased to writhe and resist the demands of the insatiable machine. He lay exhausted on the floor, plugged deeply into its whining guts. "Hey, get over here you two and get me out of this. Shit, it's sucking my balls inside ... get me out, get me out."

"Scott, why don't you...?"

"Get me out, willya?"

"Scott, why don't you just switch it off?"

The motor died, followed by a long silence, broken by Scott. "Shit!" He tugged gingerly at the machine, gently sliding his well-worked length from its grasp. The knob end emerged bright purple and inflated like a lollipop, with an audible plop. "Wow!"

"You okay?"

Scott caressed the glistening meat as it bounced slowly down, deflating and softening. "Sure I'm okay!"

"You shootin'?"

"Shit, man, I musta shot fifteen times! It wouldn't let me stop. I thought it was gonna rip my balls inside out. You gotta try this." He returned himself to the chair before the computer. "You guys shoot?"

"Sure did. Caught it in a sock!"

"All up my screen. Again!"

"Hey why don't you two guys come over this afternoon and play dirty?" suggested Scott.

"Right on!"

"Later...."

Andy and Nate logged out and Scott spent a while gently caressing and consoling his overworked shaft. "Tuck you away and rest you a while, old fella," he muttered, reaching out for his pants. He felt their dampness and sniffed them close up. "Man, I need fresh pants. Smell these crusts. They should make pants thicker to mop up more spunk. I wonder if they test them properly. They probably have guys in laboratories spunking into their pants and then they weigh the pants or wring them out or something to see how much spunk they hold. Well, if they do, I bet they only use guys with little pea- sized nuts and little pinkie peckers. I oughta get a job in one of them testing stations. I ought get fresh pants." He cast his gaze around the room but no fresh laundry presented itself, so he tugged the old pants back on. "I'll change 'em tomorrow."

Scott booted up Orgone Raider 7, where on level 5 he defeated the Evil Gribbles and gained the five keys to the mystic chamber of Orgone. His rod stirred back into life while this was happening, you can't keep a good tool down! And he absent-mindedly slipped it out of the fly and fondled it while aligning the keys on screen. With a fanfare from the speakers the stone rolled away from the mouth of the chamber and a dark, metallic voice said "Scott, behind you...."

The creature was anthropoid, bulked like a superhero, square jaw, vast shoulders, bulging biceps and thighs. And it was in Scott's room. You think this can't happen? Don't blame technology, Scott, you're in my story now, babe. Enjoy!

Scott stood up. Lean and lanky as he was, the Orgone Warrior was half as tall again. He stood amazed, unable to move, and allowed the warrior to slide a cold, metallic hand down his cheek and under his jaw. "Cute," grated the Orgone Warrior's metallic voice, the surface of its expressionless features barely moving. Its hand continued to explore the bare flesh of Scott's soft chest and abdomen, the dick still poking out at the fly of his underpants and the smoothness of his inner thighs. The Orgone Warrior pushed Scott's shoulder as an indication for him to turn around, and the hand similarly inspected his rear. It grasped the waistband of his pants and lowered them, the better to view his buns, and pinched each of these elastic mounds between its fingers. It grunted again, "Cute". Then it lifted Scott by his pants, so he was suspended in mid-air, swimming, and carried him like a

babe in the stork's beak, over to his bed. There it lowered him gently and rolled him over on his back, removing the pants as it did so. "You. Need. Fresh. Pants." it grated.

Scott lifted himself up on his elbows and gaped in awe at the huge Orgone Warrior standing between his outspread legs. "Yeah, I guess I sorta forgot to...." he trailed off nervously.

Suddenly, with a click like a rifle being broken and realigned the Orgone Warrior's tool snapped into view like an attachment on a Swiss Army knife. Scott's jaw dropped. The rod was made of a number of independent sections, each with a different pattern of indentations, and each revolving at a different speed and in different directions. The very end of the rod oscillated back and forth like the head of a toothbrush. As Scott watched, small quantities of lubricant emerged from a number of orifices along its length until the whole shaft gleamed with a high metallic sheen. The Orgone Warrior gently took hold of Scott's legs and lifted them, spreading them wide until he could feel the oscillating head pressing insistently against his tight secret muscle. He gasped as it entered, pressing forward in a single unhurried movement.

Scott was dazed by the sensations of the rotations and vibrations of the rod inside him. Looking down he was astonished to discover that the whole shaft had brightly illuminated itself like a quartz halogen bulb, and he was able to view his entire insides through skin as transparent as paper. Then it began to pump. The Orgone Warrior stood steady, not moving its hips, but the rod pumped like a piston, until Scott suddenly felt the additional sensation of his guts filling up with the Warrior's juices. The Orgone Warrior commented, as a metallic aside, "Aaah!" The rod withdrew from Scott's rear and snapped with a harsh metallic click, back into place.

"Gee, I wha.... I don't know what to say," said Scott. A pebble hit the window, followed by another and a shout from below. Scott sprang off the bed. "Would you excuse me, those are my friends arriving. I have to throw down the doorkey." He threw open the window and leaned out. "Hey, you guys, hold on, I'll throw down the key."

Behind him he heard again the familiar exclamation of "Cute." It was followed by the click that could only be the Orgone Warrior's rod snapping to attention. Suddenly it was behind him and just as suddenly it was back inside him.

"So come along," yelled Andy impatiently, "where's the key?"

"Oooh, wooh. You'll have to wait a minute. You guys won't believe this. There's an Orgone Warrior in here. Like in Orgone Raider 7. He's fucking me, man. Right now."

"Yeah, like you're hanging out your bedroom window with a computer game character shoving your ass," sneered Andy. "You sure that vacuum cleaner didn't suck out your brains along with all your semen?"

The key was within reach and Scott was able to throw it down without disturbing the Orgone Warrior's pleasure. There followed footsteps

pounding on the stairs, the sound of the bedroom door bursting open, and then the two most astonished cries of "Fuck!" that Scott would ever hear in his life. The Orgone Warrior placed its hands gently on Scott's hips to lift him from the window ledge and, without withdrawing, or even ceasing to oscillate or pump, turned to face the newcomers.

They stood with gaping jaws, lacking even the presence of mind to panic. But the Orgone Warrior suffered no such inhibitions. "Cute!" it pronounced.

"He likes you," interpreted Scott.

"Man, I can see your insides..."

"Strip!" growled the Orgone Warrior.

Andy spoke first; "A-actually, Sir, with all due respect, I'm what we Earthlings call a virgin. I don't actually do that stuff. I think I might not be any good at it...." He trailed off as a warm glow at his fly revealed the melting of his zip. His belt broke, and buttons began to jump off his shirt as if he were being roughly shaken. Nate took the hint and scrambled out of his clothes, then helped Andy to remove the last of his. As the final garment hit the floor, Scott felt the Warrior's juices discharge once more within him.

The Warrior withdrew and lifted Nate by his armpits, lowering him gently onto the rigid spike. "When were you ever a virgin?" whispered Scott to Andy as they watched Nate's insides gyrating and glowing. "I'm a virgin with metalwork," insisted Andy, "though admittedly not with plastic, candle wax, wood or human flesh." But this gap in Andy's experience was not to last for long. When the Orgone Warrior had finished with Nate, it took Andy in the same way, lifting him by the armpits and dropping him gently onto the spit. And had there been a thousand boys in the queue would doubtless have been willing to run the assembly line indefinitely.

The Orgone Warrior lifted Andy off the stake and gently set him on the floor. It motioned to the other boys to stand beside him. "What's he gonna do to us now?" hissed Nate in Scott's ear.

"Ssssh," returned Scott, who somehow couldn't believe that they were going to come to any harm. "Let's trust him shall we?"

From a pouch at its belt the Orgone Warrior produced a number of small items. Mainly they were transparent disks of a glossy material. He took one that had a small hole in the middle and pressed it to Andy's left breast, teasing and pulling until the nipple emerged through the hole and held the disk in place. He repeated this with the remaining five nipples, taking some time with Scott's, for they were tiny and underdeveloped. Another pair of disks, connected with tubing, formed a pair of goggles for each youth, which seemed quite pointless, as they had no lenses, but there were tubes hanging from them that the Warrior attached with small clips to their earlobes.

An object like an electrode, but without wires or other connections, was placed at each youth's armpits and stuck there with some kind of adhesive, Another, with a small wire probe that tickled, was placed at each navel and more at various points on the inner thigh. Larger electrodes were attached to

the dimples of their bun cheeks, and a ring of soft, transparent plastic was placed round each big toe. Then the Orgone Warrior brought out more sheets of the transparent material again with holes in the centers, and placed one on each youth's helmet. Immediately it melted with the boy's body heat to form a perfect fit, tucking itself neatly around the ridge and leaving the hole unobstructed. A further electrode was attached to each testicle.

Next the Warrior produced square sheets of the material, which he wrapped around each youth's shaft, forming a glistening, transparent collar along its whole length, and finally three crystal spheres appeared, each with a crystal rod attached, which he inserted, sphere end first, into the boys' rectums, having them touch their toes, one by one, for the purpose. He motioned to them to lie down on the bed, where there was just enough room.

The Orgone Warrior stood over the youths, looking down. It gave one expansive gesture with its left arm across them and vanished, feet first, as if erased.

"Gee, is that it?" gasped Andy after a long silence. "What was all that about...." His voice tailed off as a slight but insistent sensation pulled his attention to his breasts. Within the disks surrounding his tits small flashes of multicolored lightning began to dot here and there, gradually increasing and coordinating until they joined forces like the hands of a clock, circling in reds, golds, greens and blues and delivering the tiniest of electric shocks around his nipple as they spun. Involuntarily he squirmed and gurgled with pleasure as the sensation of this spread through him, as it spread likewise through his two friends.

By now, bands of scarlet, gold, azure and peacock green light were rising and falling the length of the tubes around their shafts, exciting them to maximum erection with a warm, electric massage and making their rods strain upwards towards their bellies and expand to the point where it seemed they must burst and explode, releasing clouds of delicate blossoms and angel dust.

Next, the tubes inserted in the youths' backsides began to glow and vibrate with a low, insistent hum like a million volts buzzing through the electric grid system like a hundred thousand monks chanting. They felt themselves expand, becoming lighter than air, floating like clouds vast beyond all measuring. It was useless to resist or even to attempt to participate. They learned very quickly to accept with total passivity all that was happening to them. Sometimes spasms took control of their hips and rocked them maniacally with a fast and frantic motion they would never have been able to achieve with their own muscles; then the force would jerk their belly muscles into outrageously exaggerated six-packs and then release them, flat and boyish again. Little flashes of colored light and spangles of multicolored stardust now began to traverse the softness of their bare skin, from nipple to testicle, from rectum to navel, and little flashes of color and crackling sound passed continuously between them as they touched and

increased yet further the intensity of the arousal they were experiencing. Scott was between the other two. His hair stood on end like a vast blonde halo and little sparks of blue and red electricity zipped and flashed within the forest of his pubic bush as he joined hands with them, palms together and fingers interlocked.

The electrical energies began to organize around the three willing bodies, collecting from all areas at the rods in their tails and pulsing with forceful thrusts that drove along their dicks and emerged at the ends, collecting each time in a little cloud of sparkling energy that hovered momentarily as an aura around each helmet.

When they came, they came together as one big pack of six nuts and one Big Bertha of a shaft. The spunk was opalescent and luminous, containing tiny galaxies of multicolored solar systems and shooting stars.

As each tingling streak splashed its way across a youth's belly, it glowed its last and gradually its lights extinguished and its luminescence faded. But it was rapidly followed by another, and yet another in an eternal heart beat pump action that never fails.

Scott felt himself in endless freefall through an ageless darkness, propelled eternally by the undying energy of his ever-pumping, ejaculating rod. Somewhere in the deeps, half wrapped in the dark and eternal lowest note of the music of the spheres a voice could be discerned chanting "I am He who creates universes and at Whose command all things tremble. I ... a ... mmmmm...."

When they awoke, it was already dark. There was no sign of the disks of colored light, but there was plenty of semen covering their bodies. "Gee," said Andy, "did we get level seven or what?"

A LITTLE EXPERIMENTATION by Peter Gilbert

"...He was breathtakingly beautiful. His butt was as plump as a pumpkin and as white and smooth as a peeled hard-boiled egg...."

Antony was only fifteen on the evening when his mother went into his bedroom to see if he had borrowed her sewing scissors. By the time John heard about it, Antony was sixteen.

"I've never been so upset in my life, Mr. Bradley," she said. "There they were, both without a stitch on and they were ... well, you know."

"I think you ought to tell me the whole story, Mrs. Mariner. I can't be an effective counselor if I don't know these things," said John.

It wasn't true of course. A little bit of sexual experimentation was normal enough and Antony wasn't the sort of boy who needed counseling. On the other hand, Antony Mariner was rather special. He was tall and you only had to look at his mother to see where that golden hair, laughing blue eyes and sensuous lips came from. On that particular parents' evening, several men's heads had turned as she walked down the corridor.

"It's all over now, Mr. Bradley. He promised his father and me that he wouldn't do anything like that again. I guess it was just a phase."

"Almost certainly, but I think you ought to tell me. In total confidence of course."

"Well, like I said, he invited Tommy Atkins round after school. He's a nice boy-or so I thought until I caught them."

"Tommy Atkins? Do I know him?"

"No, he goes to St. Joseph's."

"Oh. Carry on."

"Well, like I said, I went up to see if he had my scissors and there they were. They were both ... well... aroused if you know what I mean."

"What were they actually doing?"

"Nothing. Just standing there. Antony said they were comparing muscles but there aren't any muscles in a boy's ... well, you know, are there?"

"A cock size competition. That's what they were doing. You can be sure of it."

Mrs. Mariner blushed under her make up. "I hope you don't use such frank language to the boys," she said. "Anyway, my husband spoke to him about it and he promised not to do it again. We banned him from seeing the Atkins boy again. It was probably he who instigated it. Since then we've had no problems with Antony."

"And neither have we, Mrs. Mariner. He's a very good student. All his teachers report well on his progress. But thank you very much for telling me about it."

It was, he thought, interesting. Antony-spotting had been a favorite occupation for some six months. Antony in the corridor, hurrying to his next class with that attractive butt-rolling walk of his. Antony in the library, with his long legs stretched out under the table. Best of all was Antony coming off the sports field, making his way to the showers. Those skimpy little athletic shorts, the ones with the double blue lines down the sides. Then John would watch him from the window, first feasting his eyes on the lump in the front of Antony's shorts and then, as the boy passed, admiring the perfect roundness of his butt.

Until the interview with Mrs. Mariner it was those memories which delighted him at night. After that evening, the fantasies became rather more elaborate. Antony was with Tommy Atkins. It was just as well John didn't know Tommy Atkins. The boy changed his appearance every night: huge, muscular Tommy Atkins sat naked in the armchair in the corner of the bedroom, fondling his massive cock and growling encouragement. "Go on, John. Fuck him really hard. That's what he likes."

Slim, pretty Tommy Atkins: "Make him hard, Mr. Bradley. I can't wait to get another mouthful of his spunk."

Tommy Atkins with the bubble butt: "Let him fuck me, and you fuck him at the same time, Mr. Bradley. That'll be fun, eh?"

Oh God, a total fantasy. He hardly knew Antony, let alone Tommy Atkins.

Some three days after the interview with Mrs. Mariner, he saw Antony in the corridor, peering at the sports notices.

"I see we're playing St. Joseph's next week," he said, looking at the notice over the boy's shoulder.

"Yeah. Should be a good game."

"You've got a buddy there, haven't you?"

"That's right. Tommy Atkins. How did you know?"

"I can't remember. Somebody must have told me. With so many students it's difficult to recall these things."

"Probably my mother. She said she'd seen you at the parents' evening."

"Could be. I don't recall."

"What else did she tell you?"

"Like I said, I can't remember. Anyway, anything said at those evenings is confidential."

"He used to come round to our place after school but my parents stopped him," said Antony.

"Why? Because he's a Catholic?"

"No. Religion's about the only thing they aren't bigoted about. Something else."

"You want to talk about it?"

"Not really. We sorted it out."

"Sorted what out?"

"The problem."

"What problem?"

"It doesn't matter."

"Antony, it does. It matters a lot. I'm the counselor here. Look, it was nothing to do with school, right?"

"Right."

"Okay, so we keep it out of school. Do you know where I live?"

"No."

"Here's my card. Come round one evening. And because it's nothing to do with school, you need not tell your folks. Bring this buddy of yours too if you like."

Antony took the card, looked at it and then stuck it between the pages of one of the books he was carrying. John smiled resignedly. He had ten years of experience of working with teenage boys. It was a library book. The card would be returned with the book and fall out months–maybe even years–later and someone would wonder who the hell John Bradley was.

He was right. Weeks passed. Antony didn't visit–and yet after that meeting, Antony-spotting was no longer necessary. It was almost as if Antony were doing the hunting. The boy seemed to be *everywhere*.

"Hallo. Where are you off to?" he'd ask.

"Meeting with the principal."

"Don't forget to put a good word in for me."

"I won't."

Sometimes Antony visited him in his office, tapping lightly on the door and then putting his head in. "Just making sure you're working."

"As ever. Got time for a chat?"

"Not really. Got a history lesson. See you later."

And on one never-to-be-forgotten day, he came in wearing those athletic shorts.

"Do you have a safety pin?"

"Why?"

"The elastic in these has broken. I thought I could sort of fold them and put a pin through."

"I don't think I have. Hold on. Let's have a look."

He fumbled in his drawer. 'Let's have a look' indeed! Well... maybe. Ask him to take them off? No. Too dangerous. He found a rusty pin amongst the paper clips and thumb tacks.

"Shall I do it for you?"

"No, it's okay. I can do it. Thanks a lot. What are you doing tonight?"

"Hoping that you might visit."

For a moment, Antony looked doubtful. Then he smiled. "Could do, I guess," he said. "What time?"

"Seven?"

"Sure. I'll be there."

John had rarely felt so nervous as he did between the hours of six and seven that night. One part of his brain said that Antony wouldn't come. The other warned caution.

Seven... five past seven... ten past seven–and then the door bell rang.

"Sorry I'm late," he said. "Had to help Dad clear the cellar."

"That's okay." John's heart was thumping. "Coke?"

"Sure, if you've got one."

John went to the kitchen, poured himself a beer, and a Coke for Antony. He returned to the lounge. Antony was sprawled comfortably and attractively on the sofa."

"So...." said John. "How about this problem of yours?"

"Like I said, it isn't a problem."

"Let me be the judge of that."

Antony shrugged his shoulders. "Fair enough," he said. "I'm gay. I enjoy sex. I met Tommy Atkins. He's gay. He enjoys sex. No problem."

"And how old is Tommy Atkins?" asked John, unable to believe his ears. It had taken four years before Ralph, the last gay boy he'd known, had blushingly admitted what John had guessed for a long time.

"He's fourteen."

"A bit young, don't you think? Wouldn't you be better off with someone a bit older?"

"Not at all. He's got a lovely ass and he likes my cock in it. Like I said, there is no problem."

"And where do you manage to meet these days, now that your parents have banned him from coming to your place?"

"Oh, his place; the woods in the summer. There's no problem there either."

The boy was totally self-possessed. He showed no trace of embarrassment–unlike Ralph. They talked for a while about various things. John wasn't particularly keen to change the subject but the sight of the boy, the smell of the boy and the topic under discussion were doing things to him.

"Nice place," said Antony after a while. "Can I see the rest of it?"

"Sure."

He showed him the study, the bathroom, the kitchen and then the bedroom.

"Who's that?" Antony asked, pointing at the picture on the wall.

"Oh, that's Ralph. He was at the last school I worked at."

"He looks a nice guy."

"He is."

"Well, are you going to give me lots of good advice?" asked Antony when they were in the lounge again.

"I wouldn't dream of it. I'd only say go a bit easy. Don't get too involved with each other." He paused to think. It was a bit risky. Should he? Why not? A boy so beautiful was worth taking risks over...

"I did, once," he said.

"With a boy?" He nodded. Telling a school student on their first meeting was probably the second dumbest thing he'd ever done in his life.

"I thought you might be gay too. Inviting me round to your place and all that." Again, Antony showed no surprise or embarrassment. John might as well have admitted to having once ridden on a bus without a ticket.

"Was it that guy Ralph?"

"It was, as a matter of fact, but I want you to believe that we never ever did anything. The relationship was and is completely platonic."

"I'm not sure that I could manage that. He looks quite a cracker. Do you want to tell me about it?"

And so the counselor became the counseled. It was extraordinary. He told Antony everything. How he'd spotted Ralph on his first day at Millard High. How they had become friends over a two year period, going out together on Sundays, having picnics and sitting on a rug, miles from anywhere and holding hands. They were the happiest two years of his life.

"And you never tried anything?" asked Antony. "You're in a remote spot, on a rug with a good looking teenager, and you never at any time tried....?"

"Well.. I might have tried but he always said 'No'. He said sex would spoil the relationship. He was probably right. Anyway, it got too much for me. I found myself driving round his neighborhood during vacations, trying to find him. I even parked outside his house several times just so I could feel closer to him. So I decided to leave the school. That's why I'm here."

"Are you still in contact with him?"

"Oh yes. We write. We call each other."

"How old is he now?"

"Oh.. Let me see. He'd be twenty, twenty-one by now."

"And gay?"

"Well... yes but you're the only person I've ever told."

"He'd turn me on pretty fast. Did you ever take any pictures of him in the nude?"

"I did as a matter of fact but he wouldn't let me take full frontals."

"Shame. I guess he's got quite a tool. Can I see them?"

"No way. Ralph would go mad if he knew I'd even told you about them."

"Tommy reckons I ought to pose nude some day but he doesn't have a camera and mine's not good enough. We tried."

"I could do some of you," said John.

"Could you?"

"Sure. Tell me when you want them done and come round."

"How's about now? I've got time."

No boy had ever fallen so willingly into his hands, John reflected. It was obvious that Antony was resigned, even anxious to get laid. Very different from Ralph's constant injunctions to keep his face out of the pictures. "Just my back view. Nothing else," he'd said on that epic picnic afternoon. There

wasn't a soul for miles but you'd have thought from the way he undressed so bashfully that they were on a crowded beach.

"Sure. We'd better do them in the bedroom," he said. "There's slightly more light and it's less cluttered with furniture than the lounge."

Antony followed him and started to undress as John fumbled clumsily with the camera. f-8 or f-4? Antony was light skinned. The parts under his jeans were likely to be even lighter. He should be able to get away with f-8. Even better; try both. His mind was racing.

Antony bent down to undo his laces. He straightened up again and undid his belt. Jeans and pale blue undershorts came down together. He was breathtakingly beautiful. His butt was as plump as a pumpkin and as white and smooth as a peeled hard-boiled egg. He turned round.

"Good God! Have you really had that in a fourteen year old?" said John. Limp, it was a full six inches and hung down from a thick patch of hair. His balls appeared to be quite small but hung down temptingly.

"Sure. Pretty often," said Antony. "How do you want me?"

How indeed? "Let's try a few of you lying on your front on the bed first," said John.

Dutifully, Antony climbed up on to the bed. John opened the blinds farther and put the camera up to his eye. These had to be good. The dark colors of the Mexican poncho that covered the bed were wrong. Antony climbed down again so he could replace it with a pale yellow candlewick counterpane. That was much better.

"Lovely!" Click. "That's nice. Move around a bit. Oh yes. That's perfect." He put the camera on motor drive. "Open your legs a bit. That's right. A bit more. Oh! Perfect! That's a good one." It really was. His butt was flawless. Not long to wait now...

"Turn over, Antony," he said. Would he?

"Like this?"

"Sure. That's nice. Hold it in your hand. Make out you're going to have a wank. Smile. Make it look like Tommy Atkins is here and you're inviting him over. That's great. That's really lovely."

Antony's cock began to twitch upwards.

"That's great. Tommy really wants it tonight. Tell me what you do."

"I told you. I fuck him."

"Tell me in detail about last night. I want to get that randy expression in your eyes.

Still gently manipulating his rising cock, Antony laughed.

"Got to his house at five. His mother does the church flowers straight from work. Went to his room. Got undressed. Oh... we played with his computer first. He's got a new game."

"And then?" The camera continued to click and buzz.

"I fucked him."

"As simple as that?"

"Well, he takes a bit of persuading."

His cock was fully upright. The speed of his hand increased. John set the shutter speed accordingly.

"Got a cloth or something? Don't want to make a mess when I come."

For a moment, John was too amazed to speak. The boy might as well have been announcing the arrival of a bus.

"How about if I take over?" John asked, reaching into the box at the bedside for a tissue. "You look to be in need of a hand if you know what I mean."

Antony stopped. "No thanks. I'll do it myself."

"It's much better if someone else does it for you," said John.

"Like I said, no thanks. Give it to me. Thanks."

"Try it," said John.

Antony stared at him and, putting his fingers round the shaft, recommenced, much more slowly and deliberately. "No thanks," he said again.

"Sure I can't persuade you?"

"It'd take a lot more than words." He closed his eyes. His mouth hung open and John stood by: the starving man invited to watch the banquet. Not that he even saw the food.

Antony's breathing became panting. He suddenly raised himself at least a foot from the counterpane and clapped the tissue over his swollen cock-head. In an instant it turned into a soggy mess. Had it jetted out or streamed down over the shaft? John would never know. The room filled with its delicious odor. Antony sank back, took another tissue out of the box and wiped himself dry.

"A good one," he said.

"It would have been even better with me," said John.

"Shit no. Anyway, you're too old," said Antony. "Hey! I'd better be getting home. My folks don't know I'm here."

And that was that.

"You're too old." It was said without malice but it hurt all the same. After Antony had left and John had released the tension the boy had generated, he still felt resentful. At thirty-seven he didn't feel in the least old, but when one was sixteen or twenty-one, perhaps thirty-seven *did* sound geological.

The more John thought about it, the more frustrated he felt. He had been in love with Ralph. Now he was rapidly falling in love with Antony.

It was obvious that Ralph and Antony were fond of him and that was nice. Even nicer would be....

He fell asleep.

- - -

Ralph's next visit occurred some three weeks later. He still had the same boyish charm and enthusiasm that had enraptured John during the years at

Millard High. They went out on the town, consumed far too much beer and got back to the apartment after midnight.

"Do you remember the day when you let me do some photography, Ralph?"

"All too well. You tried every which way to get me to turn round."

"If you had they'd have come out even better. I still enjoy looking at them."

"You haven't still got them for Christ's sake?" John stood up. "I don't want to see them. Don't get them out," said Ralph but John went to the drawer, took out a packet and handed them over.

"Have a look at those," he said. "Don't worry. They're not yours."

Ralph frowned as he opened the packet. John watched as he studied photograph after photograph, sometimes picking up one that he'd put to one side and looking at it again. And, sure enough, something stirred under his jeans.

"Not bad, eh?" said John.

"Mmm. Who is he?"

"A boy named Antony Mariner. A student at the school."

Ralph dropped the pictures as if they were red hot. "How much did you give him to get him to go this far?" he asked.

"Nothing at all. He volunteered. There is nothing in any of those pictures that he didn't do of his own free will. He's gay. He admits it. He likes it and he's got a thing going with a boy in another school."

Ralph picked up the photographs again. "And he even wanked for you?" he asked.

"He did but he wouldn't let me touch him."

"Just as well. You'd have had a heart attack," said Ralph; the second wounding remark. John ignored it.

Later that night, John began to think Ralph and Antony might be right. In the old days, he could drink two or three pints of beer and not have to get out of bed in the middle of the night. This night he woke up with a full bladder. He opened the door and noticed that the light was still on in the lounge. The door was slightly open. He smiled and guessed that Ralph, equally unused to drink, had gone straight to sleep the moment his head touched the pillow. He went to put his hand round the door to turn off the light when he was suddenly aware of deep breathing. It wasn't the regular deep breathing of a man who is sleeping off too much to drink. It sounded as if Ralph was gasping for air.

Alarmed, he peered through the gap. Ralph lay naked with his knees slightly bent. He held a photograph near to his face with one hand. The other hand was occupied in stroking and fondling that which John had not yet seen – and it was a beauty! It wasn't less than eight inches long. It was thick, apparently uncut, and it grew out of a bed of thick black hair.

John's bladder problem was immediately shelved. He stood transfixed. Ralph dropped the photo and picked up another one.

He murmured something about a "little beauty" and his right hand speeded up. He lifted his butt off the couch. John could see his balls shaking. Ralph dropped the photograph, grabbed a handkerchief from the floor and clapped it over his purple cockhead. His butt sank back again and his knees straightened. He wiped his belly with the already-sodden handkerchief, threw it onto the floor and then picked up the bundle of photos and began to sift through them again.

John, having seen enough, went to the bathroom. A full bladder and the long awaited sight of Ralph's cock had done things to him. It took a long time to pee and it was painful. By the time he flushed the toilet, the light in the lounge had been switched off and he went back to bed - considerably happier.

He hadn't meant to say anything about the incident but Ralph's habit of strolling around the apartment in the mornings wearing only his shorts drove discretion away.

"You enjoyed Antony's pictures last night," he said.

"I did as a matter of fact."

"I thought of asking if you needed a helping hand."

"It does no harm to ask."

"I know what the reply would have been," said John ruefully.

Ralph laughed. "If you'd have been Antony it would have been different," he said. "You're a lucky sod to have gotten so far. I wish I'd been here on that day."

"You wouldn't have known what to do!"

"That's a counselor's job. To guide and instruct."

"I suppose I could try and get him round here." Suddenly, everything seemed to click into place in John's mind.

Ralph's attitude changed immediately. It wasn't that important, he said. Anyway, teenagers were usually pretty busy at weekends. But the more John thought about it, the better it seemed. It would do Ralph the world of good to get his rocks off and his inhibitions cast away, and it wouldn't do Antony any harm to learn that an older person–even if he was only six years older–was preferable to a lanky fourteen- year-old. He picked up the phone.,

"Don't mention my name," said Ralph as Mrs. Mariner came on the line. As it happened, Antony was at home.

"Not with Tommy this weekend?" John asked.

"No. He's gone fishing with his dad."

"I just wanted to say that my friend, the one in the picture, is here if you want to meet him."

"Great! I'll be right over."

Thirty minutes later, he was at the door. John introduced the two of them. They shook hands.

On the pretext of having to go out to buy spaghetti, he left them. He spent an inordinate amount of time in the delicatessen, wandered round two

department stores and took a roundabout route home. The likelihood was, he thought, that they would be shut in the bedroom. He opened and closed the front door as quietly as possible. The lounge door was closed. A good sign. He put down his shopping bag and carefully placed his ear against the keyhole.

"He's a fool!" said Antony vehemently.

"Or possibly we've been fools," Ralph replied.

"I can't see that."

"Methinks the lady doth protest too much...." said Ralph.

"Eh?"

"Quotation. We can't help the way we are."

"Yeah," Antony replied, "but you'd think a counselor would know about these things."

Ralph laughed. "We went on a picnic once," he said. "He wanted me to undress for some pictures. I said I'd only let him take me from the back. You'd have thought he would have got the message. I was as horny as hell. And what happened...?"

"I know. He told me. He took pictures of your back. I just don't understand him. I mean, for me and Tommy the struggle is nearly as good as the screwing. He really puts up a fight but boy oh boy–when he surrenders–wow!"

John couldn't believe his ears. All his training as a counselor; those endless lectures about teenage psychology. All wasted. Why, "Psychology of the Adolescent Male" was still on his bookshelf. He'd highlighted one sentence. *"A show of reluctance to undertake any new undertaking or activity may be regarded as typical of this age group and often conceals a desire to participate with an accompanying anxiety that the boy might not perform the task as well as his peers."*

Experience was a thousand times better than book-learning! He opened the door. They were both sitting on the sofa. The denim bulged at Antony's crotch as if he had secreted a cucumber in his jeans. Ralph was similarly aroused. Both blushed.

"I didn't know you were back," said Ralph, obviously flustered.

"Seems to me there's a lot you didn't know about me–or me about you," John answered. He stood, staring at them for some minutes. They both blushed.

"Well?" said Ralph. "What's on your mind?"

"I'm just wondering which of you I'll have first. You I think, Ralph."

"And if I say no?"

"I may not be strong enough to prevail alone. We old guys of thirty-seven and all that–but Antony's pretty strong. He'll help, for sure."

Antony's eyes sparkled. "Do I get part of the action too?" he asked.

"Sure." He put both hands on Ralph's shoulders. Ralph shook them off. "I was only joking," he said.

"I wasn't. Come on Antony. Lend a hand."

There was quite a lot in what they'd said about his age. Undressing a struggling twenty-one-year-old was difficult, even with Antony's assistance. Antony managed to get Ralph's shoes and socks off. His tee shirt was more difficult. It was rolled up under his armpits like a white tyre. His arms were flailing wildly.

"Stop struggling, for God's sake, Ralph. I'm not going to hurt you," he said.

"Oh God!" said Antony. "Will you never learn?" He stood up, dropping Ralph's socks on the floor, and brought the palm of his hand down across Ralph's face with a loud smack. It wasn't just a token blow. It hurt. You could see that.

Ralph stopped struggling and put a hand to his face.

"Now see here," said Antony. "You may be older than I am but John's gonna fuck your ass. There's nothing you can do to stop it. And I'm going to suck you dry."

"I'll get you, you bastard," said Ralph.

"That'll be something to look forward to. Now let's get the rest of these clothes off shall we? You got any cream John?"

"Sure. It's in the bathroom."

"Get it."

At any other time he would have remonstrated with a teenager who ordered him about.

"What about him?" he asked, pointing to Ralph, who lay on the sofa, panting, and with his eyes closed.

"Oh I can handle him now. He's just starting to juice up. Hurry."

He'd bought the cream a long time ago. It was behind everything else but he found it and returned to the lounge. Ralph had turned over. Antony sat next to him. One of Ralph's legs lay across the younger boy's lap. Antony was stroking it and appeared, at first, to be crooning. As John drew near, he heard the words.

"Twenty-one years! That sure is a long time to wait. But my mom says that people enjoy things more if they have to wait for them and boy oh boy, is John going to enjoy you. Aha. Here he is."

"What now?" John asked. Again it felt odd to be asking a teenager for advice.

"We get the rest of the clothes off. You can't fuck an ass through jeans."

"But maybe he doesn't...."

Antony glared at him. "Of course he does. Deep down he wants it a lot and boy, do I mean 'deep down'! Come on. Lend a hand."

Ralph fought to retain his jeans but they came off. Something ripped as Antony pulled his boxers down and threw them across the room.

"That's one nice ass," said Antony. "Oil him up now. I'll hold them open for you."

Ralph wriggled but the fight seemed to have gone out of him. Antony's long fingers held his buttocks apart and watched with an expert air as John

squeezed the contents of the tube onto his finger and touched the tightly knotted opening.

"Not too much," said Antony. "I give Tommy the barest minimum. You want to let him feel it."

The 'you' was reassuring. John had begun to wonder if Antony was reserving the pleasure for himself. He pushed the finger as hard as he could. It felt as if there was no way anything would ever get in there. Ralph struggled again. Antony let go of a buttock, slapped it hard and then held it open again. "Last minute resistance," he said. "Tommy's the same. He'll loosen up now. Press harder."

Ralph cried out but kicked his legs apart as John's finger disappeared from view.

"See what I mean about him wanting it?" said Antony. "They're all the same. I guess I mean *we're* all the same."

"And what have you got in mind for yourself?" John asked. His voice sounded strangely hoarse.

"Me? Well, if you fuck him on his back I'll suck his balls dry. He's really juicing up now. It's all over my jeans."

"Take 'em off then."

"Oh it's not the first time it's happened and who wants to take his jeans off when there are two strong men to do it for me. My turn will come after you've finished."

"So right it will!" Ralph growled. He cried out again as John's finger explored his anus.

"Oh, you're still conscious are you? Oh yes. My turn will come. From what I can feel pressing against my leg, it'll fit my ass just nicely but I'll make you fight for it."

John retracted his finger. "Okay?" he asked.

"Okay," Antony replied. Ralph said nothing and seemed incapable of movement. Antony stood up. He took one of Ralph's ankles. John took the other, but not so roughly. Together they twisted Ralph, exposing his frontal aspect for the first time.

"Gee! Get a load of that!" said Antony.

Ralph's cock stood bolt upright–all eight glorious inches of it. Viscous fluid poured from the slit. The hair on his thighs was soaked.

"Take him now. He'll come in a minute and I don't want to waste a drop," said Antony. Together they hoisted Ralph's apparently dead legs over John's shoulder. He daubed his cock with cream, moved forward slowly so that it slid between Ralph's sodden thighs. He had to help it find the right place.

Ralph spoke. "Go on," he said. "Fuck me. I deserve it."

Sliding into him was a strange feeling, almost as if he were putting his cock into a greased rubber bottle. First came the constricted neck. That seemed to open out as he pushed farther and farther in. He made a mental

note to ask Antony if they all felt like that. Antony was bound to know. Antony was the ideal person to advise....

At that moment, however, Antony wasn't in a position to give advice of any sort. He had his hands on Ralph's hips and his mouth over the tip of Ralph's cock. As John pushed the last few centimetres in, Antony's mouth descended. It seemed impossible that anyone could take anything so large in his mouth but, somehow or other, Antony managed it. John gave the first thrust. Antony's lips sank down into Ralph's pubic hair. Another thrust. Antony made a sign with his hand. John had no idea what he meant and wasn't that interested. Ralph's muscles contracted, constricting his cock almost painfully and then relaxed again.

Nothing, he thought, could possibly feel so good as fucking a mature ass. He'd forget schoolboys–even attractive ones like Antony or Ralph as he had been six years previously. Something told him that if he had fucked Ralph on that picnic afternoon, he wouldn't have been nearly so good. Hair made all the difference even though Ralph's hairy legs were rubbing against his ears, making them feel sore.

He continued to thrust away. His balls began to ache. Ralph writhed and groaned.

"Yeah! Hair! Yeah! Hair!" John gasped. Ralph's pubes extended in a thin line right up to his navel. John wondered where the tip of his cock was in relation to that deep little depression. It was almost as if that thin ribbon of hair was pointing its way forward, urging him to get further in.

He gave one last thrust. It flooded out of him, making him feel faint.

Ralph wriggled slightly and then hoisted himself upwards, pushing Antony's head upwards as he did so. Then he too lay back, panting. Antony made another sign. John watched the muscles in the boy's neck moving as he swallowed and his cheeks draw in as he sucked the last drops. Finally, he stood up and wiped the back of his hand.

"Are you alright, Ralph?" John asked.

Ralph gave a long sigh. "I guess I've waited a long time for that," he said.

John grinned. "Me too," he replied.

"As for you," Ralph said, addressing Antony. "Just wait till I've got my breath back and my cock charged up again."

Antony smiled. "You got a spare belt, John?"

"Got several. Why?"

"You're a counselor. You should know that schoolboys sometimes need a bit of discipline. This one certainly does."

SEX WITH X & Y by Tomcat

*"There's nothing quite like the feel of
teenaged cock in your mouth...."*

(Editor's Note: The author agreed to share these tales with us provided we changed the names of the boys involved. "I have to live in L.A.," he said. Thus, we will just call them X and Y.)

About three years ago, an ad in *Frontiers* magazine caught my eye. There were no pictures, but it was a headline that grabbed my attention: "Two Blond Boys, together or separate," with the usual contact information included. What could be more divine, I asked myself, and, that night, fortified by a martini, I called the number given in the ad. A pleasant-enough-sounding guy answered the phone, and explained that he and his cute blond boyfriend, who, he said, had just turned 18, would charge me $500 to come to my house near the beach, and let me direct my own porn show starring them. The only rules were that the client had to wear a condom for oral, and they would not perform anal with the client, though they would flip/flop with each other while I watched. He said his name was X and that he had done some porn videos and he asked if I had heard of him. I hadn't, so he offered to send me some pics via e-mail, said he was free the next day, and to call back if I was interested.

The e-mailed pics arrived promptly. He sent the boxcover from a video with his name in the title. I didn't recognize him, but was blown away by how good-looking he was, couldn't get the idea out of my mind that this beautiful face and body could be at my doorstep the next day. I called him back immediately, and booked an appointment for two the next afternoon.

As 2:00 PM rolled around, I was frantically straightening up the house. I heard a car pull up., I peeked out the window of my house, and saw two cute young blond kids getting out of a car at my curb. They were both so good looking, I couldn't believe my luck!

After I invited them in, we sat down on my sectional sofa in the living room. X and Y sat next to each other; I sat on the other section of the couch. We chatted for about 20 minutes about this and that; Y kept cuddling and necking with X while we were talking. Y was very quiet, by the way; he was letting his "man" do all the talking. Finally, X said, "So you wanted to direct us in a porn scene, with you in it?"

I nodded enthusiastically.

X and Y proceeded to kneel in front of me, Y on the left, and X on the right. We began just rubbing each other, some light necking, etc. It quickly became clear that X was not comfortable with much more than light necking; he would turn his cheek to me every time I tried to kiss his lips.

After a few minutes of that, I turned to my left, and started nuzzling Y's neck. Wow, I had never before kissed a neck or cheek so smooth. When I went for the mouth, he opened up his teenage lips to meet mine, gently probed with his tongue, and I was in ecstasy.

X took his own shirt off, and he began to undress Y as well. I had two bare-chested boys on their knees in front of me, my hands and mouth all over their torsos. X started getting very aggressive undressing Y. We made Y stand up, and X pulled down Y's jeans. I immediately went to work on Y's Tommy H. briefs, pulling them down while sliding my palms over his totally smooth, hairless butt cheeks and thighs. Y truly had a beautiful cock, with small tight balls positioned to show off the cock even better.

It was too much for X, still on his knees, who popped Y's dick into his mouth right off! I took the opportunity to enjoy the show, before getting up from the couch. Taking my own clothes off, I continued eye contact with Y, who was clearly enjoying having X's pretty mouth on his dick, while I stroked and massaged his boyish chest and ass.

The clothes were all in a pile on the floor now, so I kicked them out of the way, and instructed Y to sit down on the couch. X still had his jeans on, so I had him stand right in front of Y, and I stood behind X. I wrapped my hands around X's waist from behind, and undid his jeans, sliding both the pants and underwear down his blond furry legs all at once. His cock was at full attention, and Y needed no direction from me! His mouth swallowed X's dick. With my arms still wrapped around X from behind, I placed my hand on the back of Y's head, grabbed a handful of hair, and guided his head back and forth over X's cock, every now and again forcing a deep-throat and holding it there. When Y started to understand my directions on his own, I started stroking X's arms and chest.

I think one of X's most overlooked features are his pecs: they are unusually nice. From behind him, with my (now happy) cock between X's thighs, I was able to cup and massage his pecs, upper chest, arms, flat stomach, etc., and still grab onto Y's head every now and again, just for fun!

We continued this for a while, and it was fun for me just to stroke my dick against X, let my hand/lips/mouth roam their tender flesh, and just watch these two cuties get into each other.

Then I stepped back, grabbed a sheet I had hidden away for just this time, and spread it out on the living room floor. "Who wants to fuck who first?" I called out.

They both looked at me and smiled. I took Y's hand, helped him up from the couch, and walked him over to the sheet. We stood facing each other, put our arms around each other, and with X watching (stroking himself, obviously enjoying it) Y and I kissed for a solid five minutes or so, my hands all over his body. I began to massage Y's luscious butt more and more. When I finally pulled away, I looked Y in the eyes. "Get down on your hands and knees," I commanded. Then I looked at X and smiled. That

was all it took–he was on his knees behind Y, with a bottle of lube in his hand.

With absolutely no preamble, X lubed up and roughly entered Y, doggy style. After enjoying the look on Y's face (and the great sigh on entry), I moved back on my knees, next to X, and held Y's smooth cheeks apart while X just plowed into him furiously.

As they continued this heated fucking for a few minutes, I roamed around the scene, taking in different views, feels, sounds, etc. Ultimately, I asked them to flip/flop. X got onto his knees, and crouched very low to the floor, his head resting on the floor. Y lubed up, and as I held X's butt cheeks apart, he entered him in one, long, slow penetration. X was stroking his own dick at this point, and Y was clearly enjoying being in the top position. Suddenly Y said he was going to shoot; he pulled out, and shot a large load all over X's back. Almost simultaneously, X cried out that he was ready too, and he sat back on his legs, and shot well all over my sheet, even spilling over onto the carpet.

They cleaned up a little, while I stayed on my knees stroking myself. Y suddenly appeared on my left, on his knees, and wrapped his arms around me. He began kissing me, stroking my butt, chest, etc. Y's cock was still semi-hard, and he was rubbing it up against my left thigh. X positioned himself in front of me, squirted some lube into his hand, took my hand away from my cock, and began stroking me with his hand. Well, it didn't take long with these young blond boys servicing me. I shot my load all over X's chest, cock, and legs. Whew. We all cleaned up in the bathroom together, hugs goodbye, etc., and they were gone.

Over the next couple of weeks I had X come out on his own. Then, about two months after the first visit, a series of circumstances led to me having my afternoon free. On a whim, I called the cell phone number that X had given me. Y answered, and it was obvious they were in the car. Y (ever the quiet one, in X's presence) handed the phone over to his man. Remember, X and I had hooked up a couple times without Y at this point, and that's what they both assumed I wanted again. No, I was interested in both; when could we set it up? Well, they were about 20 minutes away from my house (closer than I was at that point!), and were both available. We set up a meet for about 45 minutes later, I hit the accelerator, and ran to the ATM machine!

They showed up promptly, and it was hugs and re-hellos all around. We sat back down on the couch, again with the two of them on one section, me on another watching them. After the small talk (and again, Y was just all over X), X asked if we were going to do a similar scene. Basically yes, I told him, with a few twists. I wanted to play with each of them alone for like ten full minutes before starting the group fun. Not a problem, they agreed, so I asked Y to come over and sit on my left.

As soon as he sat down, it was liplock time. Y gets into kissing, and being kissed. I reached down and pulled his T-shirt right off, hardly missing a breath. We continued to deep kiss each other, while my hands roamed all

over that beautifully boyish chest. I peeked over to see what X thought of all this, and he was watching, his dick out of his zipper, lube in hand, stroking it. I pulled Y off the couch, and put him down onto his knees in front of me, his back to X, and began unbuckling his pants, pulling them down around his knees.

While Y continued to kiss me around the chest and neck, I looked X in the eye, and started to slip my hand into Y's underwear, fondling his ass, rubbing my hand against those beautifully smooth thighs. I slipped the underwear down around his knees, spread his butt cheeks, and started gently playing/fingering around his hole, teasing X with it. I felt Y's hand drop, looked down, and saw him stroking his rock hard cock down between my legs. The look on X's face is hard to describe: I think he could have shot his load in three to five good solid strokes if he wanted to!

Before he could do that, I looked at X and said, "Put that cock back into your pants, now!" He complied. Then I looked at Y, and told him to move over to the other part of the couch, strip completely, socks and all, and stay hard while I took care of X. Y moved away, and X moved over to sit in couch spot on my left, with a very noticeable bulge in his pants!

Too bad X won't kiss on the mouth! I wanted that bad, but was content with planting small kisses all over his face, cheeks, and neck, and after I removed his shirt, kisses over his shoulders and chest as well. My hand slipped down to that bulge I'd noticed in his pants, and I rubbed it hard through the fabric. X was watching a now-completely naked Y playing with himself, as I sucked X's nipples, nuzzled his pecs, and rubbed. Once again, I think he would have shot, right into his short pants, with just a little more encouragement from me. Instead, I told him to stand up and face me, away from Y. I then ordered him to do a slow strip, making him entertain me with his front side, and Y with his backside. I leaned back on the sofa, and X did a stellar job of stripping out of the rest of his clothes, even making the act of taking off his shoes/socks sexy (which he did last, all but naked, with a shoe planted on top of my thigh for show as he unlaced it and took it off!) He showed off his cock, torso to me, and would reach around and play with his butt for Y. There were hard-ons all around.

Well, it was time for some more action. I stood up, asked Y to come over, and as I stood between these two naked boys, they stripped me, completely. Two pairs of hands undressing me, caressing me, cupping my butt, stroking my cock. The two of them sandwiched me in the middle, and proceeded to give each other a long, wet, messy kiss over my shoulder. The sensation of the multiple hard cocks, smooth skin, butts, roaming hands, is an incredible memory! I sat down, spread my legs a bit, and told Y to sit down on my lap, over towards my right thigh. X dropped to his knees (he really needs little direction), and started sucking Y. I of course, needed some kissing, so Y and I went at it again.

X took over at this point, sucking Y, and fingering Y's asshole. The next thing I knew, X had put a couch cushion under his knees, to elevate himself a bit, and was asking me to position Y to get fucked.

Y and I stopped kissing for a moment, and with my left hand under Y's thigh, and my right arm/hand around his back and grabbing his right leg, I pried apart Y's legs. X wanted Y a little lower, so I scooted him lower off my lap, causing his now-spread-apart legs to spread a bit more, and getting a nice grunt out of him as well. X told Y that he should start stroking himself, and then X took his perfectly hard dick to Y's ass, and entered. I really felt involved, holding Y's legs apart and watching X's face while he fucked Y. I made Y start to kiss and neck with me again; I wanted to be mouth-on-mouth with him while he had X's cock up his ass. The gymnastics were worth it because I was rewarded with a lot of satisfying grunts, moans, groans from Y, which I was able to enjoy with our mouths locked together. There was a definite enjoyment for me knowing that while X was just able to fuck his boyfriend, I was able to totally kiss/control/manipulate Y at my whim. Y was getting ready to come so he and I came up for air, and I was able to take in the whole scene. I knew from experience that Y gets covered with goosebumps when orgasms, I felt them popping up, so I knew he was near. Sure enough, he squeezed my left hand with his left, and with his right hand pumped a stream up his chest, moaning away, with X pounding away on Y's ass all the while.

It didn't take long for X to pull out and furiously stroke himself. I grabbed his free hand (I like tactile feedback!) and watched his face. X's face gets so expressive when he comes, and his mouth makes that perfect little pucker you read about. He shot a massive load right on top of Y's load, all over Y's chest. Before any of that could drip down the sides of Y's chest, I slid out from under him, stood up, put myself in between Y and X, facing Y. X stood behind me, and I grabbed X's right wrist from behind me, and brought it around and placed it right on my cock. He took the lead, and started to stroke me, rubbing his still- hard cock against my butt. Well, it didn't take long, and thanks to X's well-trained hand, I shot my load all over Y. Poor kid had three loads all mixed up on his chest–oh, what a sight!

X now stepped back and began to wipe his hands, looking at me in kind of a post-sexual haze. He said, "That was good!"

I said, "You can say that again!"

Three or four months passed before I called the boys again. In the meantime, I'd still been seeing X alone, and, as a matter of fact, I had seen Y alone twice as well. By the way, Y talks quite a bit when he's not with X.

This time, after the chit-chat, I told them that I had enjoyed playing with them separately, as well as together. To heighten that for the evening, before team sports, I separated them. Y and I left X in the front room, and we went to the bedroom. Y and I sat down on the edge of my large bed, Y on my left, and I put my arm around him. Immediately I put my right hand up under his

shirt, and moved up to his smooth pec/nipple. With a little pinch, I got a moan out of him, and I used that second to stick my tongue in his mouth. Good fun!

I quickly had him out of his shirt and proceeded to give that gloriously smooth chest a tongue-bath. I dropped on my knees to the floor, with Y still sitting on the bed. Without a lot of goofing around, I yanked his pants, underwear, socks, everything off of him. I'm not sure what was on my mind that night, but I went right for his semi-erect cock with my mouth. There's nothing like the feel of teenaged cock in the mouth! Well, it quickly grew to a size that I could no longer hold, I just began to let him face fuck me. After about ten minutes of this, I told him to stay there, and I left the bedroom to play with my other blond toy.

X was on the couch, reading a magazine. He'd heard Y and me, and already had a pretty good hard-on working, rubbing it through his pants. Again, I wasn't in the mood for wasting time tonight, so before anything could even happen I reached down and pulled X's shirt up and right off his back. I dropped to my knees, and kissed and sucked those pecs and nipples that I had become so fond of. I rubbed my head and face over the hard bulge showing through, and undid his pants. I pulled off his pants and underwear at the same time–getting a funny look from him. I don't think he'd seen me as an aggressive type before. I threw the clothes, shoes, socks and all behind me, placed my hands under his knees, and spread his legs apart and toward his shoulders. My goal was those balls, and I licked, tongued, kissed, and bathed them with saliva. I took one of his balls in my mouth, worked it with my tongue, and let it out over my lips slowly, getting a great vocal reaction from X. I let his legs drop down to a more natural position, but this time grabbed his wrists, and held his arms down against the couch. Then I used my tongue on his cock, and with his arms still pinned down, took it in my mouth. My saliva was on overdrive that night, I was making a big slippery mess! I let X's arms go free, and stroked his cock with my left hand, and let my right hand return to those saliva-covered balls. I told X to lift one leg up onto the couch, so I had full view. Slowly, I let my hand slip off the balls, and started to let my wet thumb circle his butt hole. I applied a little pressure to his anus with my thumb, then made eye contact with X, to see what was up. I got a little nod, so I increased pressure with my thumb, until it popped into his hole. He closed his eyes (beautiful lashes, by the way) and threw back his head, squirming around a little with my thumb in his butt. I stopped stroking him with my left hand for a second, and reached for the lube. Just a couple drops on the base of my thumb, and I was able to finger and thumb-fuck him for a few minutes, and he seemed to really get off on it. After slowly and gently disengaging, I decided we were ready to go visit Y.

I took X by the hand, and led him into bedroom. Y was sitting on the bed, leaning back against the bed's large headboard, with a huge, raging hard-on between his legs. What he had been doing to keep so hard, I'll never know!

X simply fell forward flat on the bed, and attacked Y's cock with his mouth, leaving me a pretty view of X's backside.

I was still dressed, so I quickly got naked. Watching X flat on his stomach sucking Y, beautiful ass pointing skyward, made me try and press the rules. I straddled myself on top of X, told Y to let X know everything was okay, and I lubed up X's butt, massaging it, and getting the asscrack good and slippery. Then, without entering X, and making sure everyone was cool, I laid my cock down between his greased-up butt cheeks, and started to rock and roll. Looking at cute teenaged Y, seeing X's adorable blond head bobbing up and down, my cock parting X's cheeks, was almost too much for me. I literally had to stop stroking myself in X's cheeks, the compound effect of the whole scene almost made me shoot.

I grabbed X by the shoulders, pulled him back, and told Y (now our designated bottom boy) to get to work on X's cock. I had to step back and just watch for a few minutes. If anything or anybody touched my cock, it was going to be a short visit!

Clearly the two of them were into each other at the time, and it was fun to watch. Eventually, X got up off the bed, and stood next to me. He grabbed Y pretty forcefully, and without words; put Y into a doggy-style position, right at the edge of the bed. Without any fanfare, X added a little lube, grabbed Y by the waist, looked at me, and asked, "Well, should I fuck him?" Believe it or not, I agreed! X manhandled Y around just a bit to get the perfect position, and stuck it to him. X then motioned me to stand on his right, and he put his right arm around my shoulders, leaning against me and holding me in close so I could watch him fuck Y. I had my left hand massaging and kneading X's sopping butt, my right hand working myself. Y was bent way over, shoulders down low–almost touching the bed, his arms stretched out with his palms flat down on my bed, and he was moaning and whimpering.

I slipped out of X's armhold for a moment, reached over to my nightstand, and grabbed a condom. I held it up and looked X in the eyes, seeking some sign of permission. He broke into a big grin, and nodded yes. Y didn't see any of this happening, so while I was rolling the condom on, X said, "Y, I'm going to pull out, and let him fuck you."

There was no apparent concern from Y; he just kept moaning and gripping the sheets with his hands. When I was ready, I stepped in next to X, placing his arm around my shoulders again. I looked up, he nodded again, slipped himself out of Y, and moved a little to the left. I pointed my lobed, gloved up cock at Y's relaxed hole, and dove in. Y's butt was always so incredibly tight!

Grabbing on to Y's smooth, slender waist, I started pulling him back down onto my cock. X was stroking himself to my left, and now I was the cause of Y's moans, whimpers, and pleasure. I fucked him for about five minutes, until a gentle deliberate push from X caused me to slip out of Y, and X slipped back in! Right about now, Y was practically screaming, "I'm

gonna come!" X was plowing away, and I had slipped off the condom to jerk myself off.

Suddenly, X got that pucker in his mouth again (it's so cute), pulled out of Y, gave himself a couple of jerks, and proceeded to unload all over Y's ass.

I was still on X's right. I got ready to move in closer and try to shoot on Y, but I started to have my orgasm before I could move. No matter, I shot a record distance, I could actually hear the splat when the first gush from my dick hit Y on the side of his butt. Even X's jaw dropped at that noise, and I continued to pump a few more streamers out onto our bottom boy.

Y was really stroking himself now, X was shouting, "We fuckin' came all over you, Y!"

Y was screaming, "I know, I know ... I can feel it!" right as his goosebumps started to pop up.

Y reared up a bit to finish himself off, X and I had our hands on his shoulders, cum was just sluicing off his butt and back, and he shot halfway across the bed.

After we caught our breath, Y begged to use the shower. He cleaned up there, while X and I washed up at the bathroom sink, watching each other in the vanity mirror. Every time X and I made eye contact in the mirror, we'd both break out grinning ear to ear!

Epilogue

Recounting my dates with X and Y now is a bittersweet affair. A hectic travel schedule kept me out of the country for several months, and when I returned, I saw that Y was now advertising all by himself, with some other X. On the same page was an ad for a boy new to me. "Greg" sounded too cute to be true on his voicemail ad. When he called me back it just got better and better: "22 yrs old, five-ten, blond/blue, very-very smooth (his words), bottomy, etc." When I told him he sounded too good to be true, he laughed and said he had been told he looked a lot like Nick Carter, the blond from the Backstreet Boys. He had no problem setting up an appointment for later that night: "Two hours for $100, overnight for $200." Well, damned if he wasn't already booked for an overnighter, but he came over about eight and spent two hours with me anyway. I found him to be cute, likable, talkative, smart, blond/blue and as smooth as he promised. Kissable, lovable, he kept sucking me to the point of coming a couple of times before finally taking my load in his mouth (then ran to the bathroom to spit). I didn't get around to actually topping him, but he moaned and groaned at all the right times while I played with his ass.

Two days later, I considered calling him again, but hung up when I got his voicemail.

Then, a week later, I called again and his phone number had been disconnected!

Then, suddenly, a couple of months later, I got an e-mail from Y! I must have written him and forgotten. He was very apologetic, saying he was so sorry he hadn't called or written. He said he wanted to do some business. I told him I was game, but I wasn't sure he would be worth the $300 he used to command as a single when he was being pimped by dreamboat boyfriend X. I put him off and give myself time to think about it, I told him I was busy until the following week.

Then, on a website, I saw that X had responded to rumors about him in a gossip column. He wrote, "Making videos is not easy for me. People don't see what I am really like when they watch a porn video with me in it. I am the first to admit that I am a terrible actor. I am usually very nervous when I am in front of a camera. I never did anything gay with anybody until that first video! I am really a different person than people perceive me to be. Note: 1. Rumors, about me or anybody else, are a bad thing;. 2. I am not currently escorting; 3. I am not dating my ex-girlfriend; 4. I enjoy both guys and girls; 5. I do not get *everything* I want. 6. Sex with me and the one I love now is very good. 7. Videos are visual fantasies. They're not real...." True enough, but, thanks to X, my fantasy was made real for me and I will always be thankful!

SHOWERS by Kevin Bantan

"It's raining. Let's go out in the yard and fuck."
"Are you crazy? What if someone sees us?"

I was lounging in bed, trying decide if I really wanted to go jogging that morning, when I heard the spray from the shower in the apartment next door blast on. The bathrooms are next to each other, and the shower heads have some kind of water-saving device in them that makes them shoot drops like bullets. So I can hear the shower running clearly in my bedroom. I knew who was under that peppering spray. It was my stunning new neighbor, Brandon. He and his mother had recently moved in, and I'd managed to see him twice already, by accident.

But his beauty was no accident. He was maybe fifteen or sixteen and a junior adonis with his brown features, cheek outcroppings, small nose and overgenerous lower lip.

I closed my eyes and settled in for another long shower. I imagined him shampooing the short dark hairs of his head, suds running down into his thick, nearly-straight eyebrows. Closing his big brown eyes as tiny droplets gathered on his long, fluttery lashes. Then soaping his muscular, tanned torso. I pictured him moving downward and sudsing up his randy cock, starkly white from the protection of the skimpy swimsuits he favored while sunning in the small yard behind the apartment house. Stroking himself with the slippery lather, making himself lengthen and swell ever so slowly. I pictured it hard and glistening, its magnificence pointing up toward the small, round crater of his navel. Pleasuring himself in the warm, moist cocoon of the shower enclosure. Standing with his back against the pink ceramic tiles, playing his hand up and down, eyes still closed, fantasizing. I wondered who his love object was. Naturally, I wanted it to be me. Although I didn't consider myself a hunk, other males at the college, where I was in grad school, found me quite attractive. He would be moving faster on himself now, intent on achieving orgasm. Sliding his hand more rapidly, feeling himself rising. Then freezing and spurting white cream onto the floor of the tub, the evidence of his release to be carried away down the drain by the force of the spray. Slumped against the wall, still holding himself, savoring his climax.

I saw his smooth, golden body emerge from the shower shiny with water, the image of the swimsuits imprinted on the bottom of his torso. And the healthy sex swaying as he reached for the towel, considering the big bulge the Speedo revealed when he was lying on the chaise. My own cock was tenting the sheet, but I left it alone, as if to jerk off would be to sully some intimate connection with the beautiful boy next door.

As he was toweling off, I wondered if he would go rollerblading after he dressed. Maybe not, having just cleaned up. But he did seem to take a lot of showers, so I made my decision. While the coffeemaker dripped, I dressed in a string shimmel to show some of my hard-earned abs, my tiniest nylon running shorts and my new running shoes. For what it might be worth, I took my coffee to the front door and sipped it while waiting to hear the sound of Brandon's front door close. Sure enough, less than five minutes later it did. I put down the coffee and opened my door.

"Hey, Willy. How ya doin', man? Some coincidence we're both going out to exercise at the same time, huh?"

"Yeah, sure is," I said.

He had on a pair of black Spandex shorts, which were as clingy and revealing as his swimsuits. The waistband hugged him just below his cute navel. I wondered if he had on a jock or had just carefully arranged himself for maximal exposure in the skintight pants. He was bare-chested, no surprise. He had nicely developed pecs and abs under the pleasingly tanned skin. He wore white socks, and I noticed that his feet were wide. That was a real turn on. He was carrying his in-line skates. We walked down the stairs and out onto the front stoop, where he sat to strap on the high, shiny boots.

"So, you gonna run?"

"Uh-huh," I said, stretching against the porch and railing.

"I'd suggest we do it together, but I tend to be a speed demon on these." That was no surprise, given his age. It was also why he was wearing all of the black protective accessories. He looked almost like a warrior with them on. I would accompany him into battle without a second thought. We chatted for the minute or so that it took for him to secure the skates to his feet and lower calves. Then he wished me a good run and took off down the street. I jogged after him, focusing on the strong legs and tight butt. There was no protective padding there, I was sure. I followed as fast as I could, until he turned out of sight.

When I returned from the run, I felt less horny. I showered and was walking into my bedroom, when a knock sounded on the door. I retrieved the bath sheet and secured it around my waist, before going to the door. I was surprised to see a perspiring, smiling Brandon standing there barefoot. His bronze skin looked metallic under the sheen of sweat. I regretted having on only the towel, as I threatened to respond to the captivating sight of his bare skin.

"Hey, Willy. Sorry to bother you, man, but I was wondering if I could ask a big favor. The plumber's having a time of it repairing a leak in the bathroom faucet, so I can't shower." I had seen the truck on my way in. "I was wondering if I could maybe take one over here."

"Sure." Maybe said a little too enthusiastically.

"Great. Thanks. I have my own soap. I'll be right back." I resisted suggesting that he use my soap, because that would have seemed weird. He didn't know what fungi I might be harboring. Although I was sure that a

fungus could not hope to survive a second on his healthy, glowing skin. He returned with a towel, too, and I left him to undress and shower. Okay, I admit that I did go into the bedroom and pick up his silky shorts. And smell them. So sue me. His sweat went straight to my brain and cock. It was all boy and it was softly heady. I debated trying on the garment to feel the wetness next to my skin and have his scent cling to me, but I resisted. I had just showered, and he might smell himself on me.

I dropped the shorts where I'd found them and walked to the living room, unaware now that I was still wearing the terry bath sheet. I sat in my favorite easy chair and struggled to comprehend what was written in the textbook sitting in my lap, instead of listening to the water cascading off Brandon's beautiful body.

So I was somewhat surprised when he walked into the living room, similarly, if less modestly wrapped in a towel, and holding his shorts. God, he was gorgeous! His legs had a dusting of short dark brown hairs, while his torso remained unblemished.

"Thanks for letting me shower, Willy. You're a good guy." Just then the tuck gave way and the towel fell. "Oops," he said but made no move to retrieve it. He just stared at it.

"Oh, my god," I said, involuntarily, when I saw his prick hanging down. He looked up and blazed white teeth at me.

"Yeah, I'm big for my age, I guess."

"I'll say."

"And you're beautiful for yours."

"I am?" Even though I sort of knew I was. But Brandon standing there naked and saying it was something altogether different.

"Uh- huh. A babe. You interested, babe?"

"Interested isn't the word." I put down the textbook and stood. He walked over to me and tugged on my towel.

"Ooh," he said. "Just my size," he said, looking at my endowment and then fondling it. With that he kissed me, and the pressure of that full lower lip of his was heaven. Although the last thing I needed to be doing was engaging in foreplay with my neighbor, I couldn't help myself, his body felt so good pressed to mine. His lips, his skin, inflamed me. I could feel his growing erection pushing up into my sac. He came off my lips and said, "Let's do it in the shower."

"Why?"

"Because it's fun."

He turned on the water and redirected the flow to the shower head. The plumber was going to think that a convention was going on over here. We stepped in and drew the sheer vinyl curtain. I dropped to my knees as water cascaded down Brandon's body. I opened my mouth and received a stream off his cock as if he were pissing into me. I spit it out and covered the pale head. I let myself slide steadily down the wet member until I smelled the soap scent clinging to his pubic push. I had all of his eight or nine inches in

my mouth as he played with my dirty blond curls. My free hand explored the curves and valleys of his sleek torso. Then I played with his balls as I got him rock hard. By this time his fingers were tangled in my hair, and he was moaning about how good it felt. Finally he stopped me.

"I don't want to shoot yet, man."

I eased off him and asked, "Where do you want this, then?"

"Up that pretty ass of yours." That's what I was afraid of. But I turned around and bent over as he soaped my rosebud and himself. Then he guided himself to my opening and eased it in with surprisingly little pain. Still, it felt like a zucchini was inside me. As he began to hump me, he rested his chest on my back and kissed my face and neck. A soapy hand found my sleeping cock and woke it up. "Isn't this fun?"

"Uh-huh. Lots." At first he wasn't as frantic as I expected a young buck to be, which made me wonder how experienced this kid was. Soon he picked up his pace, telling me how hot I was, how tight I was. He slammed me now, his hand working as feverishly on my slick prick. I watched him masturbate me with the silky suds. "I'm gonna come." And I saw my cream erupt from my slit. "Oh, fuck, me, too!"

We were lying side by side in bed, naked.

"That was great, stud."

"Yeah, it was. But where did this doing it in the shower come from?"

"Fair enough question. I'm on the swim team at school. Well, I used to swim in middle school, too. And this one guy, Seth, had the hots for me and said so one day in the pool. I thought he was real cute, too, so we started kissing and groping. Well, out of the clear blue he asked me to fuck him. So we dropped our suits and I took him right there in the water. Man, my first fuck and doing it in water, at that. After that we would pretend to stay after practice for more laps, but we would end up screwing when everybody left. Seth went to a different high school, so we've kind of petered out. But I met this guy, Darcy, in the locker room after I was just swimming for fun. He had been lifting weights. He's a football player, a junior, no less. Well, we started talking and ended up showering together. Man, he was sexy. And he nearly strikes me dumb, when he asks do I fuck. 'You?' I asked. He smiles and braces himself against the tiles under the shower head. Well, I didn't need any more encouragement. Willy, he has a bubble butt like yours. And it felt so good to do him under the gushing shower. We've done it a few more times, but it's hard. You know, he's afraid of getting caught, butch jock that he is. So, I guess that's why I equate sex with water. Kind of neat, huh?"

"Yeah." I chuckled. "No doubt the plumber heard our little playtime."

"Too bad. He's a troll. If he wasn't, I might have seduced him first. But it did give me a great excuse to get in here."

"Which I'm glad for."

"You know it." There was another knock on the door. Now what? "If it's him, blow him off."

I looked around for something to put on and spied Brandon's shorts on the living room floor. I put them on and answered the door. A nice-looking guy with dark hair and eyes was standing there.

"Uh, I'm the plumber. I wondered if you had any leaks that need fixing, while I'm here."

"Uh, no. Everything's fine." He looked past me and his mouth opened. I turned and Brandon was leaning against the door frame in all his glory.

"We gave in the bathroom," he said, by way of dismissal. The young man was clearly crestfallen. He left.

"He's not a troll."

"Well, he's not in our league." I belonged in the same league as Brandon?

"Hey, you look so cool in my shorts."

We spent much of the day in bed watching sports. I ordered pizzas for lunch, and we had the leftovers for supper. His mom was on an overnight trip to visit her sister, he told me. He went to his apartment, nude, to get the cellular phone for the expected call. It came.

Then it began to rain. Brandon heard it and sat up.

"It's raining. Let's go out in the yard and fuck."

"Are you crazy? What if someone sees us?"

"They won't. Not with all the bushes."

"But the rain's cold."

"So my body's not hot enough to keep you hard?" he asked, playing with me. I relented. He had me squeeze half a tube of lube up his ass and then ran outside and down the fire escape. The rain shower was not as hard now. Brandon went to the middle of the dark yard and lay down. I knelt and kissed him, knowing that doing so would get me erect, his lips were so luscious. When he had me pointing north, I positioned myself, and he retracted his legs to allow me easy access. God, those cheeks of his. As soon as I entered him it began to pour, I swear. He planted his wide feet on my chest, and I got to enjoy the feel of them as I took his body. He stroked his rain-slicked cock as we got thoroughly soaked. But he was right. He did keep me hot, because I didn't even notice how cold the rain was. He kept telling me that I was hitting his spot as he pumped himself. Even in the darkness I saw him shoot after he cried out. I followed him seconds later, filling him with more than lubricant.

As we were laughing and drying ourselves off, I knew that I would never think of any kind of shower in the same way again.

SURROGATE SEX by John Butler

"...Tim, Andy and I had been suckin' each other off as long as I could remember; hell, we didn't have much else to play with!"

Only one strange incident marked Harp's first season as an escort. He had accepted a telephone appointment to meet a prospective client at a hotel one evening, and when he appeared the client introduced himself as Rudy. Rudy was probably in his early forties, reasonably handsome and trim; Harp's initial reaction was positive. The door to the adjoining room was standing open.

Rudy explained that what he wanted was for Harp to make love to his son in the adjoining room, while he sat and watched without actually participating. Harp expressed uneasiness at the proposed arrangement, but Rudy promised to add a very generous tip to Harp's fee; he added that if Harp found his son unattractive, or his own observation of their sex acts unnerving, he would still pay Harp's fee without requiring consummation of the arrangements. Harp agreed that it seemed reasonable, and they went into the adjoining room together.

A young blond boy sat on the edge of the bed. He was rather thin, but very attractive facially–almost pretty. The boy stood, and Rudy introduced him to Harp as Don Williamson, adding, "He's eighteen. It's okay."

While he shook hands with the boy and exchanged the usual pleasantries, Harp observed a high degree of effeminacy in him that he normally would have found disconcerting. But given Don's good looks, and the extremely seductive way he looked Harp over while fondling a well-filled and promising crotch, Harp thought the sex could prove to be very rewarding on more than just the monetary level. After all, his former lover Jeremy was somewhat effeminate also, but he was still one of the hottest and most satisfying buttfuckers Harp had ever encountered.

During the many threesomes Harp had with Doug, another lover, he had often fucked someone else while Doug watched, and vice-versa. He felt sure Rudy's presence as an audience-of-one would not be a problem. He grinned at Rudy and said, "Looks like fun!" He gave Don a quick kiss and began to undo his belt; as he knelt and dragged Don's pants and shorts down he said, "Let's see what you've got for me here."

Don's cock sprang up as soon as it was released–thin, but lengthy, and throbbing in full erection. Harp looked up at Don and smiled, "This looks decidedly good enough to eat!" Don seized Harp's head and drove his cock deep into the welcoming hot mouth. Effeminate he might be, but this was a boy who knew what he wanted, and was not shy about going after it! Harp reached behind Don to fondle his soft and undulating ass while it drove his cock with a ferocity totally at odds with his apparently feminine nature.

Harp heard Don say "Thank you, Dad" just before he raised him to his feet and urged him to remove his clothing.

Harp stripped naked, and Don followed suit. Rudy had placed a chair near the bed, and sat there watching the two boys while they admired each other. By now both were completely naked, and both had raging hard-ons.

Don moaned, "My God, you're beautiful!" as he enfolded Harp in his arms and began to kiss and fondle him. After a very thorough manual inspection, Don began to lick and kiss Harp's neck, shoulders, and chest before sinking to his knees to kiss his stomach. He held Harp's cock and balls reverently in his hands while he expressed his admiration, and proceeded to lick and suck them with equal devotion. His reverence soon turned to fierce hunger as he deep-throated every bit of Harp's cock and drove his lips all the way up and down its shaft; it was clear to Harp that the youngster kneeling before him was an accomplished cocksucker.

Looking down at Don feasting on his prick, Harp was surprised to see him hold out his hand toward Rudy. Rudy leaned forward and held it in his own while his son continued to nurse eagerly. It seemed to Harp as if Don was somehow *sharing* the experience with his father. Without Harp having observed it, Rudy had also stripped off his clothes, and now sat there naked, stroking his erect cock.

Using his hands to turn Harp's body around, Don expressed awe at the wonder of Harp's ass, which he kissed and licked, and then invaded with his busy tongue. Eventually, Don stood and led Harp to the bed, where they fell together in '69.' Harp knelt over Don, sucking his cock, and Don alternated sucking Harp's cock and eating his ass with equal enthusiasm.

Rudy had moved his chair until he now sat right next to the bed. Don frequently held out his hand for his father to take; it seemed to be a gesture to invite his vicarious participation in the sex play.

After an extended period of rolling on the bed as they double-sucked, Don reversed his body and held Harp in his arms while they kissed with as much eagerness as they had brought to their sucking.

Don whispered in Harp's ear, "Please fuck me!" Harp began to get up to get the lubricant and packet of condoms he carried in the beach bag he took with him to assignations. He had only put one foot on the floor when Rudy held out a condom and a lubricant dispenser to him. *Service with a leer!*

Harp stood next to the bed and rolled the condom onto his cock, while Don moved to the side of the bed and knelt on all fours, with his toes hanging off the side. Harp applied lubricant to his own cock, then squirted it generously on Don's asshole; he worked it in, using his finger to 'test the waters.' Don groaned and urged him, "Give me that big prick! Fuck me hard!"

As Harp stood next to the bed and poised his cock for tentative penetration, Don drove his body backward and impaled himself with one violent thrust and a near-scream, "Give it to me, Harp!"

Harp fucked with all the rapacity the boy's delirious hunger invited. The head of his cock almost emerged from its sanctuary each time he drew back, while at the same time Don's ass gripped his entire prick tightly and pulled on it as he propelled his body forward. Harp's balls slapped audibly against Don's ass each time he drove himself in to meet the fierce backward shoves that greeted his thrusts–all accompanied by gasps of appreciation and hoarse exhortations to fuck harder and faster. It seemed only polite to accede to his partner's wishes, so Harp held Don's waist tightly and fucked as hard and as deep as he could. At the same time, Don often reached out to communicate and share his excitement with his father, who continued to stroke his own cock excitedly.

Nearing orgasm, Harp paused for a moment to ask Don if he was ready for him to blow his load. "No, please! Not unless you can keep fucking me after you do," Don answered. Harp considered that although he would probably have no trouble in continuing to fuck after a climax, he was in ho hurry to bring this encounter to a close–this kid was a great fuck! So they disengaged and rested for a moment, with Don on his back and Harp lying on top of him sharing kisses.

They kissed tenderly at first, but gradually they began to grind their cocks together, and their asses began to undulate. Both boys heard Rudy emit a gasp, and they looked over to see him leaning back in the chair, with his eyes squeezed shut and his head thrown back; he clutched his cock as it discharged the evidence of his excitement on his chest and stomach. Apparently Rudy thought their kissing was as exciting as their fucking. The truth was, however, that a more important factor in bringing Rudy to climax was the sight of the undulation and humping of the most sublimely perfect ass he had ever seen. Rudy had good taste.

Soon both Harp and Don were once more fully aroused, and Harp whispered, "I want to fuck you again!" Don spread his legs and lifted them, locking them around Harp's waist as he raised his ass to welcome him back inside. With one quick movement, Harp's prick was again buried in the appreciative boy, and they resumed their interrupted fuck with even greater enthusiasm. Again, their fucking grew in intensity until Harp was pounding Don's ass savagely, burying his prick all the way inside with each plunge, and the fiercely hungry ass was slamming backward to increase the ferocity of their love-making. At the same time, their mouths were locked together, and their tongues intertwined while their kisses paralleled the growing passion of cock and ass.

Although Harp did not yet appear ready to climax, Don cried out, "Get on your back, Harp–let me ride your cock while you get your load!"

Harp quickly withdrew and lay on his back, holding his cock straight up as a target. With no hesitation, Don positioned his ass over that throbbing target and sat down heavily while Harp began humping upward. After bouncing up and down as far as he could, uttering moans of ecstasy all the while, Don moved his feet forward, and leaned his body backward. With his

feet and hands, planted solidly on the bed, the boy used them for leverage while he continued his frantic ride; as he did so, his entire body rode up and down the considerable length of Harp's thrilling shaft, and his long cock bobbed and swayed in a wide arc. In only a minute or two, and without touching his cock, Don's copious orgasm began; his come was flung widely as it erupted from his wildly bobbing prick in eight or ten generous spurts. He continued his eager ride long after his load had been expended. He repositioned himself so he could kiss Harp and lick his own semen from his face, without abandoning the thrill of the large cock that continued it's rapacious invasion of his ass.

Harp began humping wildly as he panted, "I'm about to come, Don!"

Don quickly dismounted and flopped on his back as he said, "Shoot your load on my face!"

Harp seized his cock and began to masturbate furiously as he knelt over Don's chest. In just a moment, he began his orgasm, which he directed at Don's face generally. Don opened his mouth wide and managed to take most of the hot white fluid inside, and before Harp's cock had spent itself, he raised his head to take the erupting shaft inside, and suck the last drops from it.

Harp fell heavily over Don's face. Don continued to nurse on the beautiful prick that had fed him so amply, and at the same time his hands reverently fondled the succulent globes of Harp's ass.

When Don finally had to come up for air, he and Harp lay next to each other while they kissed and embraced tenderly. Don turned to face Rudy, and held out a hand to him. As Rudy took the offered hand, Don said, "God, dad, that was incredible!"

Rudy's eager masturbation had resumed, and he panted a fervent reply to his son, just as he reached another orgasm, "He's the hottest ever, Don!" With his hand still clutching Don's, and his cock discharging its load, he managed to gasp "God Harp, what a gorgeous ass, and what an incredible fuck! You boys are absolutely perfect together!"

All three calmed down, and Harp excused himself to go pee. When he returned, Rudy had put his pants back on, and he motioned for Harp to follow him into the adjoining bedroom.

"You're a beautiful boy, Harp, and I've never seen anything quite as marvelous as your ass while you were fucking Don. How I wish I could fuck you!"

"Rudy, I'd be glad for you to . . . "

Rudy put his hand over Harp's mouth as he replied. "No, you're my special treat for Don tonight. Maybe another time." He took out his wallet. "You quoted $150, here's twice your fee. Stay with Don for a while if you will. I know he'd like for you to fuck him again, if you can, and I'm pretty sure he'd be anxious to fuck you if that's agreeable." Harp began to speak. "No, that's up to you–just stay with him a while longer and do whatever you both want to. You were about to offer to let me fuck you, so I guess

you'd be willing to let Don fuck you; believe me, he's very, very good at it!" He kissed Harp lightly. "Go to him."

"Okay, Rudy, but I don't understand what . . . "

"Maybe Don will explain things to you, maybe he won't; that's his decision. Don't just fuck with him, though, Harp; make love with him. Okay?"

Harp smile. "You got it, Rudy. Another time, maybe?"

"Sure, Harp," Rudy said, and he closed the door behind Harp as he returned to the other bedroom.

Don was sitting on the bed, still naked, propped up against the headboard. "Hi!"

Harp climbed on the bed and lay down on it, opening his arms to welcome Don back in his embrace. He kissed the end of Don's nose, and returned his greeting, leading to an extended period of mutual caressing and kissing of the most tender and affectionate variety. At one point he looked down and observed that the sweet blond boy was quietly crying.

"What's the matter?"

Don laughed nervously, and swiped the back of his hand over his eyes. "It's nothin'. It's just that you're so beautiful and so wonderful, and so . . . so sweet! I'm really happy, Harp."

"I'm glad you're happy, Don. I'm happy too, you know. I really enjoyed making love to you. You're . . . I don't know, so . . . "

"Such a good fuck?" Don giggled.

"I was gonna say you're so sweet too, but yeah, I'd also have to say you're a great fuck! Any guy would be lucky to fuck you-or to get fucked by you," Harp replied.

"You wanna try your luck again?" Don asked as he smiled.

"Oh yeah!" Harp grinned, and reached down to hold Don's cock in his hands. "I'd love to feel this big long dick of your all the way up my butt-almost as much as I want to feel your hot butt squeezing mine tight again."

The kiss that Don gave Harp was passionate. "Thank you! God, that's what I was hopin' you were gonna say. Dad's always so . . . he's such a wonderful man, I just wish he'd let me show him how great I think he is."

Voicing a suspicion that had been growing steadily in his mind, Harp said, "Don, you don't need to tell me anything-I mean, I know it's none of my business, but . . . Rudy's not really your father, is he?"

Don smiled and answered, "No he's not, but he's so much better to me than my real father was. It's a long story, but if you want, I'd be glad to tell you why he was sittin' there watchin' you fuck me while he beat off."

Harp sat up, propped his back against the headboard while he cradled the boy in his arms, and said, "I'd like to know, really."

"Okay, it'll take a while, but hell, we can both be restin' up so we can work up another big load to give each other." He grinned up at Harp. "Okay?"

Harp kissed him. "Sounds perfect! Tell me about it. But be sure you're working on building up that load at the same time."

Don began his story.

"My real dad was a mean, drunk, redneck sonofabitch, and I hated him as far back as I can remember. He was always gettin' drunk and beatin' up on my two brothers; Tim is two years older'n me, and Andy's one year older. The three of us slept in the same bedroom, and I always had to watch while he slapped 'em around. He never hit me, 'cause he always said I was like a little girl, and he didn't hit girls.

"And it was true–I did act like a girl. I dunno why, I've always been like that. Anyway, he didn't hit me, and he never hit Mom either, but he was mean as hell to her. He took his real meanness out on Andy and Tim.

"Mom died two years ago, by the way, when I was fifteen, so I'm only seventeen, not eighteen like Dad told you. When I say 'Dad' I mean Rudy, of course–he's a real dad to me. We always called my real father 'the old man,' except to his face; he made us call him 'Daddy' then.

"Anyway, after my Mom died, the old man got even meaner, and was drunk even more, too. One night he came home quiet for once, so we didn't hear him, and he came into our bedroom and found me kneelin' on my bed with Tim fuckin' me up the ass while I was suckin' Andy's cock. He went ballistic, and really beat up on 'em, and told me I was a little faggot whore. Then he stumbled into his bedroom and passed out.

"Tim and Andy and I had been suckin' each other off as long as I could remember; hell, we didn't have much else to play with! I started swallowin' their loads long before I shot my wad the first time. In fact, Andy and I were actually suckin' each other's cocks right at the very moment I got my first load; Andy got so excited he blew his load down my throat while he was drinkin' mine. I musta started eatin' their loads before I was twelve! But we didn't fuck each other, even though we tried a lot, until Tim fucked one of his buddies at school. I was about fourteen by then, and Tim found he liked fuckin' butt so much, he kept after Andy and me until finally I took him up my ass, and I just flat-out loved it once I got over the pain. Tim wouldn't even let us try to fuck him; he probably drank about five gallons of mine and Andy's come, but I still think he's straight. Andy never did let Tim fuck him, though; Tim's got a really huge cock, and Andy couldn't take it–but it felt great to me. Every once in a while, when Tim wasn't around, Andy'd let me fuck him. And I really loved screwin' him, too, but I knew I liked him screwin' me even more. Tim's big ol' prick was the best, though. So anyway, when the old man walked in on us with both of their cocks inside me, it wasn't anything new–just the first time we got caught.

"The very next night the old man came in drunk, and ran Tim and Andy out of our room; he woulda locked the door, but he never let us have a lock on it. He took his clothes off and started callin' me a 'faggot whore' again, and stuff like that, and then he threw me down on the bed and said he was gonna show me what it felt like to get fucked by a real man, not a couple o'

kids. He made me show him where we kept the Vaseline, and he greased me up and fucked the hell out of me. Tim's cock is a lot bigger, but the old man's hurt a lot more–he was so fuckin' drunk and so fuckin' rough, I could hardly stand it. He shot his load in me and staggered out.

"When Tim and Andy came back and found out what happened, they were ready to go kill him, but we cooked up a plan instead. We figured the old man'd be back to fuck me again some night soon, so Tim borrowed a flash camera and hid it in the living room. A couple o' nights later, the old man staggered in wearin' just his socks, and wavin' his dick and shoutin' for Andy and Tim to get out. They left, and he started fuckin' me again, and just about the time he was ready to come, Tim threw the door open and took a picture with the flash camera, and started runnin' like hell.

"The old man jumped up, and started runnin' after Tim, naked. Well, he still had his socks on, but that made him look even more naked. As soon as they were gone, Andy came in and I got dressed right away, and we ran off together. The old man was too drunk to catch Tim, and besides he was naked, and drunk as he was he knew he couldn't go runnin' down the street that way. So Tim got to the police station, and we met him there like we'd planned. Tim told the Police Chief, who knew my old man was a piece o' crap, that he'd just taken a picture of our dad fuckin' me, and we wanted protection. The chief took the camera and had one of his people take it over for the picture to be developed that night, while he went out lookin' for the old man.

"They found him in a field, naked and passed out, and arrested him. They charged him with all kinds o' shit, and he went to prison for fifteen years. The judge was real nice to us; she put Tim and Andy with different families, and she sent me to live with Rudy. It seemed kinda strange that Tim and Andy got put with regular families and I went with a man who lived by himself alone, but it turned out that the judge was Rudy's sister, and she and Rudy'd been scared of their old man when they were kids, and he'd done pretty much the same thing to Rudy that my old man did to me. She told me that Rudy knew what I'd been through, and she knew he could never do anything like that to me. And she even said that I'd be good for Rudy!

"I don't know if I've been good for Rudy or not, but he tells me I am. And he's the nicest man I've ever known; he's what a real father oughta be like. After I found out how great he was, I asked if I could call him 'Dad,' and he broke down and cried while he hugged me an' told me there wasn't anything that'd make him feel more honored.

"I knew he was gay–and so did the Judge, for that matter. Hell, he didn't even bother to hide the porn or the gay magazines from me. He said that after all I'd been through, there wasn't much reason I couldn't see 'em too if I wanted, but not to tell anybody about it.

"I got horny as shit seein' all those hot guys in the movies and the magazines, and I was really wantin' to fuck, and suck cock again. I knew it was kinda crazy, but I loved Dad so much, and I was so grateful to him for

what he was doin' for me that I finally came right out and asked him to have sex with me, to let me show him how much I loved him. Hell, my real dad fucked me and I hated him; now I had another dad that wasn't really related to me, and who was gay, and who I loved–why couldn't he fuck me? And I mean fuck me because he loved me, not outa hate like the old man did. I really wanted him to, and . . . hell, you've seen him, he's a hot guy for his age.

"It totally blew his mind; he said he couldn't do that, but I convinced him to try. I could tell watchin' him look at videos that he was really hurtin' for sex with a guy. I asked him why not me? Wasn't I good-lookin' enough? Didn't he know I wanted him to make love with me?

"It took a long time before he came around to my way of thinkin', but one night we tried, and we watched videos together and he got horny as hell, but every time I started to suck his cock, or get him to try and fuck me, he lost his hard-on right away. He told me, 'If you were that guy in the video I'd wanna fuck you, and I'd wanna spend hour after hour suckin' your cock, but you're my son, Don. I can't do that with you.' Then he told me he loved me all the more for havin' tried to give him the most precious thing that anybody'd ever offered. That was his word, 'precious.'

"Then he said that if I wasn't his son, he'd be so hot for me he'd do anything to get me in bed. He said that any guy'd be lucky if he got a chance to make love with me. When I told him I really needed to have sex with somebody pretty soon, he offered to find someone for me.

"About a week later we drove to Atlanta and went to this guy's house. He called himself a model in the magazine, but what he meant was that he was sellin' his ass, and Dad was buyin' it for me. The guy was big, and really cute, and built like a brick shithouse, and he seemed nice, and Dad was gonna leave me there with him for a while, but I convinced him to stay there with us. He sat in the living room while I went into the bedroom with the guy, who pulled off his clothes and showed me where he was really big; hell, his meat hung halfway down to his knees! I'd never had a cock like that up my ass, even though Tim's was mighty big. But it wasn't any problem; he stuck that thing all the way up my butt, and fucked like there was no tomorrow!

"We were havin' a great time when I thought about how miserable Dad must be, sittin' in the next room, and I asked the guy if he minded my askin' Dad to watch us have sex. He said it was fine with him, and I went in and made Dad come in and sit next to us and watch. I told him to pretend the guy makin' love with me was really him, and I'd pretend the same thing. The guy didn't mind, hell he was gonna get paid either way.

"It mighta been a crazy idea, but it worked. Dad enjoyed it as much as I did; he was beatin' off like crazy, and a little while later, right after the guy we were visitin' shot this huge load all over me, Dad blew his own wad all over himself. The guy wanted me to fuck him back, which sounded great to me, but as soon as I rammed my cock up his butt and started fuckin' it, I

looked over at Dad, and he'd lost his hard-on. He never wants to watch if I'm fuckin' someone. He's doin' like I said, he's pretending he's the guy I'm screwin' with, and he said he couldn't take a guy up his butt–he had hated gettin' fucked by his father so much that he would never do that again if he could help it. But he knows I like fuckin' butt, and the reason he left us here alone was so I could fuck you, if you want.

"Dad's taken me to see quite a few different guys, whenever one of his friends tells him about one that's really hot, but who's nice too. A buddy of Dad's from Gainesville told him he'd been over here to see you, and he said you were the best. I gotta admit, he's right!"

"That's really a wild story, Don," Harp said. "thanks for telling me. It sure explains a lot. And if I'm not mistaken, I seem to remember you saying just before you started telling it to me, that you'd fuck me if I wanted."

Don kissed Harp fiercely and said, "Jesus, do I ever want! Your ass is the prettiest thing I've ever seen. Yeah, please let me fuck you, Harp!"

Harp lay on his back and spread his legs to welcome Don's invasion, and found that the boy was as talented a top as he had been a bottom; his recent orgasm lent a staying power to the fuck he administered to Harp's ass that was deliriously satisfying. By the time Don blew his load inside the sheath buried deep in Harp's body, he had been fucking steadily, and with a savagery that astonished Harp and completely belied the boy's effeminacy, for over a full half-hour! He continued to fuck with almost undiminished zeal, and without even losing his erection, for another five or ten minutes; Harp was enjoying it enormously, and considered lying there while Don worked up another load to give him, but he could not hold off his own orgasm much longer.

Harp's legs had been locked around Don's waist the entire time he had been thrilling to the boy's precocious mastery; now he spread them, planted his feet on the bed, and arched his back–and with Don's still-hard cock continuing it's work, he began to masturbate. Don took over for him, saying "When you're ready to get your load, let me know."

It took little time before Harp's orgasm loomed. He cried out, "I'm about to come, Don!"

Don immediately pulled out and leaned down to completely engulf Harp's wildly driving cock in his mouth. After only a minute or so of ecstatic sucking, the hot, delicious nectar he craved began to erupt in his throat. Both boys moaned and gasped in excitement while Harp fucked Don's mouth savagely, and delivered a load as copious as his first.

They lay and kissed for some time more, but the hour was by then quite late, and Harp took his leave. Before going he lectured Don about the dangers of ingesting come, and both expressed the hope that circumstances would find them together again soon.

Unfortunately, it was the only time Harp ever saw Don Williamson, but he did get a report on him a few years later, when he was working in Atlanta. Rudy recognized Harp at the Lenox Square shopping mall, and

accosted him. He told him that Don was now a student at Georgia Tech, and was doing well. He said he and Don continued to have sex with each other vicariously, but the stand-in for Rudy was now Don's regular boyfriend, a fellow student at Tech who was not only extremely nice, but who was as devoted to Don as even Rudy could desire. He laughed when he told Harp that Don's relationship was monogamous, but that they welcomed his audience while they practiced their monogamy!

An excerpt from the novel "model/escort," published by STARbooks/Florida Literary Foundation in 1999.

MY COUSIN LIAM by Thomas C. Humphrey

"What's for supper?" I asked my cousin Liam as he stepped out of his bedroom into the upstairs hall of the strangely quiet house. I knew Ma would be working at Sammy's Grill and Pa would be getting tanked up down at the tavern, but the noise at home usually was deafening, what with a couple of radios blaring and my brothers and sisters yelling and screaming and arguing, the littlest ones bawling and whimpering and snatching toys away from each other. Quiet was so unusual that Liam's sudden appearance in the hallway actually startled me, and the hair on the nape of my neck stood up.

Ignoring my question, Liam barked, "Where the hell you been, Casey?" He sounded just like one of my older brothers, now that he was in charge of the house afternoons before Ma got home.

Liam had lived with us in our already-overcrowded house for about a month, since his mother, my Aunt Eva, died down in Roanoke. I had been fascinated by him from the beginning, without quite knowing why. He seemed gentler than the rest of my family, and more sophisticated, having grown up in a city instead of a tiny village like us. He always had time to talk to me, though I pestered him almost continuously. I suppose I was quickly became infatuated with him, without even realizing it. But lately, it seemed that he was becoming more and more like my brothers every day.

We lived in the West Virginia mountains, in what had been a mining camp. Even though the place had grown a little after the mine closed, it still was hardly a town–just one wide street with a rusted railroad track down the middle, a few stores and shops on either side, and a smattering of ramshackle houses teetering on the sides of steep hills. Everything was still coated with a fine black dust years after the mine had closed. We were practically shut off from the rest of the world, and I didn't know a whole lot about most things.

Instead of answering Liam, I just stared at his naked torso, his bare feet, his tight jeans, noting that they were only half zipped. As always, something that I did not understand stirred within me as I gazed at him, making me shiver involuntarily.

Shifting his weight impatiently, Liam repeated his question, "Where the hell you been? It's after five o'clock. You know damn well you got to clean up the kitchen so Barb can get the babies fed when they get back from Grandma's."

"I was at my Scout meeting," I muttered. I didn't bother telling him that I had detoured to watch trout flash silver in the swift-moving stream beneath the old railroad trestle, and then had trotted down a footpath deep in the woods to see if some birds had hatched. All my excitement over earning my

First Class badge and then watching the naked baby blue jays stretch their necks and squawk demandingly for food evaporated under Liam's quarrelsome voice and angry scowl. I knew right away that he was really pissed. He wouldn't understand that I had completely forgotten about time and chores.

"I'll get right to work in the kitchen," I promised, hoping to calm him down. "But I'm starved. What's for supper?" I repeated.

He stared at me for a few seconds with a puzzling expression on his face. He stepped over to me and grabbed my shoulder with one hand and squeezed the bulge in his jeans with the other. "This is," he said, his voice strangely hoarse. "Come on." He tightened down on my shoulder until I flinched with pain, and roughly steered me toward the bedroom. When he kicked the door closed behind us and shoved me toward the double bed, I saw his girlie magazines laid out across the mattress, along with a towel.

I knew all about Liam's magazines. I'd come across them one afternoon when a ball I was bouncing in the hallway skittered into the room and under the bed. When I crouched down to get it, I spotted the stack of magazines. I pulled one out and flipped it open. My heart almost jumped up in my throat when I saw the naked women showing everything they had and men doing all sorts of things to them.

I had been very slow to mature, and I still was excited and a little scared about the changes taking place in my body. Nobody'd ever talked to me about it, except other kids who didn't know any more than I did, and, despite our overcrowded house and shared bedrooms, I'd just caught glimpses of my older brothers as they changed clothes. From the time I was a young kid, a great portion of my life was spent avoiding acceptance of the unhappiness in my family by living in a dream state that denied the reality of my surroundings. This dream state had extended to sexual matters and my own body, until changes in it began to demand attention. It seemed that my penis had started growing almost overnight and wasn't nearly ready to slow down; it was bigger every time I noticed it. It got hard several times a day of its own accord, without me even thinking about it. When I was alone and it happened, an urgency tingled through my whole body, and I ached for something without even knowing what.

After I came across Liam's magazines, I kept sneaking in for a peek whenever I figured I could get away with it, at the risk of catching pure hell if he found me in his room, and I finally stuffed one of them under my shirt and carried it to the bedroom I shared with my little brother, Mark, who was outside playing. As I lay on my stomach practically memorizing the pictures, I knew without really thinking about it that I was focusing on the naked men more than the women, curious about their adult physiques, their hairy bodies, and the varying sizes and shapes of their organs.

I got a raging hard-on and began wiggling my hips around and humping the mattress until I felt like a dam was bursting deep inside me. My dick

started bucking and jumping in my pants. I had to bite down on the pillow to keep from crying out loud as the first spurt of hot wetness soaked my underwear. Nothing like that had ever happened to me before, and when I finally calmed down, I rolled over and tugged my jeans and sopping briefs down. I milked my reddened dick, squeezing the last drop of white fluid out, and rubbed it between my fingers with a deep sigh of pleasure. Little did I know that a lot scarier but ultimately much more satisfying experience would follow only a couple of days later.

Once Liam dragged me into the bedroom, he backed up to the edge of the bed and yanked me around until I was facing him. He had a funny, determined look on his face, and his breathing was short and quick.

"I'm mad as hell about you being so late," he said in the roughest tone I'd ever heard him use. "But I'm also horny as hell," he continued. "Now, I can either beat the living shit out of you with my belt, or you can suck my dick and give me some relief."

He took my hand and guided it to his crotch and cupped it around his hard-on, which twitched against my palm, hot and steely hard. I had seen pictures of women sucking men's dicks in Liam's magazines, and I had vaguely wondered what it would be like. But with my hand on Liam's full crotch, I was afraid to find out. I also was afraid of having the shit beat out of me, though. And I knew that if I pissed him off enough, he could tell Pa on me and I would get a second licking a whole lot worse than the one Liam was liable to give me.

"Undo my pants and take it out," Liam said.

"Uh-uh," I said, taking my hand away. I knew that I was trapped in the room and that he could force me into doing whatever he wanted, but I did not want to suck his dick. Dreamer that I was, I was worldly enough to know what other boys thought of people who did that.

When I hesitated, Liam grabbed my hand and shoved it against his belt buckle. "Either take it out or take my belt off so I can give you a good beating," he said, something in his voice scaring me with its urgency.

I quickly made my decision. Hands trembling almost too much to function, I loosened his belt, unzipped his jeans, and slid them down his thighs. He wasn't wearing underwear, and his long, thick cock jumped straight out as soon as it was freed. I stopped tugging at his jeans and just stared. It was lots bigger than any I had seen in his magazines, the shaft creamy white except for a couple of thick, bluish veins running up the sides, the broad, reddish-purple head already partially uncovered. Suddenly a growing excitement like nothing I'd ever felt before battled my fear of Liam and what he was forcing on me.

"Get on your knees," Liam ordered gruffly, shoving me downward with both hands on my shoulders.

I sank to the floor in front of him, and he poked his cock in my face, the heat of it burning across my cheek as he guided it to my lips. I leaned back

and had time to see a bead of clear fluid ooze out of the tip before he pulled my head back to it.

"Suck it," he whispered, the anger in his voice now gone. He pushed his cockhead against my lips, one strong hand behind my head holding me in place.

"Uh-uh," I muttered, shaking my head back and forth.

"C'mon you little fucker, suck my dick and we'll forget about you being late," he said, the anger back in his voice. Holding my head rigid, he guided his dick to my lips and rubbed it around, forcing them open until the tip of his cock ground against my clenched teeth. As he moved it back and forth, I tasted the slightly salty, musky fluid that kept oozing from his dick.

"Open your mouth and take it," he ordered, and, not really wanting to, my heart pumping with a mixture of fear and growing excitement, I slowly opened my mouth and let him feed his big rod into me.

"Now move up and down on it and run your tongue around," he said when I had taken as much of him in as I could. "And be careful of your teeth," he added.

As I relaxed my jaws and got used to the broad cockhead pushing a little deeper on every thrust, I began using my lips and tongue to caress it, fascinated by its combined steely hardness and velvety softness. As I experimented with it, Liam shoved his jeans on down below his knees. He sat on the edge of the bed, pulling my head along with him, and then lay back and tugged me closer to him.

"Slip my jeans off," he said. After I tossed them aside, he shoved my head back into his crotch. "Now get back to sucking it," he ordered.

I kept moving my mouth up and down on his thick shaft, stopping every once in a while to lick around the head and give my jaws a rest, but after a bit they began to ache from the unfamiliar stretch of his thick cock. I quit sucking it and sat back, wiggling my jaws from side to side.

"Don't quit, dammit," he growled. "You had me almost ready to shoot my load."

"My jaws are tired," I complained. "It's too big!"

"Then play with it with your hand and lick my balls until you rest up," he said, tugging my head back down.

I didn't know anything about jacking somebody off; the only thing I'd done was hump my mattress. I grabbed his prong up near the head, barely able to encircle it with my fingers, and began rubbing and squeezing his spit-slickened knob. With my other hand, I cradled his heavy balls in my palm and lapped all over them, soaking them with my saliva. Liam lay groaning and twitching and reached down to run his fingers through my hair almost tenderly. His dick throbbed in my hand.

"Okay, you ought to be rested," he said finally. "Now suck me off."

I took his rod back in my mouth. Liam began hunching into me, driving deeper and deeper on every thrust until he was banging against my tonsils, making me gag. He threw his legs around my waist and squeezed so hard I

could barely breathe. He reached under my armpits with both hands and pulled me forward on his dick and started lifting his ass off the mattress, humping my mouth like crazy.

"Oh, shit, yeah! That feels so fuckin' good!" he said. "I'm gonna shoot right down your throat!" Without breaking his rhythmical assault on my mouth, he let go of my arms and locked his hands behind my head. "Aaaah! Aaaah!" he cried out, and his dick exploded in my mouth. I tried to twist away from the unexpected heat and force and taste of his cum, but he had me locked on his cock in a vise grip. I had to take his full load, which I thought would never quit spurting. His cock swelled and jerked and fired off volley after volley until my mouth was overflowing and some of his cum dribbled out of the corners of my lips.

Liam sagged back onto the mattress and lay unmoving, his breath deep and ragged, and held me on his dick until it began to soften in my mouth. Then he shoved me off his cock, sat up, and reached for his jeans.

"Now, you get your little ass moving, and get that kitchen cleaned up," he said.

I practically ran out of the room, spitting his load into my hands as I left.

Later, as I stood over the sink of hot soapy water, tears began rolling down my cheeks. I wiped them away, not knowing whether I was crying because of what I had been forced to do, or because of my growing awareness that in a strange and curious way I had enjoyed it.

- - -

After a few more times, I knew for certain that I enjoyed it, and Liam did, too, although he never wanted to talk about what we did afterward. Once he discovered he didn't have to threaten me to get me to suck his dick, I began letting him know I liked him and his big cock. Sometimes in the middle of one of our sessions, I'd just hold his dick and admire it. I even told him I thought it was beautiful and just how much I liked sucking it and giving him pleasure. I decided that he was the best-looking guy I had ever seen, and I thought about him and what we did together so much that getting alone with him and sucking his cock became an obsession.

Finding ways to be alone was not simple, though. Having the house to ourselves, like that first time, was pretty well impossible. And Liam had to watch the young kids almost every afternoon. He became really inventive, though. He would concoct some offense or lapse on my part that was serious enough for him to take me into his room to "talk" to me. No sooner would the door close behind us than he would unzip his jeans, freeing his ready hard-on. On Barb's days off, he invented all sorts of reasons to take me with him out to Grandma's, with a stop at a safe spot off the road before we got there, and sometimes on the way home, too.

After a while, studying the examples in his magazines, I decided I wanted to broaden our activities. One afternoon after he had parked the old pickup

off the road in one of our safe spots on the way to Grandma's, I sucked his dick for a while and then pulled my mouth off.

"Why don't you put it up my ass?"

"You couldn't handle it."

"Bet I could."

"How do you even know about stuff like that? Has somebody else been doing it to you?"

"Uh-uh. I've seen men doing it to women in your magazines. Come on and do it to me."

"You've been sneaking my magazines, huh?" he said. "Well, get your pants down if you want it, you little fart."

I hurriedly tugged my jeans down below my knees, shifted around in the seat, and scooted forward until my forearms rested on the open passenger window and my ass poked up toward him. My dick was hard and throbbing, but Liam didn't even notice.

He wiggled out from under the steering wheel and kneeled on the seat behind me, his long frame bent at the waist to keep him from scraping his head on the roof.

"You're not going to be able to do this," he said, as he spat on his dick a couple of times and slicked it up. He spat again on his fingers and rubbed them around my opening. "Tell me if it hurts too much."

From weeks of practice with my fingers, I had learned how to relax and push out instead of tightening up and sucking inward. When Liam gently probed at my sphincter with his broad cockhead, I was ready for him, and I opened up without any trouble. He sank the head of his dick in me without hurting much, but I wasn't prepared as he kept sliding inch after inch of that long, thick shaft up into me. He had already violated me deeper than my fingers could, and it felt like he had shoved a telephone pole up me, but when I reached back to feel, I found out that he wasn't nearly halfway up inside me. My insides felt queasy, and I was afraid I would throw up.

"Damn, you're hot and tight!" Liam gasped. "Tighter'n any woman I've ever fucked in my life!"

I liked hearing this but I was in pain. "Don't go in any farther," I begged. "Just do me like that. I can't take any more of it."

"Want me to quit?" Liam asked, pulling out slightly.

"You want to quit?" I asked.

"It feels so damn good!" he said, rubbing his big hands over my ass cheeks.

"Then go ahead and do it," I encouraged. "Just don't shove all the way in."

Liam took his time and gently rocked back and forth, sliding his big dick almost out and then only about halfway back in. Every time he went too deep, I flinched away, but he grabbed my thin hips with both hands and held me in position, careful not to hurt me too much, even when he started cumming and I felt his hot spunk bathing my insides.

As we drove on toward Grandma's after he finished fucking me, I tried to get him to talk about it.

"Was what we did as good as doing it with a woman?" I asked.

"Uh-huh," he grunted.

"Have you done it with lots of women?"

"Uh-huh, lots."

"How many?"

"I didn't count 'em."

"About how many, then?"

"Why do you want to know?" he asked crossly. Then he looked over at me and grinned. "Look, I'll kick your ass if you tell anybody, but I haven't ever fucked a woman."

"You haven't?" I said, disbelieving. "Have you ever done it to another boy?"

"Yeah, a couple."

"I bet next time I could take it all if we had something besides spit," I said.

"Maybe," he muttered.

"Did you like doing it?"

"Yeah, it was okay."

"You like it as much as me sucking it?"

"Yeah, maybe."

"Next time it'll be better."

Liam just stared ahead at the road for a while. "I oughtn't to be doing that to you. I ought to wait for a woman for that," he muttered finally. We drove the rest of the way to Grandma's in silence.

Next time was better. Liam surprised me the very next afternoon by hurrying me out of my school clothes, saying he needed me to ride out to Grandma's with him. After we parked at our usual safe spot, he got out of the truck. "Come on," he said, heading through some underbrush into the woods.

I followed at his heels until we reached a small clearing screened by a profusion of white dogwood blossoms, which canopied their small branches, the gnarled trunks separating the whiteness above from the equal whiteness of snow trilium, which covered the ground, punctuated only here and there by the bright red of fire pink. The whole woods smelled like wild honeysuckle.

"Kick your shoes and pants off," Liam said, already prying at his sneakers with his toes and loosening his belt buckle.

As I stepped out of my jeans, the brisk early May afternoon air stung my thighs, and I rubbed goose bumps away with my hands. My dick was standing straight up.

Liam glanced at me as he worked one tight leg of his jeans over his foot. Then he just stood staring, his other leg still in his jeans. "My God," he said, "how'd your dick ever get so big?"

"I dunno," I said, grinning with pride. "It just started growing and hasn't quit."

"If it grows any more, you'll be bigger'n me," he said. "On your little body, it looks more'n a foot already."

"You think so?" I asked, beaming, shoving it away from my body, showing it off.

Liam had already forgotten about my dick. He stood fingering his own hard-on. "Lay down on your back," he said, stooping to get his other pants leg free.

I stretched out on the cold ground and felt the snow trilium crush and tickle at my bare butt and thighs. Goose bumps popped up on my legs and butt. I was glad he hadn't asked me to take off my flannel shirt, too.

As he stood over me, his beautiful dick poking straight out, he reached into his windbreaker pocket and pulled out a little jar of Vaseline. As he greased himself up, he gave me a broad smile. "You said you could take it all if we had something," he said.

He spread my legs apart, kneeled between them, and shoved a big gob of Vaseline up inside me. Then he picked up my legs and draped them across his shoulders.

"You're going to do it this way?" I asked. Suddenly I felt vulnerable and afraid.

Liam pushed against my thighs until he had rolled my butt off the ground and had me bent almost double. He guided his cock with one hand until the broad head parted my ass and slid in. Then he turned his shaft loose and reached under my armpits to grab my shoulders. Using them for leverage, he pulled his body upward, and his thick, greasy cock slid farther and farther in me. I grunted a couple of times and then held my breath and bit down on my lip to keep from crying out. I began to believe that I couldn't take all of him, but I was determined to endure all I could before I asked him to stop.

After it seemed that he had shoved his thick rod two feet up in me, I felt his wiry pubic hair press against my spread cheeks, felt the heat of his balls against my flesh.

"I'll be damned!" he said. "You did take it all."

Without him telling me, I swung my legs outward off his shoulders. He raised his arms out of the way, and I locked my legs around his waist, squeezing to force his body down against mine. I circled his neck with my arms.

"Now do it to me," I said.

At first, he made very small moves and rotated his dick around inside me. Before long, though, his movements became quicker, and he withdrew almost all the way before he tunneled back into me full length. Every time he went all the way in, his cockhead pushed against something and my

stomach got queasy and I felt weak and trembly all over. He had stretched me so wide that my ass was on fire, but I didn't want him to stop. I squirmed around and lifted my ass up and ground my hot, stiff cock against his belly as he fucked me faster and faster, each piledriving thrust threatening to rip me open.

"I'm gonna cum! I can't hold it any longer!" he panted.

He threw his head back and let out a howl and really rammed it to me. About the time I felt his cock swell and jerk inside me, I started to shoot my own load, and my assring clamped down on his cock every time my dick spurted.

He buried his whole long cock in my ass and collapsed on top of me. I felt my insides fill with his hot cum. He rested heavily against me, gasping for breath, and, wrapped all around him, I felt completely at peace with the world.

Liam drove on toward Grandma's without saying a word. I sat fretting that he was feeling guilty about what we had done and worrying that he would never want to do it again. Finally, his chest swelled as he took a deep breath. He let it out with a long whoosh. Then he turned to me and a big smile filled his face. He reached around my shoulders and cupped my arm in his big palm, tugging me over against him.

"You're all right, you little shit," he said. "How 'bout a soda when we get to Markham's store?"

THE PLEASURE BOYS by Peter Gilbert

"How long will I have to stay there?" Alan asked.

The condom rolled effortlessly over Richard's blood-engorged penis. "Not long," he said. He'd said the same thing to the first boy. He couldn't recall the lad's name but he did remember the awful ham-fisted way he tried to get a condom over it and the three torn packets and two ruined attempts that littered the floor. These days it came as second nature. It was the only hobby he'd ever had that he hadn't tired of.

His practiced hands parted Alan's shining buns. Glistening with recently applied oil, it glinted up at him; the nicest, most secret place a young man had. He dragged himself forward, put his hands on Alan's broad shoulders and felt his cock dragging up between Alan's beautifully soft and resilient asscheeks. He didn't have to think what he was doing. It was automatic. Alan gasped. They all did. He moaned slightly as it positioned itself against his entrance. Richard felt him tense up and muttered his usual advice about trying to relax.

Alan yelled as he went in. His tight muscle ring rolled up Richard's cock in much the same way as the condom had– save that it felt tighter, warmer and infinitely more comfortable than anything made of rubber. There was nothing, he thought, quite as satisfying as a healthy youth–and he had access to any number of them.

Alan groaned. Richard stopped. He had all the time in the world. It was odd, he thought, how different young men could be. There were probably as many variations as there were tissue types. In the three years he'd been station director he'd thought many times that he'd experienced them all. There were some whose asses took a cock as easily as a glove takes a finger. There were others who had to be coaxed into opening up. Each one was a surprise. That went for physical appearance too. There were boys whose massive, pendulous cocks turned out to be only a little larger when they were in his mouth and others whose pretty little pricks changed into huge, throbbing, steel-hard shafts in a matter of seconds.

He gave another thrust. Alan sighed. At that stage most of his predecessors were sobbing loudly. Not Alan. A wildly revolutionary thought struck Richard. He dismissed it. He had another problem to solve.

He'd realized on the day Luke Mendoza arrived that he'd be trouble. When he got the message that the station had been upgraded and was due for a huge expansion, Richard had been delighted. His hard work had obviously been appreciated by Central. In six years he'd achieved a lot. The forbidding grimness of the place had been softened by green lawns and flower beds. The prisoners appreciated it. You could tell by the smiles on their faces as the transports drove them in. The criminal ones thought they'd landed up in some soft reformatory where they'd be able to get away with anything. The frightened faces of the prisoners of war changed into happy

grins. All the stories they'd heard had to be untrue. Nobody would go to the trouble of planting flower gardens in a place where young men were slaughtered and dissected so that their organs could be sent off to field hospitals at the various battle fronts.

It was just as well that they never had a chance to inspect those flower beds closely. They would have noticed the little bits of burnt bone mixed with the soil. They stepped off the transporter and into the medical examination room. They undressed without a qualm, stood under the showers for the regulation ten minutes and then lay on the benches and underwent their medical examinations with only an occasional yell as the needles sucked out samples of various tissues and fluids. The doctors were kind and reassuring and that made a lot of difference–and no less a person than the director himself was always present at those examinations, smiling and running his hands appreciatively over the best physical specimens.

It hadn't taken Richard long to strike up a beneficial relationship with Nick Mansfield, the chief examining physician. "This one looks like a reject to me," Richard would say, placing a hand on a particularly beautiful rump or penis.

"Far from it. He's a good one. Rare tissue type too," Nick would reply and then, realizing that he was talking to the one man who knew about his corneal transplant sideline, he'd grin sheepishly. "But on second thoughts you're probably right," he'd say and sign his name in indelible ink on the youth's quivering buttock.

Of course it wasn't as easy as all that. They didn't want to be parted from their buddies. Richard always took the one he'd chosen up into the viewing gallery. One glance at blind old Hans shaving still-twitching bodies was enough to convince them that whatever the director had in store for them was better than that. It was hardly ever necessary to look down into the dissecting rooms.

"What's going to happen to me?" They were usually close to fainting when they asked that question and, by the early hours of the following morning, they knew the answer–or, like Alan, half of it. Most of them stayed with him for about two months. That was as long as it took for Richard's friend Michael to fix the necessary papers and permits. Re-named and officially licensed, the lad joined the rest of Michael's pleasure-boys at The Golden Quoit.

"What if I don't want to go? What if I want to stay with you?" Alan asked again, in a rasping, breathless voice. Richard slid his fingers under the boy's sweaty midriff. Alan's cock was softening slowly in a sticky pool of semen.

"I was just thinking about that. There must be a way," said Richard and, not for the first time, he cursed Luke Mendoza. Something was going to have to be done about Luke.

- - -

"Batch one-zero-nine-two-five. Twenty-seven Australians. Is that right?" Luke asked.

"Correct," said Richard.

"That's odd."

Richard's mouth went dry. "What is?" he asked.

"I can only account for twenty- six."

"A reject obviously. Leave that. We've got fifty-three Russians to process today. Is everything ready for them?"

"Completely."

"You are aware that an anatomist can't work for more than three hours without a break? Fifty-three Ivans are going to take a long time to process."

"I've got three teams standing by."

"Incinerators?"

"Both ready."

"Help for Hans?"

"Arranged, though I doubt he'll need it. He's amazing."

"You seem to have thought of everything."

"I think so. Now, where in hell's name is this missing Aussie?"

"I told you. He must have been a reject."

"He was. There were three rejects but only two went up the chimney. I asked the incinerator people."

"They probably made a mistake. They wouldn't know if a body was Australian. I guess he got mixed up with a previous intake."

"Unlikely. The previous lot were from West Africa and the following batch was from Thailand. Why are we processing Australians anyway? Australia isn't in the war yet."

"Land clearances. Eliminate the young males and you reduce breeding and the work force at the same time. That brings the country to a standstill. Then we move in. I wouldn't worry about just one missing. There'll be several thousand more."

"I've got to find him. I won't rest until I do," said Luke.

"I wish you luck," said Richard. When he'd left for work, Alan had been sound asleep in his bed. He'd have to be moved off the station quickly. There was no doubt of that. But how?

He was still inwardly cursing his over-zealous assistant when he stood in the arrivals hall later that day, surrounded by a throng of laughing young Russians. He made his usual welcoming speech, assuring them that each of them had something special that would enable him to be integrated fully into Euro-American society. The staff, standing behind him smiled at the double meaning. The boys grinned happily as the interpreter passed on the message. Laughing and chatting, they filed off into the shower block.

"Nice-looking bunch," said a soft voice at his side.

"Good morning, Nick. I'd noticed."

"What are they?" Nick asked.

"Prisoners of war. The last remnants of the Russian Army."

They stood chatting about the progress of the war for some time. The first few Russians emerged and obediently got up onto the couches.

"I'd better start work," said Nick. "They're screaming for livers down in the far east. Some bacteriological weapon apparently. It's decimating our lads. I shouldn't really but I guess one can be spared if you feel like a change."

"The present one's giving me problems enough. My ever-efficient new assistant has discovered he's missing."

"Is that what it was about? He came to see me. He wanted me to go through the complete organ inventory. I told him where to get off. Hey! Take a look at this one!"

The young man concerned was tall, fair-haired and sported the biggest penis Richard had ever seen. All nine inches of it swung as he walked towards the nearest empty bench. Some of the others laughed. Nick went over to join his colleagues. Richard stayed a few minutes longer. The Russian boy's butt and legs were just as attractive as his front view. If only... The old adage they'd been taught in training school came back to him: "The needs of the State are paramount." Oh well... perhaps young Ivan's liver was worth more than his ass. Richard went back to his office but couldn't concentrate. Luke's place was empty but his monitor was still on so he was around somewhere–still hunting for Alan. It wouldn't be long before his search radius increased to take in staff housing.

It wasn't often that Richard's bright red "'Dragonfly" was seen parked on the roof of the "Golden Quoit." Richard had no need for the establishment's services. One evening it was there but its owner was not wrestling sweatily with one of the Golden Quoit's boys. He sat in Michael's office.

"I'm doing everything I can," said Michael, "but it takes time to get it all together. New identity, new papers, new bill of health...."

"Can't you take him and hold him here till they come through?" Richard asked.

"He's better off where he is. Surely all you've got to do is keep him out of sight? Anyway, he'll be a greater asset here when you've fucked him enough to make him enjoy it. I don't really see where the problem is. You had young Thomas for six weeks."

It went against the grain to have to explain that he was fearful of his assistant but there was nothing else for it but to tell the truth.

"Mendoza? Mendoza? Luke Mendoza," said Michael. "He's one of my customers."

"I'm not surprised. I guess most of my staff are. This is the best place for miles around."

"I'm not sure. It must be a bit like running a candy store. Most of your guys have seen more cock and ass than the average citizen has had hot dinners. Mendoza's a bit of a problem here."

"How so?"

"I shouldn't be saying this. Customers' anonymity and all that. You know young Robert, the kid who washes the glasses in the bar?"

"Vaguely. I think I've seen him once or twice."

"Your man Mendoza snoops round Robert every time he comes here. I've had to warn him twice."

"But the kid's ... how old?"

"Fifteen. He knows the score of course. He'd have to be pretty stupid not to. The fact of the matter is that I stand to lose my license if anything were to happen to him. There are certain laws in this great country of ours and that one is a hundred per cent enforced. Minimum eighteen years old, in good health and certified as fit for prostitution. That's what it says."

"I know. Maybe I'd better have words with Luke. "

"Be glad if you would. In the meantime I'll get in touch with my contacts to see if we can speed up Alan's papers."

Not all Richard's concentration was on his driving as he flew home. He almost missed the radio beacon, so intent was he on what to do about Luke. The problem was that every idea he came up with carried a possibility of retribution against himself. If he asked for Luke to be transferred, Luke would report the various "irregularities" that Richard turned a blind eye to. Ideally, it should be Luke himself who asked for a transfer but a man with a passion for a local teenager was hardly likely to do that. There had to be something he could do–but what?

He landed the 'Dragonfly" in his parking lot and let himself into the house.

"I expected you earlier," said Alan. "I've made a meal."

"That was good of you. You're not just a pretty face after all."

Alan laughed. "I didn't think you were that interested in my face," he said.

"You do have other attributes that I find more attractive certainly," said Richard. "Come over here."

Alan smiled. He'd done that very often in the last few days. It seemed to light up his face. Obediently, he stepped forward. "What did you have in mind?" he asked.

"This." The old green athletic shorts Alan was wearing were the only garments Richard had that fitted the young man's slim waist. They'd been worn by one or two of Richard's "guests" in the past but only Alan looked right in them. They set off his strong, hairy legs and his tightly muscled butt to perfection– not to mention his thick, fleshy cock. Richard slid his hand down between Alan's back and the cotton. As always, Alan's buns felt delightfully cool and slightly moist. Alan took a step nearer. Richard felt his breath. Then with his free hand round Alan's naked shoulders, he kissed him. He couldn't help it. It was the first time he'd ever done that to one of his boys and, amazingly, Alan didn't repel him. Instead, Richard felt the young man's lips part to admit the tip of his tongue. He pushed harder. Alan's arms went round his waist and his mouth opened wider.

Richard had no idea how long they stood there, clinging together, pushing their tongues as far as they could. Sucking on Alan's tongue, he thought, was almost as good as sucking his cock. It was only when the smell of something burning assailed their nostrils that he started to think logically again.

"Fuck! That's our dinner!" said Alan, as their mouths separated. He disentangled himself and went into the kitchen area. "It's not too bad. It's just about edible," he said when he returned.

"We can always have something else later," said Richard and then, after a pause. "Or we could have something else now."

"Can't imagine what you're on about," said Alan and, once again, he put his arms round Richard's neck and, for the first time since he'd been in the house, pressed his body against that of his rescuer. Richard didn't need to look down. He could feel it pressing and throbbing against the top of his thigh. Once again, he insinuated a hand down the back of the boy's shorts and, for a few seconds only, massaged the soft flesh of Alan's buns. Then he drew his hand upwards, letting his middle finger find the cleft. He pushed gently. He felt Alan's soft buttocks part to admit it and then found the spot he was searching for. There were one or two straggly hairs there. One of them snagged under his finger-nail.

"Bristle butt!" he whispered. "If it hadn't been for me, old Hans would have had them out."

"I'm glad he didn't," Alan murmured dreamily.

"So am I. So am I!"

Hans was the longest-serving member of the staff. He was totally blind, but to watch him work was a revelation. Hans could transform the hairiest youth into an egg-headed, smooth-skinned object in a matter of minutes and chatter away happily as he did so. Like most people on the station, Hans had a sideline. His was bracelets of woven pubic hair. Women wore them as fertility charms. There was no shortage of raw material for those. The bracelets he made for men were necessarily much more expensive. Hans was never happier or more chatty when the conveyor delivered a young man in his mid or late twenties.

"Maybe we strike gold, eh?" he would say and turn the body over onto its front. He'd part the still quivering buttocks and then grin, exposing the most dreadful teeth anyone had ever seen. "Oh ja! A gold mine!" he'd say and pull out each bristly hair with his forceps.

"I wouldn't want any part of you round somebody else's wrist," said Richard.

"I wouldn't mind one part of me being round some part of you though," Alan replied. As if by magic, the shorts dropped to his ankles and he stepped out of them.

For Luke, the burnt dinner and the increasing workload at the station were soon forgotten as their bodies joined, dripping with sweat, to the accompaniment of a growing crescendo of groans, grunts and moans.

When it was over, when Alan lay under him panting for breath and the last trickle of semen dribbled from Richard's shrinking cock, he realized what had happened. He had fallen in love with Alan. It was unbelievable but true. Alan was so different from all the others that he might have come from another planet. Australia was a long way away to be sure but from all Alan had said, the average Australian young man was similar to the average Euro-American, although he had more room to move about in. The average Australian went to school, fucked women and had children. The gay revolution had never caught on in Australia apparently. Alan had been born that way and it was Richard's great luck to have found him–and Alan's fortune that he was still in one piece and not packed in several insulated containers.

Suddenly, without any forethought, Richard spoke. "I'm not going to let you go," he said.

"You'll have to, sooner or later or you'll get no dinner. Stay where you are for a while though. It's a nice feeling."

It wasn't what Richard had meant but he didn't contradict him. It certainly was a nice feeling. Alan's anus was already beginning to show signs of life again and, as for the misunderstanding, there was a hell of a lot to do. Michael would have to be supplied with a replacement boy, but first, Luke Mendoza was going to have to go. Back to the old problem. How and where?

Two weeks later Alan started the chain of thought that led to the answer. He had been talking about a place called "The Bush" in Australia. Not a bar or a brothel apparently but a large open space. It was all a bit difficult to understand. Alan had been "bivvying" in the bush (whatever that meant) when his cock was sucked for the first time. Richard was only listening with half his mind. The other half was occupied by the problem that seemed more and more insoluble the more he thought about it.

"This guy was really weird!" said Alan. "Little kids turned him on so guess what he did."

"No idea," said Richard who wasn't really listening. It had been a bad day. Luke was still ferreting around to find out what had happened to Alan. Michael had called to say that he had public health inspectors on the premises and there was no chance whatever of transferring Alan to the Golden Quoit–even temporarily. Things were not looking good.

"He shaved me. Shaved me all over!" said Alan. "After that I had to make out I was a school-kid. Bloody ridiculous! I was nearly six foot tall even then. Imagine having a guy undress you saying things like 'Let's get at your dear little cockle.' Bloody hell. It can't have grown a lot since then!"

Richard suddenly became very interested indeed. "So what did he say when he saw it?" he asked.

"Oh, some shit about me bein' a well-developed boy for my age. 'I adore little boys with big cocks,' he'd say. Stuff like that. Then he'd ask what I'd been learning in school. Takes all sorts to make a world I guess."

"That's true. I like young men with big cocks. Especially hairy youths, but you've given me an idea."

Alan grinned and stood up. "Thought it might.".

In fact, sucking Alan's cock was not what Richard had been thinking about but his nose was soon buried in Alan's pubic thicket and his tongue was busy lapping up and down the silky exterior of a rigid cock. Once again, he became aware of the extraordinary change in his nature. His idea needed a lot of thinking about and working out. There were questions he'd have to put to Nick. Old Hans would need to be bribed.

With any of Alan's many predecessors, he would have been able to keep at least part of his mind ticking over on the problem whilst coaxing a reluctant cock into stiffness or massaging a resistant asshole until it opened. He couldn't do that with Alan.

It had to be said that some of the others were better endowed than Alan. There had been one boy whose balls were so big, and hung so low that Richard's chin was only a little way above the lad's knee when he licked them. Another's cock was so large and pressed so close to his belly that the only way to get it into his mouth was to rest his head on the lad's chest and slide down on to it. All of them panted and moaned. That was only to be expected. With some of the others, the sounds they made distracted him from his thoughts and he wore ear plugs. He wouldn't have considered doing that with Alan's cock in his mouth. To hell with distractions. To hell with all thoughts of getting rid of Luke-for the moment. Every breath, every moan, every gasped word was the most perfect music in the world.

"Oh yeah! Oh yeah! Oh! I love it. I love it!" and then, "I love it. I love you!" and, as Alan's semen flooded into his mouth, a wave of ecstasy, so strong that it made Richard feel faint, washed over him. He was only dimly aware that he had come himself, the first time that had ever happened. With the others he normally had enough time and energy in reserve to force the youth to suck it or at least to turn over. Even if there wasn't time to get it right in, Richard enjoyed the satisfaction of feeling his semen seeping along the lad's tight cleft and, a few moments later, seeing it run down his hairy thighs.

As for the conversations he enjoyed with his close friends when he was on vacation, Richard knew he would never dream of saying such things about Alan. In fact he would never dream of even mentioning Alan. "Fuck him till he bleeds. He'll soon get used to the idea after that." Richard could be counted on for a good laugh. There was the story of the young man whose cock swelled to such an extent in Richard's mouth that it almost dislocated his jaw. Another one had resisted his attentions so violently that he had to be chained to the cellar wall before Richard succeeded in getting it into his mouth and, because of an abstinence of over a week, he'd come so liberally that Richard couldn't swallow it all.

That was a point, he thought, as he came back to real life. Would Luke swallow the story? Would Hans concur or would he have to be forced?

Nick was no problem. Richard sought him out on the following morning. Patiently, he answered all Richard's questions, apparently delighted to do so. Previous directors had expressed no interest in such matters. "Not so much fun in my opinion but a lot of people prefer it that way. Who am I to say they're wrong," he said. And Richard went off to find Hans. That was no problem. Hans was always in his work room–even when he had nothing to work on. In fact he was just finishing off an intake when Richard walked into the room. "And vat I can do for you, eh, Herr Director?" he said. Hans had an uncanny way of knowing who had come into the room. His razor buzzed in the limp young man's armpits.

"Busy, Hans? I could come back later," said Richard.

"I can talk and vork at the same time. Vat you vant?" Richard told him. "Is no problem," said Hans. "As young man in Germany I vork in barber shop. I know everysing for vhat you vant. Vat you sink of zis one? Nice, eh?"

With a full head of hair he might have been, Richard thought. Hans hoisted the unconscious form over his knees and ran his fingers carefully over the taut torso and belly. Again the razor went to work. The chest hair fell to the ground. Then, with infinite care, the old man took off the pubic bush. It was so dense that it came away almost in one piece. That went into Hans' special box. Then he shaved the legs. "And now I look for ze special ones. I zink he have several," he said and, just as he spoke, the boy moaned.

"Now I talk not longer or he vake up," said Hans. He turned the lad over. The legs jerked. Not wanting to have to help restrain a young man crazed by fear, Richard left hurriedly.

The ideal intake arrived on the following Friday morning. For some days he had watched intakes come in and go through the system. Not one of them fulfilled all his criteria. The Friday intake consisted of two hundred and thirteen prisoners of war from Japan. As usual, Richard was there to welcome them. There was no interpreter this time. Richard had given her the day off. This time he followed them into the shower block and watched intently as they undressed, all laughing and chattering away happily. He soon found a suitable one. None of them was very tall but this one had the added attraction of being extremely slim and, apart from hair in the usual places, his skin was as smooth as that of a small boy.

Richard had to drag him out from under the shower. Reluctantly, the lad dried himself off and put his clothes on again. He had to be pushed, protesting violently in Japanese, to Hans' workroom. The sight of the electrodes, hanging like headphones, together with the copper floor in the next room shook him badly. For a moment, Richard thought he might pass out. He stopped screaming. By the time they reached Hans' workroom, he seemed to be in a trance. He took off his clothes again without demur. Richard pushed him towards the old man. Hans stood up and put both gnarled hands on the boy's head.

"I sink so," he said. His hands dropped to the boy's shoulders and then down from his nipples to his crotch. "Easy," he said. The hands went down even further. "Just a little hair on ze legs and I am sure....." He turned the boy round. "Just as I sink. Noosink. Like a baby is he. A pair of cream buns and not even a vhisper of a hair."

"How long will it take?" Richard asked. Time was important.

"Not long. You stay and vatch. Maybe you hold him still."

Once again, Richard was amazed at Hans' dexterity. The lad seemed so dazed that not much holding was necessary. He submitted to his hair style being changed and to his under-arm hair being removed. The razor moved below his navel. "I take off not all. Just a bit," said Hans but even then the boy kicked out and screamed. Carefully Hans put away the few curls he had shaved off and then worked on the boy's legs. "Zere!" said Hans triumphantly. "Since five minutes you vas Japanese soldier. Now you are Japanese little boy. Go play viz your kite, little boy." He gave the boy a slap on the behind. Richard beckoned to him to dress again. Despite all that Nick had said, he was still worried. Pruning his pubes had made his cock seem larger–far too big for what Richard had in mind. Hans was right about his butt though. He had the fully rounded, 'cheeky' butt of a younger boy.

This time, they walked round the building rather than through it. It was a longer way round but, vaguely remembering things he had learned about the Japanese, Richard had qualms about the boy doing something stupid if he were to see his compatriots trundling upside-down on the conveyor.

He was just in time. The second transport arrived a few seconds after they reached the intake receiving point. The boy recognized several of his friends and went over, presumably to tell them of the strange treatment he had received and thought was in store for them. Richard raced over to his office to see Luke. For a moment he panicked. There was no sign of Luke. He called him. As it happened, Luke was almost next door to the place Richard wanted him to be. One of the stunning units was delivering only a fraction of its rated voltage and Luke was wondering whether to delay the intake or send them through in smaller numbers. He was sorry to hear about the Director's sudden indisposition and, of course, he would go to the receiving point straight away. Richard sat back and smiled.

Twenty minutes later, Nick called. He too was sorry to hear about this sudden onset of sickness. If Richard cared to see him later when he was not so busy, he would see what he could do. In the meantime, however, there was a crisis. Could Richard go down immediately?"

Luke was sitting on a bench with an arm round the boy's shoulder. Nick stood nearby with his clipboard in his hand.

"What's up?" Richard asked.

"This lad. Ahiro is his name. He's nowhere near eighteen," said Luke indignantly. "Someone's made a mistake somewhere along the line."

"What do you think, Nick?" Richard asked.

"It's difficult to say. Dental development says over eighteen. The rest of him is more difficult to assess. That's a fully grown cock and a working pair of balls. He could be an overdeveloped kid or an underdeveloped man. I'd need to open him up to tell you and by then it would be too late."

"So we have to give him the benefit of the doubt," said Richard as authoritatively as he could. "There's no way this station is going to transgress the law. If he's under eighteen he should be in a re-training center, not here. The problem is where are we going to put him? I can't have him hanging around in here while his buddies are sliced up."

"I could take him back to my place while you call Central," said Luke.

"It's no good calling them. You know what they're like. They'll want to send people to see him."

"He can stay at my place for as long as you like," said Luke. "There's only me there."

Well, it worked perfectly. Three days later, Luke stood in front of Richard's desk looking very penitent indeed.

"I feel really sorry about this, Luke," Richard said. "Had I known, I wouldn't have burst in on you like that-even though the lad was in your care and protection. As it was... all that shouting and screaming. I wondered what the hell was going on; broke in and found you up to your nuts in his guts as they say."

"I don't know what to say. I don't know what to do," said Luke, a tear breaking away from the corner of his eye and trickling down his cheek.

"I've been thinking about that. You apply for an immediate transfer or resignation. Take the kid with you if you want. I'll cook the books at this end. As far as Central is concerned, the lad was rejected and is now helping to fertilize the flowers. We say absolutely nothing to anyone. As far as the staff are concerned, you've been given the promotion you deserve and took a few days' leave when you heard about it."

Luke was grateful-as well he might be. He came back later that day to express his thanks.

"Another thing," he said.

"What's that? " Richard was dying to get home to tell Alan that his future was secure.

"I found that missing Australian."

"You did?" Richard's heart gave a rapid double beat and his mouth dried up again. "Where?" he asked.

"My stupid mistake. There were three rejects, just as you said All three were incinerated. It's those idiots on the incinerator. They're more interested in looking through discarded clothing than in keeping a strict body check. You'll need to watch that."

"I will. I definitely will," said Richard and he stood up to shake Luke's hand.

THE STORY OF S: The New Boy In School
by Barnabus Saul

S was the new boy in the school. What you noticed first was his long, golden, curly hair, his tight jeans, and his big bulge. He told everyone to call him S. He also had all the latest computer games so I got myself invited back to his home after school.

He also had progressive parents.

We were playing Manic Raider 7 when his mother ("Call me Meadowblossom") put her head 'round the door of his room. "Have you masturbated today Starburst?" she asked.

"Starburst!" I blushed.

"Mastur...?" I double blushed.

"I have progressive parents." explained S. "No, Meadowblossom," he said.

"Well, would you mind doing it straight away," she smiled encouragingly. "We don't want you getting any nasty complexes. Perhaps your new little friend would like to join you."

I blushed once again. My jaw was sagging and even my butt cheeks were blushing. Meadowblossom disappeared

"I'll go to the john if you like," said S apologetically. "I don't want to embarrass you. They read in a book somewhere that if I don't empty out my testicles regularly it's going to upset my sexual and mental health and I'll turn into a juvenile delinquent or start using sexist language."

"No it's okay," I said. I was amazed. I mean how many guys in the world wank? Just me and a few degenerates in mental homes, right? With glazed eyes and their tongues lolling out of their mouths. So what are the chances that you're going to meet another guy who rubs his rod?

"No really, I'll just sit here. I mean if that's okay with you."

He flipped open his belt, dropped his jeans and boxers and tugged his T-shirt over his head. His dick was soft and small and balanced itself cutely atop generous balls squeezed forward on his thighs as he sat on his bed. "Got some work to do I guess," he grinned tickling the rosette of foreskin with one finger. "Come along, my little darling." His dick began to respond immediately, and so did mine. I watched entranced as he tickled and probed and tantalized the expanding length of meat until it stood proudly, flat to his belly, the helmet protruding halfway out of its collar of foreskin.

I felt my own length begin to throb inside my shorts and wished I were as *up-front* as he was so I could whip it out and start beating off. He manipulated his pecker with his fingertips, rolling the delicate outer sheath of skin back and forth in long, liquid strokes.

"Hey, pass me the Vaseline, would you?" He indicated his bedside cabinet. I opened the lid and held it for him to take a fingerful.

He greased his shaft and the palm of his hand so that it formed a nice slippery fist around his rod.

I sat watching with ... well, I guess my mouth was hanging open. I loved it. I loved the show he was putting on, though I knew it wasn't anything artificial put on a specially for me. He was really getting into the pleasure of it. It would have been the same even if I hadn't been there. His breathing began to get labored and there was a slight rasping at the back of his throat. I happened to catch his eye and he grinned. "Won't be long now! Oh this is good! You oughta join in. This is so good! Oh yeah oh yeah oh yeah!" His rippled belly and thigh muscles began to tense rhythmically and his neck and upper chest were flushing bright red. "Oh yeah oh yeah here we go, here we...."

Just then his mother cried up the stairs from below, "Starburst, have you masturbated yet?"

Starburst lost his rhythm and cursed, "Oh God, Meadowblossom," he bellowed angrily with the full force of his lungs. "I'm doing it for heaven's sake! I'm masturbating! I'm masturbating!"

The bedroom curtains were open and I saw a guy in the house across the way come to the window and look out with considerable interest.

S was still pumping his shaft gently to keep it warm. He grimaced. "Let's try again! We'll see if someone else wants to break my balls."

He increased the speed of his pump action and was soon rhythmically tensing his belly and thigh muscles again. His neck and breasts flushed almost as purple as his knob end and pretty soon the effort of the activity had overtaken him. "Oh yeah oh yeah oh yeah oh yeah," he gasped, over and over again, louder and louder until he was shouting at full volume; the bulb of his dick was glowing bright, shiny purple with every tensing of his muscles and every bellow until finally with a great shout, "Aaaaaargh!" he threw himself back on to the bed and fired several hot jets of spunk across his belly and chest.

At the window across the way the guy had been joined by two others and they broke into applause. From downstairs came. "Well done, Starburst! Now there's a good boy. Meadowblossom is very pleased."

S raised himself to his feet and made an elaborate, sarcastic bow towards the window, causing dribbles of cum to slide down his belly and thighs and to get trapped in his bush. He flopped back down on the bed breathing heavily, his firm, sculpted belly muscles rising and falling rapidly.

I took a handful of tissues from the box beside the bed and gently mopped rivulets of juice from his torso.

He obviously sensed that I was too shy to clean him too close to his private parts because he lifted his head and smiled. "That's really great, thanks very much. It's okay, go ahead," he said, nodding towards his soft but still enlarged dick. It was flopped across his thigh and he raised himself

up on his elbows and watched as I first teased the strings of juice out of his cock hair then cradled the length of his relaxed prick in one hand and wiped it gently clean, sliding the foreskin fully back and cleaning every little crevice and fold of his lovely tool. "That's really great," he said again, "you make me want to come again. Are you sure you don't want to get off?"

"No no, that's fine," I said hastily, suddenly very embarrassed at the way I had let myself get carried away enjoying S's dick. "I really ought to be going."

"Don't go yet, " he said. "Just wait a minute, please. I wanna show you something." He motioned to me to pass him a hardbound book from inside the bedside cupboard. He opened it and made an entry. He wrote the time and place, recorded that he had performed a good healthy wank, and in the comments column he wrote that his new mate, Steve, had watched him and that he had really enjoyed my presence and that I had helped him clean up afterwards

"How much goo would you say I made?" he asked.

"Oh, buckets," I grinned, looking at his balls draped across his beefy thigh. These were high-production modules.

"Thick or thin?" he prompted. "On a scale of one to ten?"

"Porridge." And I watched as he recorded that I had said he produced a bucket of porridge.

I noticed that he had also recorded a long wake-up wank, and that there were five entries for the previous day. "Do you keep a diary of all your wanks?" I asked.

"Sure," he said, and in answer to what must have been an expression of surprise crossing my face he added, "But that's nothing. Let me show you something. I guarantee you ain't seen anything like this before"

Rather than bothering to dress he kicked off his jeans from around his ankles and showed me across the hall into another room. Inside was a camera set up to point at one of the walls which had a series of marks on it. "Every day I do this," he said, "I've done this every day for over a dozen years."

He stood, positioning himself carefully on the marks by the end wall. He adjusted his pose. There was a button on the floor, which he tweaked with one big toe.

"It's something my dad rigged up," he explained. "He's called Cosmic Nirvana, by the way. He likes to keep records, I guess. This is some sort of, like, family album." I heard the camera whir briefly into action, then S went over to a video recorder on the desk and pressed the rewind button. He switched on a television monitor as the tape reached its beginning and pressed play.

There on the screen was S, in the pose he had just adopted against the same backdrop, but on the screen he was very young. "Watch," he said, "you can see me get taller and taller. And from now you can watch me pubing. Look how my little pee-pee grows and how my balls drop."

He ran the tape back and zoomed in on his groin area so we could watch the 90-second sequence of his prick lengthening and thickening, wire curls appearing and his balls bulking out. We watched it two or three times before he apologized. "I'm sorry, am I boring you? It's easy to get carried away with this 'Youth Enraptured in Adoration of Himself' trip."

"No, really," I protested. "I loved it. Really. I just wish I had something like it. I'd love to watch it again sometime."

"Anytime," he smiled. "I've got some of my erection going up and down. Really fine. Look, we can make some of yours if you like. You can run it backwards and watch your pecker suck its squirts back in! Have y'ever seen that?"

I was speechless. Finally I said, "I guessed I ought to get going." I didn't really want to, except I have to admit I was a little afraid his mother would appear and make me masturbate. Little did I know!

S showed me down the stairs, but just as we reached the bottom, the front door opened and in walked S's father. He did not seem in the slightest surprised to find his son buck naked round the house with a chum.

"Pleased to meet you, Steve," he said shaking my hand. "I hope that Starburst has been looking after you. Have you two lads been enjoying a little sodomy together?"

I felt my neck and throat start to flush bright scarlet again. This was getting to be a habit in this house. Meeting S's father was going to be even worse than meeting his mother. To see me blush, any court of law in the land would have been certain that I'd had a rod up my arse the whole day. I made a sort of negative gurgle.

"Don't be shy, Steve," continued S's father, giving my shoulder a little punch. "Sodomy is good for bonding and cementing friendships. You are welcome to come 'round and fuck Starburst any time. Isn't that right, boy?"

"Oh Dad!" wailed S. "We've just been playing computer games. Mom made me have a masturbation and Steve watched."

I blushed even more deeply. Now I was the sort of guy who went around watching other guys jack themselves off.

"But didn't you ask your friend to masturbate?" asked S's father in surprise. "Where are your manners?" He turned to me. "Didn't he even offer you a blowjob?" he asked. "I mean, really...."

I was blushing so furiously I could barely answer. "No, it's okay, Mr. Cosmic. I really ... I...." I spluttered.

"Now really, I won't hear of it," said S's father. "I won't have people saying that any member of this family doesn't know how to behave. Starburst, I am surprised and disappointed in you. You take your friend back upstairs and show him a little hospitality. You should be ashamed of yourself."

S led me back upstairs. I followed his smooth, elastic bare buttocks, wondering frantically about how to extricate myself from this

embarrassment. When we got into his room I stammered, "Really you don't have to do this."

"No, it's okay," said Starburst, kneeling in front of me and starting to unzip my pants. "I'm sorry, it was very rude of me. I should be more considerate."

My jeans and boxers slid down my legs and S tucked my shirt up just above my tits. He ran his hands teasingly up and down my thighs, over my buns, up my back, round to my front making my belly muscles tremble like there was a current passing through them, and then he started to nuzzle into my groin area. He left my prick to stiffen on its own and concentrated on licking around my ballsac and the root of my shaft until it stood a fair way above the horizontal. Then he licked it, wetting it and teasing it and making the very tip of it tingle with anticipation.

I didn't know how long I could keep it from firing off but S's fingers and tongue were so expert at this that he kept bringing me almost to the edge and then pulling me back a little ways.

He held my shaft tightly with the skin tugged back and licked his tongue all around my exposed helmet and around the ridge. Then he began to nibble and suck forcefully on the very end, as if it were a big, juicy nipple, pointing his tongue and trying to push it into the slit.

Then he clapped his hands onto my buns and took the whole length deeply into his mouth sucking it into the back of his throat. My belly was tense and involuntarily I went up on tip-toes with both of my hands holding S's head as he continued to munch on my pecker. I was vaguely aware that my eyes probably had a glazed state and my tongue was draped out of my mouth. Suddenly the door opened and S's father appeared with a tray. Didn't anybody ever knock on a door in that house?

"I brought you some milk and cookies," he said, putting them on the bedside table. "I hope Starburst is doing that to your liking?"

My breath was shuddering but I managed to gasp, "It's ve ve ve very ni ni ni ni ce ce ce! Nice! Oh, thank you, Mr. ... Co Co Co Cosmic, sir!" Now I felt one of S's hands let go of holding tight on to my bun and a finger start to probe its way up in between, heading for my ring.

S's father pulled an encouraging chummy face and said, "Well, I guess I'll leave you boys to get on with it ... unless you'd like me to stay and watch?"

"No, no, no," I said quickly and in a very high voice. I hoped it didn't sound rude, but mostly it was a reaction to getting my tail penetrated by S's finger.

"Well then...."

"No really, that's okay. Thank you, Mr Cosmic, sir."

S's dad made a fist and punched the air as if to give me a chummy punch on the shoulder. He left the room quietly and closed the door.

I couldn't hold it any longer. I yelled to S to watch it and pulled out of his mouth. My rod had gone into overdrive and I was shooting big gobs of

splash all over his face and neck. There was a long, lumpy string across his nose and cheek, and another trailing from his earlobe to his shoulder like some bizarre earring.

"Oh wow!" I gasped.

He twitched the finger that was still inside me, which made my fast-falling shaft jerk and deliver a last couple of wads of the white stuff onto his chest.

"You should keep a diary," he smirked, and his tongue slipped out and licked some of my cum from his lip.

THE BOY COOK'S COMPENDIUM by Peter Gilbert

"Do I have to?" Henry whined.

"Stop complaining, darling. It's very good for you. Thousands of boys don't have one. Daddy didn't when he was a little boy."

"But it tastes horrible!"

"You'll soon get used to it. Come on now. Be a good boy."

Michael flinched as the child's hands reached round his naked thighs, pulling him forwards. He was certainly enjoying a better life than many of his friends caught in the last round-up but he found this business as distasteful as little Henry did.

"Make it nice and stiff like Daddy showed you first. That's a good boy."

Henry's sticky fingers clasped Michael's cock. Michael wondered if the child had washed them since his morning feed. There seemed little point in the Robinson family keeping him so clean if Henry was to be allowed to drink his twice daily medicine in that condition. There was something smeared round the child's mouth too.

Thinking of Henry's lack of hygiene wasn't bringing him any closer to delivering. He gave himself up to other, more pleasant thoughts.

"Good boy!" said Mrs. Robinson. "That's much faster than this morning. You're getting the hang of it at last." For a moment, Michael thought she might be talking to him but she went on. "Now put it in your mouth dear. Don't bite it. Right in now. Now move your head like Daddy showed you."

Michael turned over in bed. That had been a long time ago. Daddy, Michael thought, was considerably better at it than his son. Mr. Robinson only had to say that he felt a bit lethargic and in need of a tonic for Michael's cock to harden. Even better were the occasions when Mrs. Robinson went off for the weekend with her "Progressive Young Mothers' Guild." Henry would be packed off to bed early and Michael would be aware of Mr. Robinson's stare; then of a hand moving up his thigh. "You really are a cracker and no mistake." That's what he'd said last time and then "Let's get these off, shall we? Let the dog see the rabbit though I fancy the rabbit's burrow tonight."

Leaving his shorts on the floor he'd allow the man to shepherd him into the big bedroom and lay him on the primrose-quilted bed. First came the fingering–cold, greasy digits sinking into him; stretching him until he was certain something vital would split. Then...

It was odd how you got used to things, he thought. Just a couple of years ago he'd been a reasonably happy teenager, living with his parents in a small, friendly little English town. Then, one Saturday morning, he went out to buy a transistor for the long range holovisor he was building. He knew about the boy-curfew but it was never imposed with any strictness in Green Vale. Not until that Saturday. Before he knew where he was, he was in the

van with six other boys, one of whom was his great friend Paul. He remembered being stripped and he remembered trying to tell the doctor that it was all a mistake. Then came the twenty-minute journey in a packed aircraft and Michael, together with two hundred and twelve other teenage boys, was on the other side of the Atlantic. He knew as much about the Progressive Republic of America as any other intelligent, fifteen-year-old boy. With over a hundred American holovision channels, not to mention its huge Cosmonet coverage, you'd have to be pretty dim not to know about it but the culture shock was nonetheless considerable.

For a start, the great climatic change had obviously been much more drastic than he'd thought. They were taken overland from the landing pad to the holding area; a twenty- four-hour journey through sheer wasteland. Yet, everybody seemed reasonably well off and well fed. The climatic change in England had resulted in a great deal of poverty and starvation, which in turn gave rise to a horrendous rise in teenage crime–the real reason, as everybody knew, for the selective weekend curfews.

The cause of American prosperity became all too horribly apparent when they were in the holding center. Transports of young men and boys arrived every day, bringing boys from every part of the world. The same vehicles left the same day, equally full. Strong young men for mines and factories. Younger boys for light industry. All of them were destined to be slave laborers; to work for nothing until they dropped and were, as one of the guards put it, "recycled" for spare-part surgery and fertilizer.

Feeling grateful for his slim build, Michael watched them go. His happiness didn't last long. Fifty boys were awakened early one cold morning and paraded naked in a vast hall. "What's up?" Michael whispered.

"God knows," said Paul. "I guess we'll soon find out. There's somebody coming now."

Four men in white coats were moving slowly along the shivering lines of boys.

"How many have you got here?" asked one of the men.

"Fifty. We've selected the best. None of them is too fat."

"Mmm. We only want four. Three for the Senate and one for the White House."

"Hear that?" said Paul excitedly. "Government jobs! And to think my old man's a shop assistant! He stepped forward slightly and smiled.

The men stopped. One of them ran a hand over Paul's chest and naked belly. "Turn round," he said. Still smiling, Paul turned. The man felt his buttocks and thighs. "This one will do for the Senate," he said. "Now we want two more for them."

Paul was ordered out of the ranks and they proceeded to walk up the line. They hardly gave Michael a glance.

Two other boys joined Paul and the men started back along the line, walking this time behind the boys. Three places to Michael's right there was a small group of much younger boys. Judging from the sparse hair at their

groins, he judged them to be about twelve to fourteen years old. They were fair-haired and spoke a language that Michael had never heard in his life. The men stopped.

"How about this one?" one of them asked. He patted the boy on the shoulder.

"We're not looking for an anatomical specimen. You can count his cutlets!" said another.

"There's time to put him on force feeding."

"No. You know what the first lady is like. Very particular, she is."

"This one then." They had moved along the line slightly.

"Now that's more like it."

The boy joined the three others and the parade was dismissed. Michael never saw any of them again. When the guard enlightened him about Paul's fate, he'd vomited for days and yet...

It was odd, he thought, how quickly one got used to the various aspects of the "progressive society." He'd been with the family for two years when he sat down with the Robinsons to Thanksgiving dinner without a qualm. He'd even helped prepare it and had enjoyed Mr. Robinson's joke as he carved the boy's bottom.

"Like a bit of bottom, do you, Michael?" Mr. Robinson had asked.

"I've never had it," Michael replied.

"More fool you. Nothing like a bit of bottom. A bit older than this for preference though."

"I'd have you know I paid a lot for that. You know how expensive pre-adolescents are," said Mrs. Robinson. "Make sure you save the special bits for Henry. They're very good for him."

He'd been lucky to have been bought by the Robinsons. They were a really nice family. True, Henry was a bit of a pain; a spoiled brat if ever there was one. Henry got everything he wanted–and, twice a day, something he wasn't so keen on receiving. As far as Michael could make out, the idea of feeding the boy with fresh semen every day had come from the Progressive Young Mothers' Guild. Most ideas in the Robinson household came from the P.Y.M.G. Whether the twice-daily doses really did Henry any good was doubtful in Michael's opinion. He was growing but then, all boys grew. It certainly wasn't doing anything to improve his character. The only times when Henry wasn't making Michael's life a misery were the morning and evening sessions when his mouth engulfed Michael's cock. By the time Henry was fifteen, Michael had gotten so used to the process that his cock rose the moment he heard the click and buzz of Henry's door opening.

It was about then that the nighttime sessions started. "There!" Henry would say, wiping the pearly spillage from the corners of his mouth with the back of his hand. "Go and wash but don't go to sleep early. I might want to play with you."

It was roughly the same shape as a rocket but it wasn't "Space Stations" that Henry had in mind. The opening of his door had the same instinctive effect even in the middle of the night. There would be a slight pause as Henry tiptoed across to Michael's room. The door would slide open.

"You're not asleep, are you?" he'd whisper and Michael, heavy with sleep, was expected to answer brightly that he wasn't.

"Just as well. What have you got the bed cover over you for? You know I don't like you doing that. I want to look at you. Take it off. That's better."

The first few minutes weren't so bad. There are many worse things than being felt all over by a naked teenager. The trouble lay in Henry's technique, or lack of it, and Michael wasn't allowed to say anything. Time after time he lay there wincing as Henry pumped his penis. Each downward stroke was agony and if he did cry out Henry just grinned and said, "This is hurting you isn't it? Good. I like hurting you. C'mon, I wanna see it come out."

Not surprisingly, Michael was never able to achieve the spurting ejaculation Henry expected and that resulted in a violent slap with a semen-sodden hand.

Each game ended the same way. Michael had to lie with his mouth wide open while Henry stood over him. He handled his own already-quite-big penis with considerably more care.

"Let's see how much you can catch," he would say. "I'll tell you when.... Any minute now. I'm coming. I'm ... there!" and Michael was expected to emulate a sea-lion at the zoo and catch as many drops as he could. More often than not, he missed and that resulted in a painful twist to his balls or having his cock tugged with such force that he wondered sometimes if it might be torn off.

Worse was to come. Henry had three friends: Trevor, Martin and Hank. All three were about the same age as Henry. Mrs. Robinson, more and more involved with the Progressive Young Mothers' Guild, was not usually at home in the early afternoon when the education center closed and, one afternoon, Henry brought the three lads home with him. Michael was in the yard when they arrived, lying out in the sun.

"This is him," said Henry.

The one whom Michael later learned to be Trevor walked over to him. "How old is he?" he asked.

"Twenty. Dad bought him when he was fifteen."

"He's not bad looking. And you have to drink his spunk?"

"Yeah. Twice a day. It's a new idea some professor invented. It makes you strong and I don't have spots on my face like Hank."

It was pretty easy to identify Hank. His acne became more apparent as his cheeks reddened.

"Get him to take his shorts off," said Martin. "Let's see the fountain."

"I can speak English," said Michael, angrily. It was a silly thing to say. Henry, obviously for the benefit of his friends, threw one of his tantrums.

"Don't you dare speak to your betters!" he said and slapped Michael's face. "That's the trouble with him," he added, turning to his three admiring cronies. "He's getting above himself."

If anyone deserved that description it was Henry himself, Michael thought. But he said nothing, stood up and slipped his shorts down to his ankles.

"That's better," said Henry.

"It's big," said Hank. "Get him to make it hard."

"Do it yourself. Suck it ... if you like. He makes plenty."

"Ugh! No thanks. But I wouldn't mind...."

Hank put out a tentative hand and touched it.

"Go on. It won't bite you," said Martin. Hank's long fingers wrapped round Michael's cock. He had soft fingers and Henry could have learned a lot from his technique. It was a pity about the spots, Michael thought, but the kid had a nice smile. If it was really true that semen-swallowing prevented acne, Michael would have been delighted to oblige Hank at any time. Hank put a gentle hand under his balls; a thing Henry never thought of doing. Inexorably, Michael's cock began to rise. He was desperately anxious to give himself up completely to Hank.

The boy was obviously kind-hearted and, despite the facial eruption, he was good looking. He stood so near that Michael felt his breath. He liked the way Hank kept glancing enquiringly at his face, seemingly asking, "Am I doin' all right?"

He cursed the fact that whereas the maximum clothing permitted to slave boys was a pair of short-shorts, Americans could wear any scandalous thing they wanted.

Despite the summer heat, Hank and the others were wearing the full rig of long pants and shirts made of "breathe-through" (but not, unfortunately, see-through) plastic. He looked down. Hank's pants were stretched to the bursting point. He wanted to reach down and open them; to let it pop out. That, unfortunately, was impossible. He couldn't avoid a shudder at the thought of what would happen to him. Hank looked at him with a worried expression and he smiled back reassuringly.

Henry, Martin and Trevor had moved behind him, the better to see Hank at work.

"My brother fucks our kitchen boy," said Trevor.

"Yeah, I know. You told me," said Martin.

"It's the only way of keeping them under control. They can't get above themselves when they've got one of us on top of them. That's what my brother says."

A picture formed suddenly in Michael's mind: an extraordinarily clear picture of Henry lying full-length and face-down, whimpering pitifully as Michael's cock pushed into his tight asshole. Hank's hand was transformed into Henry's inner lining. Michael gasped. The conversation behind him continued.

"He's got a lovely bottom. You should see it when he's got his kitchen apron on," said Trevor.

Henry had never worn a kitchen apron but he did have a nice rear. Michael had been called upon to rub cream into the boy's buttocks after the all-too-few occasions he'd been paddled by Mr. Robinson. A good fucking would do him a lot more good than a few thwacks with a paddle–not just any fuck but a really good, long, drawn out fuck like Mr. Robinson gave Michael when Mrs. Robinson was away at a P.Y.M.G. weekend conference....

"My brother says fucking a boy is the best feeling in the world," said Trevor. "And the boy getting fucked enjoys it too."

"He probably says he does, just to avoid being sold," said Henry.

"No. Honestly, I've heard them. I caught them at it one time. You can tell when a person's enjoying something. No kidding. His tongue was hanging out and he was enjoying every inch. It's a nice feeling isn't it, Hank?"

Hank's hand stopped moving and his fingers tightened round Michael's throbbing shaft.

"I told you not to say anything about that," he said.

"It's okay amongst friends. We're not all lucky enough to have such a kind uncle."

"He's not my uncle. He's a friend of my dad's. Anyway, it was a long time ago."

"Don't try and kid me. I'm not so dumb as your folks. Football practice indeed! You go there every weekend. It must feel good or you wouldn't go. Mind you, what he sees in a spotty kid like you is beyond me."

Michael's excitement peaked. He couldn't hold back any longer. Hank's grip, still tight with anger, prevented too much of a mess. The first jet splashed onto the patio. The rest ran down Michael's legs.

"Dirty bastard!" said Henry. "I'll deal with you later."

"Good for you, Henry," said Trevor. "Take my advice. Fuck him."

"Yeah, I may well do that." The three of them trooped into the house. Michael followed at a respectful distance, staring at Henry's butt and wondering how he was going to achieve his goal. He cleaned up in the bathroom and went to his room. The sign by Henry's door read "SECURE." He put his ear to the cold metal.

"We'd better not go too far. My folks'll be home soon." That was Henry's voice.

"But the door's on 'secure.' Why worry?"

"My dad will wonder why. I don't usually do that."

Trevor laughed. "Neither does my brother. That's how I managed to see him with Alan."

There was a long pause interspersed with shuffling sounds.

"When you get fed up with your uncle, come and see me." That was Martin.

"Shut up about that. Just give me a wank."

"Shall I do it to you or do you want to do it to me, Henry?" said Trevor.

"We can do each other. It'll make a change from Michael's cock."

"It's not his cock you should be thinking about. Get into his ass. Do it as soon as possible."

"Yeah. I'll do that. Oh! Gee! Oh gee, that's good."

Michael slipped into his room, and lay on the bed, thinking. If only he had a security lock he could try his plan in his own room. That was impossible. There had to be another way....

"Mum," said Henry that evening. Michael, as usual, was sitting on his stool in the corner.

"Yes, dear?"

"Why don't you make Michael work in the kitchen? Trevor Busby was here this afternoon. They make their boy work."

"There are only three of us and I enjoy cooking. The Busby's have got three sons. Anyway, that boy of theirs is trained as a cook."

"And a very good cook too," said Mr. Robinson, turning his attention from his computer for a moment. "Remember those boy chops he did?"

"Oh yes. And what about that other meal? The little things. I know what they were but what did he call them?"

"Cocklets Creole."

"That was it."

"What was it?" Henry asked.

"Oh never you mind. That reminds me. Have you had your evening food supplement?"

"No. He made a lot this morning. That's enough."

"Of course it isn't. Come on, you can do it now."

"But I want to see the program about the new Venus colony."

"It won't take more than five minutes. Michael's very quick. You can do it here if you want."

"He'll take longer tonight."

"Why?" said Mr. Robinson sharply.

"Oh nothing."

"I asked you why."

"Trevor and Martin and Hank came round and we had bit of a muck around. Hank tossed him off."

"Hank did what?"

"He tossed him off. "

"And you let him?"

"That Hank has got a dreadful complexion. It won't do him any harm," Mrs. Robinson interjected.

"If Hank's parents want to put him on semen treatment, they can buy a boy for him just like I had to. I will not have something I paid for treated as a plaything. It's a paddling for you, my son."

"He is sixteen, dear," said Mrs. Robinson.

"I didn't do any harm, honestly, Dad. I never even touched him," said Henry is a faltering voice.

"That's besides the point. You let someone else do it-no doubt for your amusement. Go and get undressed and bring me the paddle."

"Trevor Busby's brother does worse things to their kitchen boy and his parents don't mind. Trevor said...."

"I am not in the least interested in what goes on in the Busby household. Even slave-boys have some rights."

"He did it in a good cause, dear," said Mrs. Robinson. That Hank boy does have a dreadful complexion."

"I doubt if even one drop went into his mouth. Did it Henry?"

"Well...."

"Did it?"

"Well no."

"I thought as much. Go and get the paddle. I'll do it down here and Michael can watch."

"Not in front of a slave boy!" said Mrs. Robinson.

"Certainly. It'll make up for the indignity he suffered."

Both Henry and Mrs. Robinson left the room. Henry crestfallen and Mrs. Robinson seething with indignation.

"I'm sorry about that, Michael," said Mr. Robinson. "That boy needs to be taught a lesson. If he carries on as he is at the moment, he'll be confiscated for sure."

"But he's an American citizen," said Michael.

"Makes no difference now. It's mostly political of course. You can't act as police force to the entire world if your own kids are playing havoc. Unless Henry can be made to see sense, it'll be the meat factory for him and I don't fancy the thought of being invited to dinner somewhere and finding my own son on the serving platter. Ah! Here he comes...."

The door opened and Henry came in, with the paddle in his hand. Where he had found it, Michael had no idea. It hadn't been used for a year at least. Henry obviously had the same thought.

"I am sixteen now, Dad," he said in a tremulous voice. "I'm not a kid any more."

"I am well aware of that. Do you know what will happen to you if you keep on like you are?"

Henry nodded.

"You're too old for specialist training and too young for heavy labor. That means the meat factory. Now, this is the very last time I'm going to punish you. One more instance of misbehavior and your mother and I are going to have to give you up. Get up on the couch."

If he had not said that, Michael might have enjoyed the next ten minutes but the sight of Henry lying face down on the couch, together with what Mr. Robinson had said made him remember the previous year's Thanksgiving,

Thwack! The paddle landed on Henry's soft buttocks.

Thwack! That was Mrs. Robinson's hand. "Nice one," she said. "You can always rely on Mr. Blaekley. Why some women buy their Thanksgiving boys from the supermarket I can't imagine. You wouldn't get a nice tender bottom like that in a supermarket."

Henry howled. Mr. Robinson brought the paddle down again. Henry writhed.

"Don't worry about that, boys. They often twitch like that. It shows he's fresh. Mr. Blaekley only slaughtered him this morning. Feel him. He's still warm. We'll need to hang him for a few days to bring the flavor out."

"Where did he come from, Mum?"

"I don't know dear. Look on the invoice. It's on the clip."

"Scandinavian, twelve years and three months," Henry read.

"The best age. Lean thighs and a nice, plump bottom. Daddy likes them like that. And free-range too, coming from there. They get a lot of exercise."

Thwack! The paddle came down again. Henry screamed. "That's enough," said Mr. Robinson. He put a hand on Henry's left shoulder and turned him over. Tears were running down Henry's cheeks. The pain had shrunk his penis so much that it was hardly visible.

"Help me turn him over, boys."

"He hasn't got much of a cock, has he Mum?"

"It'll look bigger when I've plucked him. Then we'll put a bit of foil over his special parts so they don't go too crisp. Just like you like them, darling. Hand me down the cookbook, would you, Michael."

Henry clambered off the couch and stood, shaking visibly.

"Now then, young man," said Mr. Robinson. "I've got a surprise for you. For the next week you are going to learn to obey orders. Now, I'm out at the office all day and your mother's got her P.Y.M.G. meetings. Michael is at home, so for a week you are to do everything Michael tells you. If Michael tells you to stand on your head, you stand on your head. If Michael says 'Jump!' you jump. Is that clear?"

"But, but he's a slave-boy." said Henry.

"I know. It's just for a week and every evening I shall ask Michael if you've done everything he tells you to do and if he says that you haven't even once, I shall have to report you as being beyond control. Now Michael will help you to your room."

Michael put a protective arm round the boy's shivering shoulders. Henry shrugged it off. They reached his room. Henry lay face-down on the bed.

"The bastard!" he said. "Get the cream. It's in the bathroom cabinet."

Michael left the room, fetched the cream and turned the lock to 'secure'.

"Now rub it in. Gently, you stupid oaf!" said Henry.

"Think yourself lucky it's not salt and butter," said Michael, squeezing a large dollop of the cream into the center of the most prominent paddle-mark.

"What's salt and butter got to do with it?"

"Remember helping your mother with last year's Thanksgiving boy? You heard what your dad said might happen to you. 'Rub salt and butter

vigorously into the buttocks'. That's what the book said." Henry shuddered violently. Whether at the memory or because of the hand rubbing his right buttock, Michael didn't know.

"So you've got to do everything I tell you to do for a week. If you don't, the chances are that you'll be on some housewife's kitchen table. Maybe the Busbys'. That would be a turn-up for the books, wouldn't it? Having their famous kitchen boy rubbing your butt with salt and butter?"

Henry said nothing and lay still whilst Michael rotated his hands over the boy's tender bottom, smearing the cream into ever widening circles on each of the three bruises.

"My dad wouldn't do that," he said after a few minutes.

"I think he would. He's at the end of his tether with you and both he and your mother believe in the progressive society. The semen-swallowing, the boy-meat dinners. It's all part of the progressive society." The cream had been absorbed into Henry's skin. His butt shone under the light. Michael added some more and went back to work. Surprisingly, Henry didn't say, "That's enough. You can go now," as he had said on previous occasions. He was obviously thinking things over.

If Michael thought that if he was to succeed in what he was planning, he needed to get the boy really frightened. His cock twitched violently under his shorts as he racked his brains for something suitable to say.

"In fact," he said, increasing the pressure of his hands slightly.... "No, I'd better not tell you."

"Tell me what?"

"Well, you remember that day in the summer when the Busbys came over. You and Trevor were in the pool. I was looking after the drinks."

"What of it?"

"Mr. Busby tried to buy you."

"He didn't?"

"He did. Your Mum was dead against it but your Dad was getting interested."

"He wouldn't."

"It's the progressive society, Henry. I was taken away from my parents when I was fifteen and, as far as I know, they just accepted it."

"Yeah, but you're a slave."

"I wasn't when they rounded me up. I was just like you."

"What did Mr. Busby say?"

"I can't remember all of it. I know he said something about you being a big lad."

"Nothing wrong with that. It's true."

"Then your Mum said it was because you were on a sperm diet and Mrs. Busby said their youngest son could do with something like that. What's his name?"

"Timmy."

"That's right. And Mrs. Busby said she wasn't keen on buying a slave. It would be much better to use a real American boy. Healthier, she said it was." Michael continued to rub.

"Yeah? Go on. Then what?"

"Mr. Busby said you had a really nice butt and how it looked as if there wasn't any fat on it and how he liked rump slices without fat. It got a bit coarse after that. The drink I guess."

"What did he say?"

"He said something about how nice you would look on a serving platter with a bunch of celery sticking out of your stuffing hole."

The moment had come. Michael put down the cream tube and parted Henry's cheeks with his greasy fingers.

"What the hell do you think you're doing?" asked Henry. "He didn't hit me there."

"I'm just wondering if it would be possible. I shouldn't think so." Henry's anus looked like a little brown spot set amongst a few straggly hairs.

"If what's possible?"

"To get a bunch of celery in there," said Michael, with something else in mind. "It might be. I mean, they have to open..." He slid a finger between the soft cheeks and touched it.

"Leave off!" Henry growled.

"It's me who gives the orders this week. I can do what I like."

Henry fell silent. Michael let his finger play on the tightly puckered muscle, holding Henry's buttocks apart with his free hand. In fact, he thought, Henry had a fat ass. It rose almost vertically from the top of his thighs and then curved down to the small of his back. Instinct told Michael that it would feel soft and comfortable when pressed against his groin and a live sixteen-year-old butt was infinitely more pleasing to the eye and the hands than a younger, dead one. What did the cook-book say?

During his first year at the Robinsons, he'd been largely confined to the kitchen, attached to the wall by a long, lightweight chain terminating in a padded, steel collar. Mr. Robinson was naturally anxious that his new purchase shouldn't run away. In retrospect that was just as well. Michael thought that the "Boy Cook's Compendium" might have recipes for cookies and candy. Something to do on the long afternoons when the family were out.

He was wrong. Mrs. Robinson had returned to find him in a near fainting condition. He'd almost strangled himself trying to break the chain. It was only when she had explained that Michael was not due for the family oven that he'd been able to read it objectively. Not entirely objectively. Some chapters were a turn-on. Chapter one was a bore: "Thousands of years of inane taboos have been swept away to create our progressive society." That sort of thing.

It got interesting (and relevant to what he was doing at that moment) in Chapter Two: "Selecting a live boy.

Slowly, very slowly, his finger became less numb. Henry gave a little wriggle. Michael withdrew the finger, dipped it and its companion digit into the cream pot and then pressed them both against what the book, at one point, described as the "rear aperture." "A carrot or some similar vegetable can be used to plug the rear aperture to prevent the juices leaking during the long cooking process."

Henry was so tight that there was no chance whatever of any juice leaking from him. Unfortunately, as Michael was becoming aware, the "cooking" process wasn't going to last very long. His own juices had already started to leak.

"Oh yeah!" Henry gasped. Suddenly he writhed on Michael's exploring fingers. It was time for Henry to be stuffed. Not with a mixture of vegetables and fruit as recommended in the book but by an eight-inch, relatively thick cock that had it not been for the lecturer at Mrs. Robinson's P.Y.M.G. meeting, would have probably been sizzling in someone's fry pan a long time ago.

The fingers came out easily enough. "Oh, put them in again," said Henry.

"No, lift your butt a bit." Michael took his numbed hand from the boy's cock as Henry shuffled his knees forward and raised his behind.

"If your oven is not deep enough to admit the boy's entire length, he will roast well in a kneeling position. Baste regularly."

Henry was pretty well basted the moment Michael struggled out of his shorts. Just like the melted butter recommended in the book, pre cum dribbled over his buttocks. Michael put his hands on the boy's sides and pushed his cock between Henry's cool, still greasy buttocks. And Henry helped! He put his hands behind him and opened his cheeks. For a moment or two Michael contemplated his purple cockhead compressed against the opening. Then, with as much force as he could, he thrust forwards.

"Jeez! Jee-ee-ee-jeez!" Henry exclaimed. Michael's groin slapped against him. A momentary pause and then he gave another thrust. Henry gasped. Then Henry started to pant and he waggled his backside to and fro as if anxious to wind even more into himself. A warm, damp feeling enveloped Michael's cock and he became aware of a pulse that was not his own. Something hard touched his cockhead and, from that moment, there was no stopping either him or Henry. If Mrs. Robinson herself had come into the room at that moment, neither of them would have been able to stop. Henry squirmed and panted. Michael thrust harder and harder into him and then, inevitably, he came, squirting it deep into Henry's spasmodically contracting colon.

Henry continued to pant and writhe for a few seconds and then his head sank forwards. His long blond hair brushed the pillow and spots of his semen appeared, as if magically, on the headboard.

"Better in the rear than the mouth, eh?" said Michael, giving him a friendly slap on the rear.

"Bastard!" said Henry but somehow he didn't sound angry.

He couldn't go to classes the next day. His behind hurt too much, he said. Mrs. Robinson was sympathetic. "It's the last time he'll paddle you darling. I burnt the horrid thing last night," she said. She stayed at home that afternoon to look after Henry. At three o'clock he called "Mum!"

'Yes, darling?"

"Is Michael around?"

"He's with me in the kitchen, dear."

"Send him in."

"Oh good. You'll feel much better after you've had your feed." She turned to Michael who was again engrossed in the "Boy Cook's Compendium."

"He needs his feed, Michael. Give him a good one."

Which Michael did. The head-board, he noticed, looking over Henry's bent back, had been wiped clean. Perhaps Henry had read the book as well.

"Your first attempt will invariably be messy. Make sure all surfaces have been wiped clean before you attempt another boy."

One was enough, Michael thought, as he slid into the now-familiar channel.

They had just finished when Trevor, Hank and Martin called. The headboard had to be wiped clean again and Henry came out of the bathroom as they arrived. Winding a towel round his middle, he took them into his room. Michael waited until the door had closed and put his ear to it.

"Well, did you do it?" Trevor asked.

"Of course I did."

"Good, was he?"

"Bloody marvelous!"

"Told you so."

"Many people experience revulsion at first. This is particularly true of young people but they soon get over this and will come willingly to the table."

That was certainly not true of Henry. He came willingly to bed–either his or Michael's–regularly for the next three months. There were no more nighttime, sadistic games. The same sound of the door opening and the same padded feet, and then the same "Are you asleep?"

After that, the dialogue changed. "God! You're beautiful! Gee, what an ass!" and "Oh yeah! Do it to me! Fuck hard. Real hard. Oh yeah! Yeah!"

Then came the bombshell. Mrs. Robinson came back from her P.Y.M.G. meeting.

"I was just going to, Mum," said Henry. "Michael's washing it now."

"Don't," said Mrs. Robinson. "I don't want you sucking on that thing again."

When her husband got back from work, Michael, sitting on his stool and silent as usual, heard the whole story. Even more modern scientific research had showed that there was no benefit whatever from drinking teenage semen. Indeed, there was a strong risk of disease.

"So we'll put Michael up for sale or have him slaughtered," she said.

"He's twenty years old, dear. He'd be as stringy as old boots."

"He's got a lovely skin, though. That's all the rage at the moment. Mrs. Kershaw made some beautiful handbags out of a boy she bought. It would make a nice hobby for the winter evenings. Stand up for a moment, Michael."

Reluctantly and feeling sick, he got to his feet.

"Mrs. Kershaw made four bags out of a sixteen-year-old. I reckon I can better that." She tugged at Michael's shorts. This will make a lovely novelty bag," she said, fingering his penis. "I'll leave this on the side of the bag with the hair round it. " Her long fingers found his balls. "And there'll be a matching purse inside for small change," she said.

For the next three weeks, Michael couldn't sleep–not even after fucking Henry, who still came to his room every night. Mrs. Robinson had obviously not read the book as well as Michael had. "Slaughterers. 3 p.m." had appeared on the kitchen calendar opposite October 3rd, Henry had been told off to clean the cellar out.

"Can I watch, Mum?" he asked.

"You'll have to ask the men dear. I expect so. It's a bit messy though."

"How do they do it, Mum?"

As if she had been unaware of Michael's presence until that moment, she suddenly looked up and then ordered him out of the kitchen. It didn't take long for him to find out. When the other three boys visited next, Henry was bursting with new- found information for them.

"They'll stun him first with an electrical gadget and then cut his throat," he said. "Then they'll hang him upside down and cut his guts out. They usually cut the head off and take it away but Mum wants to keep it. She's got some idea of making a lamp out of his skull and using his hair for something."

"Cool!" said Martin.

"I'll tell you what...." said Trevor.

"What?"

"I wonder whether they'd let us. I don't see why not...."

"What?" asked the other three again.

"Let us fuck him before they do it. Now that would be really cool. One after the other. I don't see why my brother should be the only one in the family who's fucked a slave and if it's as good as Henry says...."

Henry blushed. "Yeah ... er ... it's great," he said.

"Ask your folks, then."

"Sure. When they get home."

The next few weeks went by more slowly than Michael could remember. He woke up every morning with the sickening feeling that October 3rd was one day closer.

Then, at the end of September when he was seriously contemplating doing it ahead of time and had already selected the longest and sharpest of the kitchen knives, Mrs. Robinson went away for a P.Y.M.G weekend course on decorative leather-work. Henry wanted to spend the weekend with Trevor and, as there was now no need for twice daily food supplements, his parents, especially Mr. Robinson, were pleased to let him go.

"This will be the last time, I guess," said Michael. He was lying on Mr. Robinson's bed with his legs splayed out. He heard Mr. Robinson open the cream jar behind him. For once, Michael was not even slightly aroused. There was just a hope that Mr. Robinson's finger would put some sort of spark into him but doubted it.

"What makes you say that?" said Mr. Robinson.

"October the third. My last day alive. Just over a week to go."

"That's not you. Oh, of course, they wouldn't have told you."

"Told me what?"

"As soon as the wife told Henry she was going to have you put down, he threw one of his tantrums. I can't imagine why. I know you dislike him and he treats you like dirt. However, the wife bowed down as she always does with Henry, and I must say I put my word in. For obvious reasons. Lift your ass up a bit. That's right. Get right into the burrow as the ferret said."

"Ooooh! So... er... what?" Michael asked, as the finger invaded.

"The Busbys' kitchen boy," said Mr. Robinson. "You never let them know what's going to happen to them. You were here when Henry said their eldest son was fucking the boy. I said nothing of course. I'm not in a position to. Not with you and me if you know what I mean...."

"Go on."

"With the finger or the story?"

"Both."

"Well, they found out. I told the wife that she'd make much better handbags out of him than out of you. He's got a real peach of an ass. I'm thinking of getting her to bind a couple of my favorite books in buttock-skin. She told the Busbys'. They were only too glad to agree. So it's Alan who's got the appointment on October the third. Not you. Hello, you're warming up fast."

"I sure am. Can I ask a favor?"

"Sure. What?"

"If there's enough skin, could you ask Mrs. Robinson to have the 'Boy Cook's Compendium' bound as well?"

"Sure I will. Why?"

"There's a good phrase in there. It comes at the end under Barbecues. 'Parting the cheeks carefully....'"

"Like this?" said Mr. Robinson.

"The rod should be well greased."

"Oh, it is. It is...."

"Well, then, insert it at the rear aperture and push it as far as it will ... go. Oh! Oh! Oh!"

WORSHIPING GODS by Leo Cardini

(How Jesse Got That Scar)

"...There were some men at the Mineshaft who were gods. Jesse was one of them."

Jesse. Scarface. Scarface Jesse. Lost in passionate contemplation, I would turn these names over and over again in my mind, mentally fondling them in much the same way another person might finger the beads on a Rosary.

But this was not church. Not by a long shot, though it was certainly just as much a place of worship. No, this was the Mineshaft. Or to be more specific, this was the main bar at the Mineshaft, that narrow, rectangular oasis of light illuminated from above by four low-hanging, low-wattage lamps, in stark, almost brutal, contrast to the shadowy, redlit semi-darkness that pervaded the rest of the Mineshaft. And the object of my worship was no saint or deity, but Jesse, the cowboy-bartender with the intriguing scar on his left cheek, a crude-cut, right angle of a scar consisting of two irregular, one-inch-long ridges of white tissue meeting below the outer edge of his left eye.

Ah, Jesse. There were some men at the Mineshaft who were gods. Jesse was one of them.

There was Cam, the doorman, always looking a little larger than life, who seemed to know everyone's secret sexual desires and had the knack of coaxing them into full expression at the Mineshaft, often right there at the door. There was Kurt, the muscleman-artist who tended bar in the Den, and whose well-known sketches and drawings memorialized the sexual fantasies and adventures of the Mineshaft membership. There was tall, lean, square-jawed Slater, whose eyes blazed with life and who was always in uniform: one night a policeman, on another a Swedish sailor, on yet another a UPS deliveryman. And Little Ricky, the messenger of these gods, always on the run–upstairs, downstairs, in and out of rooms–a hot-tempered, mischievous Mercury who was always getting into trouble.

And there was Jesse the Cowboy, quiet and unflappable, given to frowns when it looked like he was entering another world, a world where a scar like his would not have been such an extraordinary insignia.

What had happened to him? What was the adventure behind the scar? Night after night I would sit at the main bar along the yard or so of it that right-angled in from the bar proper, creating a short, narrow passageway that led to behind the bar, if you took a left, and to the "employees only" area behind the coat check window if you took a right. And from that

vantage point I would observe Jesse, contemplating the where, when and how of his scar, constructing action-packed, wild-West stories where rough, unsmiling men of few words-like Jesse - did whatever they damn well pleased, always coming out on top, and where cowhands-like me-always had to put up with whatever shit was dished out to them by those men when they were horny and hankering for relief.

How many hours had I spent at the Mineshaft, sitting there drinking beer, shirtless and black-leather-vested as usual, with my boots hitched onto the lower rung of my barstool as I leaned forward with my arms crossed and my elbows pressed against the bar? And every moment of that time, I would suffer the sweet ache of my insatiable, usually half-hard cock as it relentlessly teased me, begging me to just go on and slip my hand down into my crotch, unbuttoning my 501s so I could whip it out and jack off an urgent load of cum as I watched Jesse going about his work. As powerful and lithe as a caged tiger, he sauntered back and forth in that narrow space behind the bar, absolutely oblivious to my fascination with him, seemingly unaware of those occasions when I gave in to the demands of my cock and spurting wad after wad of cum against the side of the bar, quickly buttoning up again as my jism oozed down to the sawdust-covered floor below.

Ah, Jesse. Scarface. Scarface Jesse. Trim and tight-muscled. Six-foot-two or three, but looking larger than life to five-foot, ten-inch me.

He had wavy, dark brown hair parted in the middle and pushed back behind his ears, thick, menacing eyebrows, dark, searing eyes and a bushy, abundant moustache that drooped over his upper lip. He had a broad forehead and a prominent, well-defined jaw. He hardly ever smiled, but when he did, he looked meaner than when he frowned, which was frequently.

He always wore cowboy boots-usually black-and faded blue Levi's that strained against his powerful thighs and inched up into his asscrack, approaching that dark, doubtlessly hairy, region that had been the object of my meditations on so many occasions, tantalizing in its inaccessibility, for I was sure if there was any fucking to be done, he would be the one doing it. Though perhaps I could hope to earn a few moments of his approval if I rimmed him and rimmed him good, pulling his asscheeks wide apart and snaking my tongue in as far as it would go and....

But my cock's taking over my thoughts. I was telling you how he dressed, wasn't I?

He wore a wide, black leather belt-good for tanning your hide-and sometimes a red bandana tied around his neck. And always cowboy shirts: plaid flannels, faded blue denims, solid blacks with white snaps. But whatever the color or material, the sleeves were always rolled up, straining against his biceps, and the front was always unsnapped halfway down to his navel, displaying the thick, dark forest of hair that covered his chest. God, the nights I spent longing to run my hands through it, aching to feel it brush

against my fingers as I inched my way up, ascending the muscled contours of his pecs, slowly approaching the sharp stab of his hard, brown nipples....

Anyhow, to pull my thoughts away from my cock again, sometimes, on nights when the Mineshaft was particularly warm and humid, he'd remove the shirt and I could feast on the complex play of his back, shoulders, and arms as he nonchalantly went about his work pouring drinks, pulling cold beers from the bins, honoring requests for Crisco, scooping it out of a large, half-gallon can into small paper cups, all these actions meaning so little to him, while meaning so much to me that I'd sell my soul just to lap from his armpits the sweat all this activity had generated.

But whatever my thoughts, they always returned to his scar.

It looked like someone had tried to tear away a patch of his skin. Perhaps whoever did it had wished to possess it in the voodoo belief that it would give him supernatural powers over reluctant sex partners, transforming them into impassioned participants in any sexual act that pleased his fancy, no matter how cruel, demanding or bizarre.

Or perhaps it was torn away in some subconscious belief that to do so would allow a glimpse inside the man, peeking in like curious kids at a carnival looking through a tear in the tent that housed the hall of tortures, that most desirable of all exhibitions because their parents had strictly designated it as off-limits, or else.

Or maybe it was to slip inside and experience what it was like to actually be Jesse, to feel the texture of his shirt as it brushed against his nipples, or the hang of his Levis on his hips as he went about his chores, or the weight and swing of his cock and balls as they were forced to slightly reposition with every step he took.

But the most intriguing possibility to me was that perhaps it was to look through his eyes and see what he saw during those moments when he was at rest behind the bar. On such occasions he would raise his left foot and rest the sole of his boot against the top edge of one of the beer bins, balance his left elbow on his raised knee, and cradle his chin in the heel of his hand, leaning forward and looking into the darkness beyond the light that illuminated the bar. And as he looked, he seemed totally unaware that his left middle finger repeatedly traced a route along his scar, traveling back and forth and back and forth along that narrow, irregular ridge.

And I would be there watching him, feeling closely connected with that scar as I silently chanted his names–Jesse, Scarface, Scarface Jesse–drawing me into a trance-like state in which I actually became that scar, feeling Jesse's touch, plunging me into my wild-West scenarios where cowhands like me never stood a chance against cowboys like Jesse when they were hot and horny and really needed to get their rocks off, going even so far as to....

Anyhow, Jesse had fallen into one of these reveries exactly one week ago. He was resting boot-against-bin opposite two men in cycle leather, each well over six feet tall, who I found out later came to the Mineshaft because

their sex together was so loud and violent it disturbed their neighbors. He was listening to their conversation when I saw in his eyes that he was drifting off into his own thoughts. The frown on his forehead deepened and I knew he'd left these two cycle men and the rest of the Mineshaft far behind.

His left index finger was making its slow journey across his scar. In my mind the chant started up: Jesse, Scarface, Scarface Jesse. My cock pressed against my Levis with a sweet, dull ache. I became aware of my black leather vest (as usual, I wasn't wearing a shirt) clinging to my warm, sweaty back, and of my hard nipples, so sensitive it was like they were small nubs on the ridge of Jesse's scar, over which his left index finger regularly passed, transmitting waves of pleasure down to my cock.

I went into that world where the Mineshaft becomes a haze as I contemplated how Jesse got that scar. I saw him leaning against the bar in a wild-West saloon. The bartender slid him a shot of whiskey that skated down the length of the bar until it reached him. He picked it up and polished off its contents with one quick gulp. The instantaneous hard-liquor high made him all the hornier for the cowhand gagged and tied to the bed in one of the hotel rooms upstairs.

Change of scene to that very room. It was so dark I could hardly make out the objects around me. The rope that bound me held me securely in place, belly-down, with my hands and legs stretched to the four corners of the bed as if on a rack. My heart was pounding. Sweat covered my forehead and trickled down from my armpits. My clothes lay in a rumpled heap in one corner of the room. The slight breeze from the open window ran across my body, making me aware of my vulnerable state.

I could hear Jesse's footsteps outside the room, getting louder and louder as he approached. The door creaked open. He stepped inside. A few steps later he was standing beside the bed, leaning over and whispering in my ear....

"You're wondering how I got this scar, aren't you?"

The warmth of his breath against my ear as he uttered these words pulled me out of my fantasy and back into the present moment. During my reverie, Jesse had strayed from the two tall leather men and was leaning over across the bar from me.

His closeness was almost overwhelming. The lick of hot breath against my ear filled me like I had just inhaled a powerful aphrodisiac.

I didn't know what to say. I felt my mouth open to respond, but at first nothing came out.

Then, as if from a distance, I heard myself say, "Uh...yes."

"Hey! Little Ricky!" he yelled beyond me into the general area of the coat check room.

"What!" came Little Ricky's annoyed response from somewhere inside it.

"Watch the bar. Time for my break."

Ricky mumbled some indistinct complaint that scarcely reached us, but in no time he was out of the coat check and behind the bar, coughing up a cloud of marijuana smoke as he passed by, silently offering me a half-smoked joint.

I took it and inhaled as Jesse picked up the practically empty beer can in front of me and shook it to see if anything was left in it.

He tossed it into the trash and pulled out two fresh cans of beer from the bin. He opened one and slid it across the bar towards me, and then opened the second for himself.

I held out the joint for him. He took it and inhaled as he walked out from behind the bar, silently nodding for me to follow him.

Beer in hand, I jumped off the bar stool and followed him across the room towards the second-floor entrance to the Mineshaft, my heart beating in anticipation of whatever was going to happen.

Cam was seated on his own barstool just inside the entrance. His boots were hitched onto its lower rung, forcing his legs apart. We stopped as Jesse passed the joint on to Cam. While he took it, my eyes were drawn, as they always were, to the interesting bulge between his legs that was almost hypnotic in its sway over me. I felt a flash of vertigo, like I was going to fall headlong into his crotch.

"Thanks," Cam said still holding in the smoke, as he held out the joint again for Jesse.

"Keep it," Jesse said.

"How you got your scar?" Cam asked.

"Yeah."

The two of them smiled at each other knowingly.

"C'mon," Jesse ordered me as he walked out onto the landing.

Now, opposite the stairs that ascend to the rooftop, there is a recess in the red-painted brick wall, perhaps three feet wide and two feet deep. A pay phone hangs on the right, surrounded with all sorts of scribblings, most of them more fitting for a men's room wall than a pay phone.

Jesse seated himself on the desktop-high wooden shelf that had been fitted into this recess. With his right foot he pulled over the open metal folding chair that was resting nearby, scraping it across the floor until it was close enough for him to rest his foot on.

He took a final, hearty swig of beer and rested it on the shelf beside him with an "Ahh!" of slaked thirst. Wondering what I should do, I followed his lead and took a swig of my own beer as I stood in front of him.

Spreading his legs apart and leaning forward, he rested his left hand on his left thigh, and entwined his right arm around the outside of his bent, right knee until he could grab onto his booted calf. He looked over my right shoulder and into his thoughts.

I stood there, staring at the tantalizing geography of his crotch, where a mere thin layer of worn denim separated me from the subject of so many of my meditations. I had the sudden urge to cast off all my apprehensions and

get down on my knees and bury my face in it. But I checked myself and looked back up into his face.

Our eyes met. It was clear he'd caught me staring at his crotch.

"Hmh. So you want to know about this scar?"

The way he said it, it sounded more like a challenge than a question.

"Uh...yeah."

"You sure?"

Suddenly, I wasn't so sure anymore. But at the same time, I wanted to know more than ever.

I nodded yes.

He looked back out into his thoughts.

"It happened about ten years ago–after the Stonewall, before the Mineshaft."

I could see him settling into his memories as he paused to take another swig of beer. Feeling like I'd been offered a slight respite, I took another swig of my own.

"There used to be this kid. Looked kinda like you."

Jesse's eyes left his thoughts again to size me up. I could feel my chest heave and my cock stiffen as I tried to look at myself through Jesse's eyes: short blond hair, clean-shaven, hazel eyes, regular facial features and standard good looks, except for that quarter-inch gap in my right eyebrow that some said made me look sexy, others evil, and still others both at once.

So I was shorter than average. Did he care? Or did he appreciate my muscular, broad-shouldered physique too much to care? Hell, I'd worked hard enough at developing it. Yeah– a classic case of compensation. So what?

When he, or I, or both of us, had finished this inventory of my physical assets, he half whispered "Yeah," which I interpreted as a sign of approval.

And in response, I could feel my nipples sensitize, two stiff, pinprick stabs against my leather vest.

"Go ahead," he urged, as if reading my mind. "Take it off."

As I removed it, draping it over the bannister behind me, Jesse lifted his booted foot and used it to nudge the chair over several inches towards me.

"Sit down," he ordered.

I obeyed.

"Anyhow," he continued, "there used to be this kid. Those days Cam and I hung out at this place called The Saloon. You've probably never heard of it..."

I hadn't.

"...since it was a private hangout. No advertising. No listing in any guide anywhere. You had to hear of it by word of mouth. And to be allowed in, you needed a sponsor."

Jesse's eyes glazed over. He was back in The Saloon on some post-Stonewall, pre-Mineshaft evening. And there I was also, watching him from across the room.

"Anyhow, it seemed like whenever I was there, he was too. Always alone. Always sitting by himself on this bench that ran along the wall opposite the bar. And always watching me."

Jesse's words came slow and deliberate as his voice got murderously deep.

"At first I didn't pay him much attention. But after a while his stare got to me, like I could feel it crawling all over my skin."

He paused and fixed his forehead in a frown.

"Finally," he continued, "one night, I'd had enough. I looked over at him. There he was, sitting in his usual spot, leaning forward with his forearms resting on his thighs, and his hands hanging between his legs.

"Well, I got up and walked over to him real slow. His eyes were burning into my crotch like he had X-ray vision. With every step I took I could feel my cockhead, like he'd over-sensitized it, rubbing against my Levi's. And no mistaking it, I was getting a hard-on.

"Finally, I was standing right in front of him. Like he was hypnotized, he just continued to stare at my crotch. Christ, he didn't even blink.

"I could feel my heart beating fast, and my temper rising. And I knew that any second I was going to boil over inside.

"See something you like?"

Jesse's query echoed low and menacing in my mind, crowding out all the other sounds at the Mineshaft, as he stood up in front of me, his crotch barely a foot away from my face.

Open-mouthed, I stared straight ahead of me.

"And you know what he said?"

I knew I should've looked up into his face, but I just couldn't tear my eyes away from his crotch. My throat was dry–so dry, I didn't even try to answer. I just slowly shook my head no.

"He didn't say a thing. Not a fucking word. He just continued staring at my crotch.

"'I asked you a question, asshole.'

"But he still didn't say anything. He just gathered up a wad of saliva in his mouth, and spit it out onto the floor, right between my legs!"

Suddenly, Jesse's right hand flew up, the backside of it coming down just as quickly against my left cheek with a loud, sharp smack. It was so forceful and unexpected it knocked me off the chair, which went noisily scudding across the floor behind me as I fell onto my knees, breaking my fall with the palms of my hands.

The next thing I knew, Jesse had his hands clamped on either side of my head, pulling me up onto my knees and angling my face so I was forced to look up at him.

There was sweat on his forehead and he was breathless. Odd that I should have chosen just the moment to notice the day or so's growth of desperado's beard that shadowed his face.

"No, I don't think you meant that, kid. 'Cause if you did, you'd be in deep trouble ... deep trouble."

He paused to let it sink in.

"As if you ain't anyhow," he added with a sneer. "No, I think you do see something you like. Right here!"

Suddenly, Jesse yanked my face into his crotch and held it there. His hands were pressed against my ears and the sounds of the Mineshaft sounded muffled and distant.

My nose was pressed against the prominent bulge in his crotch. I inhaled. Its dirt-denim-and-sweat odor filled my head and spread throughout my body like a potent drug, making every inch of my skin feel super-sensitive. I felt that sweet feeling below my balls that I always get when I'm real horny. My cock began to stiffen, desperately rubbing against the denim in my Levi's, greedy for the little relief it afforded, draining me of all thoughts and desires, except for one - Jesse!

I felt like I'd been pushed headlong, not only into Jesse's crotch, but someplace in post-Stonewall, pre-Mineshaft time to a private club where, if things got too rough, nobody but its members would hear your desperate shouts, and you couldn't count on them to come rushing to your aid.

My first impulse was to push my face even further into Jesse's crotch, if such a thing possible. I wanted to move beyond the denim that separated me from his warm, sweaty body, beyond the skin-deep barriers of his ballsac and the taut outer covering of his hard cockshaft, burrowing deep, deep, deeper inside, assimilating myself into this mean cowboy, becoming one with him.

And then, a split second later, a second impulse washed over me. I wanted to rebel against all this arrogant abuse. Who the fuck did his think he was, slapping me across the cheek, forcing me down onto my knees, and pushing my face into his crotch?

I tried to scream, but it was useless. I tried to pull my face out of his warm, stifling crotch, but Jesse held me firmly in place. I wrapped my hands around his legs and struggled to push myself away from him, but with no luck. The harder I tried to break free, the more firmly he held me in place, a captive on my knees, imprisoned in his crotch.

Suddenly, I felt two hands reaching from behind, clamping down hard and tight around my wrists. Whoever it was, he was much too strong for me, and in no time he had my hands painfully wrenched behind my back.

And my head was still forced into Jesse's crotch! I never felt so helpless and abused in my life. And yet, that sweet aching feeling deep down in my balls refused to go away–if anything, it was intensifying.

I finally gave up trying to resist. Jesse released my head, allowing me to pull my face out of his crotch.

"Hey, there!" from behind. It was Cam's voice, sounding just inches away from my left ear. The thought of this unexpected intimacy–Cam kneeling on his haunches behind my back, his body just inches from mine as he held me

in painful captivity in front of Jesse-exceeded anything in even my most self-indulgent fantasies!

I twisted my head to the left and met Cam's hard-smiling face.

"Remind you of anyone, Cam?" Jesse asked.

"Back in The Saloon, when you got that scar?"

"Yup."

"Then I guess you could say he reminds me of any one of a dozen guys."

With this, they shared a mean laugh, though I didn't understand what was so funny. And what made me think this wasn't the first time they'd been through this scene together?

Jesse looked down at me, moving his right hand to his crotch, fondly massaging the bulge there.

"This is what you're after, isn't it, kid? The same as that other kid back there at The Saloon."

I clenched my jaw and tightened my lips, resolved I wouldn't answer. But there was that crotch. And there was Jesse's hand massaging it.

Cam pulled up on my right arm. The pain increased.

"Isn't it!" Jesse demanded.

I said nothing. But sandwiched between Cam's forceful persuasion and Jesse's captivating crotch, I felt my resolve weakened by a deep, pervading lust.

"I said isn't it!"

I broke out in a sweat.

"Hell, you're not the first kid to get all hot and bothered about this."

He gave his crotch a tug.

"Go ahead, admit it!"

But I still said nothing.

Then Cam gave my arm another yank

"Yes," I finally capitulated in a whisper, my eyes glued to his crotch.

I leaned forward, prevented from falling by Cam's restraining support. I stuck out my tongue as far as it would go and lapped the back of Jesse's hand. After several laps, he turned his hand around and held me by the chin, raising my head until we were eye-to-eye again.

"Good boy," he said, like I was nothing more than a damn mutt.

Then he led my mouth forward until it was about an inch away from his crotch, and released my chin.

I stretched out my tongue and lapped the underside of that denim-enclosed bulge in Jesse's Levis. I could tell from the slight give that I'd planted my tongue on his ballsac. Appreciatively, I lapped it again and again and again.

I pulled away to admire it once more. Ah, yes. I could see through the denim that his cock was growing larger, snaking down his left leg just inches from my face. I leaned forward again and ran my tongue along it, feeling that hefty log lengthen and expand.

Cam relaxed his hold.

"Yeah, that's it, kid," he coaxed as I continued to lick the denim covering Jesse's cock. He was so close to me I could feel the warmth of his breath as it tickled my ear. "Show him how much you like to taste good, hard, cowboy dick."

As Cam looked on, witness to my profound appreciation, Jesse slowly and deliberately unbuckled his belt. Then the top button of his Levi's. I pulled away to watch. My mouth hung open and my breath was shallow in anticipation. My sensitive, hard cock pressed urgently against the denim in my crotch.

His fingers expertly moved from button to button, following their accustomed route, as he slowly opened his fly. The worn denim parted, revealing the narrow trail of hair below his navel that descended his taut lower abdomen until it lost itself in the full forest of his dark pubic hair.

The last button freed, his fly stretched open, spilling over with pubic hair. And in the center, the first few inches of his fat cock–fatter than I ever would have imagined–stood revealed, only to be lost in denim again as it burrowed down his left leg.

I felt Cam loosen his hold on me.

"Yeah," he said to Jesse, "that cock of yours has got him drooling. I don't think you're going to have any trouble with him now."

"For his sake I hope not, or he's gonna be in hotter water than that kid at The Saloon ever was," Cam snorted in reply:

"I just hope you can suck cock as good as he could," Jesse threatened, "because that's what we made him do next."

Cam released my hands. I carefully planted them on Jesse's boots, moving my face closer to his crotch.

"Though we didn't trust him the way we're trusting you right now. No, Cam just stayed right there behind him, giving his arms a friendly little twist every time it looked like his enthusiasm seemed to be waning."

I could hear Cam getting up behind me. From above, he said, "If he gives you any trouble, Jesse, I'll be nearby."

And with that, Cam moved back just inside the doorway, barely five yards away from us, to let in two guys who'd been patiently waiting for him to return to his post. Yeah, while I'd been forced to lick Jesse's crotch on threat of punishment, there were two men standing nearby watching, not lifting a finger in my defense!

When we were left alone, Jesse dug his left hand deep into his jeans and hoisted out his hefty cock, holding it in his clenched fist right in front of my face. There it was, fat, rubbery and half hard, the first several inches of it spilling out of his grasp like it was as curious to examine me as I was to examine it.

But before I had the opportunity to admire it in detail, Jesse released it. His cock plopped down heavily in front of me, scarcely coming to rest when Jesse once again dug his fingers into his Levis, this time pulling out his balls.

His cock and balls fully liberated, he just stood there in front of me with his legs spread apart and his hands on his hips.

"Yeah," he said, clearly appreciating my open-mouthed, cock-hungry stare, "The way you'd watch me at the bar, I could tell whenever you wondered how I got this scar, maybe your thoughts always began up here..."

His left hand moved up to his cheek, where his forefinger traced the right-angled route of his scar.

"...but whether or not you were even aware of it, they always ended up..."

His hand moved down to his cock and he wrapped his fist around it once again, aiming its piss-slit at me.

"...here."

I stared and swallowed hard.

He released his cock. Unhampered, it jerked upwards towards erection as his left hand returned to a resting position on his hip.

"Go ahead," he coaxed, an undertone of challenge in his voice, "take a good look at it. You've wanted to long enough."

His cock slowly began to rise farther, gradually ascending towards full erection just inches in front of my face.

I looked down at his balls, egg-shaped and practically egg-sized, hanging heavily in their low-slung sac. My attentive gaze rose along his thick, light brown cockshaft, networked with prominent blue veins, rising up to an expanse of pinker, paler terrain, finally ascending through that narrow pass that led to this flaring cockhead, which towered majestically above my brow like an exotic purple fruit, overripe and fresh for the plucking.

And as I stared in awe at his–What? Nine or ten inches?– I undid my own jeans, pulling them down mid-thigh and yanking out my own rock-hard cock. In a moment of distraction from admiring Jesse's cock I wondered if he would even bother to glance down between my legs to size me up. I don't mean to brag, but I do have eight inches of fat, cut cock that stubbornly arcs downwards, even when hard, like it was right then, and a smooth, practically hairless, baseball-sized (well, almost!) ballsac, which snugly encased my two large nuts.

"Now, this kid," he said, pulling me out of my reverie, "I had to force him down onto my cock, and hold him there. But I don't think I'll have to do that with you."

In my imagination, I refused to obey, leaving him no alternative but to take my head between his hands again and impatiently force my mouth onto his cock. But I wanted him too much for that.

So what I did instead was to lean forward, stick out my tongue and plant it on his cockshaft, giving it one slow, ascending lap, luxuriating in the smoothness of the skin stretched taut against the veined hardness of his erection.

"Good boy."

His left hand lightly tousled my hair.

"Now take it in your mouth."

And as I wrapped my lips around his cockhead, I closed my eyes and traveled back in time and place to The Saloon, inhabiting the body of that rebellious kid who had to be forced to suck Jesse off, feeling the strain of his every muscle and every movement as he was coerced to comply with his captors' wishes.

I slowly lowered my lips down along his cockshaft, savoring the moment as I descended into bliss. I felt the thickness of his cock as it filled my mouth, then the fleshy fullness of his cockhead as it slipped into my welcoming throat, and finally the tickle of his pubic hair bristling against my nose. I achieved all this only to reverse direction, a return journey over familiar, welcomed territory, gradually dismounting until I was back where I had started, with only his cockhead remaining in my mouth, running the tip of my tongue along his piss-slit and feeling his cock twitch in response, jerking against the constraint of my lips.

A drawn-out, gravelly "Umm" issued from his closed lips and I knew he was pleased with my efforts, which only encouraged me to try all the harder to satisfy him, travelling more slowly, and with tighter lips, up and down his cock, familiarizing myself with every detail of it, each time taking a little bit more of him in until soon his cockhead was regularly slipping down my throat with ease as my nose pressed against his hard abdomen, lost in the sweat-smell jungle of his pubic hair.

At the same time, I worked on my own cock with long, slow strokes, my knees positioned wide apart so my nuts hung tight as coconuts in a tree close by my exposed asscrack, so sensitive it seemed like the very air was stroking me with silky fingers between my spread-open legs.

And all this time men were entering and exiting the Mineshaft, just feet away from us, where Cam stood guard.

Suddenly, Jesse pulled me off his cock.

"Still sure you want to know how I got this scar?."

At that moment, cruelly and desperately separated from his cock, I vigorously nodded yes, panicking over this sudden withdrawal. *Yes! Please, yes! Just give me your cock again!*

"It's a long story," he teased.

I shook my head up and down like it was going out of control. I was furiously pumping on my cock. My mouth hung open, my heart was beating doubletime, and sweat streamed down from my armpits. At that moment I would've done anything he demanded of me. My mind reeled with a dizzying collage of images: I was fucked in the ass; I was crawling on the floor; I was in a crouching position, licking his boots; I was under a table while he and his whiskey-swilling friends played poker and was thoughtlessly kicked and pushed back and forth between their legs, then forced to suck them off.

"Okay, then!"

He pushed me onto his dick again. His cockhead abruptly invaded my throat. Then, with his hands on either side of my head, he took control of

my suck-strokes, forcing me up and down on his cock like I was no more than a jack-off tool, some senseless object whose sole purpose was to bring him to orgasm whenever he felt the need.

Not that I minded. Oh no, not at all! I just gave in to his demands while furiously stroking my own hard cock, a helpless but oh-so-willing victim to my own approaching orgasm.

"Ohh! Ohh!" from above while he tightened his hold on my head.

I could tell from the slight forward thrust of his cock as he tensed his legs that he was clearly on the verge of orgasm.

Then it happened. Spurt after spurt of hot, scalding cum shot out of his cock and into my mouth. In my mind, sprays of his cum gushed across galaxies in stunning arcs, filling my universe, upstaging the rest of creation, so pale and insignificant in comparison.

Then suddenly, he pushed my head back, forcing my mouth off his cock. It jerked up in front of my eyes, drooling cum. He grabbed it with his left hand and dripped the last drops of his spewing jism all over my face.

At the same time my own cum flew out of my cock, landing between his legs in a series of milky-white pools.

A silent, prolonged "Ohhh!" streamed out of my mouth, as if to fill the void left by Jesse's cock.

Then Jesse was still. I remained motionless on my knees in front of him, fascinated with the descent of his cock softening in his hand, a final bead of cum embedded in his piss-slit. I was about to lean forward and dislodge it with my tongue when he broke the silence.

"Yeah, I faced-fucked him as hard as I could. I wanted to make sure he'd never forget what it was like having my cock down his throat. At first he tried to struggle against it, but he was no match for me and Cam. Go ahead, lick it off."

With the tip of my tongue I removed the drop of cum from his piss-slit.

"But do you know what he did after I pulled my cock out of his mouth?"

I looked up at him. He was frowning at the recollection. I nodded no.

Jesse's eyes were blazing again as he continued.

"He spat my cum out on the floor! Right there in front of me!"

Suddenly, so quickly that I couldn't even tell you exactly how he'd managed it, he reached behind me, twisting my left hand behind my back and yanking me off my knees. The next thing I knew I was flattened against the wall at the foot of the stairs leading up to the roof, my right cheek pressed against its rough, cool surface. My Levis had dropped to my ankles and Jesse's body was so hard against my own I could feel his chest heave with anger.

This shirtless guy wearing a Stetson was descending the staircase at that moment. He was so perfectly tall, narrow-waisted and broad-shouldered, he looked more like something Kurt would draw than a real flesh-and-blood hunk. He stopped, backed up a few steps and looked on curiously.

Jesse's hot, threatening voice vibrated in my ear as he whispered to me.

"Yeah. He was really asking for it. And I gave it to him, all right."

With his free hand, he fondled my butt, evaluating it like it was his own personal property.

"Such a pretty butt," he said, slipping his hand up my ass crack. "Yeah, just like that kid's, though I don't know if you could take what was in store for him after he had the cheek to spit my cum out. It began with me ramming my cock up his ass..."

He removed his hand and pressed his crotch against my ass. I could swear he was hard all over again.

"...but you could tell he really dug that, and I realized it would take more than just a fucking–no matter how heavy-duty–to bend him to my will..."

He tightened his grip on my arm. An exquisite wave of pain coursed through my body.

"So I said to him...."

He wrapped his free arm around my chest, crushing the breath out of me as he pulled me hard against him.

"'You just come with me.'"

A wave of panic passed through me. In my mind I saw a room with no witnesses. There I was, bound and gagged. And there was Jesse, just about to...

"Hey, Jesse! Get the fuck back here!"

Little Ricky's shrill voice, full of annoyance, cut through the air and arrested Jesse's actions.

"How long you gonna break for? I got a line a mile long at the coat check, man!" he yelled from behind the main bar.

"Yeah, yeah," he called back, loosening his hold on me, clearly annoyed at being interrupted.

He pushed me against the wall again and whispered in my ear, "I see I haven't gotten to the point where I got this scar. Tomorrow night, if you dare to show up here, wait for me to take my break, and I'll get to it."

I nodded in compliance.

"Hey you," he barked at the tall stud on the staircase.

"Me?" the guy mouthed in surprise, pointing at himself.

"Yeah, you. You look like you got a really *big* piece of equipment there."

Jesse was right. He was stuffed into tight, tight Levis, with this huge cock-bulge pressing against his right leg, looking almost too large to be real.

"Do me a favor, will you? Fuck this kid for me. And fuck him good and hard. If he gives you any trouble, just yell for me –Jesse. I'll be behind the bar."

"Yeah. Sure." Stepping down towards me, he rubbed his left hand against his bulge like he was warming it up for action.

I was passed from Jesse to my new captor with several rough, efficient gestures, pinned once again between a warm body and a rough wall.

Twisting my head around, I watched Jesse saunter back to the bar, looking like nothing of much consequence had happened during his break. That's how little I meant to him!

Well, Mr. Stetson gave me a fucking I won't ever forget. And when he was done, catching his breath without withdrawing his oversized cock from my ass, Little Ricky came over and said to him, "Jesse says to pass him on to some other guy who needs to get his rocks off, and when you're done, come over to the bar and he'll treat you to a beer."

I left the Mineshaft real ass-sore that evening. And the bar must've taken a loss on the free beers Jesse handed out.

But I was sure to return to the Mineshaft the next night. However, before Jesse could get to the part about how he got his scar, his break was over again. That was six nights ago. Every night since then Jesse's continued the story during his break.

Well, over this past week I've sucked Jesse off, he's fucked me up the ass and tortured my tits, I've lapped the sweat from his armpits, drilled my tongue deep into his ass, crawled across the sawdust-covered floor to lick his boots and ... well, then it gets worse, or better, depending on your point of view. But I can't get into it all right now.

I will tell you this, though: I still haven't found out how he got his scar!

Well, maybe tonight.

LEAVE WELL ENOUGH ALONE by Antler

Let Christianity say what it will,
Let Islam, Buddhism, Hinduism
　say what they will,
Let Judaism say what it will,
Let Native American spirituality,
　African-American spirituality
　　say what they will-
In awe of boyhood cock-awe I advance.
Jack off boys with the hands of the dead
　who can no longer jack off boys,
Jack off boys with the hands of the unborn
　who can not yet jack off boys.
Give blowjobs to boys not with your mouth alone
　but with the mouths of all the dead
　and the mouths of those still to be born.
Why not blow a boy's big cock in a single blowjob
　with all the mouths of all the cocksuckers on Earth
　　alive or dead or yet to be?
Stack all the Bibles and sacred texts ever written
　on top of each other so they reach
　　from Earth to the Moon and back
　and place next to them a teenage boy's
　　exquisite dick: hard, throbbing, lubricating-
There's no question which most proves
　the existence of God and life after death.

STARK NEON MEMORIES by K.I. Bard

Early Saturday morning.
Dressed in pajamas and robes,
Michael and I invaded
his father's fish room.
The lowest level of the house,
usually off limits,
was a masculine retreat,
leather-chaired,
an imposing desk,
luminous fish tanks
lining the walls.
Aged ten, we couldn't resist
certain temptations,
risking the forbidden,
pulled by forces
with tendril roots
that penetrated deep,
beyond what we understood
to cause excitement
in what was otherwise fear.
We were, as so often,
after secrets.
What we searched for
we didn't know
other than as a buzzing feeling
buried in the belly-pit.

At ten, the most commonplace
mystery could provoke
a chill-thrill zip along the spine.
An early morning invasion
of the fish room
equal with bolder escapades.
In stealth, we crept inside,
opening and shutting the door
a whispered sigh in the gloom.
Inside, no light but the tanks,
like being underwater,
rows of tanks
quietly bubbling
while we stole

in slow motion silence
across the carpeted floor.
We floated and drifted among the tanks,
Michael having his favorites,
as I had mine,
but we both agreed on how it should end,
in meeting before
the largest tank
where huge Angels cruised,
their long fin-tips
trailing.
The Angels were special,
his father's prizes,
pampered,
their individual beauties
set off by colonies
of dazzling Tetras,
tiny neon jewels
adding swift glories
next to their bigger companions.
Once again we were drawn
before the largest tank
where majestic Angels cruised
among darting neon gems.
We stood in awe.

Perhaps more than we realize
begins in wondrous awe
that tingles the belly
like a silver bell
connected to an unseen wire
pulled jerking through one's core.
More than floating Angels
drew us to side-by-side
merger,
our fingers, hypnotic as the mood,
following the floating fish,
our shoulders bumping
without pulling away,
our breath fogging the glass
as we bent,
peering into the mysteries.
Sharing the room's invasion
we shared the guilt,
a comforting reality if caught

doing the forbidden,
our fingerprints on polished glass.
Mutual risk
a reassuring presence,
another nervous heartbeat
to echo one's own.
A calm pervasive as the hum
of aerator pumps buoyed us
in happy suspension
that neither sank to the bottom
with fear
or broke surface
with useless mirth.
We hung in poised suspension,
our bodies leaning in relaxation
one against the other
while our gazes drifted,
beyond the glassy barrier of separation.

Watching the fish glide,
I wondered what it would be
to cross the glass
to inhabit a fifty gallon planet.
Without realizing the implication,
I imagined Michael joining me,
the two of us, mer-boys, alone,
except for the dazzling Tetras,
companions to joy.
Even through layers of robe and pajamas
I felt his easy warmth relax against my side.
It was a feeling I welcomed,
wanting more.
Being near him made me want something
I didn't understand.
An unfathomable want not limited
to the confines of a tank.
Each time I felt it I experienced its spread
inside and then beyond me.
It was something too big
for comprehension.
It was a presence
to be experienced
only in parts,
the connections between pieces
or episodes,

known to me only
as spine-tingles and belly-flutters.
With Michael breathing quietly
at my side,
I felt it again
and recalled last night
in his tub.
I wanted, once again, to pass my wandering hand
over his underwater flesh
as we played a game
of our own invention,
Find The Soap.
In the tank of his tub
I searched for the hidden soap,
his eyes guiding me,
encouraging,
fluttering in delight.
We took turns hiding the soap,
which slowly made the water cloudier.
Clouded water hid us,
excused our touching.
We blushed
while our eyes sparkled,
dancing in revelation.

Was that the first time
I knew
I loved him?
Was it then,
that weekend,
sleeping over
I first knew?
Was it the tub,
the fish tank,
or feeling him near me in bed?
Was it then,
with dazzling Tetras darting
that first I knew,
suspected
what lay in my deeps?
No.
I'd known months before
when an older boy
pulled me aside
lured me with unaccustomed friendliness

until I dropped my guard.
With a smile
he kneed me in the groin.
Clutching myself and groaning,
I fell onto my knees
while through resolve
not to let him see me cry
tears crept free with my moans.
Which pain was worse?
The one between my legs?
Or between my ears?
"Little fairy." He hissed,
bending low to sneer.
"Yer nothin' but a little fag."
That was when I first knew,
a message so clear
that when I touched Michael
my hand trembled.
Cold neon fright
glowed in the deeps,
showed itself
through the murkiest
soap-clouded waters.
There was no hiding
and no escape
from its fluorescent joys
or stark neon pains.

ODE TO BOY by Kevin Bantan

Your smile is innocent and genuine,
Radiant in an unblemished face.
Your eyes glint with the naivete of youth.
Above, your hair shines like emerging corn silk.

Your smooth skin is delightful to the touch,
surpassing the finest fabric; its surface flawless.
Beneath, your sinews are imbued with power;
They flex and stretch without effort or protest.

The emblem of your maleness rests handsome and proud
between your solid thighs;
Your source of intense physical pleasure;
Its nerves instantly responsive to your youthful whim.

 You are the idol to which silent prayers are sent by those beholding your countenance.
 You are the altar on which desire longs to be consecrated.
 You are the essence of human beauty.
 You are boy.

jesus + the turtles by Carl Miller Daniels

(this fantasy is so peculiar it surprises even me)

i thought that
if i ever prayed again
i would ask jesus to look out
for the
turtles
crossing the highways
i'd ask jesus
to protect all the turtles
to make all
the drivers
kind + considerate
so drivers wouldn't
squash any more
turtles
ever
then
i'd ask him if he
cared to join me for
a drink
he'd say
yes + we'd be
sitting outside at
a cafe or something
i'd have to
show him how crass
i really am
i'd ask him for 10 million dollars +
he'd just laugh +
then we'd talk
about kindness
+ homosexuals
+ he'd say
he's all in favor
of kindness
to everybody
in this fantasy
i'd still be single
perhaps i hadn't even

been introduced
to my lover yet
but still i'd be
kinda afraid
i'd wonder why
i was
afraid to
ask jesus to go to
bed with me
who taught me
that jesus never had sex
and that he wouldn't if
he coulda
still though
i ask him
anyway to
go to
bed with me
and i'm
surprised when he says yes
but positively
startled to find out that he's
into S/M, and
i don't believe him
when he tells me
that turtles all over
the world
are busily copulating
messily
at exactly the
same
instant
that we are.
it bothers him
that i don't believe
him
about the turtles
+
i'm afraid
that when we
part, it's
on
the
shakiest
of terms.

CELEBRATION by Carl Miller Daniels

he was
troubled
by TOTAL JOY as he
and 5 other high-school-boy/JOCK/athletes
treaded water and celebrated his
18TH BIRTHDAY. it was
almost midnight, the water WARM,
hyper-friendly.
girls' body parts were
discussed with general ignorance
as if by EXPERTS.
UNDERWATER ERECTIONS
occur in secret in the
warm GENTLE-current water.
minnows swimming silver silent
TOO MUCH LAUGHTER
dwindles to silence
and BEER on the crescent sliver sandy BEACH
6 boys in the warm night, one of them
TURNED FRESHLY 18
and nothing like sex
except for the way the hot wet air
clings to the WET YOUNG SKIN
yet/yes oh yes/it's
a SEX-FREE ZONE
all candy strictly
off limits!!!!
shhh

*Beyond love,
beyond obsession,
there hides something
quite beyond reason...*

BEYOND IMAGINING
by JOHN PATRICK

An Erotic Roman a Clef

STARbooks Press
Sarasota, Florida

> "In Hollywood, if you don't have happiness, you send out for it."
> - Film Critic Rex Reed

> "In L.A. when you meet somebody... it's not, 'Are you attracted to me?' it's 'I wonder what they want from me?'"
> Doe Gentry, Singles Correspondent

> "Who cares to define / What chemistry this is? Who cares, with your lips on mine / What ignorance bliss is?"

PROLOGUE

The schoolboys developed an unprecedented enthusiasm for singing in the Christmas cantata. It exhilarated their director, Lucius Bonner, to observe their progress under his tutelage. One boy stood out: Sam Saxon. Sam looked the part of the angel he was portraying, and, best of all, he had the voice of an angel. It was amazing, given that he was such a little devil in reality.

Was the performance, as Sam's pounding heart told him, really the chance of his lifetime? He sang as if it were, and when he appeared to take his curtain call, the whole room rose. It was a night without precedent.

Lucius had done a remarkable thing, taking these juvenile delinquents and making them stars, at least for one night. Lucius approached Sam, saying, "I take a personal pride in the whole thing because I always maintained that you had a first-class talent. Only we didn't know exactly what it consisted of. Now, of course, it's clear. You're a singer. I don't say that you should necessarily go on the stage, but maybe we should arrange for a recording. I don't know. We'll have to see. We'll have to look into things."

Now Lucius felt like one who had been awakened from a deep sleep by the sudden rattle of a shade being snapped up. He was awed by Sam's talent. He knew that he had been the presence of something special. Just how special, he could never have imagined.

It had only been a few months ago that he had seen Sam sitting there, in the back of the classroom, sneering at him. It was as if Sam hated school, hated him, hated everything.

Boys like Sam scared Lucius, and he kept his distance from the boy. Then Lucius happened to be cruising through the park one mild spring day. He

seldom made such journeys, and when he did he usually just looked at what was on display. Once a year, at most, he might be so overcome with desire that he actually approached one of the boys who was on parade. He had too much to lose if something went wrong.

When he first saw the kid standing near the fountain, Lucius couldn't believe it was really Sam. He drove around again and again, then parked his car. He got out of his car and approached the boy with a mixture of fear and desire.

"I had to be sure," he said.

Sam smiled at Lucius. He had seen the boy flash that smile on the girls in class, but this was the first time the boy was aiming it at him. "Well, well...."

Sam, chuckling, got in the car. Lucius sped away.

They were silent for a couple of blocks, then Sam said, "I've known about you from the first day, but you never made a move."

"I'm a terrible waster of time," Lucius said. Then he chuckled. It amazed him how some guys could always know one when they saw one. He'd never developed that talent. Obviously, he'd had no inkling Sam was available. Of all the boys in the class.... "At least I know you're not a cop," Lucius said.

"You've had trouble with cops at the park?"

"No, but I've heard stories. Terrible stories. That's why I don't make a habit...."

"Don't make a sound," Lucius whispered as they entered the house and slowly made their way to the basement "playroom." Lucius still lived with his mother and he said she would be sleeping and he didn't want to disturb her. Sam said he understood perfectly.

Sam noticed there was something different about Lucius' voice now. It was too soft, too honeyed, like the voice of a corrupt priest saying prayers while fondling an acolyte in the confessional. Even as a part of Sam was terrified being in Lucius' company, with his mother upstairs, there was another part of him longing to be touched, touched the way other horny men had touched him.

Lucius closed and bolted the door to his private sanctuary and dropped to his knees before Sam. Sam was glad all Lucius seemed to want was to worship his cock. Sam had been with other men who wanted something more, something different, when all Sam craved was a quick blowjob.

Sam remembered a guy who wanted to treat him to "lunch." They went through the drive-through at Wendy's, then the man drove to the edge of town. They got out of the car and went deep into the woods.

It was peaceful being in those woods, nobody but them, and they ate their hamburgers. "What do you want to be?" the man asked Sam.

"What do you mean?"

"Life," he said. "You know, what you want from it." Sam thought about that for a while. Nobody had ever told him he could have a choice. He knew what he did with men would be considered criminal by some and knew that wasn't what he wanted. Lucius had told Sam he could be whatever he

wanted to be, but Sam hadn't really thought much about the future. The man had asked Sam what he wanted out of life, so Sam answered: "Freedom." And Sam thought he knew how to get it–through sex. He told the stranger that he was the son of a single parent struggling to make ends meet. Then his mother remarried a truck driver who thought the iron fist was the only way to deal with teenagers. The strait-jacket of rules was driving Sam over the edge. He was only happy when he was out of the house and someone like Lucius was paying him compliments.

The stranger, whose thick hair was blacker than shoe polish, worked on his hamburger as if he hadn't eaten in a week. His face appeared to Sam to be ridiculously fat, and he had a bad shaving nick on his cheek. Still, the man was being nice.

The man told Sam he well remembered that feeling of being trapped by rules, rules, and more rules.

"I guess I want to go to New York City," Sam answered thoughtfully. "See if it's as big as they say. After I did that, checked it out like, I could sit down and try to figure out what's what."

Sam didn't know running away would probably just get him into worse trouble. But the man knew.

Done with his lunch, the man moved closer to Sam. "Well, before you make the big time, how about a hug," he said. "The way your daddy does." Before Sam could even open his mouth to say his daddy never hugged him, in fact his daddy had died when he was two, the man locked his arms around Sam and gripped him. He said, "You're such a beautiful boy." He ran his hands down Sam's legs and licked his ears. He said, "I love you. I love you." Then the man started chewing on Sam's neck. His voice got an edge. "Sweet boy," he said. "You're going to suck my dick till I explode." It was a weird thing. Sam had heard stories from other boys about how some men wanted them to suck them off, but Sam had never met anybody that wanted any more than to fellate him. He knew, sooner or later, it might happen, but now that it had, he was unprepared. He was shocked, and it seemed that he wasn't in his body anymore. Then it was like somebody had thrown a switch. Sam didn't know where it came from, but his fists started pounding the man's body. When the man fell, Sam started kicking and kicking. By the end Sam was bawling like a baby and the man wasn't moving and blood was coming out of his mouth and ears and nose. Sam ran, and he didn't stop until he got to the main road, out of the woods.

Now, in the basement, Lucius, who had said he was a terrible waster of time, was wasting no time with Sam. He ran his hands up Sam's thighs. He unzipped Sam's jeans. He saw Sam's briefs were sticky with pre-cum. He caressed him, and Sam's throbbing hardness sent a current through his fingers, and up his arm. He pulled Sam's trousers down and ran his fingers slowly up his thighs, returning to that hot, wet place. He nuzzled the bulge, breathed in the musky smell. He kissed the bulge, which began to protrude from the fabric like a mountain. He licked him through the material. Sam

clutched his head, pulling him closer into his scent, grinding his crotch into Lucius's face.

"Please..." Sam begged. "I've had to wait so long...!"

"Me, too," Lucius said, as he pulled down the briefs, and began licking the magnificent cock that sprang from the fabric. Sam's pre-cum was dripping all over Lucius's face. Sam's grip on Lucius's head grew stronger, and the thrashing wilder, as Lucius continued to make love to that delicious cock. His tongue was bathing it, adoring it, relishing Sam's boy-taste. Soon his mouth was working harder until Sam was aching beyond even his vivid imagination. Lucius teased and taunted, and silence became impossible. Sam groaned louder, but Lucius took his mouth off of it and said, "Not yet."

Sam begged, "Please... please...!"

"Tell me this is what you want," Lucius said.

"Oh, I do. I need it bad." Sam soon became breathless with desire as Lucius went back to sucking it.

"Mmmm" was then all Sam could manage.

Lucius's fingers stroked the erection in a thousand different ways it seemed, until finally Sam came. Lucius did not take it in his mouth again; he simply watched the sperm fly out of the beautiful cock onto the floor. He kept stroking it, squeezing out all of the pent-up cum, and then, when he thought Sam was finished, he went back to kissing it and sucking it and adoring it....

After that memorable night when Sam expressed an interest in singing in the Christmas program, Lucius saw it as a chance to bind Sam closer to him, increasing the opportunities to perform fellatio on the lad, and Sam saw it as his chance to break into show business.

ONE

It was a bit of a shock to Tony Taylor to find, after the memorial service, he was at last alone in the limousine with his mother. Mona was entirely in character: no tear glistened in her eyes; no throb altered her usual tone of voice. They might have been leaving one of her favorite matinees on Broadway.

"I had quite a time with the bishop," she told Tony. "He wanted to eulogize your father. But I told him I find that I lean toward Rome. No flowers, no special prayers, no laudations. Corpses are all equal. If there's a God, He knows what you've done."

"I felt as if He was there," Tony ventured, after a moment of hesitation.

She gave Tony a brief, faintly pitying glance. "God, I hope not." And then she smiled−triumphantly, Tony thought.

It was then that Tony fully realized she had probably never been happier in her life than at that moment. She had accomplished what she had always wanted: she had outlived the old man. She, one-time starlet from Philadelphia, and she alone, had control of what she called "the whole shebang." Yes, Tony realized, Zachary Taylor's long-suffering wife had had the last laugh.

At the memorial service, Tony noticed George Simmons, the screenwriter and one-time actor he had originally met in New York. As they were getting in the limousine, George approached the car and hugged Tony. "Thanks for coming," Tony said. "I'll call you."

George smiled, his sober hazel eyes showing a twinkle of excitement. "I'll be waiting."

When Tony had first returned to Hollywood, he found George had a lover, so visits to his place would be a problem. After Tony's brother Tommy died, Tony entertained George at the Taylor house in Beverly Hills, but on the last such occasion George told Tony that he didn't think they should meet again. Tony said he understood, although he did not. He thought it was because of George's lover, when, in fact, George had begun to feel that Tony was only entertaining him because of his cock. Tony, it seemed, never wanted to see George for any other purpose than sex. As much as he liked fucking Tony, George began to feel slightly degraded by the whole scene.

After Mona flew back to the Taylor house in Greenwich to supervise the burial of Zachary at the new family plot she had purchased, Tony was at last all by himself and he was lonely. He called George. George swallowed his pride and said he'd drop by.

George's young lover had been giving him problems and he was almost as horny as Tony, so when Tony hugged him at the door, George immediately started to peel of Tony's clothes. When they were nude, Tony examined George's amazing cock, as if he were reacquainting himself with an old friend. The cock was wider at the bottom as it reached a flat base, and tapered until it flared out again at the rounded pyramid of the head.

"Oh c'mon," Tony said, and he led George into the living room and sat himself down on the white couch and threw his legs in the air.

George stood over Tony and slid a finger in. He smiled when he realized Tony had already prepared himself. He dropped to his knees and drew Tony's body forward to meet his throbbing erection.

When George entered Tony, Tony moaned, not used to the enormous size of him, and George started to withdraw.

"I'm sorry," Tony said. "It's been a while."

"I'm the one who's sorry. I rushed it." The cockhead rested at the entrance to Tony's ass.

Now Tony pulled him closer to him, holding him fiercely. George's cock was back in him, and George then began to fuck, filling him. It was gentle and loving and it kept building until became frantic and demanding. They

went to the floor and suddenly it was beyond anything Tony remembered from his previous fucks by George. It was ecstasy, an unbearable rapture, a mindless animal coupling. Tony had forgotten just how great a lover George was. After George came and withdrew, he turned to gaze at Tony. He looked warm and disheveled, yet he was still incredibly attractive to the older man.

George hugged him tightly and said, "Oh, I've missed you, Tony."

As George cuddled with him, Tony remembered why all this had started in the first place–how he had been stunned at the hugeness of George's cock, couldn't get enough. But then he made the mistake of going to George's place and meeting his lover.

"How's Mike?" Tony asked.

Tony remembered that Mike, George's lover, was barely out of his teens. He was handsome, in a dim, farmboy sort of way.

George smiled. "Restless. You know how kids are. He keeps wandering off."

"Why would he want to leave this, even for a moment?" Tony asked, squeezing George's sopping, semi-hard cock.

"Well, I can only get this thing up once a day, Tony. Mike needs it more than that. I can understand it, but I don't need to like it."

TWO

After George left, Tony sat alone thinking about how difficult it must be for George to have a lover who flaunted his unfaithfulness. Still, some people can overcome it. Tony was always amazed that his father's drive to bed woman after woman had seemingly ceased to trouble Mona years ago. Yet, despite his continuing flings with women, the elder Taylor could be very jealous of Mona. Once, when they were still in Hollywood together, they attended a premiere and Mona was smoothing her gown so that she could be photographed. One of the photographers dropped to his knees to rearrange a batch of cables and wires near her feet. Zachary misinterpreted the gesture and grabbed the young photographer by the collar, ready to punch him in the nose. Only Mona's quick intervention kept the men from fighting.

Zachary had a terrible temper and made scenes in public, and these embarrassed her because she disliked open displays of temperament. She also resented the way he bullied people and scolded them in front of others for stupidity, and she felt particularly angry when he reacted to the sight of a beautiful girl in an overtly sexual way.

From the manner in which he treated the younger actresses at the studio, contemptuously slapping them on the butt, stroking or caressing them, curtly silencing them when he was not in the mood, pushing them around,

she became convinced that he really regarded all females as a lesser breed, just sexual objects. And it was true.

Mona once told Tony that Zachary said those girls he saw were "just tarts-girls to be played with and thrown away. Toys. Why get so worked up? What have they got to do with you or me?"

Mona had the distinct feeling that she was being treated like the senior wife in a well-run harem. She was awarded affection and respect, as the honored mother of the master's children. But there were no signs of heat or the tactile contacts that indicate physical passion. For those who heard the rumors around Hollywood of Zachary's extramarital activities, that was hardly surprising. Sexually speaking, everyone who worked in the studios knew that Zachary had a roving eye and the ability to act upon it, and the principal speculation among Mona's friends was how much she knew about it. Tony suspected she knew quite a lot, and that she well understood what her friends were talking about when they sometimes slyly referred to Zachary as "the stray lamb." They also suspected she had come to accept the situation, and she and her husband had an arrangement, an unspoken one, that worked for them.

In the beginning, Mona's whole life had centered on Zachary's activities. She shopped for clothing to make the right appearance when she went out with him. Her frequent attendance at luncheons and charitable events-obligatory, she seemed to feel, for the wife of such an important man-kept her away from home nearly every day.

Marriage relieved her of the daunting problem of constantly trying to find work as an actress. There was no longer any question about what her next role would be. She had found her role-she was Mrs. Zachary Taylor, the mogul's wife.

Zachary, she knew, would never get serious about any of the other women. To him they were merely pleasurable breaks in the day-like polo, lunch, and practical jokes.

Wherever Zachary went, women were eager to light his cigar and help him put on his ski boots. He sometimes dated Italian and Swedish actresses, but observers noted that Zachary seemed indifferent to them..

Zachary was unhappy without female companionship. Eventually he left America to free himself of domestic entanglements but found little more than disorder and disillusionment in Europe.

Most of the time, Zachary lived in Paris in a suite at the Ritz. In New York, he stayed at the St. Regis and in London at Claridge's. He almost never visited Monarch's offices, choosing instead to read scripts in his rooms and summon stenographers who would take down his thoughts for transmission to executives. The Monarch office in Paris took care of many of his personal needs. Though Zachary was no longer in charge of the company, he still participated as the major stockholder. Movie production work, which had engulfed so many of his hours, slowed to a trickle. He always had many new properties in development, but few actually made it

to the screen. He began drinking heavily and spent a good deal of time watching old movies on television.

In some ways Mona was relieved that Zachary had taken a mistress, Genevieve, but when Zachary returned to the States after Tommy's death, the affair was over and the actress had her memoirs serialized, prior to publication in *Paris-Match*. The book was less a memoir of Genevieve than an indictment of Zachary Taylor. He was held up to considerable scorn and derision. She made fun of their romance, of his jealousies, of his habits.

Zachary had been livid. He immediately set out to do something about it, instituting a suit against Genevieve for false statements and invasion of privacy. Genevieve and her lawyers panicked, stopped publication of the book. But the damage had been done, to Zachary but mostly to Genevieve. In a curious turn of fate, the memoirs rebounded against her. As she stated to the press later, "Everyone in Paris is saying, 'She's a bitch. She's horrible.' Paris is thinking of me as mud and shit."

Genevieve had brought new shame on the Taylors, something they didn't need after Tommy's drug overdose and death. She was the first to recount, in her memoirs, that before she met him, Zachary frequented Parisian brothels and was a client of Madame Claude, whose exclusive call-girl service catered only to the wealthiest and most powerful men in France. Madame had built a career cultivating and training girls of perfect stature and physical appeal to mix in the upper echelons of French society. Zachary's sexual tastes tended toward the unconventional. What he particularly liked, according to Madame, was watching women make love to each other. Viewing them would arouse him and then he would choose one and have sex with her.

These revelations about his father brought Tony greater acceptance of his late brother's strange sexuality–and his own.

THREE

After Zachary had returned to Hollywood, Tony had been given some responsibilities. He continued his studies at the U.C.L.A. Film School, but he also worked on the labor gang, constructing sets, and occasionally in the cutting room.

Eventually, Tony would sit in on most of his father's meetings as an observer. "I don't want you to get cut up and hung out to dry," his father would lecture him. But if he thought his father would accept his lifestyle, he was mistaken. Tony felt deflated by his father's fame–not enhanced, as he had always hoped to feel, but momentarily invisible. Zachary, especially when he returned to Hollywood, was the luminous center of attention at most social and professional gatherings, where people milled around him, obviously excited, doing their best to make conversation with one another

while awaiting their turn to have their time with him. In Zachary's presence they became mysteriously childlike: animated, eager, deferential, anxious to gain his interest and approval. His words, even his most casual remarks, were heard as profoundly meaningful, because of the reverence accorded their source.

Since his return to power at the studio, it seemed everyone had been intent on idealizing Zachary, seeing in him someone much more important and powerful than themselves. People would ask Tony, "What is he really like?" and Tony knew they wanted their fantasies confirmed, not an honest answer about a real human being.

Or, upon first learning that Tony was Zachary's son, someone might say, "Really? Can I touch you?" Tony felt he could never be respected for himself. This was one of the many ways in which Zachary's fame diminished him and his sense of his own place in Hollywood.

To make matters worse, many of Tony's efforts to please his father fell flat and any praise was hard to come by. Even attention was a dear commodity–but Tony was used to that. When Tony was growing up, his father rarely put in an appearance at home because his work at the studio was so demanding. Weeks would go by when Tony would never see him, even though they lived in the same house.

Tony could see now, looking back, that it had not been his father's deliberate aim to make him unhappy, though it was hard to believe that he did not derive some unconscious pleasure from it. But his professed intention following his brother's death was to make his second son replace his first as the heir apparent. To accomplish this he subjected Tony to myriad tests and humiliations. Everything Tony did was immediately graded and contrasted with a simultaneously created higher standard. His appearance, his clothes and his manners were constantly criticized. If in a meeting he ventured to join in the discussion, he was apt to be checked with a curt, "I wasn't aware that anyone had asked your opinion, young man."

But for the first time Tony listened to his father's ranting stony-faced, and he refused to excuse himself. Tony continued to obey him after that, but there was no further pretense that his compliance was anything but submission to *force majeure*. Zachary's cold, cruel jokes grew meaner than ever, but he still seemed to know exactly what buttons to press to make people leap happily to do his bidding. He remained loyal to the final product. No matter how disastrous a movie seemed to be, he declared it the best, the greatest, or the first. When he visited neighborhood theaters to screen a movie and gauge the audience response, he would invent an excuse if the reaction was negative. When the viewers coughed and wheezed, indicating that they were bored to tears, Zachary would tell his staffers, "Terrible cold season. Everyone has the flu." Once when huge numbers of people got up and left in the middle of a movie, he remarked that they were night-shift workers leaving for their jobs at a nearby factory. When he was a child, he could not be held in check by parents, grandparents, or teachers.

Later, when he was a young man, people scorned his efforts to break into Hollywood. But he smashed through the gates with self-confidence and gall. He styled himself as a writer, a producer, a man of action. He always said, privately, that he was "more Jewish than all the other moguls put together." The other moguls, such as Mayer, Cohen, Selznick, were all Jewish, of course.

At school, Tony struck his classmates as a vaguely romantic character, solitary, at times morose, seemingly eaten up by an inner turmoil. His good looks caused those who didn't know him well to think of him as a kind of prince whose family riches might one day make him a formidable figure in the film world. But he seemed to alienate others by keeping aloof, by working hard and, worse, by associating with the gayest of the class. Of course, this was an obvious way to get back at his father.

Tony saw first hand that, like him, his father had no close male friends. His father, he began to see, was really quite lonely. He didn't trust anyone. And it had gotten worse in the years Zachary had been away.

Zachary Taylor, and his father before him, ruled Hollywood during a different time, when fear had not been the overwhelming mode of operation in the movie business and the art of filmmaking had not been not as important as the art of cutting the deal. Tony began to think that he could take over if he had to. Once exposed to his father on a daily basis, Tony saw that he spent most of his time on the phone. "I can do that," Tony told himself. "Talking on the phone all the time, this I can do."

Meanwhile, to avoid his father as much as possible, Tony stayed on the move. From city to city, bed to bed, indulging his two addictions: wanderlust and flesh-lust, the passions of his life.

At one point, Tony went to Hamburg for the slave auction he had read about. It was held in the basement of a sex club, and offered nude or semi-nude men, willing participants all, being auctioned off for an hour or two of use in one of the private rooms in the establishment.

It was Tony's first visit to Hamburg, and, his flight having been delayed, he regretted the necessity of rushing directly from the airport to the club. He preferred to savor a city at leisure and at length.

But once he arrived at the club, he was glad he had hurried over. He was told that the evening's prize, a youth from the Philippines, an unskilled laborer who loaded and unloaded cargo on the Hamburg docks by day and indulged his taste for S/M by night, was scheduled to be "auctioned off" in a few minutes. Intrigued, Tony was intent on bidding on him. Edgy with anticipation, he sat alone at a back table of the club, sipping Courvoisier. A pair of young blacks were being auctioned off first, sold to an older, professorial type in bifocals and tweed. Then a young piece of beefcake, with tattoos and an enormous bulge in the crotch of his jockstrap, was sold to a rotund man in the front row.

When the Filipino boy was finally brought on stage, Tony let the bidding rise, then quickly bid a sum so large no one ventured to try to top it. As he

was going to the cashier to pay before collecting his slave, Tony felt himself being observed. Turning slowly, he saw a platinum-haired young man with green eyes watching him from the bar. He wore a silk shirt and loose-fitting black satin vest, and a diamond earring. His flesh was so pale it looked translucent. When their eyes met, the boy raised his drink, a tiny cordial glass containing what appeared to be a gold liqueur. Tony gave him no acknowledgment. Pretty though the youth was, at the moment, Tony was consumed by his desire to experience the charms of his new slave.

Minutes later, alone with his slave, Tony quickly forgot the haunting, pale features of the boy at the bar. He took the slave who, he was told, was called Santos, to an upstairs room, where he initiated the proceedings by licking every inch of his glossy, nut-brown flesh. Through it all, the slave uttered not a sound, which disappointed Tony somewhat; he liked to have his sex partners appreciative of his efforts.

"Yeah, you're a pretty one," Tony said as he ran his hand over Santos's smooth chest. "Tony likes you." He pinched one of Santos's nipples hard. Santos jumped beneath him. "Oh, did you like that?" Tony cooed. As Tony sucked on the nipples, Santos's breathing became more shallow, and his nipples swelled. "You like what Tony's mouth can do, eh?"

Tony smelled his after-shave, spicy and mixed with the natural male smell of him. He planted small soft kisses on the skin as he worked his way down to Santos's groin.

Slowly the heat began to build. He continued kissing Santos over and over. "Oh, my," he said, his eyes roaming over his body. "You're really beautiful."

Santos spread his legs, making it easier for Tony to reach all the places he wished to be kissed. He tried to tell him everything with his body, and Tony learned quickly.

Slowly he insinuated one finger into Santos's ass. "That feels good, doesn't it?" he said as Santos gasped. Slowly a second finger joined the first. He leaned over and licked his nipple. He lightly closed his teeth on Santos's tender flesh.

Tony dipped his head and, as his fingers drove in and out of Santos's asshole, Santos spread his legs wide and Tony flicked his tongue over Santos's erection. Tony kept pulling Santos along, knowing he was bringing waves of pleasure to his entire body. Soon Santos was spasming, and Tony took the cock fully in his mouth. As the man continued to spasm, Tony's cock throbbed. Tony crouched over Santos for just a moment, then drove his hard cock deep into him. "Oh God," Tony cried.

Tony's back arched and he groaned as he slammed into Santos's ass. Harder and harder he pumped until, with a roar, he came deep inside the slave. Santos's legs held him tightly against him until Tony's shuddering ceased.

They lay still for a while then, breathing the heady, pungent odors of orgasm, hearing laughter and applause from the auction still continuing

downstairs. One hand idly petting Santos's healthy young cock, Tony said, "You are quite good."

Santos smiled and shrugged. It occurred to Tony that perhaps he spoke no English. Summoning up what meager Spanish he possessed, Tony persevered, but Santos remained silent. Santos's cock, however, was far more communicative. Nearly erect again, it pressed lewdly against Tony's belly. Tony mounted him. Grinding against his slave, he reached back to fingerfuck his own anus this time. Then he lifted up and squatted over Santos. Slowly he slipped the erect cock into his ass. For several minutes Tony indulged himself as he hadn't in weeks, bouncing up and down on the thick cock. For the first time in months, Tony was able—for a little while—to forget about his troubles back in Hollywood.

They lay together afterward, and eventually Santos's cock, well-drained, slid out of Tony with a soft smacking sound.

When Tony returned to the bar, the blond was still there. He appeared even more pale now, with heavy-lidded green eyes with tiny pupils—as if he had seen visions. "Hi," he said, a desperation about him. He hugged Tony and Tony felt his shoulder blades through his damp shirt.

"Sit there," the blond ordered, patting the stool next to him with his hand. A drink was in the other hand.

Tony expected him to focus on his face, but instead he was interested in what was happening on stage. It was the finale, wherein men were invited on stage to fuck one of the slaves. The fuckee of the night, introduced as Lee, stepped onto the stage. He was delicately formed, small like a child, but his shoulders were broad, his wrists were thick.

"You'll love this," the blond said in heavily-accented English. "In fact, if you hadn't already been with Santos, you might want to join in."

"Oh, it'll be fun just to watch. I've heard about this show."

The blond placed one arm gingerly around Tony's waist and held his hand with the other. He pressed against Tony, slowly moving closer until his mouth was against Tony's ear. "Ummm," he purred, moving his hand to Tony's crotch. "This is nice."

"And we're in no hurry," Tony said. But Tony could feel his growing hunger and he kissed the stranger's cheek gently.

Everyone was staring at the stage with lust-clouded eyes. A velvet bench was brought on to the stage. After bowing to the crowd, Lee allowed the announcer/auctioneer, a thin, balding man in his early thirties, to remove his jockstrap, leaving him gloriously naked. Lee stretched out on the bench on his back, his arms at his sides, his legs spread. Mirrors reflected his image from above and around the bench, and a video camera projected images on two large screens. The room lights dimmed and spotlights brightened to illuminate the body on the stage.

As the group watched, the auctioneer tied Lee's wrists and ankles to rings in the bench with soft velvet strips. Then he invited the customers to come forward. Four men bounded onto the stage; all had erections.

"Take your places," the auctioneer said. Each man moved to a different spot, one to Lee's head, one to each side, and one between his thighs. The auctioneer provided a silver bowl of condoms and each man unrolled one over his cock. "Now, you all know the rules. First you will rub oil into Lee's skin, all over his body. Then each of you will slowly take Lee, one in his mouth, one in each hand, and one in his tight ass. Then you will remain unmoving while Lee does whatever he can to make you climax." He looked down at the audience. "Those of you who want to get off while you watch what is happening may certainly do so. 'Whatever gives pleasure' is our motto here."

Lee lay on the bench, listening to the auctioneer give his speech. "Gentlemen," the auctioneer said, giving each man a bottle of oil, "you may begin."

Lee closed his eyes as eight hands rubbed warm oil on his belly, his pecs, his thighs. Hands kneaded, stroked, fondled, and pinched. Several fingers invaded his ass, opening him, readying him for what was to come.

After a few moments, "Enough," the auctioneer said.

And Lee was filled. One cock slowly thrust into his mouth, the latex not diminishing his pleasure. One cock was pressed into each waiting hand and he closed his fist around each. And finally one slowly filled his now-well-lubed ass. Then each of the men stood completely still and the auctioneer said, "Now, Lee will work his magic."

Lee licked the cock in his mouth. Since he couldn't move his hands because of the bonds, he squeezed his fingers, one after another, to pump those two cocks, and he clamped his anal muscles to squeeze the cock so deep in his ass. His own cock was throbbing.

The cameraman was moving around the bench, taking close-up shots of the cocks. Tony found this tableau one of the most exciting things he'd ever seen, this vision of Lee's body invaded by so many men.

Lee increased the movements of his hands, mouth, and his boy-pussy muscles. Only moments later, the men's groans and howls filled the room, as one after the other came. It was a spectacular display. The men at Lee's sides were the first to come, and they bent over and each took one of Lee's nipples in his mouth. The man at Lee's head cupped the lad's head in his hands, holding him still while he pumped into his throat. Several men in the audience moaned as they came as well. The room began to stink of sex and sweat and animal lust.

Over and over men's cocks invaded Lee, men moving around the bench taking additional pleasure from his mouth, his hands, and his anus. When they were finished, the auctioneer pulled off his robe and, unrolling a condom over his exceptionally large cock, he moved between Lee's legs. Lee watched as he removed the bindings on his legs.

"Oh, yeah, fuck it," Lee said, his still-hard cock throbbing with his own need to come. As the auctioneer held the tip of his cock against the steaming, puckered opening, he rubbed Lee's cock with his other hand. Then in a single, slow stroke, he filled Lee. Lee came with the first stroke, screaming his pleasure for all to hear. The auctioneer pulled back, then thrust into Lee again. Over and over he filled and emptied Lee's ass until he, too, succumbed to the steamy pleasure of the fuck. As he pulled out, someone announced that anyone who still wanted to come forward could do so.

The blond again whispered into Tony's ear, "If you want to, I'll understand."

"Oh, no," Tony said. "I've found what I want."

They kissed. Without breaking contact with the stranger's mouth, Tony slid his hands between their bodies, unbuttoned the blond's shirt and pulled it off of his shoulders. His chest was hairless and surprisingly smooth as Tony slid his palms over his skin.

The stranger's eyes watched Tony's hands as his fingers played with his nipples, his breathing becoming ragged. Tony pinched gently but firmly. The blond finally held his gaze and said, softly, "We will be a lot more comfortable in my room upstairs."

Both naked to the waist, the two walked upstairs hand-in-hand.

Once in the dungeon-like little room, which had only pillows strewn on the floor, the blond kissed Tony full on the mouth. "You're quite something," the blond said. "Not what I expected at all." He pressed his lips to Tony's.

Tony, now more sure in his motions, pulled away and said, "I want you."

"You can have me, sure." He reached down and started to unzip his pants.

"Let me," Tony said, moving the blond's hands aside. He deftly unfastened the blond's pants and, in one motion, pulled down both his slacks and his shorts until he stood naked except for his socks. Tony knelt and pulled them off as well, his eyes now level with the stiffening penis. Tony gulped as the cock soon pointed straight out from a thick patch, darker blond than the hair on his head. Tony saw that the cock was huge, perhaps even bigger than George's. At first he resisted the urge to take the hard cock into his mouth, preferring to examine it closely with his fingers. He drew the foreskin back and found the boy had perfumed himself; it was a delightful, cinnamony scent. Then Tony started sucking it as if it was a giant piece of candy had been given to him to enjoy. The adoration of the blond's cock lasted several minutes until Tony could stand it no longer. He stood and removed all of his own clothes. The blond lay on the pillows, stroking his erection. Tony joined him on the floor and moved against him until the length of his body was against the length of the stranger's. He stroked the blond's throbbing cock. Then he maneuvered so his body was beneath his,

his legs spread, the tip of the blond's erection against his anus, still lubed from his encounter with the Filipino boy.

The blond pushed his hips forward, sliding his cock deep inside Tony's ass. Tony cupped his buttocks and held him still for a moment, then moved, in the rhythm of the music they could hear from downstairs.

It was only moments until the blond came, his hips pounding against Tony's. "Oh, shit," he bellowed. He collapsed against Tony, then rolled onto one side, his cock sliding limply from Tony's body. "Oh," he groaned, clutching Tony against him. "Too fast. I'm sorry."

Tony took the cum-coated cock in his hand, squeezed it, and said, "There's plenty of time."

So enamored was Tony of the mysterious blond, whose name he found out the next morning was Christopher, that he asked him to accompany him on his travels. They went from Hamburg to Munich, then south to Marseilles and Andorra, and across Spain, stopping in Granada and Seville. In Gibraltar, they took a hydrofoil across the channel, arriving in Morocco at Tangier, then took the train south to Fez, where they explored the myriad maze-like streets of the Old City, glorying in the exotic squalor of the Quarter's sights and sounds and odors.

The first night in Fez was like all of the others. Although Christopher did have a problem with premature ejaculation, he was good for three or four a day, and when at last they went to bed to sleep, Tony spent considerably more time sucking the heroic cock than being fucked by it.

The second day, Christopher said he had some shopping he had to do, and he could only do it alone. Tony accepted this, and set about to enjoy the city on his own. He found a bathhouse of sorts where, Christopher told him, sex could be had. But all the people Tony encountered seemed in a kind of stupor, like sleepwalkers who, upon meeting each other in a darkened hall, fucked or sucked more from habit than desire and without ever being aroused sufficiently to become fully awake.

As the afternoon wore on toward dusk, Tony found some of the men interrupted their sex to follow him a bit, but they were slow and clumsy, their unsavory caresses easy to elude. In some of the rooms, men offered their slicked cocks, parting their cum-soaked thighs. Tony was repulsed. Then Tony came upon a lad ripe with youth. The boy led Tony on a merry chase until they reached what was obviously an orgy room. Here, the lad's cock came within inches of Tony's mouth before the youth saw a friend and disappeared into the shadows with him. Tony wandered on, appalled yet mesmerized by this frustrating scene. Finally, Tony left, hurrying back to the hotel. The streets grew steeper, narrower, and when he reached his rooms at the hotel, with its damask curtains and faded silken spread, he was exhausted. Waiting for him was Christopher, reclining on the bed, incense burning, the room reeking of spices and hashish. Christopher's eyes were closed, his wondrous genitalia covered with a corner of the rumpled spread.

A halo of smoke drifted up from the pipe between his lips. In the dim light, his pale hair framed paler features, but his strange beauty was an intoxicant to Tony after such a frustrating afternoon.

After Tony slid the chain lock into place, he turned to see Christopher's eyes were open, his gaze strange, unfocused. "You're late," Christopher spat.

"I didn't know I had a curfew."

"If I'd known you were going to be so late I would have gone back to that Frenchman's room."

"What Frenchman?"

"Some fairy I met in the men's room of this very hotel. I told him I couldn't go to his room so he paid me to let him give me a blowjob right there. He came while he was blowing me, but I couldn't come." He sighed theatrically and dragged on the pipe. "He didn't get his money back, though. Fucking faggot."

He offered Tony the pipe. "Please, go ahead. The experience will be so much nicer for us both."

Tony hesitated, then took it, pulling the sweet, narcotic smoke into his lungs and holding it until he felt the irritation seeping out of him, replaced by a warm and scented glow. He took another hit. This time the smoke didn't just fill his lungs, but traveled through his bloodstream in ways he had never felt before.

"What the hell is this stuff?"

"Opium."

"My God! But it's quite nice."

"I think so. The only thing that's better is to have sex while you're doing it."

Tony took another toke. "We can do that." His head turned and he started to lie back. Just then pillows, sheets, and mattress seemed to all fold round him. Christopher crawled over to him. Up close, the opium made Christopher's face seem so beautiful to Tony it was almost frightening. Tony leaned forward to help the blond remove his shirt, then reached up idly, ran a fingertip along Christopher's chin. His gaze lingered on Christopher's face. Now it seemed as if there were something askew there, although Tony was at a loss to know exactly what. The eyes, something about the eyes. That charmed-snaked look. For an instant, it had made him think of–Tommy.

"There's plenty more where this came from," Christopher said, offering Tony the pipe again when he got Tony completely naked.

Tony took the pipe, sucking first from it, then on Christopher's cock, which dangled appetizingly in his face as the blond leaned across him.

In a drug-induced haze now, Tony permitted Christopher to bind his arm to the bedpost.

"Now your other arm," Christopher said as he lifted away the pipe.

"What are you...?"

"I'm sure this isn't anything new for you," said Christopher, securing Tony's other wrist to the bedpost with a scarf. "But this time will be especially memorable for you, believe me. Before we go on, would you like another hit?"

"I don't think so."

"Please. Go ahead."

He put the pipe between Tony's lips; Tony drew in the fragrant smoke.

"There may be parts of this that are difficult for both of us." Christopher leaned across the bed and put his mouth to Tony's. When Tony breathed out, Christopher caught the smoke in his own mouth and held it.

"Oh?"

"Yes." Christopher began rummaging around inside his suitcase. Tony watched, the narcotic effect of the opium blunting his perceptions in a way he found increasingly distressing. He resolved not to give in to panic but to simply accept his fate for the moment and await the next development the way one allows a nightmare to run its course. He knew enough to relax into the game, submit, and enjoy it.

"You see, I fear I've grown too fond of you for my own good," Christopher said, and he turned around and the effect of the narcotic in Tony's system made his eyes appear more feline than ever, gold-green slits that would have bewitched him entirely had he not been suddenly distracted by the sight of what was in Christopher's hands: the biggest dildo he had ever seen. It was black, with life-like veining. Its beauty was hypnotic. Tony couldn't take his eyes off it.

"I bought it in the bazaar, just for you. Lovely, isn't it? When I saw it, it made me think of you. Unlike me, it can never go soft on you, Tony."

He took a pair of underpants from Tony's suitcase and plugged Tony's mouth. "I don't want you to wake the neighbors when I start fucking you with this."

Soon Tony's body was trembling, out of control, and his ass was starting to throb painfully. He knew he would be raw when Christopher finished, his ass red and swollen. But he didn't care. Right now he needed this, wanted it with all his being, and felt helpless to stop the process. The dildo invaded him slowly, and had really only gotten a little way in when Tony came, unassisted in any way. Yet he was still hungry. He cried out. His eyes filled with tears of gratitude. He tightened around the invading latex automatically. Christopher only needed to thrust twice and Tony came again. Tony's mind turned to mush. He lifted his head to look behind him while Christopher thrust the dildo in and out of his ass. It was glorious, the sight of that huge cock impaling him, and all he could do was take it. But the fucking continued, on and on. Christopher was insatiable, unstoppable. Just then, another orgasm rocked Tony, leaving him limp and mindless.

"Since you don't seem to be enjoying this," Christopher chuckled sardonically, "I might as well enjoy myself." He pulled the dildo out of Tony and began withdrawing objects from his pants pockets. Hypodermic syringe

and powder. Soon he was busy with the paraphernalia of his habit. He tipped a bit of heroin from bag to spoon, then cooked it with a cigarette lighter held underneath. All this Tony watched with stricken eyes, wishing he could stop him. He forced his eyes shut, and eventually drifted off to sleep.

"How are we, pretty little one?" crooned Christopher, mincing across the room with a breakfast-laden tray. Tony didn't have to look to know the contents: toast and milk, half a grapefruit, a jar of honey. Christopher said he had this same breakfast every day. "How do we feel now? Better?" He set the tray down on the desk. "I will not let you leave here again without me, Tony. The world is such a dangerous place. You might hurt yourself."

Tony blinked as Christopher stood beside the bed and unbuttoned his trousers.

"It's been so long without your ass."

"Oh, no," Tony pleaded. "Please. No more."

Christopher grabbed Tony's hand and pressed his fingers to his groin. Christopher's magnificent prick was dripping pre-cum.

Before long, despite Tony's pleadings for mercy, Christopher had pulled apart Tony's thighs and was inserting his cock in Tony's ass. Pain seared Tony. Christopher's merciless cock filled his rectum until it felt stuffed to bursting. Sweat poured from his quaking body, and he offered himself up to him in complete submission. Christopher accepted the offering as if it were his right to take it, as if Tony existed simply to be taken by him. The orgasm that rocked Tony as Christopher fucked him left him trembling, panting, his vision blurred. Suddenly Christopher pulled out, came on Tony's belly, as if to show him he could. Now there was the pain of abandonment. Tony was sore beyond what he would ever have imagined possible, and yet needy still.

By now, Tony was terrified of what Christopher might do next. But terror, as Tony had long known, was the most potent of aphrodisiacs, and sex with this hustler was sex magnified a hundredfold, each orgasm an intoxicant that bewitched his mind for days. In a moment of clarity, Tony decided enough was enough.

Tony told Christopher he had to return to the States. Christopher made it easy for him, deciding to go with him as far as Tangier, where he knew he would find ready buyers for what he had to sell.

That last night, as they fucked in the moonlight, they kissed each other goodbye. Christopher had no orgasm at all, but Tony did, and then Christopher held Tony all night in the bed. He held him fiercely, not the way Tony had expected, as if they had this single night of reprieve before they had to return to real life.

FOUR

Even though Tony had used "the press of business in California" as an excuse to escape Christopher, he was not exaggerating the importance of his return. After Zachary Taylor's death, the Monarch board had elected Stanley Allen studio chief. Allen had been an agent and then production head at Monarch when Zachary left for Paris. He had long campaigned to have the studio sold to his friends at Tatsuya Electronics in Tokyo, but Zachary always turned down that prospect. Now Allen had his chance. Over several months, Allen and his lawyers brokered a deal which left him, and the Taylors, fabulously wealthy, but left Tony feeling that his days at the studio were numbered.

Upon Tony's return, a meeting was set on friendly turf. Allen was frank when he met Tony at the Polo Lounge for breakfast. Allen showed up wearing the Saville Row dark blue suit and dark silk tie that were his trademark and the trademark of all his top people. In fact, he had twenty such suits, and virtually no other clothes. Tony preferred to dress casually, which always seemed to rankle Allen, but today he wore one of the Brioni suits he favored, simply because they never needed to be pressed.

"The Japanese are very conservative, you know," Allen stressed, after complimenting Tony on how handsome and rested he looked after his European vacation, "and your name has come up during our discussions of executive personnel...."

Tony interrupted him, not wishing to prolong the agony: "I'll resign. Resign whatever the job is that I have. I have never considered 'Vice President-New Acquisitions' to have been a job in the real sense anyway."

Allen smiled. "No, no. That will not do. You certainly have a place in the company. You will always have a place in the company. I have another idea that I think would persuade the Japanese you are a serious player."

Tony was shocked to find that Allen was offering him the presidency of the studio's recording division, Groove Records, which they had acquired years ago but never done much with. Allen told Tony, "You don't have to listen to the bands that agents bring you, and you don't have to like their sounds, you just have to sell their products."

"Sounds interesting," Tony lied. The thought of working in the record business instead of the movie business unnerved him. He knew little about music, didn't even really care for much of popular music. Jazz piano was about his favorite thing, along with Broadway show music. Groove specialized in what was called bubble gum rock, and their top moneymaker was a kid named Sam Saxon, who Tony had heard was nothing more than a cute juvenile delinquent from Boston with an average voice who was a lot of trouble.

Tony left the meeting feeling beaten, and there was no telling what sort of state he might have worked himself into had his mother not suddenly arrived from Greenwich. She burst into the mansion, a lovely flurry of blue silk (she said she would wear mourning only at the memorial service), and hugged her son tightly and at length before she uttered a single word. She apparently knew of the battles going on at the studio; she always seemed to know everything before Tony did. Tony often wondered who her spy was. Finally she said, "It'll be fine, Tony. You'll see."

Mona always had a strong layer of common sense beneath the sparkle and froth of her exterior; she knew where her priorities lay. She was bored with all the press attention her husband's death had brought upon her. She had learned to be adept at handling reporters. "Tell them everything, but don't tell them anything," she told Tony. She did make the pronouncement that there was nothing she could do about the dead; her job was with the living. And, as usual, she set about at once to pull her son out of his bad case of the blues.

"I think I'd like to see Tokyo," Mona said at dinner. "See who is investing all this money in *our* business."

Tony knew Mona could really not have cared less about Tatsuya. Since Zachary's death, her motto had become "Money only makes you happy if you spend it," and she was spending it as fast as she could.

Tony agreed to take her along with him to Japan; they would enjoy each other's company. They would leave at once. She was jubilant boarding the JAL flight to Tokyo, but Tony could tell she was worried about him. Tony admitted he was down, having being shunted off to Groove, and it wasn't like him to let things depress him, but the past few months had taken a greater toll than he was willing to admit. "How on earth are you going to deal with the wily Orientals in your present frame of mind?" Mona asked him. Tony mumbled something in reply, but he really had no answer.

But Tokyo proved to be a restorative, and a "Wily Oriental," in the formidable shape of Mr. Okira, the "President of Entertainment," was the perfect host. With his photographic memory, Tony had quickly made himself knowledgeable when it came to the entire Groove library and he knew about the advanced technologies that the Japanese were bringing to their ownership of Monarch. Mr. Okira seemed delighted that such a young man had a thorough grasp of the business, and such a charming and beautiful mother besides. Business was conducted in a gracious and leisurely manner, quite at odds with the hustle and bustle of Tokyo.

The Tatsuya Film Company studios, on the outskirts of the city, were reached by helicopter from the pad on top of the mid-town skyscraper that housed the executive offices. Mr. Okira gave Tony and his mother a VIP tour through the dozen or more stages crowded with martial arts films, modern dramas, musicals, and costume epics in the making. Lunch was attended by a neat young man with a calculator who did not partake of the food or, indeed, join in the conversation unless he was addressed. Tony's

shy, respectful manner was in perfect synch with the Japanese way of doing things; typical Hollywood aggression seemed to be bad form. Mr. Okira listened with willing politeness to Tony's vision of the future of music. Tony said that with the advent of cable television, particularly MTV, music videos had become the product of the future. The Tatsuya facilities would be a great advantage, Tony told Mr. Okira. Meanwhile, the neat young assistant was working permutations on this calculator and playing to Mr. Okira. When the tour was finished, Mr. Okira expressed the hope that Tony would do him the honor of being his guest that evening. He wanted to show him some of the delights of the city. Mona begged off, saying that, these days, traveling tired her, but Tony knew she really just wanted some time for herself. She had made this trip for him, but she always wanted some time to sight-see. She insisted "you boys" go off and have fun.

The "sights" began at the Orsen Bath House. "You do not visit Tokyo without visiting a bath house, and this is my favorite," Tony's host explained.

Tony was ushered into a private room. There was a steam cabinet, a small pool, and two delicate girls with fingers of steel in attendance. The massage was sweet agony, and at its climax had one of the girls walking barefoot up and down Tony's spine.

From there, his host took him to a restaurant where no foreigner could be admitted except as the guest of a Japanese. His shoes were removed and slippers substituted. Tony was delivered to another private room where this time they sat cross-legged on cushions at a low table and were served many delicacies by perfumed and twittering geishas, with their chalk-white bobbing faces and their scarlet rosebud mouths. Every now and then Mr. Okira made reference to their business discussion, and Tony felt encouraged that he had been accepted despite his young age. While course followed course in a masterful orchestration of different tastes, Mr. Okira on several occasions repeated how honored he was to have representatives from the studio call on him. Sake was drunk with the meal, and occasionally one of the geishas would sing a plaintive song, accompanying herself on a three-stringed instrument. Afterwards games were played, childish but innocent Tony thought, punctuated by Mr. Okira's deep-throated growl and the girls' silly giggles. All of it was quite incomprehensible to Tony, but he found himself relaxing at last.

After the meal, they got back into Mr. Okira's chauffeured Rolls-Royce and made their way to the Mikado nightclub, a vast, glittering place of cabaret featuring five dozen showgirls. The last business word was spoken there with some difficulty because of the raucous atmosphere; Mr. Okira assured Tony he would discuss Tony's proposals for the record company with his colleagues and have an almost certainly positive answer for him in a day or two. Meanwhile two hostesses fluttered around Tony. They had the faces of flowers and soft voices. They had, Mr. Okira stressed, raised the pleasing of a man to a fine art. Tony was amused to see that the girls

seemed to always come in pairs whether in a bath house, a tea house, or a nightclub

Throughout the evening, Mr. Okira refused to let Tony pay for anything. "When I come to Hollywood," he said in his curiously growling English, "I will be your guest, correct?"

"Indeed," Tony said, amused.

Mr. Okira, looking more Buddha-like than ever, said that now that they had finished their business talk, the best entertainment was yet to come, and took him to the House of Pleasure. Kimonoed girls–two, of course–led Tony into a room where candles burned. He found himself alone there in a large sunken bath filled with warm, sweetly scented waters. Delicately the girls disrobed him, giggling a little like children at play, and put him into the bath where they laved and soothed him with oils and soaps. After a while they let their kimonos fall and got in with him. The game continued as they glided around him like oriental mermaids with hands like fast fish and firm buttocks and breasts. Tony couldn't help himself, he had a hard-on. They made signs for him to get out of the bath, and a large, soft towel was produced, big enough for the three of them to dry each other. Then they laid him down on the nearby couch, making him understand he was to leave everything to them. They spread oil on each other; then they slithered all over him until he glistened like they did. He felt their practiced hands work on his erection, finally laying their smiling faces close to it. Their two tongues replaced their hands, flicking up and down its full length, until their lips met at the tip to enclose it in a passionate kiss. They were pros, and they sensed Tony was close so they backed off for a moment, their delicate fingers closing like a vise around the throbbing root of Tony's cock. Again and again they postponed his orgasm, but, finally, he could hold back no longer.

As the girls were toweling him off, all Tony could think of was that now, at last, he had a true story of straight sex to regale his new record company business associates back home, but he wondered if anyone would really believe him.

Back in Beverly Hills, Mona didn't even unpack. "I think I'll go back to Egypt," she said. "I'll take Mother with me. Oh, Tony, you must go up the Nile one day. It's so glorious!"

A few hours later, Mona was off, after a phone call was made to the studio to commandeer the corporate jet for the trip back to New York. Tony was astonished at how diplomatically she could engineer these things: "This is Mrs. Taylor. Can I hitch a ride on the plane?" Tony knew damn well nobody could ever say no to Mrs. Taylor.

That night, lying awake into the wee hours, Tony resolved that he was not going to allow his poor misguided father to have died in vain. He decided to profit by his example. He would resist all temptations that would endanger his health and happiness. He would seize from life all that it had to offer.

And he would continue to have beauty in his life, wherever in the world he had to go to find it.

He reached for the phone. He held the receiver in his hand, wondering who to call. While he had been in Tokyo, Harry Griffin had called and left him a message. He didn't want to see Harry again. Not after what had happened.

It had begun when Tony was briefly assigned to read scripts for the story department. He didn't mind this a bit; in fact, he had at one time toyed with the idea of becoming a writer. That was how his father had started out, working for *his* father in the forties before he went into the Army, and there had always been stacks of scripts around, which Tony had enjoyed reading them as a child.

On his first day on his new job, Tony and met Harry Griffin, who was writing press releases in the publicity department under the supervision of the studio's long-time official mouthpiece, Bradley Lewis. Lewis was one of those brilliant, effeminate men who study from childhood how to adapt themselves to the world of their more masculine contemporaries, and end by dominating it. There was nobody more adept at controlling the media than Lewis, and it was obvious he was enamored of Tony from the time Zachary first brought the boy to the studio when he was ten. But later, from all appearances, Tony had been usurped in Lewis's affections by Harry.

Tony's sudden appearance in the story department now was bound to cause a stir, and it did.

On a Saturday, at three o'clock in the morning, sometime after Zachary's death and Tony's move back into the Taylor mansion, Mrs. Olmstead, the housekeeper, shook Tony into wakefulness. An old age pensioner, the woman occupied a downstairs bedroom. But she did little else but occupy it, and very little in the way of housekeeping. Fortunately though Tony required little, and consequently paid her little. So one hand washed the other. She wasn't a very bright woman at best, and she was far from her best at three in the morning. But Tony gathered from her babbling and gesturing that there was an emergency somewhere below, so Tony hurried downstairs only to find that a very drunken Harry had slammed his new Corvette into one of the palms that lined the driveway. Mrs. Olmstead helped get Harry into the house and they lay him out on the couch. Miraculously, Harry was unhurt, but he was terribly upset, sobbing, pleading with Tony not to call Bradley.

Tony left Harry on the couch and went back to bed. In the morning, he was awakened by Harry, nude, in bed beside him. Harry was about twenty-five, lean and muscular like a swimmer, with a thick head of black, straight hair, cut conservatively. His dark body-hair covered his chest like fur. Tony had been attracted to Harry from the start, but Harry had always spurned his advances. Now Harry had ended up in his driveway, in a mess that was going to make Bradley crazy. Tony was furious with Harry, but he

couldn't resist playing this scene for all it was worth. He ran his hand across Harry's chest and down into his crotch, where his immense cock lay sleeping against his thigh. Now he knew what Bradley saw in Harry.

Harry stirred when Tony began to suck it. "Stop," Harry told him, "it can wait."

"Sure it can," Tony responded, one hand moving up to caress a nipple. Harry moaned as Tony continued sucking while he twisted each of Harry's nipples. A long moan escaped from Harry's throat, and he begged Tony to let him up so he could pee. In the bathroom, after Harry finished peeing, Tony bent down and started working on the prick again. "No, Tony, not like this."

"You came here for a reason. This must have been it. I'm only giving you what you want."

"You're *taking* what *you* want. That's what you do, just take, take, take. Bradley told me all about you..." Harry went on telling Tony more than he needed to hear about how selfish and irresponsible he appeared to be to others at the studio.

Soon Harry was hard again. Tony turned around and, his asshole greased, backed down on the nearly nine-inches of prime prick. "Please, Tony, let's go back to bed."

"No, I want it this way. This is the *only* way."

So they fucked standing, Harry's hands holding Tony's ass to elevate it, and Tony dropping his head back in ecstasy as he came, the veins in his forehead throbbing as the cum gushed from his cock and splattered on the floor. Tony wouldn't let Harry finish. He pulled free and climbed into the shower without saying a word. Dumbstruck, Harry walked back into the bedroom, and got dressed in last night's clothes. He opened the door to the bathroom, leaned his head inside, letting out some steam. "I'm going to take a cab home. I'll send somebody for the car. Sorry I bothered you." He couldn't keep the irritation and nerves from his voice. Mostly, he was upset with himself because he had come to the Taylor house for a reason. He had been seeking someone kind to talk to, a shoulder to cry on. He and Bradley had been at a party, had a fight, and he had left alone. He happened to be passing the Taylor house and pulled into the drive, a fateful move that he would come regret for the rest of his life.

No, Tony would not return Harry's call. In fact, he went down the list of the men he'd slept with. Every one, he realized, was either married to a woman or had a lover. He himself was the only person he knew who was single! When he was pursuing Harry, Bradley had given him a business card. "If you get horny, just call Hal Lindsey." Tony knew he was only trying to keep him away from Harry, but still it was thoughtful because Tony had no idea that particular "talent agent" actually could be one of the most successful pimps in Hollywood, serving up the popular porn stars of the day to the highest bidder. Having Bradley recommend such a person

meant that the agent could be trusted-as far as anyone could trust anyone in Hollywood.

At first, Hal couldn't believe the youthful heir to the Taylor fortune was calling him and asking for some entertainment to be put on his American Express Corporate Card. Hal thought that if Tony Taylor couldn't get laid, what hope was there for anyone? He called Tony back to confirm that, yes, he had someone Tony might find "amusing," and he could be there in an hour.

"No," Tony said, "I can't entertain anyone here. Doesn't he have a place?"

"Well, yes, but-I tell you what, why don't you come here? I have three guys living with me now and you could just take your pick and go to his bedroom. How's that sound?"

"Like music to my ears," Tony said.

Hal's house was set back on a steep slope, with a very treacherous driveway, just off Sunset Boulevard-with a garden of roses out front, and a swimming pool along the side behind a stand of eucalyptus trees.

It was a rambling one-story house, with four bedrooms, and so much foliage blocking the windows that curtains were not necessary. The decor was eclectic, with lots of wicker and throw rugs on the tiled floors. It was a very secluded, private place, the kind of house people didn't just drop into. It appeared to be, as Hal said, "a safe place."

Hal greeted Tony warmly, ushered him into the sparsely furnished living room. Hard-core videos were being played on the TV, and Tony was introduced to a blunt-faced blond named Rick, "just in from Atlanta," Hal said. Rick, Tony was told, would be starting his first porn movie in two days. Rick was quiet, almost sullen, intently watching the TV. Tony, attracted to Rick's bulging crotch, moved onto the couch next to him and put his hand in Rick's lap. Rick said nothing, just leaned up and started kissing Tony. The taste and feel of Rick's lips and tongue made Tony's dick throb, and Rick rubbed it.

Tony massaged Rick's cock, then unzipped his jeans. He manipulated the large head of Rick's cock and was about to start sucking it when Hal walked in with two more guys, both of whom looked a bit apprehensive. They shook hands with Tony and introduced themselves. The blond, taller one was named Kip and the shorter, cuter one, with a pony tail, was named Brian. Kip said, with a chuckle, "Don't stop what you were doin', dude. Rick loves a good blowjob."

Hal, chuckling, went over to the bar and started mixing everybody a drink. A sideboard was stocked with liquor, with stacks of plastic glasses and bottles of mix. Hal poured himself a Dubonnet and topped it with ginger ale. The two new guys settled into the armchairs across from the sofa.

Tony continued to fondle Rick, whose hard-on had not died down. The cock was cut, about seven inches long, and quite thick. It was oozing a bit of pre-cum, which Tony wiped away.

"Like Rick's do ya?" Brian said.

Tony swallowed hard, let Rick's cock free. "It's a nice one, I must say."

"So what you into?" Kip asked, spreading his thighs, giving Tony a good view of Kip's own lewdly bulging crotch.

"Everything," Tony answered.

"Cool," Brian said.

"This is Tony's first visit," Hal said, delivering a drink to everybody but Tony. "I think you guys should show him a good time tonight." He radiated his warmest smile and turned his attention to Tony. "What can I get you?"

Tony smiled. "Nothing, really. I gave up drinking after–well, a long time ago."

Hal laughed. "Okay, how about a little coke."

"Sure," Tony said.

But the coke Hal had in mind was not for drinking. White powder was laid out on the coffee table, and a golden straw was passed around. Each of the guys snorted a bit and, when it was Tony's turn, he demurred.

"God, you're a fuckin' choirboy," Hal roared.

"I have only one addiction," Tony said.

"I bet I know," Brian said, "you're addicted to sex. That's why you're here for chrissakes!"

"That's right," Hal said, smacking his forehead in jest. "That's what he's here for, for chrissakes! How dumb of me. He didn't come here to drink or snort or do anything but fuck!" He pulled himself up and prepared to leave the room. "Okay, I'm gonna leave you guys to work it all out."

Just then the phone started to ring. Brian laughed. "Well, now it's starting. The phone won't stop ringing until three. I'm glad you came over, Tony. That way we're booked and we don't have to go out again."

Tony blinked. He had been told he would have his *choice* of these guys. Apparently, he'd had his choice made for him, and it was every one of them!

The guys passed the straw around a few more times while Tony continued fondling Rick. Brian stood up and walked over to Tony. He started to kiss him and grope at his fly. Sticking his tongue in Brian's mouth, Tony willingly surrendered to Brian.

Kip took out his huge uncut cock and began stroking it.

Brian left Tony's mouth and went to his crotch, tearing open his pants and quickly kneeling down before him and sucking his rigid prick. Tony was so horny he began face-fucking Brian while still pumping Rick's fat dick. Rick got up on his knees on the couch and allowed Tony to begin sucking his cock.

Kip watched from across the room, jerking his tool.

Brian pulled Tony's pants down and began to rim him, getting his asshole wet and ready. Tony moaned and deep-throated Rick's dick.

Kip stood up and moved over to the couch, presenting his dick for Tony to suck. Tony left Rick's cock and took Kip's into his mouth. Tony

somehow managed to take in every inch, nearly gagging on the impressive length of it. As Kip pumped Tony's face, Brian parted the perfect rectangular slabs of Tony's asscheeks with his hands, then probed it with his tongue.

Rick left Kip on the couch and kneeled down beside Brian. Kip leaned back and moved Tony so that Tony was lying on his back on the couch. Rick inspected Tony's asshole, finding it a perfect purple rose, puckered and wet from earlier explorations by Brian. He licked it, then made way for Brian's erection, which began poking his cheek. Kip continued to stuff his cock in Tony's mouth while Brian pulled Tony's pants completely off his body and prepared to fuck him. At first Brian pumped his cock very slowly, then with an increasing rhythm into Tony's hole. Brian was great at fucking, Tony realized, and his erection slid in and out smoothly. On every stroke, he pulled his cock all the way out and then he would plunge deeply back inside Tony.

Rick watched the intense fucking for a few minutes, then tapped Brian on the shoulder. He wanted a turn at fucking Tony. Brian reluctantly slid out of Tony's ass, but he saw that Rick had become crazed with lust, and it was as if the force of his lust gave off a scent that was palpable even in a room that already reeked of sex. Rick moaned as he positioned himself between Tony's legs and entered him. Tony shuddered with the assault and tightened his ass around the throbbing pole. Rick's balls slapped against Tony's ass as he fucked him.

Kip pulled his cock from Tony's mouth, pulled at it, and with a few more strokes, he could not hold back, and he shot a load of cum onto Tony's chest. Brian replaced Kip at Tony's mouth. Tony took Brian's swollen cock in his mouth and rolled the big head around on his tongue. Seeing this made Rick all the more excited, and he plowed into Tony until, grunting, he came after just four fast, strong thrusts. Tony pushed forward and pulled backward, being stimulated from both ends, and coaxed out a heavy load from Brian's cock. It shot into his mouth and rolled down his chin. Kip and Brian left the room, and Rick continued screwing Tony's ass.

Now the most extraordinary thing happened: Rick maneuvered Tony so that he was perched on the edge of a sofa cushion and he took him in his arms and began kissing him passionately while he screwed his ass. Rick was a wonderful kisser, Tony thought, and being kissed this way while being fucked by a perfect stranger was exhilarating for Tony. Tony reached down and started stroking his own cock furiously while Rick continued kissing his lips, his cheeks, his neck, his shoulders. Rick pulled back and watched Tony jerking off with his own cock imbedded in Tony's ass. "Oh, I love you," Rick gushed. "I just love you." Rick was big-boned, his yellow-gold hair cut short. In return, Tony liked Rick, who seemed trusting, open, ready for a good life.

Tony couldn't believe how sweet this fuck was, and his orgasm was intense, with cum flying all the way up to his chest, joining the dried cum

that had already been left there by Kip. Knowing he had pleased Tony, Rick now stepped up his attack, and he too quickly came, pulling out and watching as the juice streamed out onto the tiled floor.

Instead of getting up and joining the others, wherever they had disappeared to, Rick took Tony back in his arms and began kissing him again. Tony never would have imagined being treated so warmly by a paid-for stud.

It took Hal to break the two apart. "I got a call for Rick," Hal said. "Sorry."

"Now?" Rick asked, incredulous.

"Yeah, now. Get showered and dressed. Brian'll take you over to the hotel."

Shaking his head in disgust, Rick grabbed his clothes and began dressing. "You want a shower, Tony?"

"No, thanks, I've gotta be getting home."

"You got a..." Hal hesitated, winked. "Roommate?"

"No, just a maid and a gardener."

"What, no chauffeur?"

"Too tempting," was Tony's reply.

FIVE

Much as it is today, Hollywood in 1946 was the film capital of the world, a magnet for the talented, the greedy, the beautiful, the hopeful, the crazy and the downright weird. It was the land of palm trees and Rita Hayworth and the Holy Temple of the Universal Spirit. It was a con game, a whorehouse, an orange grove, a shrine. It was all magical to twenty-two-year-old Hal Lindsey. Tall, slender, and good-looking, Hal thought Hollywood was where he was meant to be. He arrived in town with an army duffel bag and three hundred dollars in cash, moving into a cheap boardinghouse on Cahuenga Boulevard. He had to get into the action fast, before he went broke. He had read all about Hollywood; it was a town where you had to put up a front. Hal went into a haberdashery on Vine Street, ordered a new wardrobe, and with twenty dollars remaining in his pocket, strolled into the Hollywood Brown Derby, where all the stars dined. The walls were covered with caricatures of the most famous actors in Hollywood and Hal could feel the pulse of show business there, a sense of the power in the room.

Hal had not just wandered in there by chance; he had a lunch date with an old Army buddy, Bill Lawrence. Lawrence was more sincere than most agents, and his client list ran the gamut. He had a one-man office and was constantly on the move, servicing clients in London, Switzerland, Rome and New York. He needed some help, he said, and he was willing to give a pal a chance.

Lawrence had a reservation at the eatery, but he was running late; Hal was told by the waiter he was to wait. An hour and two martinis later, Hal watched as the door opened and Lawrence bounced in, elegant in a beautifully tailored suit. He walked up to Hal, extended a perfectly manicured hand and said, "Hey, old buddy. How's every little thing?"

Lawrence was always envious of his buddy's huge cock. Lawrence boasted to whores everywhere that Hal had "the biggest dick in the Army," and the two had participated in three-ways dozens of times. Hal didn't mind. In fact, he got his biggest thrill out of watching Lawrence fuck a girl while he lay on the bed on his back having his hard-on serviced orally while watching Lawrence's normal-sized prick giving pleasure to the bitch doggie-fashion an watching that always made him come.

It was Hal's voyeurism that eventually led him to the porn industry, and, once he got into it, there was no turning back. Lawrence fired him, but he didn't care. There was far more money to be made in representing porn stars, and renting them out for all kinds of scenes than in being someone's flunky. He had found a need and it was thrilling to him to be able to fill it.

Hal had benefited more than anyone from the emergence of a gay porn industry. He rented boys to directors and, once they had appeared in a flick, to customers. With the advent of video, he invested in a sophisticated system to make his own home movies, surveillance tapes actually. On the night of Tony's visit, Hal had been watching the scene in his living room while he was answering phones in his office. His closed circuit cameras captured everything that happened in every room of his house. His friends at Malibu Video edited the tapes he made and maintained his private library for him. He had captured some high-powered individuals on tape and, although he had, at this point, no need to access the library for anything but his own voyeuristic pleasure, he found comfort in the fact that he could use the tapes if he had to. Now he had one of the hottest videos in his entire archive: he had little rich kid Tony Taylor getting fucked by three guys! Tony, he reasoned, now belonged to him.

It wasn't surprising to Hal when Tony called him a week after he had been to his house. He was, as Hal expected he would, asking for Rick.

"Rick's not here. If you want to come right over, I have Roberto. New boy, nice dick. Hot little ass."

"Sounds good."

- - -

Hal's new boy, Roberto, appeared to be in a terrible hurry. "Let's go do a line," he said.

Tony shook his head, but Roberto would not take no for an answer, and he took Tony's hand and pulled him down a long hall to his bedroom at Hal's. There was a huge, very cheap oil painting on the wall and it made Tony chuckle. Roberto ignored him and took out a small vial of coke and set

it on the night table. Then he pulled the pants off Tony, a little roughly, but Tony didn't mind. Tony was excited by the new boy, and his cock already stood erect, the pink crown bobbing against his flat belly.

Roberto rolled Tony over on his stomach, then dribbled a spoonful of coke on the exposed top of each of Tony's smooth buttocks. Then he could feel Roberto's nose and chin against his skin, his tongue licking him clean. Roberto began fucking Tony's asshole with his tongue, making delicious noises. The muscles in Tony's legs and ass were tight. Roberto stuck two fingers up him and whistled softly at the tightness. Tony began moving against him, groaning as he began to enjoy the finger-fuck.

Suddenly there was a knock on the door, and Hal asked if Tony was okay.

"He's fine," Roberto grunted.

"Don't forget, you have a date," Hal reminded Roberto.

"Okay, okay. This won't take long."

Roberto massaged Tony's back and lit up a joint to take the edge off.

"This is an incredibly thick joint here," Tony said, putting a hand on the bulge in Roberto's jeans.

"You want some?"

"I want some dick, man," Tony said. "I came for the dick."

Roberto sensed Tony's anxiety, the urgency for sex. He tried to reassure Tony to let him know exactly what he intended to do to him, but he was so soft-spoken, Tony had to keep asking him, "What?"

Roberto took off his clothes slowly, letting Tony appreciate his lean, hard, hairy body. Roberto's cock was uncut and thickly veined, leading to a pair of heavy balls lightly furred with black hair. Roberto stepped over to the bed and Tony sucked the hefty knob into his mouth, relishing the salty tang of pre-cum on the crown. He moved down, slurping saliva across the heavy balls, then going back to work on the head again. Hunger, at once terrible and thrilling, welled up and overflowed within him. He gorged himself on this big, thick cock, but he grew frustrated when he could not seem to get it hard.

Roberto got on his back on the bed and let Tony continue, his cock delicious but still soft in Tony's mouth. Finally, Tony moved his tongue to Roberto's ass. The funky smell seemed to turn Tony on even more. Tony moved up and rubbed his cock against Roberto's ass. Roberto pushed back onto him. "Fuck me," Roberto begged.

Tony's cock slid in. "Oh, that feels great," Tony said. Then Tony started to moan and fucked Roberto harder. Tony came and he let go of Roberto. "Now I gotta wash up and go," Roberto said perfunctorily as Tony lifted himself away.

They got off the bed and went into the bathroom. Roberto started to get into the shower and Tony asked him if he could shower with him. Roberto agreed and they showered together, Tony telling Roberto how nice it was to fuck somebody for a change. Tony also told him how nice it was of Hal to save Roberto from the streets.

"Yeah, like some old fuckin' queen is my salvation," Roberto chuckled. The water ran down his back and Tony started playing with the uncut cock, again trying to get it hard. Tony took Roberto's cock into his mouth. Roberto started fucking Tony's face. The cock was finally getting hard, at least hard enough to stick in Tony's ass. Tony stood, hands on the wall, getting ready for Roberto to fuck him. "God you're hungry," Roberto said. He slid it in Tony's ass and started to pump. He rubbed Tony's stomach while they rocked back and forth. Slowly Roberto's hands traveled up Tony's smooth chest. Roberto's semi-hard cock was sliding in and out of Tony while the water sprayed his back. His hand snaked up around Tony's neck and suddenly Roberto's cum was shooting up Tony's ass.

Pleased now that he had gotten the stud off, Tony turned the water off and got out of the shower. Roberto followed him and they dried each other. Tony stood in the bedroom and watched Roberto pulling on his jeans and sweat-shirt. "That was great," Tony said, starting to put on his own clothes.

"Hey, all in a night's work," Roberto said.

As he left the room, Roberto's fingers found a jutting nipple, tweaked it hard enough to hurt. Tony gave an appreciative shudder. "So, you gonna see me again?" Roberto asked.

"Oh, sure," Tony said, buttoning his shirt.

"That'd be good," Roberto leered, his long black locks sweat-slicked to his face. Tony followed him as Roberto stumbled out into the night to his car.

"Have a good time?" Hal asked, catching up with Tony at the front door.

"Always," Tony said.

SIX

Besides the Monarch stock and a huge portfolio of other investments, most of the Taylor fortune was in real estate, land bought by Tony's grandfather in the 1920s and 1930s. Now, in Southern California, real estate prices were escalating by the month. For those who already owned land, homes, or commercial buildings, the local cliche was that you could simply fall out of bed in the morning and earn a bundle. Money filled the air, and for the Taylors, Tony and his mother, it was a time of fiscal abundance. *Forbes* magazine estimated their net worth at more than $100 million. Tony could have had a career in just keeping track of the Taylor investments, but he needed the excitement the entertainment business offered. Yet, in the new era of Ronald Reagan's presidency there was a creeping meanness everywhere, and it sickened Tony. Music had definitely gotten meaner. Black rap was edged with violence, and some elements of white rock or heavy metal were simply ugly. Tony couldn't take the fact that tastelessness and bad manners were growth industries. At least his new stepchild, Groove, was selling relatively harmless bubblegum rock to teenage girls.

Tony recalled something one of his favorite professors had said, that "most of the best things that happened to me have been detours–something on the road to something else. Just be open to what's out there."

Tony was determined to stay "open." He knew better than anyone that when you'd had a wealthy father who had been famous, there's an extra need to forge your own identity. It was a burden that went along with all the money. To be taken seriously, you have to work twice as hard. Being a record producer was something he had never considered before, and it took him some time to warm to the idea. What he liked best about the deal was that he could operate virtually his own.

Tony discovered that the label's best selling artist was Sam Saxon, who was now being promoted as every mother's nightmare, the boy she feared her daughter would fuck but never bring home. This was a conscious business decision on the promoter's part, matching the tenor of the times. When Sam was first signed by Groove, the producers said, "In Hollywood, image is everything. Who you *seem* to be is more important than who you are. We need to get rid of the choirboy image. That's the trick. Ditch the halo. Clip his wings." The halo was gone, certainly, but nobody could ever clip the wings of a boy who flew as high as Sam Saxon did..

The chain of events that led up to the intimate relationship between the heir to the Taylor fortune and Sam Saxon was really quite mysterious and incomprehensible.

In no sense should their business relationship have led to what it did in fact lead to; such an affiliation would normally not call for such an intimate relationship. Indeed no grounds seemed to exist for a relationship between them at all. They were such different people, from extremely different backgrounds. But yet, it happened.

Their perverse affair was preceded by an initially formal, business-like relationship, but what brought them together was something else, something unfathomable, something beyond human reason, something that went beyond Tony's even wildest imaginings.

Before he actually met his biggest star, Tony flew to Florida to attend one of Sam's concerts. He was surprised to see how short, Sam was only five-foot-six. His band, three black boys, whom he called "homeboys," towered over him. But Sam had an undeniable appeal to teenage girls. He was trim, athletic and exceedingly boyish in appearance. His tanned, unlined face was cherubic. Yet he had developed a routine that called for his pants to slide down during his concert so that, by the end of the show, he was running about the stage in his briefs. Girls threw their panties up on the stage at the finale, many containing hotel room keys, Tony noted. It was a gimmick that started out as an accident. The band was doing a show at Magic Mountain and Sam had been wearing an old pair of jeans that, after he'd been working out in the gym, were a size too big, and he just couldn't keep them up. So he let them drop altogether and danced out of them. Everybody thought it was hilarious so they kept it in the act, and Sam's reputation as a "bad boy" act

grew. What radiated from the stage was a sense that the group was thoroughly enjoying itself.

Tony anonymously sat through a press conference where sexy-as-hell Sam held center-stage, answering the small group of reporters' questions with great humor. At one point, when a pretty young girl passed by outside in the sunshine, Sam lost his concentration and stared at her. He grinned at her and then had to ask the reporter, "Excuse me, what was your question?"

Sam articulated the group's philosophy: "Music should be fun. It's easy to be miserable. Music should help lift you outta that." He related how his mother had worked for years as a singer in lounges, struggling with agents, owners and managers. He said he remembered how his mother was always broke and how he learned a lot from that. Now, he said, he spent as much time on business as he did on making music.

That night, back at his hotel, Tony tried to sleep, but he couldn't. He was too excited. He sat straight up in bed sweating, with Sam's words and voice pounding all through him. He couldn't get over just how ambitious Sam was as he always had his eye on the money. All the next day he felt feverish. It was sick, he thought, this obsession with Sam. Not since the days when he was having sex with his brother had Tony wanted anyone so much. The memory of those episodes with Tommy haunted him still. *But it won't happen*, he told himself. Tony was sure Sam was, in his own strange way, as fucked up as he was. He kept telling himself, *Can you imagine the two of us together? Fucking each other up?* But when Tony saw Sam on TV or heard his voice on the stud's first album, he couldn't think clearly. Sam had touched a nerve, touched that which was impossible to put into words.

After their initial meeting in Tony's plush new office at the Groove Records building, Tony lost no time in calling Sam and inviting him to the mansion on Kensington Drive, behind the Beverly Hills Hotel. Tony was in the process of renovating the place, and when Sam arrived, an electrician had just hung a new chandelier of extraordinary proportions in the baronial dining room, an antique chandelier, made of porcelain, with forty-eight bulbs and numerous delicate petals and pendants.

Sam stood about under the chandelier, the light making him glow. He was admiring the delicate craftsmanship that had gone into it, and Tony beamed. Despite his rough manner, Sam apparently appreciated beautiful, expensive things. Then Tony gave Sam a tour of the mansion, and it became obvious that Sam was not eager to get away. He told Tony how lucky he was to live in such a house. Sam was as dazzled as any boy from the seamy streets of Boston would be seeing one of the remaining examples of the design style of one-time film star and famed decorator Billy Haines. The house hadn't been touched since Mona had had it done over in the 1960s, when Haines was also busy with the homes of Barbara Stanwyck and Robert Taylor, and Betsy and Alfred Bloomingdale. But instead of Lucite and Plexiglas, fashionable in those days, Haines kept to his proven mahogany and crystal

themes, and the house became a plush retreat for Mona until she pulled out most of the art and the priceless antiques to furnish the Greenwich mansion. Now Tony was enjoying working with one of Haines' disciples, William Cody, to fill the house again with fine furniture and art. For Tony, it was like coming home and being able to do things his way. The big wrought-iron gates at the street entrance were still there, now controlled with a card or remotely from the mansion; the guard from the studio, who Tony's father had always posted at the entrance was long gone. The driveway's canopy of sycamore trees were still illuminated at night by soft hidden lights, and the fountain in the brick courtyard still gurgled. To live in such a place had always been a dream of his, Sam said, and Tony was determined to make that dream come true–as soon as humanly possible. "They don't call Hollywood the Dream Factory for nothing," Tony told him.

Accordingly, the peculiar relationship between Tony and Sam proceeded to develop quickly. They had wine by the pool. Tony told Sam about Haines, who had been a leading man in 1930, and when he had refused to give up his male lover he was blackballed by Louis B. Mayer. "Luckily, he had an antique store, and from there he started decorating the stars' houses, beginning with Joan Crawford," Tony explained. This led to a discussion of Crawford, with whom Sam was vaguely familiar. Tony showed Sam a photo of his mother with Crawford at an awards show in the 1950s. That, in turn, led to a discussion of "pussy," and, loosening up, Sam told Tony about all the "cunt" that was thrown at him on the road. Although Sam was inarticulate about it, Tony sensed that what Sam felt most was the desire to love and be loved, but that he had had no luck at all, that no one would take him seriously. Tony was smitten with Sam's honesty. He could see that he wasn't the only one who was alone in a crowd.

Just when Tony thought he might be getting somewhere with the stud, Sam brought the conversation to a close, and what was beginning to seem like their mutual seduction ended for that day, with Sam going out, the chandelier tinkling above him, and Tony closing the door behind him.

For a long time afterwards Tony sat frozen in his bed, re-living every minute Sam had been in the house.

After that, Sam began to phone Tony, or Tony would ring Sam for no particular reason, to ask him how things were going, or to tell him some snippet of gossip he'd heard. Finally, another meeting was arranged at the mansion in Beverly Hills.

Tony smiled his gratitude when he had Sam back in his house, sipping wine in the living room, close together on the couch.

"You're nervous," Sam said.

"You're making me nervous."

"Don't be. We can do this right," he said, pinching Tony's knee affectionately, watching him intently.

"Do you always speak in riddles or am I just incredibly thick tonight?"

"I'm not usually this forward, you know, but this has been building. You know it, I know it."

"Yes, it has. I'm not sure it's the right thing."

"I'm not either, but you intrigue me."

"Meaning?"

"Meaning I haven't been around anybody who wanted me as much as you do in a long time. Shit, I don't think I've ever met anybody who's wanted me as much as you do. Why don't you get down to business, Tony."

"I don't know."

"Look, you didn't invite me over just so we could chat and then go on about our business."

Tony confessed, "No, I didn't."

"Well, just why did you? Tell me, Tony."

"You're not really going to make me say it?"

"Fuck, yeah. I want you to. I want to hear it. In fact, I love hearing it, if you must know."

"What makes you think this is more than two guys having a drink or two? People do stop by other people's houses for a drink or two."

"Hey, look, I've been around...."

"Okay. You know my secret."

"It's no secret, Tony Taylor. You know what they told me when you took over at Groove?"

"Ha! I can well imagine."

Sam moved closer. The wine had emboldened him. "You have nice arms, Tony," he said, running his hand down Tony's forearm. "Firm, hard. They say a lot about you. Is that how you like your men—firm, hard?"

Tony blushed. Sam watched him blush. Sam knew he could make Tony blush.

"Yes, that's how I like my men."

"Good. You like it hard and I'm harder than anybody you've ever met. I'm hard all the time, Tony." They smiled at each other. "Do I frighten you?"

"No. Not really."

Sam ran his hand down Tony's arm until he reached his hand, covering it with his, then he lifted it up. "Not really?" He smiled, and forced Tony to sticking his fingers slowly one by one in Tony's mouth. Tony tried hard not to quiver but he did as he sucked Sam's fingers. Sam was the most incredible seducer Tony had ever been exposed to.

Sam felt Tony yielding. He wanted to make Tony quiver. He wanted to make Tony come right there, come in his pants just thinking about it, about sucking his cock, not his fingers, with the slightest effort on his part. He had done it before—more times than he cared to count. Just the thought of sucking Sam's cock had caused many men to come in their pants, and he knew it.

"I can feel your heartbeat," Tony said, aware of its rhythmically drumming pulse underneath his hands as he moved his fingers to Sam's chest. "Are you as nervous as I am?" Tony could feel his own heart beating too, much faster even than Sam's.

Sam said, "No. Should I be nervous? I've done things like this before, you know. I'm no stranger to this."

"Please, let's go upstairs," Tony begged, pulling away.

"If that's the way you want it."

In Tony's bedroom, they undressed separately, watching each other. They stood naked in front of each other, not yet touching. They were drinking in the differences between their bodies. Sam was everything Tony had fantasized he would be and more, because now Tony could see what they never showed in any magazine–Sam's smallish but oh-so-perfect cock, hanging semi-hard while Tony's was fully erect and seeping pre-cum.

Tony knelt before the stud. Sam had not told him to do this; Tony just knew this was the way it had to be. Tony's hands caressed the light hairs on Sam's thighs. He discovered Sam's cock was a surprise package, practically doubling in size as it hardened.

"Oh shit," Tony moaned, taking the nicely-cut penis in his hand. He wanted to please Sam so badly he ached. He had spent so many nights thinking of it, of wanting it, and now, here, he had the chance to get down-and-dirty with this stud. He began by running his tongue over the heated, ever-so-slightly inflamed skin, then gently sucking it.

"Yeah, yeah," Sam groaned.

Tears stinging his cheeks, Tony sucked hard, trying to bring Sam to orgasm. Yet humiliation burned his face because this stud was not one of his hired fucks; he was, for all practical purposes, a contract player like those that his father had fucked in his office during his infamous "lunch breaks." But somehow this was different, because he was the servant here, on his knees before the stud. There was no hesitation, however, despite his reservations.

But Tony didn't want to wear this passionate stud out before he got what he wanted most. Tony held back his own orgasm as well, even though he ached with wanting, pulsing and beating with a heartbeat thundering through him everywhere at once. He let Sam's cock slip from his mouth and he started to beg Sam to fuck him, but he couldn't get the words out. No, that would be the ultimate humiliation and Tony was not quite ready for that.

Smack. Sam slapped Tony with his sopping erection. Then again, harder, on the other cheek. Tony's head turned with the impact, though his body remained trapped on his knees. He breathed, open-mouthed, and licked his lips once over with his tongue. "Please," Tony managed to squeeze out through clenched teeth.

Tony's eyes riveted on Sam's darkening, intense face, Sam slapped Tony lightly across one cheek, a little more playfully than before.

"Oh Sam, please...."

"Okay, get on the bed," Sam ordered. "What the hell...."

Tony got on his stomach and handed Sam the lube. Soon Tony could feel the hardness of Sam's finger, and clenched the muscles of his ass around the digit. He was shivering with anticipation of what was to come, easily moving toward a climax unlike any other, with the man of his dreams.

"Open up," Sam said in a low, seductive voice next to Tony's ear. Then, with an edge he added, "You want it and I got it for you, Tony."

The sweet pressure of another finger being forced into him took Tony to an edgy, desperate place of longing that blocked out his surroundings. It was obvious Sam couldn't resist a slave to passion. Now Sam focused completely on Tony's ass, pressing his fingers just barely in, then out, until, with a gentle push, he could feel the throbbing and pulsing of Tony's ass all around the fingers, and he began to massage and tease Tony unmercifully.

Soon Sam gave in to his lust and had mounted Tony. "Oh God," Tony cried out in desperation as Sam's erection began pushing at the entrance to his ass. Tony moaned, reached behind him to guide the cock into him. Tony's ass accepted the invasion like a mouth sucking in a shiny, cool jawbreaker. Tony drew in his breath and closed his eyes, every nerve focused on Sam's entry. With a slight whimper in his voice, Tony begged Sam to go all the way in. He raised his hips ever so slightly up against Sam's probing.

In a few moments, Tony moved his hand away, to jerk his own cock. He relaxed his ass muscles, and Sam plunged his tool in with long, steady thrusts. Before long Tony swore and screamed into the room as his ass was filled to the bursting point. Half delirious, half ashamed, Tony cried out when Sam's thrusts became harder and faster.

"Yes, I'm so ready! Fuck me good! "

"Greedy little shit!" Sam murmured, enjoying Tony's desperation. Sam's cock was working away like a machine. Tony began thrashing against Sam as he jerked himself. "Man, what a tight boy-pussy," Sam sighed.

Tony looked behind him to see Sam intensely concentrating on his tool slamming in and out of Tony's pink asshole. Tony felt his body slowly liquefy as he gave himself to Sam, the memory of Tommy ebbing with each thrust of Sam's cock. He *could* love again, and the realization made him feel as though he'd shed ten pounds . He couldn't hold off orgasm any longer. The ripples quickly swelled to rolling waves and Tony rode the crest-he was coming like he hadn't in months. Like a volcano kept simmering for way too long, Tony was exploding with passion. It was a wild display of hunger, intention, and lust. He was still basking in his newfound freedom when he felt Sam's mouth on him-firm, wet, gently coaxing, then more demanding. Tony was on fire, his ass was on fire, as Sam climbed towards his own climax.

Tony thought Sam was simply incredible, his skin shining with sweat and the muscles in his stomach rippling as he thrust and pulled out, thrust in and pulled out, faster and faster now.

Sam grunted and growled as the pressure of his approaching orgasm shimmered over his flushed skin, and Tony raised his hips.

"Yes! Yes! Fuck oh, oh," Tony groaned and forced his strong hips in tight against Sam, with Sam thrusting the cock in just as deep as it would go and, finally, filling Tony with his cum.

Exhausted, Tony lay quiet on the bed. Sam lay sleeping, and Tony regarded him objectively as if for the first time. It was remarkable the way some celebrities seem to shine in the day and glow in the dark, the way their faces are etched in blue shadow, and how differently they appear from every vantage point. But there was one important difference: meeting Sam in person wasn't a bit anti-climactic, it was a truly thrilling experience. It was almost a mythic experience–like seeing Paris or Manhattan for the first time–that did not fit within the confines of mere language.

Tony knew now he would never tire of trying to describe just how beautiful he found Sam Saxon. But now that this had happened, he would have to be on guard. Since his brother's death, Tony sometimes felt he was being watched by everyone in Hollywood. Hollywood was a City of a Thousand Watchers: A thousand listeners and thinkers and rememberers. Tony knew their secret would be impossible to keep, but he simply had to have this time with Sam.

- - -

The need to be discreet in public meant that, in private, Tony became utterly shameless. Often he and Sam didn't fuck; Tony would just suck Sam until he orgasmed. Having Sam's penis always there, always hard, gave Tony the most intense feeling of physical longing, the longing to kiss it, lick it, suck it.

Late at night, when Sam would get romantic and kiss Tony's neck and bare shoulders, Sam's erection would press against Tony's leg, the thick, smooth shape, the reddish color, pressing into his imagination. Tony adored Sam's cock. He loved looking at it, tasting it, touching and holding it, smelling it. An incredibly weighty, living object. Sometimes at night, after Sam went to sleep and Tony was lying awake, suddenly feeling fearful and guilty about how grand all this was, he would just open his mouth and put his tongue on the cock, licking the little crease and then running his tongue under the cap, marveling always at the perfect shape of it. He would often jerk himself off as his mouth kissed and sucked Sam's cock while Sam slept.

Before long, Sam moved into the mansion where, he told his band buddies with a wink, he could keep better track of their residuals. Behind

his back, they joked that Sam was sleeping with his "bossman," but they were used to Sam's ambivalent sexuality. "Hey, whatever works," Shark, the best-looking black in the band, had said.

Two weeks after Sam moved in, he had to join the band's tour to promote their album, and he flew East. Sam called Tony back in Beverly Hills from the pay phone of a gas station while the rest of the band peed and raided the candy machine. "I had to tell you this," he said. "When we were on the bus yesterday, we went past this cornfield, and I was just staring at it and I saw this little tabby cat walking between the rows. It made me think of you. The way it walked was so fine." He heard a quick intake of breath, followed by a soft, tremulous silence. "Like you."

Tony gulped. Imagine, he thought, how many teenage girls would thrill to have Sam saying that to them, and here he was calling him, teasing him.

Tony told Sam what mail had come in during his absence, what messages he'd returned for him. Sam rang off, telling Tony to "have a good time," but he knew Tony wouldn't go out, that he was the most faithful lover he'd ever have. For now, for Tony, there was only Sam. For Sam, there was Tony, and then there was everybody else.

Later that night, a slutty-looking girl threw herself at Sam. He was standing at the bar, wiping his face with a wet cocktail napkin, when she emerged from the ambient murk. She had long black hair and a fancy little strut that suggested uncomplicated, competent sex. They made out against the wall, and she nonchalantly pressed her pubic bone against him. He was going to suggest that they go to her place, but realized that would complicate things. Besides, he wanted to show his homeboys he was still on the game. The girl stuck her hand inside his shirt and circled the rim of his navel with one cold finger.

"Let's go," Sam said, making sure the homeboys saw him leave with her.

In the cab, however, Sam decided he really didn't like the slut's looks after all. "I can't do this," he said. "I have to get up early tomorrow." The irritated slut was drooped off at the nearest corner and Sam continued on to his hotel. Back in his room, free to revel in the thrilling notion that he hadn't lost his power over women, he masturbated to the image of what would have happened had he brought the girl back here, but, before he came, he was obsessing over Tony again. Tony wouldn't leave him, and it had begun to spook him.

In the morning, he called Tony and told him what had happened.

"You shouldn't have done that," Tony said mildly. "That girl was probably really hurt."

"Oh, she was just a groupie," he said. "The point is, I didn't care how hot she was. I wanted you."

"You should have fucked her, Sam. You shouldn't let me change your life."

"Okay. If that's the way it is, I won't."

After that call, Tony began to feel pity for Sam. Fame, while commonly perceived as a gift, or an achievement, is actually an accumulation of losses. First you lose your privacy. Your face and body become public property. Next, you lose your friends. You lose the privilege of being entirely honest; anything you say can be used against you.

After three weeks on the road, Sam returned to Beverly Hills. The road tour, although short, had been exhausting. Tony told Sam the tour was a big success, though the sales of the album were climbing again. Tony was pleased; the board of directors was pleased.

"Show me just how pleased you are," Sam said before Tony had even finishing pouring him a welcoming drink.

But this was a new Sam, a different Sam. Sam stopped Tony from dropping to his knees. He pulled Tony up into his arms and it was then they exchanged their first kiss. It was so totally unexpected Tony began shaking. Then Sam forced Tony to his knees. Tony hung onto Sam's torso. All over again, he felt ashamed of the need he was revealing to Sam, embarrassed by the wanton lust he had long recognized in himself. It was humiliating that he, Tony Taylor, would be forced to beg, not for pity, but for a fuck.

"Please!"

Unable to stop himself, Tony let out a sigh of both relief and frustration.

Leaning forward, Sam smacked Tony's face with his dick until Tony looked up at him. "Suck it!" he ordered. "Show me just how much you missed it."

Tony held back, enjoying the game for once. Tony kissed the balls, stroked the penis, but hesitated to put the cock in his mouth. When Tony didn't respond, Sam forced the head of the cock between Tony's lips. Surprised, Tony didn't have time to lock his jaw before the thick shaft was pushing into his throat. He gagged as he attempted to take it all in.

"God, you love it!" Sam teased, pumping his hips a little so that the cock slid in and out of Tony's mouth. "I can't get over how much you love it! Yeah, show me how much you love it!"

Tony was helpless as he was fed more and more of the prick. "You're just a natural cocksucker," Sam taunted. "Now do a good job, and maybe I'll fuck you."

Tony's mouth worked up and down the length of Sam's luscious dick. At first, Sam simply fucked his mouth. Then he pulled out, forcing Tony to lean forward and take the head between his lips. "Tease it," he ordered. "Use that fairy mouth of yours on my big cock."

Sam slid a finger into Tony's asshole and felt the walls contract tightly around it.

"Do you want me to fuck you?" he asked.

Tony didn't answer; he could tease too.

Sam slid his fingers in and out again, keeping Tony on the brink. "Well, fairy-boy, do you want me to fuck you?" he repeated.

Tony nodded almost imperceptibly.

"I can't hear you."

Tony sobbed, "Yeah! Please, fuck it. Fuck it now."

Sam smiled and slammed his cock into Tony's ass, driving it home in one swift stroke. Tony rose off the bed, a howl ripped from his throat, as Sam's dick impaled him. Sam knew Tony hadn't had anybody for three weeks and it must hurt him, but this only increased his excitement. Pulling back, then shoving forward, Sam hammered Tony's ass with vicious force, pumping away at him in swift thrusts. Grabbing Tony's legs, he hoisted them over his shoulders and toward his head in a classic porn film position. He liked the view this gave him of Tony's ass and of his cock slipping in and out of it. "God, what a hot fuckin' boy-pussy," he said. "Makes my cock feel *real* good."

Tony was moaning, his head thrown back as Sam fucked him. Tony felt his body begin to tense as he neared his own climax.

"You really missed me, eh?"

Tony answered him by coming in a long, shuddering orgasm. His whole body tensed, and Sam plunged one last time into Tony's hole, cum gushing into Tony. When it was over, Sam smirked as he looked down at Tony. "Yeah, you did miss me."

Tony kissed Sam's cheek. Next, his neck. And finally, his soft lips and warm tongue found Sam's. They embraced and kissed for what seemed an eternity. Then Sam gently caressed Tony's arms as he pulled him atop his masculine form. He wrapped his tongue around one of Tony's nipples, which caused Tony to gasp.

They continued to explore one another as they left no limb untouched, no hollow place undrenched. It was the first time that Sam had toured Tony's body so thoroughly, and when Sam was done he was hard again and he moved inside of Tony once more and Tony closed his eyes and held on tight. As Sam's breaths came quickly, Tony's gasps kept pace, and Tony squeezed him so tight that he thought he might suffocate him. Sam continued to methodically fuck Tony's ass. Tony opened his eyes slowly as he wondered what expression Sam's face held when he was close to coming. There was that charming smile, those strong hands that never left Tony's body, and those soft lips that now kissed him so completely and so well.

For a few short moments, Tony had forgotten who this stud was, what he was. Sam was not the singer contracted to Groove; Sam had just become a giver of incredible pleasure. Tony didn't care that even now he didn't really know Sam's full life history. But what did matter? What was important was that they had found and enjoyed one another, even if for a short while. This had been the best fucking of his life. Yet Tony couldn't avoid thinking about their affair in cinematic terms, that it was like the Hitchcock movies he had written a term paper about, how often things started so calmly and then quickly spun out of control.

In the morning, well before sunrise, Tony woke up beside the stud. Sam was sleeping soundly and Tony lay next to him, admiring him. Sam was a star with the makeup he always wore still on, and Tony could smell Sam's still-pungent, citrusy cologne. Sam the quality that often defines a star: the capacity to suggest so much more than you actually are. Tony reached around in front of Sam, touching his nipples almost imperceptibly, gently teasing. When Sam moaned, rolled over, Tony pulled back the sheet. Sam was hard, as usual. Tony kissed the cock. The cock was still a bit smelly from the night before, even though Tony himself had cleaned it after Sam had fucked him. Waking up to Sam was always an adventure, after a night of sex during which Tony's fantasies would have come true.

The stud moaned himself awake, nipples stiffening in Tony's fingers, and for a moment Tony felt like a victor, except he was never sure what he had won. Or that, with Sam, there even was such a thing as winning.

With Sam, Tony always found himself trying to get somewhere, but where? Tony wanted to help Sam, to do everything he had promised he would do for him: get him into the movies, get him into modeling, get him publicity, make him rich. Could he make good on those promises? He would, he decided, or die trying.

Sometimes Tony and Sam talked the whole night long, especially after those road trips of Sam's. Tony's curiosity was as insatiable as his need for Sam's sex. Sam would tell Tony about his various women, comparing them all with Tony, and Tony couldn't get enough of it—he'd drag every last detail out of him.

And Tony said he understood everything, that it reminded him of his brother, how Sam talked so casually about women he'd fucked, just before or just after fucking Tony.

It was these stories of cunt-fucking that revealed how, over the past few weeks, Sam had become more disconcerted about his strong attraction to Tony and where it all might lead. Sam refused to even consider the possibility of being bisexual, but these days the lines had definitely become blurred. He found himself kissing Tony back when he had his cock deep up his ass. He was holding Tony like he would hold a girl. He wasn't sure what he wanted to do about Tony's infatuation with him or why he needed to do anything about it at all. He did not like the fact that he seemed less drawn to women. That scared him. Fucking Tony didn't mean he had to change his life. It would just add something to it. Sam had to admit he had never felt such emotional intimacy with anybody, man or woman. He felt torn, and berated himself for not just going along with what he felt. But he wasn't really sure what he felt, other than lust. That seemed strange enough in itself: lusting after a man's body. He found himself getting hard every time he thought about Tony's ass spread before him, Tony's mouth on his cock.

The relationship began to worry Tony as well. Even though a great many other details of his life had long since become common knowledge, this

affair was the most serious threat to Tony, yet, because he knew nothing in the end gets hidden from people, that one way and another everything comes to light. Still, his desire for Sam was overwhelming, and he was willing to risk everything to keep him.

SEVEN

"Christmas," Mona always said, was a time to "forgive and forget." But for Tony the holidays had become a waste of days that always lay ahead of him–the intolerable emptiness of spending them at home with his mother, and not at the studio or the office or even in Manhattan. He had to do something about it. But Tony was expected, at least for the long weekend. Sam was not going home, he made that clear; he had become estranged from his parents after the last holiday he had spent with them. Despite Sam's success, his truck-driver stepfather continued to be impossible, now a drunk besides everything else. Sam could stay only one night before he had had enough.

Tony wanted nothing more than to spend the holidays with Sam. He asked Sam if he would go to New York with him, see some Broadway shows, then go to see Mona. Sam said, "You sure you want to introduce me to your mother?"

"Oh, she'll love you," Tony said.

"I don't know. I don't want to be checked out by a bunch of stuffy rich people."

"You won't. It'll be just us."

Sam thought about it for a long moment. Then he smiled. "Well, okay."

Tony had resolved now to go home and see how his relationship with Sam played with his mother. Sam, he felt, would charm Mona and certainly make his case for "live and let live." She had unexpected tolerances as well as unexpected rigidities; one could never be quite sure what would surface. But Tony was also convinced that she loved him better than anyone else in the world, and she would want him to be happy. He did not know how much she knew about his secret life, but her recent silence on that subject was surely an indication that she was watching and waiting for something. Little could he have imagined that something would be Sam Saxon.

The Taylor place in Greenwich was an enormous old house, built in the early 1900's by a local millionaire. One of the directors of Monarch, owned it before Zachary took it off his hands a couple of years before he left for Europe. It had gray gables, five fireplaces, oak paneling, leaded-glass windows and fifteen rooms.

Sam was shown to Tommy's old room, which, he noticed immediately, which meant he and Tony would share a bathroom. They showered together, and before they toweled off, Tony sucked Sam off. Refreshed, Sam dressed for dinner in the new Armani suit Tony had bought him in New York.

Tony left Sam and his mother alone while he helped Florence prepare the annual egg nog.

Mona and Sam had seated themselves on a huge burgundy pouf near the fireplace. Sam was nervous, knowing he was not much of a conversationalist except with his own pals, but he tried his best. Mona opened a great silver box on the table and took out a cigarette. She put it between her lips and waited for Sam to light it, then inhaled the smoke deeply. "I am delighted that you're with us, Sam." She smiled at him. "Tony looks so happy in your company."

"He is happy. Happy that he's been such a help to me in my career."

Mona nodded. She understood completely. She didn't like the fact that Sam was using Tony to further his career, but it was a fact of life in Hollywood. Yes, they seemed to understand each other at once. Mona had seen Sam's pictures in the fan magazines she devoured, and from what she read and heard, she could see how her gay son would be excited by this stud.

"Oh, Tony is such a good boy," Mona went on. "Do you know that he's been very good at everything he has ever taken up?"

"I'll bet," Sam said, thinking immediately of Tony's skill at fellatio.

"Why, all through school, whatever Tony wanted, Tony got."

Sam snickered. "I'll bet."

"Yes, why we never thought of failure. My other son, however, was another matter altogether. Tommy was like his father. He was the most ungrateful, impossible young man ... He never showed any respect for his father's wisdom and judgment. He was rude to his father, and impossible with me."

Sam nodded, smiled. "Tony's never rude to anybody. He's the nicest guy I've ever met."

Mona return the nod, and the smile. But she had to look away. Sam was simply too beautiful, in a crude sort of way. She could not quite explain it to herself, but for the first time in years she was responding to a man–a *young* man. But it seemed Mona always found something "young" to stare at while she thought about growing old; usually it was an inanimate object, like a blooming flower. Rarely did a man interest her.

Sam was, as usual, at a loss for words, but Mona's hand was close to his on the bench, and he took it and pressed it warmly. She returned the pressure, gazing off into space. Sam, having once taken her hand, did not know how to get rid of it, so he continued to hold it as they sat there, both of them silently staring straight ahead. Sam was overwhelmed by this flood of confidences and seized on the first subject that came into his mind. He started asking Mona about her days in Hollywood. She said she missed the social scene there at first but not any more. "Oh, I miss California, but I don't miss Hollywood. There's a lot of life out in California–but in Hollywood they just make movies with it. Nothing means anything."

Sam sat, literally, on the edge of the settee while Mona reminisced; the intensity of his expressions was almost stagy. He moved, the way precocious children do, from the serious to the flirtatious, then struck an appealing balance. Mona pulled her hand away finally to take a drag on her cigarette, and Sam wiped his palms on the settee. He was perspiring now.

Tony came into the room and had the distinct feeling he had somehow disturbed them, his mother and Sam! But Tony accepted it good-naturedly; he had learned that Sam did this with everyone, and would flirt with anybody if he could get a reaction out of them.

Tony served the egg nog and they all toasted each other. A few moments later, Florence came into the room to announce dinner and Tony insisted she have a cup of egg nog too. Sam had been amusing Florence, a large, pecan-colored woman, after they arrived and it was obvious he felt much more comfortable in her presence than he did in Mona's.

As Florence was leaving the room, she said to Tony, "That Sam. He do make me laugh."

"Yes, he's a funny one all right."

They all crossed the hall to the dining room, a vast room paneled in gray. The table could stretch to accommodate eighteen or twenty, though tonight it was closed to serve four, and therefore seemed like a toy in the enormous room. The service plates were fine silver, as were the knives and forks, and the holiday bouquet in the middle of the table filled a silver-plated swan.

Florence served the turkey with all the trimmings and they took their time enjoying the meal. Mona did most of the talking, about her travels to Eygpt. She recommended dining at Justine, ordering fillet of lamb with ratatouille or the curried chicken with pineapple. And she told Sam the best place to stay was the Mena House Oberoi Hotel and Casino in Giza. Her favorite room there, she said, was the Montgomery Suite, No. 706, which had a triple canopy bed, a bronze whirlpool tub set in marble, fine antiques, and a terrace looking onto the Pyramids. Tony thought how sad it was she would have such a magnificent place and be alone. He pictured himself there, with Sam. What a trip that would be! His reverie was disturbed when Mona started reminiscing about a recent visit to the estate of her friend Claudette Colbert in Barbados, one of her few actress friends from the old days.

At one point, Mona caught herself gazing at Sam. She said, "You are blessed with talent and looks and everything that a star needs. I can imagine the past years have not been easy for you, but I think that's all over."

With such words from such a great lady, Sam was equally smitten.

After dessert, Sam excused himself, saying he was still suffering jet lag. But what was troubling Sam was that his instinct told him that a press of the hand from Mrs. Taylor meant more than a kiss on the mouth from an ordinary woman. He felt it was all too crazy, too much beyond him. He took a hot shower, followed by a cold one.

Meanwhile, Tony and his mother went into the library and Tony poured his mother a brandy and sat with her. She began to question Tony about

Sam, how long he had been staying at the Beverly Hills house, how long did he plan to stay, who were his friends, and on and on.

Finally, Tony said, "I thought you would understand. You've always fancied yourself a romantic." His eyes were plaintive, rather appealing.

"But, my darling boy," she questioned, recalling what Sam had said to her earlier, "is this really so romantic?"

Tony looked away. Maybe his mother didn't get it after all. Or maybe she was harboring some romantic notions of her own for Sam. Or maybe she understood things better than Tony gave her credit for.

Mona fell silent, then rose to go to her room. She kissed Tony good night–a gesture that Tony surrendered to reluctantly for the first time in his life. Then, with a glance of sympathy at Tony, she left.

In his room, Sam tried to read, but he was unable to concentrate and was relieved when Tony entered, coming through the bathroom to the bedroom where Sam was lying naked on the bed.

Tony decided it was better to face the facts than to suffer what his mind was conjuring up. "See, I told Mother would adore you."

"What are you talkin' about? They *all* love me," Sam chuckled, rolling over onto his stomach, hiding his groin from Tony.

Tony jumped on the bed. "I've never imagined my mother having sex with anyone before, but that's what I started to think about."

"Ha! If you weren't here, I'd be in her bed right now."

Tony tugged on Sam's waist and Sam rolled over, his cock lolling tantalizingly against his thigh, just inches from Tony's face.

"I'm tired, Tony."

"Please?" Tony asked, running his hands up Sam's thighs. "It's Christmas, and you haven't given me my present."

"Just blow me again. I'll fuck you in the morning."

"You promise?"

"I promise."

"Okay," Tony said, lowering his face to Sam's groin.

Before long, Sam began to pant softly as Tony's mouth moved up and down the length of his stiffening prick. Sam placed his hands behind Tony's head at one point and pushed him down until the entire length of his erection was buried in Tony's throat. Relaxing his throat muscles completely, Tony opened his mouth wider and allowed Sam to fuck his mouth hard.

"Oh, yeah," Sam muttered.

Tony began to beat himself off as Sam continued to slide deeply in and out of Tony's greedy mouth. Tony's prick was painfully hard, his cockhead swollen and throbbing wildly in his palm.

Moments later, Sam pulled Tony's head off his prick and lifted Tony's chin up so that Tony was looking him in the eye. "Oh, what the hell," Sam said. "I wanna fuck it."

He turned Tony around roughly, pushing his legs apart. A few scant moments later, Tony found himself grunting aloud in excitement as Sam's fingers pried apart his smooth asscheeks.

Tony nearly lost his load when he felt Sam's tongue darting out to lick along the length of Tony's asscrack. Then Sam pulled Tony's ass open completely, exposing his tender pink hole to his mouth.

The sounds of Tony's short, sharp breaths filled the bedroom and reverberated off the walls as Sam's talented tongue slipped into the tight opening of Tony's asshole. Tony let go of his cock and relaxed. He could hear Sam stroking his cock as he ate Tony's ass out, and he groaned when Sam took his tongue out of Tony's asshole and pressed his body against Tony's. Tony pushed his ass back against the probing cockhead. "Put it in me, Santa."

Not wasting any time, Sam pulled his cock back a bit, spat on it, and pushed it against Tony's asshole. Tony clenched his teeth as Sam's thickness pressed into him.

"Oh, yeah," Sam whispered into Tony's ear as his prick slipped into him. "Here comes Santa Claus, right down Santa Claus Lane...." Sam sang out.

"Yeah," Tony cried, pushing his ass back against Sam again.

Sam began holding on to Tony's hips to balance himself as he drove into the tight butt with long, deep strokes. Soon Tony could hear the familiar lewd squishing sounds as Sam plowed in and out. The moment Tony reached down and began to jerk his cock again, he knew he would come. Tony's ass tightened and began to spasm around Sam's prick, and Sam pulled him against him as hard as he could. Soon a series of cum splashes flooded Tony's asshole. As Sam's prick began to soften inside him, Tony pulled a few more times on his cock and finally let loose with a climax that shook his entire body.

Panting, Sam pulled out and flopped beside Tony on the bed.

"Merry Christmas, Tony," he said finally.

Tony smiled and, as he relaxed into Sam's sweaty embrace, he knew Sam, in his own way, really did care about him. There was still so much unanswered between them, but Tony did not care, as long as Sam kept on performing so magnificently.

In the morning, careful not to disturb Sam, Tony slipped out of bed and stood under the shower to clear his head, and try to come to a decision. He toweled himself dry, shaved and dressed. He wanted to leave immediately, to go back to Manhattan, but he was determined to brazen it out, and his bright cheerfulness was impregnable. He went downstairs to find his mother. She had wanted to go to the Taylor family plot but Tony said he needed to get to New York as soon as possible.

Mona's heart sank, and Tony could tell she was disappointed. She said she had ordered a big new monument for the Taylor burial plot, but she didn't want to go alone.

So once Sam was awake and had eaten, off they went, Tony driving his mother's Jaguar, with Mona beside him, Sam in the backseat. Mona gave Tony directions, while Tony wondered how Sam would act at the graveside. Would he stay in the car and let Tony and Mona go to the gravesite, or would he lend his support? When Tony stopped the car, they had to walk up the grassy hill to the plot. Tony said at once that he would walk ahead so as to find the exact spot. Mona went over and took Sam's arm as Tony, on the hilltop, waved. Mona felt a tingle of joy. Tony was so happy, and he and Sam were so young, so full of life, and she hoped there were so many, many good days ahead for them.

Tony interrupted this reverie by saying, "I think the headstone's too small."

But Mona disagreed; she thought it was gigantic, an awful thing, really, a phallic symbol of deep red granite poking up from the earth. Sam moved away from Mona to get a better look. "It is really rather interesting," said Sam reverently. Tony weighed in with, "Father would have been pleased."

Mona put her hand on Sam's arm. "I am sorry that you never knew Zachary," she murmured. "He would have liked you."

Tony wanted to laugh. Zachary would certainly not have cared for Sam if he had the slightest hint of his relationship with his son. The elder Taylor always thought that homosexuality might have been all right for his friends but it would never have been acceptable for his sons.

The three of them stood there in silence, looking at the stone. Suddenly, to the astonishment of everyone including Mona herself, Mona broke into tears. "Oh God," she sobbed. Then she put her head on Tony's shoulder. Tony rose to the occasion. He put his arm firmly around her waist and patted her back. "There, there, Mother," he said soothingly. Over Mona's head, he and Sam exchanged pitying glances. Poor Mona seemed uncharacteristically lost. Tony gave her a gentle kiss on the cheek and took her firmly by the arm, saying, "Mother, we must leave. This is too sad for you." He led the still-weeping Mona down the hill and into the car. Fortunately, the drive back to the mansion was short because again they were silent.

When they were back in the house, Mona asked Tony to come with her into the little room she used as an office. They sat down on the one small leather sofa and, when a moment had passed, Mona spoke. "It was so strange back there at the grave."

"You were upset, that was all–and quite naturally so."

Mona gave him a penetrating look. She had a feeling that she had somehow made a fool of herself, and she felt relieved and, affectionately she took his hands in hers and said, "I waited to go to the grave to see the new stone until you came."

Tony looked at her fondly. "It was very thoughtful of you. And it was very moving for me too. I cared for my father. I owe everything to him."

"This has been such a short visit, and now you're leaving. What are your plans?"

"Well, back to business, I'm afraid."

Tony had been touched by this rare glimpse of vulnerability.

At last Mona rose, dropping Tony's hand, and she announced they would have a late lunch.

By 5:30 Tony was worn-out and glad to escape. Sam and Tony were seated in the rental car and, as Tony started to close the door, Mona said, "Be careful, you two."

As Sam drove off, Tony turned to see her walking slowly back into the house, her head down. All that money and she seemed so unhappy, Tony thought, and he felt protective of her for the first time. Maybe he should have stayed out of the way and let Sam seduce her. It seemed absurd, but why not?

EIGHT

Once Tony and Sam returned to California, they started work on Sam's new album, which would feature only romantic ballads. It was a solo album, really, but Sam's group was included on every cut. Sam worked hard on the album and at night Tony worshiped at the shrine that was Sam's body. Sam's lifelong commitment to fuck everything he possibly could was still a threat to Tony, but he seemed content for the moment letting Tony kneel before him. Occasionally, Sam would disappear and Tony understood that he had to make love to a woman once in a while, but only if it was readily available. He didn't want to go out and look for it.

Sam loved all the attention Tony lavished on him and his career, and, for his part, Tony felt appreciated. Further, after being fucked by Sam, Tony felt more fulfilled than he had with anyone else. Yet, speaking about homosexuality, Tony understood, was unacceptable to men like Sam, though it was okay to partake of unspoken things because it felt good. Sam was devoted to his orgasm. To Tony, Sam became symbolic of sex. Their sex became a ritual, something they did regularly and out of necessity. If they had sex in the daytime, Sam would position himself so he could watch his gorgeous cock going in and out of Tony's body, either his mouth or his ass. Watching Sam looking down at himself or reflected in the mirrors in Tony's bedroom turned Tony on. Other than the missionary-position fucks Tony so loved, another of their favorite positions found Sam kneeling on the bed, slowly letting himself fall back, resting on his elbows, so that his magnificent penis jetted rakishly upward and glistened in the light. Tony would kneel before him and caress his thighs and his hard abdomen and pecs while he serviced him. After Sam came, Tony would pull back and jack himself off, his cum usually landing amid the residual cum on Sam's cock. Then Tony would lick it all off as Sam stretched out on the bed and closed his eyes.

If they went out at all, it was to strip clubs. Tony went along, indulging Sam, but he couldn't understand why Sam was so fascinated with slutty women. The truth was that Sam had some time earlier stopped functioning very well with girls who weren't patient and easy. From years on the road, Sam had a big reputation among strippers as having one of the laziest pricks in showbiz. His cock was big but lazy; it needed a lot of work to get off. Sam was easily bored; his friends had to be fun-loving, hard-drinking and able to attract women who were experts at fellatio. Every city they played had a strip club, with plenty of sluts ready to perform oral sex on the hottest new act in show biz.

In Los Angeles, Sam's favorite haunt was a sleazy strip joint on Sunset. It was the type of place where the girls walk right up and grab hold of your cock and ask if you want to buy two beers and a lap dance for fifteen dollars. "Hey, who can refuse?" Sam always said with a snort.

One night, Tony went with Sam, and Sam ended up fancying a big-busted mulatto girl, whiled Tony had a rough-looking blonde named Precious. The girls took them to sofas behind a partition. Precious told them the owner would kick them out if he caught them, so they had to be quick about it.

Sam sat there drinking his beer while the mulatto worked her hand into his pants. He felt her tits while she rubbed him. Precious rubbed Tony. These events had become foreplay for Sam and Tony. They didn't come, saving it for when they returned to Kensington Drive, where Sam would fuck Tony. That was the benefit, Tony saw, of indulging Sam. Once Sam got worked up, the only way to work off the rush was to fuck, and Tony was happy to spread his thighs and let Sam assault him.

This night, Tony caught up with Sam in the shower. "Let me scrub it," Tony offered, dropping to his knees to worship the stud. Tony scrubbed the cock and balls with vigor and Sam moaned, then turned off the water.

Tony took a few big, gulping breaths as Sam shoved his thick cock deep inside Tony's worshiping mouth. Sam grabbed hold of Tony's hair and slid his cock in and out of the open mouth. Tony almost gagged, but Sam slid his cock all the way down Tony's throat. "I swear to God you're the best damn cocksucker in the whole wide world, Tony."

Sam was using Tony's mouth mercilessly, and Tony, as always, loved it when Sam aggressively face-fucked him. The cock pounded into the back of Tony's throat with quick, sharp strokes, then, when Tony's jaws were beginning to ache, Sam pulled the cock from his mouth. Tony began tonguing its veiny underside. "Let's go to bed, baby," Sam cooed.

Tony stood, breathed deep, and tried to steady his trembling body. By the time Tony was in bed, Sam was snarling, "What do you want?"

"Oh please, oh please, please fuck me."

He eased Sam's cock, limp again, into his mouth and was met with a moan. He started to suck Sam again, a little faster this time than before. Sam was panting hard now. Despite himself, he was almost over the edge. Tony's own cock was hard, aching for release. Tony felt like it was getting

larger and larger. He couldn't ignore it anymore. He moved faster, harder, not caring anymore that Sam was about to come.

"Oh, shit," Sam was saying. The end of the word trailed off into a cry, and Tony could feel him coming, spasms shuddering through his body from his cock, his head turning from one side to the other and back. The warmth radiating through Sam from the end of the cock smashed against Tony's throat. Sam thrust inside of Tony's mouth again and again, all of Tony's attention focused on that one point, the meeting of Sam's cock and his mouth. And he swallowed Sam's cum.

Sam's cock still in his mouth, Tony jerked himself to orgasm.

Resting against Sam's thigh, Tony mused that it hadn't been the fuck he'd been waiting for but, after all, you can't *always* have everything you want.

NINE

The advancement of Sam Saxon's career became Tony's new obsession. Tony did things he would never have done if Sam hadn't been part of it. For instance, when he heard designer Barry Beringer was in danger of losing his blue jean and cosmetic empire unless he got a fast infusion of cash, Tony arranged a bond offering of $80 million. He had met Beringer only twice, at media parties in New York. Tony was impressed with the designer, finding his intensity came across the minute he started talking to him. Tony saw Barry was, like himself, a passionate individual, making mental notes of everything he saw, felt and touched. Their meetings were short, cocktail party-type encounters, but at one point Barry mentioned how important his mother had always been to him, and Tony recognized a soulmate.

"You know, that's all people in Beverly Hills ever ask me about. My mother left her mark, let me tell you." Barry acted as if he had some idea of who Mrs. Zachary Taylor was, but Tony doubted he really knew anything about him or his family.

It was quite a shock to the designer to have his problems solved so easily. He placed a call to the Coast and left word for Tony to call him. Barry knew there must have been something Tony wanted in return. Sure enough, when they finally connected, Tony got right to the point. He asked for a favor. "I would like you to meet Sam Saxon, you know, our number one recording star?"

"Yeah. He's cute."

"He's gorgeous. He'd look great modeling your jeans."

"Okay." There was pregnant pause. "Sure."

An interview was set for Sam at Beringer's vast summer home in Southhampton. Tony and Sam flew to Manhattan in Monarch's jet and they settled in at the apartment Tony inherited from Max. By this time, Sam realized just how wealthy his new lover really was, and the tables turned a

bit. Sam was less inclined to abuse his benefactor. Still, it was what Tony was used to. He didn't want Sam any other way. Tony's fantasy of being "raped" by the bad-boy stud remained undiminished, and had never lost its fascination. Sam was a bit slow, but he was bright enough to see exactly how he could keep pleasing the one person who had been kinder to him than anyone in the business. Regarding his career, Sam let Tony call the shots.

They had barely settled in at the apartment before Tony was tearing at Sam's clothes, wanting to feel Sam naked against him. Tugging Sam's shirt out of his pants, he tore Sam's pants open. Tony sucked him like a starving savage.

Tony's ass was now fully exposed. Waiting for Sam, wanting Sam. It didn't take much coaxing tonight for Sam to fuck Tony. He slid his hands underneath Tony's hips, lifting his ass up just a little. "Mmm, perfect, baby," Sam murmured. Sam thrust his cock deep inside Tony, so deep that Tony cried out.

Tony's first orgasm had barely ended when Sam started fucking him again.

Tony was rocking and bucking against Sam's front. "Uh...uh...uh," he grunted as the stud fucked him. Riding him to the point of no return, Sam fucked him every way possible. It became an orgy of sights and sounds and pleasures. Sam ignored Tony's pleas that he stop, fucking him over and over until he knew Tony was raw and sore, wanting to make certain Tony would be limping the next day. They pushed on into each other, their fingers in each other's mouth, their sweat slippery and their eyes and hands all-consuming as their bodies began trembling with incredible simultaneous orgasms. Finally satisfied, Sam pulled out of Tony. Tony was still spread out over the bed panting and gasping.

A satisfied expression on his face, Sam said, "That should hold you till I get back."

"Where are you going?" Tony demanded.

"To take a leak," Sam said. "That okay with you?"

Tony smiled. "Anything you do is okay with me."

Sam was laughing when he entered the bathroom and shut the door behind him.

Sam would sometimes throw back his head and shake it in disbelief, as if the world he inhabited was quite beyond his comprehension. What on earth was to be done? Just look how long he'd been telling these lies, making the whole thing up, pretending he didn't get off on fucking "the boss," as he sometimes called Tony. Sam didn't know what on earth to do about this relationship. His "homeboys" saw the situation Sam had got himself into was, in their minds, utterly absurd and stupid, but no one could find it in his heart to say anything to him. They knew full well Sam would somehow work it out, and they kept their silence.

When Sam was away, Tony was tempted just to give up on the whole strange business between him and Sam, but he was helpless in the face of his own carnality. Tony, in his own way, loved Sam dearly–and love has its own inscrutable ways, totally illogical.

- - -

From New York, Tony and Sam flew directly to Tokyo, where Tony introduced the studly singer to Mr. Okira. The cordial meeting occurred backstage before the concert Tony had arranged to promote the debut of Sam's new album in Japan, where it was being released in advance of the U.S. In addition, Sam was going to film a music video at the studio.

Tony stood with Mr. Okira while Sam did his opening number. Then Tony heard Sam say, "This is for someone who's become very important to me, and I want that person to know it's time."

And the next song began:
"It's time.
It's time to hold my hand/and take a chance
It's time to pay the band/and start to dance
We hear the melody/we know the song...
It's time to risk it all/and shoot the moon
Just let go and fall/it's not too soon..."

The lovely words seemed to reverberate in Tony's entire being; he wanted to hold them, keep them. Sam's voice had a breathy quality, as though it required amplification simply to be audible. It was a sexy voice, and a sexy lyric, and Tony wanted Sam more at that moment than at any time in their short relationship.

After an hour, the concert ended and Mr. Okira left in his Rolls. Tony was standing near the backstage door and he saw that dozens of adoring fans had quickly surrounded Sam, seeking his autograph. Tony would have to get used to sharing Sam with the public. Sam would be playing Amsterdam soon, and Tony said he would accompany him for the concert.

Tony had always wanted to visit Amsterdam, where he heard you walk down cobbled streets with beautiful whores seeming to float above you in glowing red windows, green-eyed cat deities perched on sills among the tulips. Sam had said, "I've heard you can smoke hash as rich as black chocolate." The memories of Christopher and those drug-filled days still haunted Tony and he had said, "Whatever you want to do," but he hadn't meant it. Not after living through Tommy's losing battle with dependency.

Their first night in Amsterdam they went to an infamous "underground" club. In contrast to the cool, stormy weather outside, the club was steamy and dimly lit, with a central stage and dance floor. Tony ordered a Coke and Sam got a tall bourbon. Sam tipped a waitress to secure a tiny table on the stage.

After they had been in the place a few minutes, Tony noticed a couple of guys standing not far away, against a nearby wall, one in front of the other. The one nearest to Tony was pressing his ass into his partner's groin and they are smiling and chatting. Then the one behind reached round and started stroking his lover's dick, which, Tony could easily see, had became hard. The slow stroking excited Tony; he could hardly believe this was such an "open" club. Sam noticed where Tony was looking and smiled. "Well, I see you've found some entertainment of your own."

Just then, the speakers in the walls were blaring the "Mission Impossible" theme and a girl clad in leather wheeled a bike on the stage, to huge applause. She writhed and teased the bike with her cunt. She rubbed herself over the bike, fucking it. She wore dark glasses and her leather cap so far down over her face all they could see was her painted lips. She gyrated some more and pretended to rev the engine.

The music changed—"Rock the Boat," which struck Tony as terribly funny. The girl was now off the bike and danced over to Sam, who grabbed her ass and pretended to perform cunnilingus on her. She lifted her leather skirt and draped it over Sam's head. Tony saw the girl was naked underneath, and Sam had his face right on her pussy! Sam was kneading her naked ass, and she was grinding her pussy into Sam's face. She gripped Sam's head and fucked his face with real fierceness, and the audience roared. Sam gripped her and she went rigid, then, slowly backed away. The crowd applauded. The air had become heavy with sex; they could almost smell the excitement in the air. Now Sam was throwing his head back and laughing in time to the music. He was dizzy from the strong drink and sexual excitement. Tony was, surprisingly enough, so hard he thought he just might come in his jeans. He turned and saw that the gay couple had vanished.

Sam said the smell of the cunt was pretty strong but it wasn't really offensive to him. "You don't know how good that felt," Sam said.

"Good thing," Tony muttered.

They watched the next act, a black girl with a fake snake, when Sam noticed the biker-girl was sitting at the bar, legs smooth and seductively crossed, and he told Tony he wanted her. The waitress sent the woman over.

"Hi, there," Sam said, punctuating their first kiss with a low whistle.

"How about you, cutie?" the girl asked Tony, rising, pushing Sam back and leaning over him.

Both her hair and her pear-sized breasts grazed Tony; *God*, he thought, growing short of breath, *what next?* He didn't have wait long to find out; they were soon headed back to the hotel. The cold rain had stopped; the night was at its zenith. In the cab, Sam and the girl, who could speak decent English, talked with an ease and familiarity that inwardly surprised Tony.

In the hotel room, Sam got naked and let the woman start blowing him. Tony went to the bathroom, and when he came back into the bedroom, Sam told Tony to join him in bed.

But it was hard enough getting naked for a woman, to say nothing of mind lying back and letting himself go.

"I'll just watch you," Tony said, sitting in a chair near the large double bed.

Tony thought all the girl would do was to fellate Sam but for some reason, Sam decided he wanted to fuck her from behind. Then they started screwing. Tony smiled because he could see, true to form, Sam's cock was not fully hard. The poor girl winced as he was shoving it in her and Sam said, "Are you okay?" and she said, "That really hurts."

After a while she calmed down and finally they started moving together. Tony had his hand on his cock and he got really excited watching Sam fuck her from behind. They kept moving together and it was wonderful, watching Sam fuck. Eventually, Sam lost interest in the woman; he decided he didn't want to fuck her anymore. He didn't come, and when she offered to fellate him, Sam begged off, paying her and sending her on her way.

"I guess we should get some sleep," Sam suggested grudgingly.

They got in bed together and Tony rolled away from Sam, trying to ignore him. Sam said, "I'm sorry you're hurting."

"It's not me that's hurting. I think you really hurt her."

"Fuck her."

"You did."

"Not very well. She was too loose. She was a real slut."

Tony felt like telling him they were *all* sluts, but he held his tongue.

Before long, their bodies melded together. It was almost as though the presence of another body, the comfort of it, the longing for more had overloaded Tony's senses. He felt tingly wherever his body touched Sam's. Involuntarily he began caressing the smooth thigh that brushed up against his own. His strokes were soft and rhythmic. Sam stirred, moaning quietly from the pleasure.

"I love you," Tony said softly.

"I know." Sam said. His smile was gone and his face was somber, older, in the flickering golden light of street outside the windows.

Sam put his hand on the back of Tony's neck and drew him down into his crotch. Tony fought him, because Sam still smelled of the pussy. "Lick me off. Lick that bitch off me."

Tony, tears forming, obeyed. And when Sam was ready, Tony swallowed his load.

Backstage after the concert the next night, a girl in her early twenties came over to Sam. Tony had seen her before. She was in a notorious video for some punk band, naked and supposedly "slaughtering" the lead singer in the video. Now she leaned forward when she was introduced, giving Sam a good view of her large breasts and deep cleavage. Sam embraced her.

Tony ran for the door and stood outside in the rain. He would never get used to having these bitches push themselves on Sam. After a few minutes,

a composed Tony went back into the theater, only to hear the news that Sam had left through another entrance, with the girl.

Riding back to the hotel in the limo alone, Tony was comforted by the fact that, somehow or other, no matter where he set out from, Sam always did seem to make it back to Tony. Despite Tony's recognition that it would never work out between them, he loved Sam, loved him unfathomably, beyond his wildest imagining.

TEN

Tony returned to Beverly Hills alone. When the tour ended, Sam began to spend more time away from Kensington Drive. It had got to the point where Tony absolutely had to have something to fill those empty evenings. He could feel it coming on him physically.

Tony took to driving down Santa Monica Boulevard just to look at all the young boys-whole clusters of them seemed to have ripened all the time that he had been with Sam. These boys appeared to be ready for everything, and aggressive. But Tony felt the danger, and never stopped.

The last straw came when Sam invited Tony to go to a strip bar where the latest chick he fancied, Lola, was dancing. Tony at first refused to go, but then gave in, as he always did to Sam. He felt Sam was doing this only to spite him, to put him through even greater torments. But Sam didn't seem to think this was cheating, everything was out in the open if Tony met the girl. Tony wasn't up to these psychological subtleties. He accepted the girls and even felt that Sam wasn't all that interested in them, that they'd be no match for him in bed, and that the zigzags wouldn't last long.

Tony gradually discovered that Lola was hopeless; she didn't understand a thing in life, hadn't a clue about anything-decent underwear, books, good food. She just felt her way blindly, sensing warmth and kindness through the pores of her skin and heading straight towards them without saying a word, without even changing her expression. Tony found out she had several inconclusive affairs and even a pregnancy that had resulted in a stillborn child.

Two nights later, Tony, wanting to demonstrate that Sam's tawdry affairs with women didn't make a difference to him, and even admitting a grudging respect for Lola, hosted the couple at the mansion. Tony sent Mrs. Olmsted home so the threesome could dine alone on the Regency chairs at the table that could seat twenty-four. At one point, as Tony was going out of the room to fetch the coffee from the kitchen, he glanced in passing at the hallway mirror. The mirror reflected part of the dining room, including the table where Sam and Lola were sitting. He watched Sam cautiously, as he would with a child, stroking Lola's chin with his cupped palm, and Lola take his hand and place it on her breast, then shove it down between her legs. Then they kissed. Tony kept a grip on himself, but it was so terrible to

him because Lola was such a nobody, a complete nonentity, who could never help Sam's career, only hinder it.

That night Sam took Lola home and, for some reason, returned. It was one in the morning and Sam was completely exhausted, worn-out, beat. Tony didn't touch him, didn't say a word, because he knew, at that point, all Sam cared about was a shower and some sleep. If Tony had said something to him and thrown him out he would have gone to sleep in his car, the Porsche Tony had bought him in a moment of weakness. Or he could have gone back to Lola's and stayed with her. But for some reason Sam had returned to him; all was not lost. It meant that they hadn't yet reached the final stage; that Sam had just embarked on a new zigzag, nothing more than his usual protest against "perversion."

Still, Tony was disheartened when he bent over to give Sam a hug as he lay, bathed and tucked up, in his bed in the semi-darkness. Perhaps, Tony reasoned, he owed this sense to Tommy, who'd taught him to expect betrayal.

Before dawn, after tossing and turning all night, Tony could stand it no longer. He kissed Sam and awakened him. Sam had a piss-hard-on. Tony squeezed it, then started sucking it. The constraint he had felt melted in a hot rush of desire. As he traveled every crevice and plane of Sam's magnificent body, he knew it was obvious to Sam once again how Tony hungered for it and waited for it and craved it. Tony savored Sam's smooth flesh and filled himself with him, and still could not get enough.

He climbed over Sam and lowered himself on Sam's wet erection. As Sam pushed into his ass with his cock, Tony cried out, but the pain he caused him was so blissful he could only beg for more and clasp him close and tight. The fuck was thirty minutes in duration, an extraordinarily long time for Sam, and Tony enjoyed every thrust.

Later, as Tony sat drinking his morning coffee, Sam entered the kitchen.

"It'll work out," Sam said gently, taking the cup from Tony's fingers and setting it aside. He gathered him into his arms and hugged him close. "It'll all work out. You'll see."

Tony let his hands sneak inside the sweater Sam wore unbuttoned. His arms slid around his lean waist. He nuzzled his cheek against his black Barry Beringer T-shirt, one of dozens Sam had in the closet, taking comfort in the solid muscle beneath the soft fabric. He noticed Sam didn't say "give it time." Time was not on their side; he knew that. But Sam offered Tony what he could, and Tony loved him for that.

"Here now, enough of this," Sam said, standing back from Tony, seeing that Tony had a hard-on now. There was a devilish twinkle in his eye. He squeezed Tony's hard-on. "I know you can't get enough of me, but I can't spend every minute with you."

"I know." A crooked, self-deprecating smile tugged up one corner of Tony's mouth.

Sam took Tony's hand and placed it on his cock. Sam too was hard. Truly, fully hard this time. Tony's heart swelled as well, with unending, undying love for the stud. Sam turned and roughly seized Tony's hand, pressed it until it hurt and then hoarsely thanked him for his patience and adoration. Oh, Sam rejoiced, what a difference Tony had made in his life.

"I love you, that's all." Tony sighed.

Sam shook his head. "Then don't make me leave you, Tony. Please." He pulled away and was heading toward the garage.

"Where are you going now?" Tony asked.

"Work. I do *work*, you know."

"You do?"

Sam shook his head. "God, you can be an asshole!" He raised his voice, angry now. "Yeah, I've got a go-see. You set it up, for chrissakes. Now it's time for me to go. I gotta go."

Tony stood still, made no effort to follow him. Yes, Tony had forgotten all about Sam's audition. Sam in the movies. Tony could hardly wait.

The lyrics of Sam's best song came back to Tony now, causing his eyes to well up with tears. How quickly it was "time" for Sam to go.

"It's time to risk it all / and shoot the moon
Just let go and fall / it's not too soon..."

Now Tony was left, stunned and groggy, with the sense that it really could be over. Tony still ached in his heart at the thought of it, or rather at the thought of how long and hideously he might have ached had he never had Sam in his life. "Just good sex isn't good enough for you," Sam told Tony once, and it was true. Tony wanted a relationship, something Sam simply was not capable of, at least not with another man.

But as so often happens when men are involved together in business, the final break occurred not because of sex but because of money. Sam's deal with Groove had been signed before Tony took over. Tony was unable to do anything about the contract without calling undue attention to his relationship with Sam. He tried to explain to Sam that music contracts are based on giving the artists advances against future income. Sam had two albums that had sold well, but he was still $100,000 in the hole. Tony showed Sam the computer print-outs. Sam was incredulous: "My lawyer told me it was a good deal. My manager agreed."

Tony tried to explain to Sam that nobody ever mentions all the pitfalls of major label deals to the artist. But, to be fair, the artist rarely wants to hear about it. Tony knew that Sam was told that once he become a big star he could negotiate almost all of the pocket-picking clauses out of his contract. Tony also knew that an artist has years to prepare material before he is signed for his first record, but only a year to prepare his second record, and six months to prepare his third. The absurd time constraints make it nearly impossible for the artist to keep this production schedule at all, let alone

with any degree of quality. When an artist is touring for six months out of the year, he is almost doomed to find himself in breach of contract. If he doesn't comply with the label's schedule, then he doesn't get the royalty increases promised him. Tony knew it was all a fraud. It was worse than the movie business, where every production, no matter how big a hit, never seems to recoup its cost and make a profit.

But Sam was not to be consoled. In a rage, he began throwing what was left of his clothing into his suitcases. Trembling, Tony left the room, went out to the pool.

In a few minutes, Sam was about to leave, and he came to say goodbye. "I'm sorry, Tony. You know I think you're the nicest guy I've ever met, but you want too much from me. You want me to be here to fuck your ass. But when I'm done, then it's back to business-back on phone, back at work. Damn, you're always working! You don't ever have to work another day in your life, but you're always working. I can't figure it out."

"Oh, I know. It's a lot easier to figure out some stripper's life."

Sam was about to slap Tony but held back. "Look, Lola's had a hard life, and she needs a break. Give her a break."

"*I'm* supposed to give *her* a break?"

"Give *me* a break, then. I need a woman, Tony. You know that. I can't handle this queer shit." But despite his words, he gave Tony a look of love and grief. Tony had disappointed him; he thought Tony was looking after his interests and, now it appeared, that simply was not the case.

"Whatever," Tony shrugged. "You are hell to live with anyway."

"Thanks." Sam looked lost now, abandoned by his benefactor. An unbridgeable gap had opened.

ELEVEN

Feeling guilty about the financial screwing taken by Sam and his band, Tony, behind the scenes, did everything he could to further Sam's fledgling acting career. He kept calling casting agents around town to help Sam get jobs. Sam's modeling for Barry had made him recognizable outside the music world and Tony had no trouble lining up auditions for some minor parts in three upcoming films. Further, Tony enlisted Bradley Lewis's aid in promoting Sam. Sam had a naturalness before the camera that everyone said was "magical." Tony laughed at that, but he knew the magic in their relationship was gone, yet Tony could not help hungering for Sam's body.

Without Sam, Tony was going crazy; he was constantly horny. It was like the days long before Sam, when he always seemed to be alone and in need of a fix. He called Hal's number. Roberto answered.

"Ain't you heard the news, man?"

"No."

"Hal's in the slammer, man. Rick got busted and spilled the beans, man. They came and got Hal and his Rolodex, just a few hours ago."

"God...!"

"It'll be on the news tonight, and in tomorrow's papers. But I'm takin' care of certain customers, whoever calls, you know? You need bein' taken care of, man?"

Tony didn't answer; he was momentarily confused, then embarrassed. Finally he managed to stammer, "Ah, no. Not right now. Where is he?"

"At the county jail, man."

"I'll get back with you."

In moments, it seemed, Hal was calling him, collect, from County Jail. "I need a favor," Hal said, calmly.

"Okay."

"Hire me a lawyer. All my money's tied up. They've seized my bank accounts."

"I'll see what I can do."

"I know you will. It'd be horrible if everything came out."

"Everything? Like what?"

"I have records."

"What records?"

"Tape. I tape everything at the house. Security measure, you know. I have 'em tucked away, safe."

Tony was speechless; he couldn't believe what he had just heard. He had read about such treachery, but never thought he would be a victim.

"Well?" Hal asked after a few moments of silence.

"Okay. I'll arrange it."

Tony was angry by the time he got Bradley on the line. "What does this mean?" he hollered into the phone. He rarely lost his temper. To him it was like losing his keys, and he never did that either. When he was angry he was a person he was not comfortable with.

"I don't know. Just the fact that they have your name doesn't mean anything."

"That isn't all. Hal says he has tapes."

"Tapes?"

"Yes. I guess everything was taped."

"Where?"

"At his place."

"You went to *his* place?"

"Yes. I didn't want anyone here."

"Oh, shit." Bradley gasped automatically but went on talking, without his customary enthusiasm, as if he were pondering something, as though something else-some bitter thought or other-was distracting him at that particular moment.

Bradley remained cool; he agreed to obtain counsel for Hal, but, more importantly, he was going to find the stash of tapes. "I have friends," he said.

"How well I know," Tony sighed.

Hal, people in Hollywood knew, was the best friend one could possibly have, but could also be the worst enemy. He loved settling scores, and he had a very long memory. Besides, he had a Rolodex filled with names, numbers, and now, Tony knew, he also had those closed-circuit tapes, crude but effective.

Finally, Bradley said, "Don't worry your pretty little head, kid."

But panic had set in. Tony couldn't sleep, didn't even feel like going to the office. He thought of getting drunk, of finding some drugs, even thought of suicide. He was terrified out of his wits, as if everything were caving in, everything about to shatter in pieces. Waiting around for Bradley to "take care of it" would drive him crazy; he knew that much. He called his secretary and found that the Monarch plane was taking Allen to a meeting in Miami. Tony told her to call MGM Grand and book a seat on the next flight to New York. What did he still have the apartment in New York for anyway, if not to escape to it when necessary? He hadn't been there since Sam and he had stayed there for two nights on the way back from Europe. What a happy time that had been, he remembered, betting he could still smell Sam in the bed, and find Sam's album on the stereo where he left it in the middle of another great fuck. He got hard just thinking about Sam. He went to his bedroom, where he kept all Sam's music videos. He had had them all put on one tape.

Lying in bed masturbating, watching Sam vocalize on TV, Tony found the lyrics to the song "Don't Explain," which Sam had co-written, had a special poignancy:

"Hush now, don't explain
Just say you'll return
I'm glad you're back
Don't explain...."

Tony watched Sam's face and he swallowed several times, remembering how incredibly tasty the stud's cock was. He longed for it, wished for it ... and he came, harder than he had in weeks.

TWELVE

Before going into Manhattan, Tony went to Greenwich. Seeing Mona would raise his spirits.

As Tony poured his mother some champagne, she said, "This spring I'm going to London with Lydia. You should come with us."

Tony waited a moment to gather his wits. "That's wonderful, Mother," he said, clearing his throat. "But much as I would love to, I don't believe that I can get away."

Mona shrugged her shoulders impatiently. "It's easily arranged," she said. Her motto was, If you see what you want, get it. "I think you need a change." With that, she closed the discussion, and said good night.

Tony went to bed but slept very little. He hated to disappoint his mother, but the idea of a month with her and Lydia was appalling. A month in London would be soothing, but not stimulating. It would not change his mood. He needed something more vital. He tossed and turned, remembering in his restlessness the last time he had been in this house, and how well Sam had fucked him in this very bed.

He tossed and turned and slept only as dawn began to break.

Back in Manhattan, depression again settled around him. He took long walks and, before long, he was beginning to see the city in a new light. Sure, sections of Manhattan were wretched, streets lined with deserted, boarded-up buildings, and, on warm nights, the city smelled of garbage, auto exhaust–Manhattan was still alive, still fighting, still creating, still on the cutting edge. Before long, Tony was happy to be there. He felt a new freedom, decided to do nasty things he hadn't done in a long time. He went to the Show Palace. He crept up the stairs and entered the small theater. In the darkness he found the row with the fewest occupants and sat down.

The spotlight played on the stage, then froze on a bronzed musclebound stud wearing a hard hat and ripped jeans. He began gyrating to some hot, pumping music Tony couldn't identify at first. The dancer slowly unzipped his fly and soon revealed his thick, semi-hard cock. Tony looked on, wide-eyed, as the stud moved to the music, stroking himself, and Tony shifted uneasily in his seat. The stud was quickly joined on the tiny stage by another stud wearing only a jockstrap, who bent over and wagged his hairy ass at the crowd. The audience whistled, cheered their approval. The jockstrap stud was faux-fucked viciously by the musclebound dancer.

Tony now noticed the guy who had been two seats down had moved next to him, and was shifting in his seat. He should, Tony thought, have been on the stage: all muscle, a tight white T-shirt straining to contain his huge chest, hard nipples visible through the thin material. Tony's eyes wandered down to the tight Levi's, and the stud's hands, which were placed on either side of his huge bulge. Tony watched as the stud's hands moved ever so slightly, his gaze fixed on the guys on the stage.

Tony watched as the man popped the top button of his jeans and wiggled his ass in his seat, then slowly undid the rest of the buttons, each one revealing a bit more of the hard cock. When he finally had all of them undone, the huge tool flopped out in all its glory. The stud sensuously ran his fingers along its considerable length, the motion making his cock jerk with pleasure. Tony licked his lips, reached across the seat to grab the throbbing, cut dick, enclosing it in his palm, enjoying its smooth hardness. Perspiration and pre-cum lubricated his strokes. The stud did not look at Tony, just leaned back and sighed, reveling in the touch of another.

Dizzy with excitement, Tony bent to take the cock into his mouth. The stud groaned as Tony ran his tongue up and down the shaft, pausing to luxuriate over its mushroom head. While his tongue was flicking at the tip, then licking the glans, Tony was simultaneously tugging at the stud's balls.

Tony looked toward the stage, saw that a leather-jacketed stud had joined the other two, and noticed the three of them were taking turns simulating sexual activity. The sounds of their enjoyment filled the theater. Tony took the cock deep into his throat, then released it when he felt the stud start shuddering as he climaxed. Tony pulled back and watched as the cum spurted over his hand and ran down onto the stud's balls.

Tony leaned back and wiped the cum off his hand with his handkerchief. Quickly, the stud buttoned up his jeans and, without saying a word, moved away.

A boy who had been watching Tony blow the stud moved over and began groping Tony. Tony leaned back and closed his eyes. He was horny and what the youth, who he doubted could have been of legal age, was doing felt so good. Tony gripped the kid's head with urgency and the kid speeded up the suck. Tony groaned louder, the kid's tongue worked harder on the cockhead and his fingers went into a faster stroking of the length of the cock. Tony's cum started gushing out and the kid closed his mouth over it, his hands rubbing up and down Tony's arms, then thighs. Tony's juice filled the kid's mouth. The kid spit the cum on the floor and raised up, then raced out of the theater without saying a word.

Tony watched new dancers on stage for a few moments, but he was tired and decided to leave them to their fake sex. When Tony left the theater, he pulled back the sleeve of his sweater to check the time and realized his Rolex watch was missing. At first he was angry with himself for being so stupid, then he started laughing. This was the first time he had ever been robbed. "That was the most expensive blowjob of my life," he said almost out loud. Then he remembered he was well-insured.

Tony started laughing long and joyfully just the way he used to do, as if all his strength had suddenly returned to him and he'd become a kid once more.

But a joke's a joke and a laugh's a laugh, as an old unmarried librarian loves to say; yet still the heart bleeds and still it aches, and still it seeks revenge.

THIRTEEN

When Tony returned to Los Angeles, all evidence of Sam's having lived on Kensington Drive was gone, but the Porsche was in the garage; Sam was apparently taking nothing from Tony, and Tony sat in the car in the garage and sobbed. For the first time in his life, suicide crossed his mind.

Occasionally, Tony would resume his late-night cruising along Santa Monica Boulevard, checking out the action. There was no shortage of possibilities, despite the publicity surrounding what was variously called AIDS or "the gay cancer." Tony had even begun to store condoms in the glove compartment should he be moved to partake. One Saturday night, near midnight, he thought he recognized the blond lad on the corner near

Circus of Books. He drove back, then passed the boy again. When the boy passed a brightly-lit storefront, Tony was sure of it: it was Hal's troublemaker Rick. Tony's curiosity got the better of him. He slowed the Mercedes, turned at the next corner and waited.

Rick was quick to approach the car. Tony lowered the window. Rick smiled. He was carrying a knapsack, wore tight blue jeans, faded at the knees and seat. He no longer appeared so youthful. He had, Tony assumed, fallen on pretty hard times. He was probably on probation, yet here he was back on the streets. Rick was happy to see a familiar face. After sliding into the car, he explained to Tony that after he had snitched on Hal, he was a pariah to all the gay porn producers. Hal's other escorts wouldn't speak to him either. He had no alternative but to try his luck on the Boulevard. Since Rick didn't even have a place to stay that night, Tony told him he would rent him a room at the Coral Sands, a gay-operated motel just north of Sunset Boulevard. Rick said what he really wanted was enough money to get a bus ticket back to the small town in Georgia where he came from. Tony said he'd take care of it, and besides, if he stayed a couple of days at the Coral Sands, he'd turn enough tricks to buy a plane ticket.

By the time they reached the motel, Rick was smiling again, humming along with the Diana Ross music Tony was playing in the car.

Once in the room, wanting to break the tension, Tony said, with a little laugh: "Well, it's not the Beverly Hilton."

Rick's hands began roaming hungrily up and down Tony's torso. He began kneading Tony's swelling erection with such intensity, Tony felt faint. Rick unzipped Tony's pants and let them drop, then stared at Tony appreciatively. Gently he pushed Tony onto the bed and proceeded to take off his own clothes. From this angle, Rick's uncut erection looked enormous against his wiry form. He might not be able to get hard for the camera, Tony smiled, but in this setting, he was a real stud. Tony leaned forward, thinking he was supposed to suck Rick now, but Rick dropped to his knees and knelt before Tony, put his mouth on Tony's belly, lightly circling his navel, then moved down and rained passionate kisses all over his throbbing cock. He bit and licked Tony's inner thighs before lifting Tony's legs and turning his full attention to his asshole. With the tip of his long tongue, he licked around the outer edges, then he worked his tongue deep inside Tony, moving it in and out with what seemed like superhuman force. Tony had never felt anything like it. Rick continued tongue-fucking Tony while Tony jacked himself off. Tony came, thrashing and moaning, and Rick just kept pressing his tongue into his ass. Tony was panting when Rick climbed on top of him and thrust his cock into Tony's ass, crudely pounding away for several minutes until he too climaxed.

Daylight found Tony on his knees waiting for Rick when he came into the bedroom after showering. Tony immediately began exploring Rick's cock

with his mouth and tongue. As he was savoring the fresh smell and taste, Rick pulled on Tony's hair, pushing his face between his legs.

"Oh, yeah, suck it," Rick begged.

Then Tony noticed that the curtains were open and that two men were standing outside watching them, jerking off.

Rick had seen them and was playing to his audience, as if he were back before the cameras.

"C'mon, man, show 'em how good you can suck it."

A thrill danced up and down Tony's spine. He had never performed before an audience. He pushed Rick back a bit so that they could see the prodigious member Tony was sucking on, then began again, giving it his best. He lapped hungrily at the long, slick cock. He played the scene for all it was worth, excited by the thought of men's probable reactions. He bobbed his head up and down on Rick's cock.

"That's right. Show 'em what you can do. Show 'em how much you love it."

Rick's words excited Tony even more. He fingered his own cock furiously, feeling the mounting excitement.

They both came within moments of each other, Rick pulling his cock out just in time to give the men at the window a good view. Then Rick pulled Tony up and held him. They kissed for their audience. When they finally parted, the men had vanished.

Rick's hands clenched Tony's buttocks and pulled him to him, but Tony said, "Let's have breakfast first."

Over breakfast, Rick told Tony his parents were dead, but he would be able to stay with an aunt and find work back in Georgia. He had originally gone to Atlanta from his home town, gotten a job as a bar boy, then as a stripper at a gay club. There, an agent spotted him and had his pictures taken. He hadn't heard anything for a year, but then Hal called him and said if he could get the money together to come to California, there were parts waiting for him.

"Last time I saw you, you were just about to make your first porn film."

"Yeah. My first and last." Rick's grin spread from ear to ear; he flushed crimson.

Tony felt that maybe it was a good idea, after all, for Rick just to go home.

"What was the name of it?"

"I think they called it 'Farm Boys.' I don't know. I never saw it. I was supposed to top but I couldn't keep it hard so I had to bottom. I musta been pretty good because they called me back the next day to bottom again. But I still couldn't keep it up. And it took me forever to come. So Hal said that I should just go out on calls for a while."

"And then it happened."

He nodded. "Hal blames me, but it was his fault. He shoulda checked the guy out. They'd been watchin' him for a long time, Roberto told me, and were just waitin' for the right time." He shook his head sadly. "I didn't know I shoulda just kept my mouth shut and Hal woulda gotten me out of it. I didn't know. I'd never been arrested before–"

"You're a good kid," Tony said. "I knew that the day we met. I wouldn't have stopped last night if I still didn't think that."

Rick finished his toast, then looked into Tony's eyes expectantly. "So you think I can earn enough to get a plane ticket?"

"I think so, provided we can go back to the room so we can say goodbye properly."

Rick's face brightened. "You got it."

They fell to the bed, clothes somehow being unbuttoned and peeled off. The food had charged Rick again, and, as a consequence, Tony as well. Rick was on top, kissing Tony all over. Then Rick buried his face in Tony's shoulder, digging his teeth into his skin. Tony responded by raking his fingers across Rick's back, and when Tony felt Rick's hard-on jabbing at his asshole, he moaned, arching underneath him.

They kissed for a considerable time before Rick got up and Tony gobbled Rick's cock into his mouth, sucking it as if he would never let go. He did, eventually, but only long enough to enable him to slip a condom over his erection, then to slide up his slick body and shove the cock into him, in an incredibly smooth motion. They moved against each other, limbs locked, hearts racing. When Tony came, he came screaming. When Rick came, he was nearly silent.

They lay there naked for a while. Tony finally let go of him, and rolled away, got up. "I've got to go," Tony said.

Rick looked hurt at that, an injured puppy.

As Tony pulled his clothes back on, his stomach was roiling; saying goodbye to Rick was harder than Tony had thought possible. *If only*, he thought.

Rick rolled over and covered his head with the pillow.

Tony said nothing more to him. He left two hundred dollar bills on the bureau and walked out of the room, leaving Rick behind him.

FOURTEEN

At Groove, instead of dealing with glamorous artists, Tony found himself dealing mostly with lawyers, accountants, managers, business affairs people, label promotion personnel, distributors, and executives from the corporate ranks. If Tony's heritage didn't impress the occasionally intimidating people he met, he would force himself to relax by trying to imagine them naked; all their grandiosity would instantly wilt.

But there was one special man Tony thoroughly enjoyed thinking about in the nude. His name was Derek Gardner and he was the most promising young executive at the label.

Derek was known as one of the "Groove Guys," the ones who searched for new talent to sign for recording contracts. Derek had been with the company for several years before Tony joined the group. He was a broad-shouldered, solidly built man with dark, fine brown hair, side-parted, that fell into his eyes. The eyes were blue, with crinkles around the edges, caused in equal parts by laughter and worry; he always seemed to be in fear of losing his job.

Once Tony took over, Derek went out of his way to put himself in the company of his cute young boss. Although Tony found him incredibly attractive, Derek was off-limits as an employee and, besides, the man was married and had a couple of kids.

Then one day, Derek burst into Tony's office raving about a new band he had just heard. While Tony rarely went out to clubs, he agreed to accompany Derek to the group's show that night. It was late when Tony and Derek made it into the Limelight. The Metropolitan Blues All-stars were playing, and the air was thick with cigarette smoke and the smell of beer. The music was dark and bluesy–beautifully executed, Tony thought, but far too loud for conversation.

Derek staked out a tiny table for two in the back left corner, the only empty seats left in the house. The All-stars packed 'em in, even on weeknights. Tony found the crowd fascinating–a mix, spanning the college and thirty-something generation. A noisy group of men and women in chinos and mini-skirts sat at a long table in the middle of the room, generating enormous activity at the bar. The women watched the dance floor wistfully; the men pretended not to notice. Lawyers, Tony decided.

"Tony, you want a Coke or something?" Derek asked, knowing Tony's aversion to alcohol after the death of his brother. Tony nodded, then focused on the kids at the tables in front, wondering if any of them were gay. He had begun to undress every man, letting his imagination work overtime.

After the show, Tony wanted to leave. They had taken Derek's car so Derek assumed he was going to be taking Tony back to the office. But Tony suggested they have a bite to eat at a place he knew of close by. Derek readily agreed, telling Tony that he was in no rush to go home since his wife and the kids were away for the weekend visiting his in-laws.

Tony knew the French Market had a mixed crowd so Derek wouldn't feel out of place and Tony could boy-watch. After they were seated, Derek decided he wasn't hungry, but he was "thirsty," as he put it and he ordered another drink. Tony had never seen the man this loose, and the more Derek drank the friendlier he got. Tony was beginning to get nervous; he had never approached any of his employees and he wasn't sure he wanted this to escalate out of control.

"So how's Sam Saxon?" Derek asked, out of the blue.

"Fine, I guess. I don't see much of him any more. He's concentrating on his movie career."

"Is it true he swings both ways?"

Tony took a long sip of his coffee. "I have no idea."

"Didn't he live with you for a while?"

"Yes, when we were working on the second album, you know, the one that bombed?"

"Yeah, that was too bad. I thought it was pretty good myself."

When they got to Derek's car, Tony could see Derek was really in no shape to drive. He'd had three drinks while Tony had eaten his omelette. Tony convinced Derek to let him drive him home. "How will you get back to the office?" Derek asked, falling into the passenger seat of the Toyota.

"I'll call a cab."

Derek lived on a hill high above Sunset, in a small tri-level house that would have been new about the year Tony was born. The hazy glow from the streetlights showed the house backed up to a condominium building. The front porch light was on. Tony parked the car in the short driveway. The street was lined with parked cars, giving the neighborhood a tight, squeezed feeling.

Derek fumbled with the house key; Tony wondered if Derek was as nervous as he was. Derek looked over his shoulder, scanned the dark street as if he were looking to see if they had perhaps been followed. The house was dark, just a light over the sink in the kitchen. The blinds were open and the streetlights gave the room a degree of illumination.

"I've really got to go," Tony insisted.

"I'll call you a cab."

Derek closed the front door and locked it. Tony moved toward him, not quite touching. Was he really going to do this? Tony studied his face, shadowed by darkness. Yes, he was.

Derek had to make the first move and he did; he pulled Tony to him. Tony didn't exactly welcome the embrace, but he didn't resist either. He simply let himself be scooped up, averting his face at the last moment, offering his cheek up for a brotherly kiss of affection. But Derek had something else in mind. He brought a hand up to hold Tony by the chin, turning his face back, holding him steady while he planted a direct, full-mouthed kiss on Tony's gaping mouth. Tony stood there, his hands limp at his sides, letting himself be kissed, nibbled, caressed; then, slowly, his arms come up, automatically rising in instinctive response to that loving embrace, wrapping around the young man's torso.

After a while Tony broke free. They stood still for a moment, breathing deeply. "I've wanted to do this for such a long time."

"Really?"

"Yeah, but I figured if you were with Sam Saxon, hell, what would you want with me."

Derek put his hands on Tony's ass and pulled him tight against his body.

"Oh, shit...."

"Yeah, I know what you like, Tony," Derek said.

Tony closed his eyes, feeling Derek's warmth, his hardness, the beat of his heart against his chest. Derek traced the line of Tony's neck and shoulder with the thick pad of his thumb. Tony placed a finger against Derek's lips, parting them slowly, touching his tongue, lightly grazing the bottom edge of his teeth. With his other hand he unzipped Derek's pants. They shed their clothes quickly, awkwardly. Light spilled in from the street and turned their flesh milky white. Tony sat on the couch and pulled Derek close in front of him, took his throbbing erection into his mouth. Derek wrapped a hand in Tony's hair. Tony's sucking continued and soon Derek's breath came in short gasps, and the hand tangled in Tony's hair tightened into a fist. Derek backed up a bit, twisted his hips, rubbing his hefty, cut prick all over Tony's face, letting him feel his urgency, his need, his desire.

Derek eased back a little more to give Tony room to work him over. Tony continued his devotion, covering every inch methodically, until he had Derek squirming helplessly, uncontrollably, driven to distraction by the exquisite feel of that unrelenting tongue. Now Tony extended his talented tongue until the very tip touched the sensitive underside just below the crown.

"God, I don't want to come yet. Come upstairs," he said.

The stairs were bare wood and caught the light. Tony stroked Derek's cock as Derek guided him through the open hallway toward the bedroom. Outside, a car door slammed.

Derek jerked away.

"You okay?" Tony asked.

"Yeah, just jumpy."

It was dark in the bedroom, blinds drawn tight. Tony saw the white glow of a digital clock. Derek put both hands on Tony's shoulders and pressed him back against the edge of the bed. He pushed his legs back till his knees were high, then traced the inside of his thigh with his tongue. Tony grabbed the headboard and shut his eyes while Derek rimmed his ass. Tony heard a drawer open and close, the crinkle of a foil packet. Derek climbed back into bed. Placing the head of his cock squarely on Tony's vulnerable asshole, Derek pressed inward until the tight ring of rubbery flesh yielded, and the crown of his cock forced its way up Tony's writhing bottom.

"This is what you like, isn't it, Tony?"

"Yes," Tony sighed. Derek's entry was swift and painful and made Tony jerk.

"Sorry," Derek said, pausing for a moment before he resumed, relentless and slow. He moved on top of Tony.

Tony grabbed his shoulders. "Yeah, fuck it."

Tony was whimpering as Derek forced his cock up the tight channel until he was about halfway in. Then, with a furious thrust, he lunged, burying himself deep. He pulled back and then again lunged with his hips, driving

all the way in. Tony's sensual squirming only fired his excitement and he pounded into him. Tony's asshole spasmed, clutching the thick prick, sending delicious sensations coursing through Derek's body. Tony could feel him shudder with pleasure as he pumped wads of cum into the rubber.

Derek collapsed onto the bed, and he fell draped over Tony's trembling form. Derek's softened cock slid from the anus, which still twitched with the quivers that ran through Tony's body. Tony began stroking himself furiously, urgent to have his own orgasm.

Tony was stunned when Derek lifted himself from the bed, got another condom and slid it over Tony's erection. Derek swung his legs over Tony's hips and sat on top of him. He put a hand on Tony's belly, and slowly eased Tony's prick into his ass. Once the cock was all the way in, Derek rocked on top of him, slow and sure. And then Tony was overwhelmed, suddenly, and closed his eyes as his cum filled the rubber. Derek sank slowly to Tony's heaving chest. He put his arms around him, scratching his back lightly, making him shiver and smile.

"You still gonna call a cab?" Derek asked as Tony's cock slid from his anus. He sounded sleepy and peaceful.

Tony grimaced, then smiled. "Yeah, I better."

"Why don't you take my car back to the office. I'm not gonna need it."

"You sure?"

"Yeah, just park it in my space."

Derek took his hand, leading him down the stairs through the dark silent house, and they laughed for no particular reason. Tony felt like a child who was getting away with something.

Back at his office, Tony found it familiar, yet strange–his desk unnaturally clean, no messages on the answering machine. He smelled old coffee and felt like he'd left yesterday and a hundred years ago.

FIFTEEN

Tony was growing tired of the music business but, mostly, tired of having to live in fear. First came the fear of being exposed, and publicly humiliating his mother, his late father's memory, and his heritage. But now there was new fear: AIDS. Men were dying by the thousands. A few homosexual activists had raised their voices against the Reagan administration, in the hope that it would pay more attention to this problem, but their early efforts had gone nowhere.

Tony saw the most depressing thing was that once someone got sick, he really had nowhere to go. Tony knew his mother had an interest in several vacant office buildings and some apartment complexes in Los Angeles that could easily be converted to homes for these men. He flew to Manhattan to

see Martin Bernbaum, his mother's counsel in New York, who advised him to set up a foundation and then recruit others to contribute to the effort.

Barry Beringer, who held Tony in high esteem since the Sam Saxon advertising campaign, met with him for lunch at the Oak Room. Tony had seen a copy of *Vogue* in which Barry had, finally, come out. Tony thought this a courageous thing to do, but Barry said, "Everybody told me I was crazy, but, really, it's more embarrassing for me to play the piano than to tell people I'm gay. Most people knew anyhow, and they tolerated it. My message was that we have to do more than just tolerate homosexuals these days. I want gay people to embrace their homosexuality. And I hate that word tolerance. Who the hell just wants to be tolerated? I want to be loved, to be accepted."

Tony nodded. "It's funny, ever since I grew up, I've been amazed at how much homosexuality there is, really. I've lived in New York and in Hollywood, and I've traveled. I've been lucky to be able to do that, and it's taught me so much."

"You are lucky. You have no idea, really. I'm a poor kid from Brooklyn. You're–"

"A Hollywood brat," Tony finished the thought, afraid of what Barry might say.

"Such a cute brat though." Barry smiled, then took a sip of his mineral water. He batted his long eyelashes, and asked Tony, "But how is the brat these days?"

"Fine."

"Sam was glorious, wasn't he?"

"Yes. It was one of those things that you're glad you had happen. Despite everything."

"I can't imagine how it must have been for you to be with him for so long."

"Exhausting," Tony laughed. "Emotionally, mentally...well, every way."

Tony admired Barry at that moment. Barry would never allow himself to fall under the spell of someone like Sam. Not a single day of his life had ever beaten him. He was tall, thickly built, his head set solidly, rather defiantly, in place. One might say he gave the physical impression of being the kind of man who, if condemned to hang, would dangle and kick for an exceptionally long time. Hardly the popular image of a fashion designer.

Barry raised an eyebrow. "He never stopped being trade, I take it. He never dropped that mask?"

"No, not really. But that was the charm of it." Tony had always wondered whether Sam had let Barry suck him off, but he decided it didn't really matter. It was better for him to assume that Sam had let everybody in the world who could do him some good in a business sense suck it and go on from there–which was probably close to the truth.

But then Barry seemed to answer the question by handing Tony a business card. "I owe you one, Hollywood brat," Barry said, smiling.

Tony took the card, read the name, the phone number.
"A new BB briefs model?"
"Fuck, no. He'd bulge too much!"
"Seriously?"
Barry's smile grew even wider, and he said, "I thought you might enjoy it—I mean, him."

- - -

James J. Jackson, a sleekly muscular black man, neatly dressed, with angular shoulders, sat a table in the late afternoon lull of the Ramada Inn cocktail lounge in midtown. Other than a smooth-faced young boy busing tables, he was the only black man in the midst of the ice-clinking, quiet conversing of late diners and early drinkers. James watched the boy moving table to table, the slow sweep of the sponge in his hand, the symmetrical positioning of chairs, how he butted them against the tables with a push of his thighs. The boy would sneak glances at James as he worked.

As the boy lighted the candle in the red, netted-glass globe at James's table, the match tumbled at the wick between his blunt-edged nails. He winced as the flame caught and rode up against the pads of his fingertips, then drew back quickly, flagging the match into smoke as he lowered the candle to the center of the table. The boy lifted one finger to his lips. He paused, then dropped his hand to his side, and James was filled with desire once again. He could never explain why little boys turned him on so.

James leaned back in his chair, and smiled at the boy in the white kitchen uniform with his finger to his lips. James was wearing his favorite jeans and a starched, pale blue shirt with silver-rimmed pearl buttons. Without a belt, the jeans rode low at his hips, and they were faded down the fly and worn through at one knee. At his collar, a black bolo tie met in a noose beneath a polished oval of rose quartz.

He dressed carefully, wanting to look good for this new customer, whoever he was. James knew the man who called him, made this date, was somebody important. He also knew that anybody who used Barry Beringer's name paid higher than the going rate, plus being a good tipper.

Under ordinary circumstances, he would have spoken to the little busboy, but he was working, and he had to conserve his energies. Even though he had danced most of the night at the bar, he had slept until two, so he was rested, ready for action.

He noticed the busboy making his way to the restroom, pausing before he went in, looking back at James, getting no response, then disappearing. Just the thought of how eager that busboy would have been made James's cock twitch in his jeans.

Meanwhile, Tony was getting in a cab a few blocks away. He was running late, and he hated being late, especially for a date. Less than twenty-four hours before, he had called the number Barry had given him.

The card said only, "JAMES" followed by the phone number. When he called he had no idea the man on the other end of the line was black. They made a date for the next afternoon, and then James said, "You coming to see my act?"

"Act?"

"I dance at the Olympic."

"Oh ... What time?"

"Ten till two, usually."

"Okay. I think I would enjoy that."

There were several dancers, but none named James. Then "J.J." was introduced as the last "star" of the night. Tony thought that this had to be him.

Tony was shocked that J.J. was black. A stunning black, for sure, with a complexion the color of an unshelled almond, with thick lips. He remembered Halston had this thing for blacks, straight blacks, and for all he knew maybe Barry did too. But Tony had never, in all his travels, bedded a black. He had been tempted a couple of times, in London, even here in Manhattan some years ago, but he had always been afraid. Now, if Barry was recommending this man, he needn't be afraid, at least of being mugged. As J.J. stripped to tiny leather shorts, it was obvious from the obscene bulge at his crotch that if there was anything Tony had to fear from J.J. it would be being ripped apart.

J.J. slid his tongue out from between his lips and quite deliberately let it journey the length of his upper lip, then his lower lip. His eyes went from one man to the other and finally settled on Tony as he slowly began to unzip the zipper of the tight leather shorts he wore as part of his notorious act. The leather was old and worn and fit his body like a second skin. Slowly, very slowly, he pulled the zipper down, down, down. Tony was surprised to find how fascinated he was, watching J.J.'s long, slender fingers tugging gently on the zipper. Too slowly, Tony thought anxiously. Much too slowly. Tony was engrossed, his eyes riveted to that little zipper that was being pulled, dragged so slowly, down. Tony was entranced, captivated, unable to pull his gaze from that silver zipper that glimmered each time the light hit it just so. J.J. urged the zipper teeth apart, exposing more of his dark pubic hair. The music was perfect, Marvin Gaye's "Sexual Healing," with J.J., moving his hands away from the zipper exactly in time to the music, to let more and more of the cock be exposed. Oh, Tony thought, it would be overwhelming, that cock. He just knew it now.

J.J. was still watching Tony–only Tony–as if he knew Tony was the one who had called, and this dance was just for him, a preview of what awaited them the next afternoon. J.J. slowly glided in time to the music and dropped to his knees before Tony. Tony took a deep breath, felt a stirring between his legs. He shifted in his seat, just as J.J. thrust his crotch into Tony's face. Teasingly, tauntingly, he rubbed the bulge in the shorts, which seemed to be hardening before Tony's astonished eyes. Tony could see only the pubic

hair and an inch of the dark shaft. The rest of the tool was hidden by the leather.

J.J. turned again, undulated his hips to the music, then turned back to let the crowd, and Tony, see that the head of his cock was now fully in view, peeking out from the hem of the shorts. He knelt again in front of Tony, began moving his hips very slowly-hypnotically tugging and rocking, tugging and swaying. He was asking Tony to touch it, but Tony only shoved a ten dollar bill in the gap made by the opened zipper. J.J. smiled and danced away, down the bar. He made a bow, and then disappeared.

The other dancers were circulating, making dates, but J.J. did not reappear. Tony decided this was somehow appropriate, that the man had made a date and had given a preview, now the customer had to calm down, get some rest, and get ready for his own private matinee.

Now James's hands formed a tepee at his chin, and he breathed deeply and made a slow, circular sweep of the room, his eye on the door. He sat perfectly still with his lips slightly parted, lifting his hand to his neck. The quartz warmed in the tracing of his fingertips. He studied the people who come in and out of the bar, the men and women carrying slim leather briefcases, calling out to one another, shaking hands, meeting for drinks and business.

James was comfortable here, waiting for an important man. He had lived among whites all his life. He knew when to talk and when not to. "You playin' the game," his brother complained. "No, man," James argued. "This is business." "Yeah, you playin' white men's games, nigger." James just shrugged at such talk. He knew what he had to do and he did it–besides he loved it, loved every fuckin' minute of it.

James smiled when he saw Tony enter the bar. He remembered him from the night before, had hoped that it was he. Seldom did he entertain anyone in his early twenties. Tony, with his Italian silk suit, his perfect hair, his manicure, his tan, was wealthy, that much was obvious. How important a man he was, James could only guess.

"Hi," was all Tony had to say.

They shook hands and Tony sat across from James. He waved the waitress over. James ordered a brandy, Tony a Coke.

"That was some act," Tony offered.

"Glad you enjoyed it."

They chatted about the weather, which was clearing after a drizzling rain. The waitress delivered the drinks. James wanted to know where Tony was staying. Tony explained that he had an apartment in Manhattan but that he preferred meeting people on "neutral ground" before having them to his home. James nodded, sensing Tony's nervousness, despite the neutrality of the location.

James finished his brandy quickly. He seemed to be in a hurry, and Tony decided that, for a stud like this, time was money. Without further

discussion, they left the bar and took a cab to Tony's high-rise. Riding up in the elevator to the 17th floor of the Carlton, Tony felt small next to the taller, hunky black. He backed up so that he could lean against the wall and take James in. Tony could detect the outline of cockhead and fat shaft through the denim.

James smiled. "Like it?"

Tony looked up, into his face, and nodded. "You are one handsome man, J.J."

"You ain't so shabby yourself, Tony. Why–?"

Just then, the elevator stopped and the door slid open, sparing Tony the indignity of once more having to explain why someone like him had to hire his sex by the hour.

They entered the apartment, and James stood at the window enjoying the view of Manhattan, stroking the bulge in his jeans. James seemed to be in no hurry now, but Tony kept thinking about how time was money for this guy and, besides, he had worked himself in a state thinking about what James's jeans concealed.

"Can I get you another brandy?" Tony offered.

"No, thanks." James stopped rubbing the bulge and started to unfasten the button that held the jeans on his hips.

Tony stopped him, saying, "Let me, please."

Tony lowered James's zipper and looked into the gaping fly, shaking with anticipation. He opened the jeans and let them slide down thick, dark thighs. They went to his knees, and Tony moaned in appreciation when he saw the cock close-up.

Tony's hands moved quickly to unbutton James's shirt, and when everything was released, Tony tugged the clothes from the stud's ebony body. James's cock was semi-hard by now and Tony desperately wanted to touch it but he held back. He quickly undressed and knelt before the stud once more. Tony sighed at the sight of James totally nude. Moving forward, he let his tongue move down over the smooth flesh of James's abdomen.

James's body trembled as Tony's mouth got close to the now-throbbing cock. Tony himself was already so aroused that he was nearly ready to come. He massaged the swollen prick, then fondled the heavy balls. He kissed the head of the cock, now almost fully hard. It was a masterpiece of a dark chocolate-colored cock: heavily veined, very thick, a bit nine inches, Tony guessed, and cut. Tony's body became tense with fear at the thought of taking it up his ass; he had truly never seen anything quite like it. Tony kissed the cock over and over, then drew back and just stared at it, then started stroking it gently. He leaned forward and rubbed his cheek against it. Then he touched it with his tongue. The thing bounced and jerked in Tony's face as if it had taken on a life of its own.

"Suck it," James pleaded.

"I want you to fuck me," Tony gasped. "I want to be fucked by this cock more than anything else in the world."

"I don't do that very often."

"Please?"

James hesitated. Then, smiling, said, "Well, that'll be another hundred."

"Okay." On the phone the day before, Tony had agreed to pay $150, but had no idea that was just to suck James's cock, but money was no object at this point.

In his bedroom, Tony lay on his back and spread his legs wide. James positioned himself between his legs. "You got a nice ass, man. I like eatin' white boy ass . . ." He seemed to be apologizing for his next move, but it needed no apology, for Tony loved what James was about to do. Moving downward, Tony felt James's talented tongue working over the flesh of his buttocks, gently at first, then more vigorously. Then, when James was sure that everything was in readiness, he took his fingers and separated the cheeks.

James moved his wet tongue downward and he taunted Tony with it. Tony lifted his hips, letting the black savor his asshole if that was what he wanted. And that was what James wanted. Indeed, James pushed his tongue in, then flicked it with the expertise of a true connoisseur, pushing it in, working it forcefully, until it was fully inside. Tony moaned with delight. The sensation of the wiggling excited Tony so much he began to tremble and thrash about wildly. He had to stop jerking himself or he would come.

"Oh, shit," Tony groaned as James continued working methodically. No one had ever tongue-fucked his ass like this. Rick was good, but James was simply awesome.

As good at rimming as he was, it was, for James, just preamble. He was as anxious as Tony was for the main event. He withdrew his tongue and replaced it with the tip of his now fully-hard cock. Spitting on his fingers, he rubbed the warm saliva over the massive shaft, then forced the head into the puckered opening. He held that position for a while until Tony became accustomed to the pain.

"Ready?"

Tony had propped his head up with the pillows so that he could watch the entry and he nodded, his eyes riveted on the erection in James's hand.

"Yes, but, please, put a rubber on it." Tony pointed to the silver packages on the nightstand.

James said he hated them, but he knew it was better to be safe than sorry. He rolled the condom over his prick and then got into position again.

It took only three lunges before James had penetrated Tony completely.

Working more deliberately now, he rammed the prick deep into Tony's body, burying the cock all the way to the hilt. Tony gasped, "Oh, my God...!"

Soon James was breathing hard and Tony could feel his heart pounding furiously as he eased his body down and pressed his whole weight against

him. When James fucked a man, he usually wanted him on his stomach, but Tony had wanted it this way and now James did what he always did with a woman: he took Tony in his arms and began kissing him. His fingers ran through Tony's hair as he took Tony's breath away with his kisses. Tony felt strangely drawn to this man, by his fierce arousal, by the very fact that something so wonderful was happening. Then James hugged Tony to him and buried his head beside Tony's on the pillows. Tony held James tight; with a feeling that was surely not quite love yet was something like it.

Working his hips expertly, James began panting loudly. Tony thought he could actually feel the cock swelling; he knew that James was about to explode. James rammed his cock in deep one last time, and suddenly he felt heavy and strange in Tony's arms. Tony closed his eyes when James lifted himself away, the rubber filled. James raced to the bathroom without uttering a single word.

Tony lay still, unfulfilled, hurting from the assault on his anus. He heard the toilet flush, then the shower being turned on. He rolled over and began stroking himself. His cock glistened with pre-cum. He was frustrated. He was disappointed he had not come while he was being fucked so expertly by James.

Suddenly the bathroom door opened and James emerged, toweling dry his magnificent cock. Tony sighed as he gazed at it again. He longed to suck it now. James seemed to read his mind. He said nothing as he approached the bed. He simply climbed over Tony and took Tony's head in his hands. He drew Tony forward and Tony licked and lapped at the semi-hard cock.

"Okay, now you're gonna suck me," he said.

"Oh, yes," Tony gasped as he nibbled the prick, which hardened fully, nearly doubling in size. It took great persistence to deep-throat it, but Tony managed. Again and again, Tony nuzzled and then sucked upon the rigid black prick. James bucked forward, jamming the cock in Tony's mouth as he heaved a groan of release. When he withdrew the prick, cum spattered on Tony's chest and even splashed his neck and face. James smiled with shameless satisfaction at having given what he thought Tony had wanted the opportunity to make him come twice in an hour. He had already risen from his conquest and was preparing to depart when he noticed Tony was still jerking his cock.

"Oh, shit," James said, again kneeling on the bed, his now- soft but still substantial prick dangling in Tony's face. He ran his fingers through Tony's hair, pushing Tony into his crotch as a shudder of restless anticipation shook Tony's body. Tony's fist tightened as he squeezed out an arc of white spunk that splattered against James's arm.

Tony had come, but he was not about to give up James's cock. He kept sucking and sucking, knowing the meter was running, and this was going to be one expensive fuck. But he couldn't care less, because too much of a good thing was still not enough for Tony.

SIXTEEN

Back in California, Tony was ever more frequently asking himself what he had accomplished with all his advantages and privileges. He had not brought sound to movies the way his grandfather had; he had not produced the serials and comedies his father was famous for. He had really produced nothing. He couldn't even produce a smash album for the greatest love of his life, Sam Saxon. What could he do to make any difference?

Whatever victories Tony had were only temporary phenomena. He now had the perceived problem of a fellow traveler in the ranks, an employee he had been intimate with. Derek tried to make dates with Tony, but Tony decided it would be best to avoid him. Weaving and dodging had become part and parcel of Tony's life. After each fresh blow he had to pick himself up, and go on.

He began accepting invitations to parties that he would have avoided in the past. He wanted to squelch the rumors about the mess with Hal. You could keep scandal out of the news, but, Tony knew, no matter what you did, you couldn't stop tongues wagging. And now he had Derek to worry about.

One balmy night, Tony went to a party hosted by a TV producer. The house by the sea in Malibu was full of stout, tanned men in denim suits, and of tall, tanned women glowing like oranges from too much California. All the faces seemed anonymously familiar: from soap operas, perhaps, or supporting roles in long-running series. Tony picked his way through the thicket of self-possessed guests, and found a perch at the bar from where he could scan the scene. Suddenly, he felt eyes on him. He looked across the room to see a glorious youth watching him with an intensity that should have disturbed him but did not. Their eyes met and, for a moment, both of them hung suspended in the same slice of space and time. Then the boy turned away.

Tony felt a sagging disappointment. Something had passed between them that could not be ignored. But part of him was relieved, because this was not the right time, not the right place, and very likely he was not the right guy at all, despite his undeniable beauty.

Tony sipped his Coke, lowered his butt to a convenient bar stool. Suddenly, the beauty was at his elbow.

"How are you?" the boy asked, sitting next to Tony.

Tony smiled. "Couldn't be better."

They sat in silence for a moment.

"I know about you," the boy said after a while. His voice was low, almost a whisper.

"You do?" Tony's voice, too, was low and slow. What did he mean by that?

"You and I are alike."

"Oh yeah? How?"

"We both love sex."

Tony's eyes popped open. He stared at the youth, whose eyes were cracked in slits. Cat's eyes, Tony thought. Stalker's eyes. "How do you know that?" This was getting too heavy. He felt his pulse in his neck. "You don't know me; we've never met before."

"Oh, but I know who you are. And I know myself. And I sense a kindred spirit in you."

This was true, because Tony sensed the same thing; it was undeniable. Tony wondered what time it was; it was getting late. Yet he had just arrived; he couldn't really use that excuse. They subsided into quietude again. The boy got a glass of wine from the bartender and drained the entire glass in one long gulp. "Come with me," he said, setting his empty glass on the bar.

They walked along the beach in front of the house. It was a cool night, a comfortable night, and Tony was pleased to discover the beauty at his side was in the business, so to speak. He was Andy Lang, lead singer with the group EX-plicit, which Derek had been bugging Tony to see. Although he looked fifteen, Andy was nineteen and was a big fan of Sam Saxon's. He was also a big fan of Derek's, and Tony quickly got the drift. Derek had set this up, telling the lad that if Andy wanted a recording contract with Groove, he would do well to show up at this party. But of more immediate interest to Tony was just how well Andy knew Derek. However, as much as he wanted to ask, he didn't, preferring to wait until he had personally sampled the boy's charms himself. That time was to come quicker than Tony could possibly have imagined.

The Taylors had been rich for generations, but they didn't call it being rich; they spoke of wealth. They spoke of managing their wealth. And wealth, Tony came to realize, was not about money but about power. Wealth was noticing how people treated you when you said your family's name. It was not about having actual money of your own to spend or having access to the millions that sat, paper quiet, in banks all over the world. It was about what you could do once people knew who you were. He did not have money of his own, but he had power, and thus he had wealth. But wealth brought responsibilities. Zachary had told Tony, "In your position you will need to be very careful about the motives of people around you." Tony remembered those words now as he drove towards Beverly Hills with Andy next to him. The singer was looking at him with a hunger that scared Tony. Andy had moved too fast, and he continued the seduction, caressing Tony with his words. Tony knew what Andy wanted and he knew how Andy thought he could get it: through sex. The idea energized Tony; he knew the boy would be at the top of his game.

At the mansion, Tony turned on the stereo, filling the game room with Diana Ross complaining of her "Love Hangover," which had become

Tony's favorite song of late. It felt like New Year's Eve as Andy took Tony in his arms and they both felt an electric animal energy pass between them.

Andy could not control his rising passion. In no time, his tongue found a warm reception as his hands encircled Tony's tiny waist. Their swirling kisses were accompanied by mutual squeezings and rubbings until Andy firmly gripped Tony's straining prick through the coarse fabric of his pants.

Tony had been unaccustomed to such a fearless advance. He gasped for air as he squeezed one of Andy's asscheeks and whispered, "And I thought I had a cute ass. You have the cutest ass I've ever laid eyes on."

"Okay," Andy said, "let's see what you want to put in that cute ass." Rudely, Andy pushed both hands into Tony's pants, unsnapping them, forcing the zipper down. He pulled Tony's T-shirt up, then he stripped off Tony's shorts and shoes. He stroked Tony's cock, but he didn't kiss it or suck it. Instead, he made Tony sit down on the couch while he disrobed, slowly, swaying to the music as if he were a stripper. When his cock was exposed, it was semi-hard, and he waved it in Tony's face.

"You're cute everywhere, Andy," Tony said, reaching over to it.

Andy danced away, teasing Tony.

Tony was not to be denied. When Andy danced back into range, Tony grabbed him, and began sucking his cock. Andy's legs turned to water, and his back arched, and when the cock was erect, he turned around so that Tony could see just what a fine ass he did have. Tony spread back the dewy, slightly hairy slit with two fingers. He began to brush the opening with a gentle, rhythmic frigging. The lad broke a sweat and began begging Tony to fuck him.

Tony spat on his erection. Andy lowered himself over Tony and Tony nudged his cock into the crack. This was quite a change, and Tony was thrilled by it. He eased his throbbing organ into Andy, slow and slick, as his hands explored Andy's chest, smooth and firm, then his youthful penis.

Tony almost swooned when Andy grunted and he hugged Tony's penis cock tightly deep in his ass.

The rest of the night was not quite in focus for Andy. After the fuck in the living room, they went to Tony's bedroom. Tony confessed that he was, really, a bottom, and Andy said, "That proves my theory."

"Oh?"

"Yeah. There's no better top than a great bottom."

Hearing this, Tony fancied, for the moment, that he had fallen madly in love with this youth.

"Have you ever been in love?" Andy asked Tony.

"Oh," said Tony, "all the time. But perhaps I don't love enough, or something. Anyway, it's too big a subject for me to altogether understand."

"I agree."

"If we loved enough"–Tony was struggling, kneading Andy's exposed buttocks with his hands–"then perhaps we could forget to hate."

"Whom do you hate?" Andy asked very carefully.
"Myself at times."
"Me, too, for being like this."
"It's not so bad."
"Not if you're rich, like you. For me, well, it's a struggle. Do your parents know?"
"My father's dead. My mother knows. You'll have to meet her."

Tony suspected Andy was waiting to trap him in more love-talk, yet now, here, it seemed so natural–and right–to talk this way. Tony had loved, but not wisely. And there was a pattern to his affections, no question about it.

Now he wanted to be fucked.

"You aren't too tired?" Andy asked.

"Hell, no," he said, as he rolled over eagerly, getting on all fours.

Andy got behind him, kneeling with his cock poised just at the entrance to Tony's ass. Andy drizzled lube onto his cock, sliding it up and down. Tony wriggled against it, nuzzled his ass down over the cockhead, opening up for it. He squirmed his way down onto the shaft, feeling Andy's body move slightly back so that he could watch as the ass all of his cock.

Andy finally began to move his body against Tony's, pulling his cock out part way, then pushing it into Tony rhythmically.

The fucking continued for several minutes, Tony's pleasure increasing with the violence Andy brought to the physical act. At one point, Andy begged Tony to roll over so he could fuck him in the missionary position. After just a few moments of this, Andy threw his head back and wailed, an incredible orgasm exploding through him, but he kept fucking Tony, pounding between his spread thighs, as he stroked Tony to orgasm.

Although he was trembling from the intensity of the fuck, Tony went to the pool, just to soak, to recover from the shocks to his system.

He submerged himself in the warm water but then he saw Andy was standing in the doorway, waiting for him. Andy opened his arms. "Aren't you sleepy now?"

Tony smiled and climbed out of the pool. At once Andy engulfed Tony, and led him back into the mansion.

They lay together in the bed that had belonged to Tony's parents, then later occupied by Tony and his brother and then by Tony and Sam. The bed had seen a lot of fucking, but nothing quite like this, Tony thought. They kissed each other all over their faces, and Andy began to cry with happiness. He told Tony he had never been so happy in his entire life. "Look at me, in Beverly Hills with Tony Taylor. And we have fucked each other senseless. It's fuckin' unbelievable!"

Seeing him so happy made Tony happy as well, and they kissed some more. By this point their smeary faces were melting together.

As they lay in the vast bed, they seemed to flow together, and the morning promised to be a sticky one.

Andy was worried about how Tony would react in the morning. Had he been too selfish, too eager, too demanding? Was he just waiting for him to leave so he could have a good laugh about him, about his ambitions?

Andy awoke alone in the huge bed. Slowly he made his way downstairs, fearful he would run into a servant or two. He found Tony in the kitchen. Tony smiled at him and told him to sit at the table, which had been set for two. Tony poured him a cup of coffee. Then Tony laid out two bowls of granola. "How are you feeling today?"

Andy picked up his coffee and said, "Fine." His voice caught in his throat. He took a sip of his coffee.

Tony sat across from Andy and they ate in silence, not looking at each other directly. Why did it feel so damned awkward? Andy wondered. He was scared by the silence between them. Instead of embracing Andy, Tony was serving him breakfast.

Andy put down his spoon. "Last night was great, but–"

Tony raised his eyebrows. "But...?"

"Well, I'm thinking maybe this is just some little adventure for you. You're on the rebound. You're lonely. You had a few drinks–"

"I don't drink," Tony inserted.

Andy smiled, continued: "And so you fell into bed with some kid..." He ended with a shrug.

Tony's heart was pounding. "Don't you know how long I've waited for last night?"

"And what about today?" Andy said. "Now that you've gotten what you wanted."

"Oh, I want more."

Tony's hands were resting on the table. Andy found it difficult to move, but he found the courage to place his hands over Tony's

Andy said, "No regrets?"

"My only regret," Tony said, looking directly into Andy's eyes, "is that I didn't meet you until last night."

"I'm glad."

"Finish your breakfast," Tony said. And he watched until Andy picked up his spoon and began eating his cereal. Then Tony slid down in his chair and disappeared under the table. Andy felt Tony's warm hands on his ankles, sliding up his calves to his thighs. He pushed his chair back from the table as Tony's tongue slid up his thighs, to come to rest in his groin. Tony began sucking Andy's cock, which quickly swelled. Once it was erect, Tony left it and kissed his way up Andy's body, between his pecs, up his throat and his chin to his lips. They kissed passionately before Tony returned to Andy's cock and sucked him to orgasm.

- - -

While Andy was showering, Tony called Derek at home, since it was Sunday. Derek played a demo so Tony could hear how the boy sounded. Tony wasn't impressed. Derek explained that Andy sang simply, loudly, woodenly, but he was direct, sincere. He exuded a vulnerability that it was right for a teen idol. He was taut as a violin string when he sang, seeming to strain every nerve and shudder ever so slightly at the rhythm of the song. Andy was, Derek thought, no Sam Saxon, but he did have promise. With the right song, he just might make it. Derek said he was sure Tony would like Andy if he met him. Tony chuckled. "Well, I have met him. That's why I'm calling. But you knew that already."

Derek chuckled as well. "I'm glad you had a good time."

"Thanks to you...."

Just then, Andy came out of the bathroom. Tony hung up the phone and spread his thighs, to show Andy he had an erection.

Andy bounced on the bed and took Tony's cock into his mouth, working it reverently. With Tony's moans of satisfaction ringing in his ears, Andy feasted hungrily. Tony's scent intoxicated him as his fingers moved up and down on the penis. Tony arched against him, and gripped him fiercely. When Andy realized he was close to coming; he backed off, but it was too late; the first pulse of Tony's orgasm spread out from his groin like buckshot. Andy took the load.

"I'm sorry," Andy said as they lay in each other's arms.

"It's okay. We've got all day."

Andy still looked disappointed; he jerked on Tony's spent cock and sighed, "Oh, Tony, I wanna get fucked so bad."

Tony smiled and rolled away. He pulled out the dildo Christopher had given him from his night table. As it had been for Tony, its hugeness and black beauty was hypnotic to Andy and he couldn't take his eyes off it. "My God," Andy gushed as Tony coated the thing with a generous dab of lube.

Tony lifted Andy's legs up, exposing his ass, and eased the dildo in and out of Andy's tight ass.

Andy moaned as Tony suddenly slipped the dildo out of him. Tony set it aside and reached for a latex glove. "Now for something even smoother." A lubed fingertip caressed Andy's anus. He twitched.

Tony laid his hand on Andy's belly. "Be calm."

Andy drew a ragged breath and tried to do as Tony told him. A finger entered him. He squirmed. Then two fingers, then three. The finger-fucking that followed was relentless, the pain finally yielding to incredible pleasure.

At one point, Andy's eyes snapped open and he stared at Tony. His mouth opened in astonishment when he realized Tony had his entire hand in him. A shudder shook his whole body. As the fisting continued, sensations rioted through his body. Tony stopped jerking himself and began to jerk Andy's erection. Now, after what seemed to an eternity to Andy, Tony's probing slowed. Tony realized Andy was close and he wanted to fuck him before Andy orgasmed. Andy gasped as Tony replaced his fist with his cock. Andy

now relaxed into Tony's rhythm and floated. Smooth, slow strokes built shared excitement that both fed and increased the hunger. Andy's eyes closed as he was swept up in the intensity of the moment.

"Come for me." Tony begged.

Andy sighed. The strokes were all in the right place now. "Oh, Christ," Andy groaned despairingly. "Come with me, Tony. Come *in* me!"

Andy began to tremble as Tony's thrusts came more rapidly. Andy felt himself pass the line where climax becomes inevitable and he let out a long scream of fulfillment.

Andy's cock jerked, emitting drops of ejaculate, some of which struck his face and hair. As his climax peaked and began to subside, he realized Tony was coming; it was a climax that was incredibly long and intense considering he had just come minutes before.

When silence descended, they stared at each other a moment before Tony pulled slowly out. "God, that was good."

"That was fucking unbelievable!" Andy cried.

Tony smiled. What was happening to him was wet-dream material. A long overdue rite of passage, the pig bottom becoming an accomplished top.

- - -

The next day, Tony called Leonard Pierson at *Teenybopper* magazine, who agreed to schedule Andy for a photo shoot and cover story. A bit later, looking at the proofs and reading the story, Tony realized both the reporter and the photographer must have desired Andy.

Leonard smiled. "It'll be love at first sight the minute we begin running pictures of him. All the teenage girls will start swooning."

Tony read the subhead of the story and chuckled: "His face is almost angelic, but there's a hint of mystery there that makes him irresistible." Little do they know, Tony thought.

SEVENTEEN

The news of Andy's lucrative new recording contract–and the rumors that Andy had moved in with Tony–traveled fast at Groove, and, it appeared, no one was more concerned about it than Derek.

One day, Tony was leaving a recording session of the All-Stars when Derek appeared at his side. "We should talk," Derek said as Tony unlocked the door of his Mercedes in the parking lot.

Tony smiled. "Why? Are you alone for the weekend again?"

"Yeah."

Later, when they arrived at Derek's house, Derek accused Tony of avoiding him.

"I just think it's too dangerous– " Tony countered.

"We both have a lot to lose," Derek said, pouring Tony a Coke in the bright kitchen of his house. Tony sat at the tiny table and looked about the cheerful room. He couldn't believe he was here in this married man's house again, especially since he had just had been fucked that morning by Andy.

"I guess that's the attraction then, isn't it?"

Derek nodded as he set the soda before Tony. He began to rub Tony's shoulders. "Do you get everything you need at home?"

"Do you?" Tony asked, bringing his hand to Derek's.

"Ha! Does anybody?"

They went into the living room and, while Derek pulled the blinds, Tony made himself comfortable on the couch, kicking off his shoes and unbuttoning his shirt.

Derek finished undressing Tony, stopping occasionally to kiss him, then he left him for a few moments to pee and get some condoms. Tony sat on the couch playing with himself.

Soon Derek was back, nude except for his underwear, and Tony watched Derek skim down his briefs, freeing a penis that was stiffening with eager anticipation.

Now Derek stood before Tony once more, a vision of sheer manliness. Tony became painfully erect, aching with a throb of longing to again possess the married man with two kids. Tony held him there for a moment, relishing the anticipation of sucking that cock once again, letting it build slowly. Tony had learned an almost-theatrical sense of timing.

Derek's cock was as big and wonderful as Tony had remembered, the wrinkled sac of the scrotum already tightening, contracting, with fear or with excitement ... or both. Tony knew how badly Derek had wanted a rematch. He also knew how badly Derek wanted to please, to make this continue. Derek's cock seemed to cry out to be sucked and fondled.

"Do I really please you?" the stud asked, somewhat rhetorically, Tony thought, since Derek could see that Tony's prick was already obviously answering that question. Derek stared wide-eyed as Tony knelt and took his cock in his mouth. A surge of lust rose up in him as his prick responded to the stirring sight of Tony sucking him.

Tony could only suck it for so long, however. He really had to have it in his ass. He leaned back into the pillows and spread his legs wide. As Derek moved closer, Tony felt the intensity of his powerful masculine need, and he couldn't take his eyes off Derek's delicious, swaying prick, which was heavy and swollen as Derek applied the rubber to it. It lost a bit of its hardness but it was soon again rising before Tony's eyes. "God, I love your cock," Tony said, taking it in his hand, guiding it to his asshole.

As Derek leaned over Tony, his tongue eased between Tony's lips. Tony's mouth opened more as Derek leaned against him. The thrusts of his tongue took on a purely sexual rhythm. A low, feminine moan urged Derek on. Tony was as hot for him as he was for him. Derek pulled back, his eyes glistening, his sensuous lips moist.

"I like it when you kiss me like that," Tony said.
"Like what?"
"Like you really want me."
"Oh, I want you, Tony. I've missed it. You'll never know how much I've missed it." Slowly Derek shoved his cock into Tony's asshole. "That doesn't hurt, does it? It feels so good to me."
Tony heard anguish in Derek's voice and sized up the situation. Derek needed to feel loved, desired. Most people were mentally divorced long before they were legally divorced, Tony knew. Poor Derek probably hadn't felt loved in years. What a waste.
As the fuck continued, at one point Tony said, "I can't believe we're doing this again."
"I want you to thank me for Andy."
"I do. I do. I just can't believe this."
Derek was determined to make Tony a believer once more and he refused to rush. He stroked Tony, reveling in Tony's soft moans. He thrust upward just as he pulled Tony down, penetrating him to the hilt. Tony grasped his shoulders with both hands. "Oh, Derek," he moaned against Derek's lips. They kissed as Derek let himself go, clutching Tony, thrusting fiercely. Derek held Tony for some time after he'd climaxed, gasping for breath, Tony kissing his face.
Finally Derek lifted up and his cock slid from the opening. He took Tony's erection, dripping with pre-cum, in his hands. He kissed the head of it, then applied the condom. He turned around and slowly lowered himself onto Tony's erection. He bounced up and down on the cock until a thundering orgasm overtook Tony, racking his thin frame from head to toe with a massive, convulsive shudder. He arched up, straining to hold Derek, to cling to the heights of rapture just a moment more. Held there, Derek twisted in ecstatic abandon, crying out as he again teetered on the edge, jacking his cock. And then, with a long, plaintive moan of shivering passion, Derek came once more. He lifted himself off Tony and collapsed gratefully to the couch. They lay there, content, lost in the blissful aftermath of their second major orgasms of the day.
Tony lifted Derek's arm, put it around him, and fell against the stud. He sighed as Derek embraced him, and Tony silently thanked him again for Andy.

EIGHTEEN

Tony loved to observe the young girls as they watched Andy and his back-up group perform. Tony stood in the back of the auditorium in San Diego, leaning against the wall, with one foot crossed in front of the other, arms folded, left over right. Andy was up on stage, of course, looking very much like Sam, swaggering across the stage, to smile and wink at the crowd . Music filled the room, and he opened his mouth to begin the first song.

Girls gasped, they swooned, they inched closer to the stage in one hungry wave. Tony could practically hear the disbelief churning through their minds: "Can a man as gorgeous as that sing too?"

Andy worked the microphone the way he worked Tony's cock, drawing it close to his lips, his tongue caressing it with his hands, all the while singing words of undying devotion. Tony could about feel all the teenyboppers in the auditorium breaking out into a sweat. What would they think if they knew Andy was going home with Tony tonight?

Tony watched Andy flirt with a girl in the front, close to the stage. He pretended he was singing to her, only to her. He dropped down on one knee and extended his right arm. Andy pretended she was everything he had ever wanted and more. He pretended that he would never hurt her. Would never lie to her. Would never leave her. Tony imagined the girl thinking about how wonderful it would be to have Andy between her thighs, fucking her into ecstasy each and every single night of her entire life.

But the girl would never know the truth, of course, that Andy's life was pure and simple lust, that nothing else mattered to Andy but that. And, fortunately for Tony, that lust was aimed in his direction.

Andy danced away and Tony imagined the girl was wondering if he meant it, if she should go backstage afterward and rap on his dressing-room door. Every girl in the room wished she were that girl in the front. Andy was back again, taking her to the edge, reaching out with his fingertips as if to stroke her face, and then in a split second he turned and focused all his attention on someone else in the crowd. Every girl was supposed to think she had a chance with Andy. He finished the set and promised to return. As he disappeared backstage Tony wandered through the crowd, listening. He liked to hear what they said about his newest star.

The house lights went down again and Andy was back. This was the part of the show Tony liked best. First the girls were standing quietly, politely, then they began to clap and cheer; and then, just before their eagerness might very well have turned to annoyance, Andy emerged. Like everything else about him, his timing was perfect. There was a pause, a heartbeat of silence, and then they gasped. Andy had changed into his skintight white jump suit. He was truly, utterly beautiful. He began to sing, and as he did he began to slink across the stage, perfectly at home. He picked a girl from the audience and wagged his finger at her. She tried to step forward, but her legs were shaking. Her girlfriends shoved her forward, and before she knew it she was on stage. She danced with Andy for all of two minutes before the song ended, and she was led off-stage. Three numbers later, it was all over. The encore Tony's cue, and he hurried through the crowd, to help Andy change for the short drive to the hotel. Tony was the one who got to see through the illusion.

The show was just foreplay to Andy. What was to happen at the hotel was the main event. The minute they were alone, they were all over each other,

ignited by the power of desire. All those girls wanted what they couldn't have, because Tony was having it.

Tony undressed Andy as if he were a child. He lifted him onto the bed and laid down gently beside him. Finally they were together, naked, and they began touching each other everywhere, fingers stroking, mouths caressing, skin on fire. When Tony entered his ass as if on cue, Andy sang out to him. Tony pulled him up to look at his face, so close, so naked, so sexy. Andy's clever eyes grew brighter and yet deeper too, more secretive. Andy loved the old songs and one of his favorites he sang now, "Who cares to define / What chemistry this is? Who cares, with your lips on mine / What ignorance bliss is?"

And Tony sang back, even though he couldn't sing to save his life, and they laughed together, then they kissed, as only lovers can, knowing the little secret between them was safe.

EPILOGUE

Tony decided he was doing fairly well. Andy still brought up his past a bit, but he had learned to live with that. Tony had also learned to live with the idea that he could never have Derek as often as he wanted him, but it was an arrangement that suited him.

Tony had also learned to live with the idea that if he wasn't exactly at a place where he'd thought he might be when he was younger, he kind of liked that. He had decided one can't expect things to go the way you dream. He was still uncertain what he wanted to do with his life, but he felt he'd achieved a bit of inner peace at last. He even found it possible to see Sam again.

Tony discovered that Sam had snared a supporting role in a military drama being filmed on the Monarch backlot. He decided to swallow his pride and see Sam again, ostensibly to ask the stud to appear at the upcoming AIDS benefit concert he was organizing.

When Tony reached the location, he was told Sam was in his trailer. Tony knocked. Sam opened the door slowly, saw who it was, and flashed his most radiant smile. "Hey," he said, opening the door wide.

Now Tony saw Sam was naked but for a towel wrapped around his waist. The sight of Sam nearly nude again gave Tony pause. "Are you busy?"

"Just got out of the shower. Perfect timing. But then you always had perfect timing."

"Me?" Tony asked, entering the trailer.

Sam locked the door behind him. "Yeah, you always seem to come along just when I need you."

Tony looked about the trailer. It was not very glamorous; after all, Sam was not the star of this picture. Still, Tony was impressed Sam was doing

well as an actor, but then, Sam did everything well that he set out to do. Sam had, in Tony's imagination, entered the realm of myth.

Sam leaned back against the door, his hands behind his back, allowing Tony to gaze upon his superb body as long as he wished.

Tony gulped. This was going to be harder than he thought. Sam was now even more glorious than Tony had remembered. "I can only stay a minute–" Tony started.

Sam laughed. "You mean you've stayed away for six months and now you gotta run off?"

Tony sat in the chair at the vanity table and explained why he had come. Sam listened politely, quickly agreeing to do the benefit: "Whatever you say, Tony," he said, stepping closer and closer to him.

"You must be working out again," Tony said, enjoying the splendid view.

"Every day. Got a good trainer."

"Yes, you look better than ever."

"Thanks."

Flustered now, Tony started to get up, but Sam stopped him. "You coulda just asked me to come to your office–"

"I–" Sam's hands were on Tony's shoulders, pushing him back down.

"Or called me on the fuckin' phone."

"Sam, please..."

"You've been missing it, right?"

"No...I mean, yes, of course, but I have somebody else now."

"Andy Lang. I know all about it."

Tony blinked. "Well, then–"

"Well, then, all the more reason. You're tired of the junior league. You miss the big league." Sam drew Tony's head forward, directly into his crotch.

Tony shook his head in defiance; Sam held him steady. "Go on, Tony. Take what you came for."

Tony managed to look up at Sam, past the incredible pecs, to the grinning face, the laughing eyes.

Seeing Sam now made Tony's ass ache. God, he wanted to be fucked again by Sam. Sam's hold over him was never scarier than now, yet Tony knew he couldn't stop himself. And though he didn't want to respond, he had to. His body pulsing and surging beneath the stud's strong touch, Tony pulled the towel away.

"Oh, shit," Tony said when he saw the cock again. No cock had ever turned him on the way Sam's had.

Sam began to fuck Tony's mouth with his semi-hard cock. Tony tried to pull away, but Sam held him in place. Sam's cock was back home, in the mouth that loved it the most. Tony continued to shake his head, but all the while the cock was thrusting in and out of his mouth. Tony unzipped his trousers and yanked out his own cock. Just a few strokes and he was

coming. His own excitement sent wave after wave crashing over him. He cried out as he climaxed, and Sam backed off.

But Sam was not satiated. His angry need drove him to lift Tony up and tug down his pants. Tony stepped out of them, eager for it now. Sam dipped his fingers into some grease he had in a jar on his dressing table. Then he plunged his fingers into Tony, preparing him. Sam stood still and Tony backed up, impaling himself with Sam's hard-on. Tony fucked himself with the cock, so deep and so hard that he screamed when he felt Sam's orgasm burst inside him. But Sam kept fucking Tony; his need was savage and heartless. Tony didn't mind because Sam was telling Tony what he knew he wanted to hear: how much he missed him, that he had stayed away from all other men, that there would never be another man in his life.

Dizzy and weak, Tony swayed and swooned, trying to hang on to Sam, not wanting to let go. Not yet.

Sam ground harder and harder against him, then changed positions, putting Tony on his back on the carpet of the tiny trailer, his legs spread wide.

"You fuck him, don't you, Tony?"

"What?"

"You fuck Andy. Isn't that it?"

"Yeah."

"That's why you came here, to get fucked like only I can fuck you, right?"

Tony bit his lip as Sam knelt between Tony's thighs and entered him. It hurt Tony, as it always did, because Sam was not fully hard, having just come.

"That's right, isn't it, Tony?"

"Yes, yes!" Tony moaned, finding comfort in knowing Sam still wanted him, wanted him so badly.

"Yeah, nobody fucks Tony like Sam...."

"No, nobody, Sam. I love it so...."

Sam kept on, and even though he knew it was hurting Tony.

Tony accepted the punishment. Their mutual need was too strong to deny. Sam did not kiss Tony, but he did hold him tight eventually. Tony kissed Sam's bare shoulder and gasped as Sam stepped up the pace. Sam's cock hardened and soon he was close to orgasm again. Tony felt the thunder of Sam's heart, beating strong and steady against his chest. Sam pulled his cock out and came onto Tony's chest. Tony rubbed his fingers through the cum, the sticky warmth of it so familiar. "Oh God, thank you for that, Sam. I love it so much ... I love watching you come!"

Sam lifted up on his knees, then stood. This was always the hardest part, the part Tony dreaded. How could they part, just like that. How could he say goodbye to this? Just then there was a gentle tapping against the door, and Tony knew it was time; Sam had to report to the set.

"You can stay," Sam said, hurriedly dressing.

Tony did not answer him. He was still lost in the thrill of Sam's brutal fuck. He lay quietly on the floor for several moments after Sam left the trailer, his body still tingling in the steamy afterglow of their lust.

But finally Tony rose to leave; he knew he dared not stay a moment longer.

The Contributors
(Other Than the Editor, John Patrick)

"Leave Well Enough Alone"
Antler

The poet lives in Milwaukee when not traveling to perform his poems or wildernessing. His epic poem *Factory* was published by City Lights. His collection of poems *Last Words* was published by Ballantine. Winner of the Whitman Award from the Walt Whitman Society of Camden, New Jersey, and the Witter Bynner prize from the Academy and Institute of Arts & Letters in New York, his poetry has appeared in many periodicals (including *Utne Reader, Whole Earth Review* and *American Poetry Review*) and anthologies (including *Gay Roots, Erotic by Nature,* and *Gay and Lesbian Poetry of Our Time*).

"Ode to Boy" and "Showers"
Kevin Bantan

The author now lives in Pennsylvania, where he is working on several new stories for STARbooks.

"Stark Neon Memories"
K.I. Bard

The author's first story for STARbooks appeared in *Juniors 2*. Future stories are in the works. He lives and thrives in Minnesota.

"The Adventures of Father Michael"
Frank Brooks

The author is a regular contributor to gay magazines. In addition to writing, his interests include figure drawing from the live model and mountain hiking.

"Surrogate Sex"
John Butler

The author of the best-selling erotic novels *model/escort* and *WanderLUST* contributed this excerpt from the former for this edition.

"Worshiping Gods"
Leo Cardini

The celebrated author of the best-selling *Mineshaft Nights*, Leo's short stories and theatre-related articles have appeared in numerous magazines. An enthusiastic nudist, he reports that, "A hundred and fifty thousand people have seen me naked, but I only had sex with half of them." His previous tale for STARbooks was in *Fresh 'N' Frisky*.

"Jesus + The Turtles" and "Celebration"
Carl Miller Daniels
This new contributor of erotic poems lives in Virginia. Carl's first chapbook, *Museum Quality Orgasm*, is currently available from Future Tense Books, Portland, Oregon. His new chapbook, *Shy Boys at Home*, is available from Chiron Review.

"Mr Brother, My Love"
Peter Eros
The popular author's work also most recently appeared in *Play Hard, Score Big, HEATWAVE, Boys on the Prowl,* and *Sweet Temptations.*

"Boy Cook's Compendium" and "Twins Have No Secrets" and "R.I. Min" and "A Little Experimentation" and "The Pleasure Boys" "
Peter Gilbert
"Semi-retired" after a long career with the British Armed Forces, the author now lives in Germany but is contemplating a return to England. A frequent contributor to various periodicals, he also writes for television. He enjoys walking, photography and reading. His stories have swiftly become favorites of readers of STARbooks' anthologies.

"Ripe Fruit" and "A Singapore Surprise"
Rick Jackson
An all-time favorite author of erotica, Rick's collection *Shipmates* was recently published by Prowler Press in London.

"The Promise"
Ronald James
The author is a graduate student in Fine Arts at a university in St. Louis, Missouri. He is working on more stories in this vein for STARbooks. His first story appeared in *Fresh 'N' Frisky.*

"My Cousin Liam"
Thomas C. Humphrey
The author, who resides in Florida, is working on his first novel, All the Difference, and has contributed stories to First Hand publications. A memoir appeared in the original *Juniors.*

"Adventures of Billy Bob"
David MacMillan
The author was born in London, England, and entered the U.S. after the Korean conflict. He earned his masters degree from Columbia University and returned to England as a political analyst and organizer as well as a stringer for a number of publications before returning to America

permanently in 1977. His writing efforts are devoted to crime fiction, historical fiction, and dark fantasy. He is the well-trained pet of Karlotte, a 16-year-old calico dominatrix. She strokes him on average once a week–but only if he has followed his assignments faithfully and with at least some creativity. He has contributed to *The Mammoth Book of Historical Erotica*, and is editing books for Companion Press and Idol, London.

"The Last Taboo"
Jesse Monteagudo

The talented columnist and editor wrote this story especially for this edition, and recently contributed another tailor-made tale for the "Summer Camp 2: Tent Mates" segment of the upcoming *Fever!*, our Spring 2001 anthology.

"In the Gang" and "Greater Than Being Alive"
Jack Ricardo

The Florida-based author's last tale for STARbooks appeared in *Fresh 'N' Frisky*.

"A Very Special Delivery"
Rudy Roberts

The author's previous stories for STARbooks have appeared in *In the Boy Zone*, *Pleasures of the Flesh*, and *Secret Passions*.

He lives in Canada.

"A Strange Life"
Sonny Torvig

Based in London, this is the author's latest work for STARbooks. His stories have appeared in *Pleasures of the Flesh*, *Intimate Strangers*, and *Naughty By Nature*.

"Caught in Cyberspace" and "The Story of S"
Barnabus Saul

The author, based in the U.K., have appeared in *Juniors*, *Smooth 'N' Sassy*, and *Fresh 'N' Frisky*.

"Straight to Bed"
Mario Solano

A few years ago, Mario submitted some stories to STARbooks for consideration. We chose five of the stories and returned two with a note which read, "These two stories are too 'over the top' for us." Mario called and suggested we publish a book containing "over the top" stories and Mario suggested we call it *Taboo!* Obviously we liked his idea and his one story was the first story chosen for this publication. Mario tells us that on

his computer is taped a quotation which reads, "Fantasy is just another word for fearless. There will always be a place in the world for rebels. The key to creativity is yanking convention inside out." With this publication, STARbook Press is happy to prove that we have done just that.

"Sex with X & Y"
Tomcat

This Los Angeles resident frequently uses escorts and relates his experiences in print on occasion in *The Best of the Superstars* series. We asked him to contribute a more detailed account of his long-term relationship with two of the sexiest twinks ever created and he agreed, provided we did not identify them. "I have to live here," he said.

ABOUT THE COVER

The fine photography for this edition was provided by David Butt, whose photographs may be purchased through Suntown Studios, Post Office Box 151, Danbury, Oxfordshire, OX16 8QN, United Kingdom. Ask for a full catalogue. (http://website.lineone.net/~suntown1.)
E-mail at SUNTOWN1@aol.com. A collection of Mr. Butt's photos, *English Country Lad*, is available from STARbooks Press. *Young and Hairy*, David's latest book, is enjoying huge success currently and is also available from STARbooks Press.

ABOUT THE EDITOR

JOHN PATRICK was a prolific, prize-winning author of fiction and non-fiction. One of his short stories, "The Well," was honored by PEN American Center as one of the best of 1987. His novels and anthologies, as well as his non-fiction works, including *Legends* and *The Best of the Superstars* series, continue to gain him new fans every day. One of his most famous short stories appears in the Badboy collection *Southern Comfort* and another appears in the collection *The Mammoth Book of Gay Short Stories*.

A divorced father of two, the author was a longtime member of the American Booksellers Association, the Publishing Triangle, the Florida Publishers' Association, American Civil Liberties Union, and the Adult Video Association. He lived in Florida, where he passed away on October 31, 2001.